SELF/LESS

SKYLAR CHEUNG

This book is a work of fiction. Names, characters, businesses, organizations, places, incidents and events are either the product of the author's imagination or are used fictitiously. Any resemblance to actual persons, living or dead, business establishments, events or locales is entirely coincidental.

Designed by Euan Monaghan

ISBN: 979-8-4825149-2-4

First Edition: December 2021

10 9 8 7 6 5 4 3 2

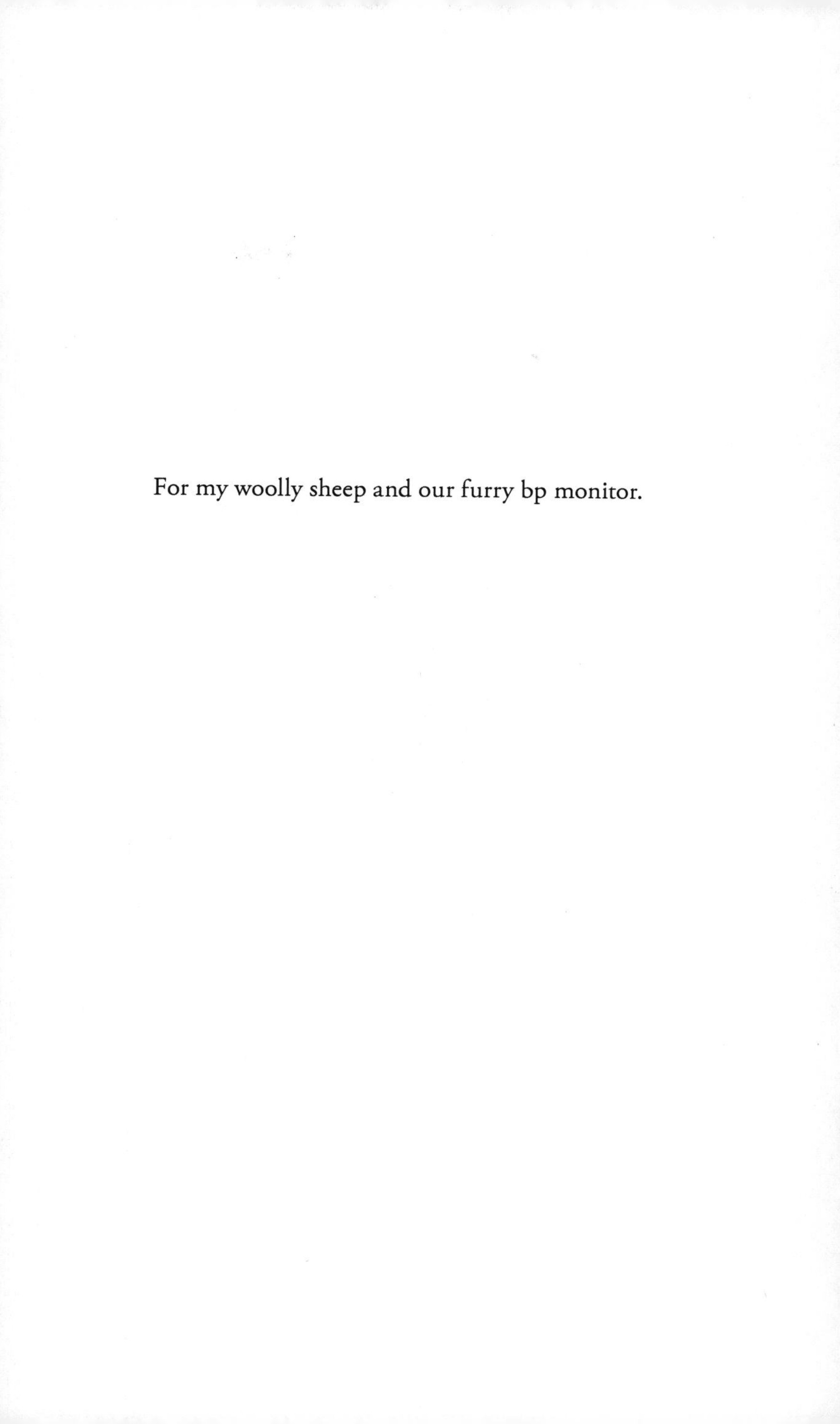

For my woolly sheep and our furry bp monitor.

SELF/LESS

prologue

"Let me in! How dare you lock the door, you worthless girl! This is *my* house! You're done when I say you're done!"

Each blow on my bedroom door feels like it is connecting with me instead of wood. I press my body into the corner where the headboard meets the wall and pull my knees into a tight hug, my breaths falling out in hot, rapid gushes. The door handle rattles just meters away. I squeeze my eyes shut. One side of my face burns.

I don't understand how it all went wrong so fast, not when the afternoon had started off so well. To the delight of the entire Kruger Preparatory School tennis team, the coach had taken ill and canceled practice, so I came home early. She wasn't meant to be back for hours, and I was to luxuriate in the peace of an empty house for the afternoon; yet there she sat, in the dining room to the left of the entryway, working on her flyers. One moment she was interrogating me about why I was home early, the next she was doling out a hard slap across my cheek. Aiming for the face is rare—a mark might betray our family's lack of perfection to others—but today, she couldn't help herself. Either she had a slow day showing houses or a bad one. Both are excuses to contemplate her life and all the ways it doesn't satisfy. And I am first on that list—her daughter topping it by bottoming out in life.

As the bedroom door shakes on its hinges, the poster taped there starts to peel and droop. I scramble around my bed to the study table. Shoving aside my geometry textbook, I grab the paperweight underneath and duck back in my corner, huddled on the ground, head between my arms, clutching the smooth grey stone. The harder she bangs on the door, the more strained my grip becomes. I am shaking.

"Just you wait until I get in there! I am not done with you!"

Then, the pounding stops.

The house falls deathly silent. I am familiar with this routine. It isn't long before she's back. What follows is the sound of metal scraping at my door and a lock which will not turn. I drop the paperweight and reach into the wardrobe on my right in search of the sharp corners of a small black box hidden in the back. I feel it between my fingers, drag it out and fling open its cover. There they are. Keys to my room, gleaming in the corner. None of the keys on her massive bundle will fit the metal slot on my bedroom door. She will grow impatient, she will blame it on her luck—the bad luck that permeates her life for all things related to me—but more importantly, she will leave me alone. I count my breaths, trying to steady them with this knowledge. They won't obey. They come shallow and rapid, out of control.

My eyes fall on a metal container in the black box. Gingerly, I extract from it a cool, thin blade. Something slams against the door. I jump and nearly cut myself. The door trembles, but it doesn't budge. Silence, again.

Like clockwork, the blade rests on the skin of my forearm, ready to do its job. It is always ready. Sometimes, it will be new lines etched between the old. Right now, I feel like opening old scars.

The tip of the metal breaks the surface. A pinch. Biting. I take a deep breath. It doesn't matter how many times I do this; it still hurts. The only difference is that now I know it has to hurt before it gets better. Still holding my breath, I begin to drag the blade through flesh, the sting giving way to a familiar pain. It is only a moment before the blood rises. Tears blur my vision—alone, finding neither comfort nor solace in my solitude.

How can I be so desperate to need this?

My right hand trembles as I ready myself for another cut. The thoughts are building in my mind, stacking like blocks, one atop another, growing heavier. I silence them by ripping a second line through a scar.

How many times have I wished away the feeling of desperation? Hoped to find a better alternative and realized there is none? I can't leave. I can't live. I have no way out of this life—a life my mother gave to me, only for her to make living it the hardest bit of all.

I grip the blade with a now-steady hand. The third cut, no hesitation. A translucent white line appears beside the first two. One beat of my heart, and the line turns red. Another beat of my heart, the red starts spilling onto the pale underside of my arm. I stare, transfixed. The pain of each cut conflates into one another until a numbing feeling settles. My surroundings fade.

Finally, I can breathe.

part / one

CHAPTER 1

I down my second pint of beer and idly watch as a couple slow dances in the middle of Element. In a couple of hours, the floor will be a sea of bodies, pressed up against each other, hot, heavy, sexual. As far as the patrons of Element are concerned, this Friday night is still exceedingly young. Right now, students are camped out in their halls of residence, ploughing through their own alcoholic concoctions, and the working crowd is bidding farewell to their last civilized hour of the week before debauchery ensues.

"Can I get you another?" The bartender leans over across the bar for my empty glass, her hand closer to mine than it needs to be.

"Yes, please."

The bartender has her blonde hair pulled back into a loose ponytail. Her t-shirt accentuates her slender neck, and the sleeves bunch up at her shoulders as she pulls the pint of beer.

I slide a fiver across the bar. "Good night so far?"

"If everyone behaves and I don't have to break up any bar brawls, then I'll have a fantastic night."

"Point taken. I'll be on my best behavior."

"Oh, you can misbehave if you like. I have no problems with that." The bartender winks as she hands back my change. I feel the heat rise in my cheeks. "You passing through?"

"Nope, studying here."

"At Rockton?"

"Good guess."

"It's not hard, Rockton's closest. I've seen a lot of their students come through. Haven't seen you around before though. So home is…the States?"

"Good guess again."

"As long as you don't make me guess which state you're from," she says, laughing. "You're a long way from home, love."

I am. The distance between London and Havenford is greater than the entire length of the United States coast to coast, and I crossed it without a second thought, all to escape a life which, the longer I lived it, the more it hurt.

When it became clear that I wasn't good enough for an Ivy League college, nothing could prepare my mother for her shame. It was wholly unfathomable to her that *her* daughter could fail where so many other Asian daughters have succeeded, so much so that when I brought up the alternative of studying law in England, she was all ears, ready for any option which could serve as the perfect coverup story to my academic ineptitude. It didn't take very much to convince her, not when our relatives in Singapore had already done most of the legwork with their constant boasts about the prestige and wealth that accompanied their children who studied medicine or law here. It was a convenient way for my mother to deal with her Ivy League conundrum. Plus, if I succeed where I failed previously, I would finally give her a reason not to be embarrassed by me. My leaving for London was as much my mother's lifeline as it was mine.

I smile at the bartender. "It is, but I have no complaints."

The couple on the floor is still dancing. Element is a gay club in London. There is nothing exceptional about that—if you know where to look, there are plenty of other gay bars and clubs to be found—but it does so happen that Element is the nearest one to Rockton, short for Rockhampton London University. The club spans two floors with a spacious outdoor beer garden and comes with the usual cheap furniture and seizure-inducing strobe lights. It even comes with a token dance pole on one of its three dance floors, although nobody is ever quite as good at it as they imagine themselves to be. When I first walked in a few weeks ago, I thought I had entered a parallel universe. Women holding hands, men kissing each other, completely open and completely at ease. I haven't had any issues being openly gay in London, but still, the sense of belonging that comes from being surrounded by so many others like me, it made me wonder if I ought to have been looking for a place like Element a lot sooner.

"Gang's here, Skye." Alison slips into the seat beside me.

Alison and I met in our first year in Rockton. We were in the same halls of residence and we quickly hit it off the moment we realized that we shared something in common—we both liked girls. It wasn't until recently that Alison insisted that we attend one of Rockton's LGBT+ Society's weekly lunches because it was, as she said, deeply embarrassing that we were nearing the end of our second year and had zero gay friends.

Now, she stares at me.

"What? Do I have something on my face?"

"Just thinking how much I would love to pull my hair into a ponytail like yours right now. It's like a boiler room in here tonight." Alison's hair is a short bob, not quite brushing her shoulders.

"Wait till it fills up."

Alison groans. "Anyway. See that girl in the corner?" She points surreptitiously. "Blonde. Reading a magazine. She's sooooo fit."

I throw a glance across the room. The blonde girl holds up the magazine she is reading and I chuckle when I make out its title—*Dyke Times*. "Yeah, she's fit. You going to make a move on her or something?"

"Skye! Alison!" A hand claps against my back. It's Cam, a diminutive dynamo who can often be found at Element with students from the LGBT+ Society, a.k.a. the gang Alison was referring to. We met at the weekly lunch where it soon became clear that Cam was *the* person to know because she came with a massive social circle. "What no-good-business have the two of you been up to?"

Alison opens her mouth. "Nothing—"

"Checking that girl out," I say.

The three of us look at each other before breaking out in giggles. Cam follows my line of sight to *Dyke Times* girl. "That's Octavia. Med student. Give it a few minutes. The rest of the gay medical fraternity will be here in a bit. You'd imagine they would be sick of seeing one another by now, all that time studying together, but what do they do instead? They party together. Oi, Octavia!"

The girl looks up, and Cam gestures for her to come over, and then makes swift introductions.

"Where's the girlfriend? Not out tonight?" Cam asks Octavia.

"Nope. It's a Tuesday. She doesn't really do parties in the early part of the week. Too exhausting."

The girlfriend sounds like she's ninety. Shame. Fit girl like Octavia taken by the ninety-year-old girlfriend…

"And this was pretty last minute." Octavia shrugs. "There wasn't enough time for her to psych herself up and get in the mood, so it'll be like pulling teeth if I tried to get her out of the house."

Scratch that. It's a ripe, old age of one hundred and ninety for the girlfriend.

"Can't imagine why she wouldn't be here when you are." The words are out of my mouth before I even have the chance to stop them. I cringe internally. It sounded like such a cheesy come-on. Unforgivable, especially when I have only had a couple of pints.

There is, however, a flicker of interest in Octavia's eyes. "You at Rockton?"

"Yeah."

"Studying?"

"Law."

"Mmm, lawyers and doctors. They have a symbiotic relationship you know."

Octavia's comment piques my interest. "And why is that?"

She grins. "I get into trouble, you get me out of it."

There is just the barest hint of suggestiveness in the way Octavia responds. I raise an eyebrow and shelve that moment—including the one where I noted a flicker of interest in her eyes—for the future. Cam lets out a tiny squeal of surprise as she is pulled into the arms of another girl who proceeds to plant a massive kiss on her lips. The gay medical faculty has, as Cam predicted, descended upon us, and they have come ready to party as hard as they study.

/

Alison stumbles towards her room, crashing along the hallway. She wakes nobody, maybe our neighbors, but who knows. We live alone in our apartment, opting for the peace of not living in a massive house with our ex-flatmates. We loved the apartment when we found it: bright, airy, and with a short entryway which leads into one long corridor. My room and the lounge are on one side, and the bathroom, kitchen, and Alison's room are on the other. Simple. My bedroom window faces a street notorious for late-night stumbles and fights, but the slanted ceiling and beautiful skylight forgive the window's shortcomings. It is otherwise a standard square room with the door in one corner and a basic-looking study desk, double bed with a nightstand, and wardrobe in the other three. Excluding the room in my halls of residence, it is smaller than any of the bedrooms I had growing up, but it is the most at home I have felt in my entire life.

"Oh my god," Alison calls out. I hear the solid thud of her body hitting the bed. "Those doctors can drink. I am going to be so hungover tomorrow. Goodnight, Skye."

Collapsing into my own bed, I let myself relish the soft fold of the mattress. The door, however, remains wide open. I ponder getting up to close and lock it, but the bed is so comfortable. *It's just one night. You're safe here.* I let the problem go.

Alison wasn't joking when she said the medical fraternity could drink. The only reason they stopped was the bar closing for the night. But the best part of the night had to be Octavia. Cheery with a flair for the dramatic, she doesn't just study medicine; she lives and breathes medicine. I lost track of the number of jokes she cracked which only someone from her field would get. I also lost track of the number of times I laughed politely and pretended to understand. She doesn't strike me as someone I'd be taken with, yet I stuck with her throughout the night, oddly enamored. She isn't Alex, but then again, who could ever be?

I stick my hand out for my wallet on the nightstand and retrieve the photograph inside. I have long committed it to memory, but still I'd wanted to look at it. Alex. Me. Her leaning into me as if our closeness was the most natural thing in the world, unguarded. The smile on my face relaxed, free, happy.

The longer I stare at the photograph, the weaker my heart feels. Weary from all the work it has done to keep itself safe from the hollowness that hasn't closed with time, it caves into the pull of memory. I brush the photograph with my thumb. My heart remembers the chains around it, tightening out of habit. I draw in a jagged breath. I don't know what it would take for the old pain to go away. I can't understand why I remain so bound to her. Worst of all, I'd sooner hate myself before I'd ever know to hate her.

CHAPTER 2

Havenford

I will never forget the day I met Alex.

It was morning in Havenford High School's gym, where the entire school had gathered for the principal's briefing on "exciting developments" unfolding in the new year. I had only been in Havenford High for a few weeks, having recently transferred at the start of junior year. My dad was an accountant who had been relocated to the office in town and my mother could technically work out of any location—she was in real estate—so there I was, with the only absentee member of the family being Richard, my older brother by eight years, who had already flown the nest. I was fine with his absence; we weren't close.

Time was starting to drag, and while I didn't suffer the heavy-head syndrome like some of the other students, the length of the principal's speech felt criminal. I stared at the clock. It was broken. I didn't have my watch or phone on me, having forgotten them in the mad flurry of getting ready for school. Nudging my classmate beside me, I asked for the time.

"Lemme check—" He started to reach for his bag.

"It's 8:30."

The girl seated on the bench directly in front of me hadn't even glanced at her wrist before speaking. I couldn't see her face, only that she had dark brunette hair.

"Thanks," I said and noted the slightest nod of acknowledgment.

It was a cold day, and despite the sweater I was wearing, the gym was draughty. I raised my cupped hands to my face and blew. "Urgh, it's so cold."

"Yeah, it is."

It was the girl again. There was nothing sarcastic about her tone, just matter of fact. I craned my neck forward, hoping to catch a glimpse of her expression, but her whole face was out of my line of sight. I gave up.

Another reason I didn't fall asleep was the dull throbbing on my arm—fresh cuts beneath my sweater. I balled my left hand into a fist and grimaced when the tensed muscles amplified the pain. I sometimes wished my "hobby" had the ability to make me permanently forget every word and action in the minutes leading up to it: the look of disgust on my mother's face, the cruelty and harshness of her words, the raining blows of her hands. It never did. And like every drug, the high of the cuts would eventually wear off and I would be left stranded with pain, the cold wet slap of loneliness, and the reality of my situation.

A loud crash brought me back to the gym. In the sudden upheaval of bodies, I was momentarily disorientated. The principal was finally done. People were surging towards the exit.

I stood up. "Well, *that* was riveting," I said to no one in particular.

"*Totally.*" Her sarcasm matching mine, the brunette girl rose from her seat, threw a glance backward and flashed me a quick smile before she joined the masses filtering out of the gym.

That was the first time Alex smiled at me. She had the prettiest smile, and caught in between an inexplicable draw towards a girl I had just met and the erratic skips of my heartbeat, as far as my darker days would go, Alex became the brightest spot in my life.

/

Emma was my first friend in Havenford High. On my first day, barely two minutes into our first class together, Emma was there, beside me, trying to engage me in banter. After Kruger Prep—where I attended until my dad's relocation—all I wanted to do was keep my head down, duck most interactions, and get by. But despite my very evident reluctance to engage, Emma wouldn't be denied. With time, I discovered that she was rather well-liked by most of Havenford High, and that her popularity cast an invisible protective dome around me. I was left alone, undisturbed, and I could quietly come and go—just as I had hoped.

"Remind me again why I agreed to let you drag me into this?"

Emma and I were surrounded by pages and photographs, some neatly taped onto a board on wheels and others strewn on the tables in the room. I reached out and lifted a slim A4 booklet: *Glyph*. Havenford High's very own school newspaper. We were in *Glyph*'s newsroom.

"You love me? You want to support me? This would look good for college admissions, if you actually thought about it? You secretly want this as much as you love me?"

I rolled my eyes and grunted. Emma's exuberance was not catching.

"Oh, come on, Skye! It's the school newspaper, not *purgatory*!"

"Fine, fine. So where's everyone? I thought we were meeting people."

"Well, they did say to meet here, but…we are kinda early…though that's kinda my fault. I thought we needed to make a good impression."

As Emma continued to rationalize, one of the clippings on the table caught my eye. I pulled out a piece of paper containing a mishmash of excessively juxtaposed alphabets snipped from newspapers and magazines to form the words, *Riddle Me This...*

"What the fuck?" I held it up over my shoulder so that Emma could see it. "Ems. This sounds like shit a serial killer sends you to toy with you before he makes you realize you never stood a chance. Are you sure this is the school newspaper?"

Emma snorted, and from behind us came soft laughter.

"Could be a she too, no?"

I spun around, and I felt my breath catch. Up close, at five feet four with a lean frame, dark brunette hair swept up in a bunch to reveal those high cheekbones, soft lips, and a delicate jawline, stood the girl from the gym. She locked eyes with me. They were a deep, chocolate brown. The edge of her lips curled into a smile of recognition.

"Alex!" Emma bounced on the balls of her feet. There was a giggle. She seemed flustered, nervous even, but more importantly, she put a name to that face.

Alex's gaze lingered before she shifted her attention to Emma. "Hey, Emma. Good to see you again. Are you up for joining us?"

"Are you kidding?! I mean, yes, yes! I'm definitely up for it." Emma punched my arm. "Just convinced good ol' Skylar here to join as well."

Emma *never* called me Skylar—too long-winded, she said. And she *never* punched my arm—too jock-like, she said. However, what was more fascinating than these odd behaviors was the fact that she had started to blush a bright, beetroot red. She was starting to behave like a giggly schoolgirl who just met the hunk of her dreams—and gay, Emma definitely was not.

"Trying. You're still trying," I said with a sardonic smile.

Emma glowered, but I was saved by the creak of the newsroom door opening and the excited chatter of students pouring in. "Emma!" someone called out.

"One second, guys," Emma said.

Alex's eyes were squarely on mine even as Emma walked away, behaving as though it had always been just us in the conversation. There was a seriousness that made her focus intense. I felt a little fazed by it but held her gaze nonetheless. If someone was going to blink first, it wasn't going to be me. My heart, on the other hand, responded in secret by beating twice as fast.

Alex was the first to look away. She nodded at the paper in my hand. "That was meant for the paper's weekly quiz. Someone thought that it would be...eye-catching. I vetoed it on the basis that it looked like a serial killer's signature."

"You vetoed it? So you..."

"Are part of this little club, yes." Alex broke into a smile that reached her eyes. I loved that smile. "So has Emma convinced you to join us then, Skylar? Come over to the dark side? Or the light, depending on the kind of journalist you are, I suppose..."

I wanted her to say my name again.

"Nah...I don't think this is for me." Alex cocked her head. "Wait, hang on, I don't mean it in an 'I'm too good for this' kinda way. I just mean you guys seem pretty cool and social and that's just kinda not my thing, you know? Anyway, I really don't think I'm what you're looking for."

I wasn't usually like this in front of girls—awkward, tripping over my own words. I've had girlfriends, and one of them even called me "effortlessly cool," although frankly, I think she had just misdiagnosed my emotional detachment as something I did on purpose, but it was appalling just how little game I exuded in front of Alex.

The smallest hint of a smile had started to form on her lips. "I haven't even begun to tell you what I'm looking for."

"True, but trust me, I'm not what you're looking for."

"Saying that twice doesn't make it true. You *know* that, right?"

I laughed. That was funny. *She* was funny.

Alex cast a look behind her. The newsroom was filling fast. She gave a quick nod to the front of the newsroom. "I gotta—"

"It's cool, don't let me keep you."

"Think about it? About joining. I mean, you just said I'm cool, and I've got an image to maintain now, and being rejected doesn't help." She shook her head with mock seriousness.

I let out a short laugh. "Sure, I'll think about it."

"Don't take too long." A wink, and she was gone.

Only then did I realize we had really been talking about what *she* was looking for. My heart galloped again.

"Oh, is Alex gone?" Emma returned, looking crestfallen.

"Yep. Ems, *who is Alex*?"

"Oh! Alexis Clarke. Senior. Co-editor-in-chief. Between her and the other editor-in-chief, they're like gods, I swear."

That was a rather over-the-top compliment for students in charge of a school newspaper.

"Um, why?"

"Because our newspaper got like this super-massive redo slash makeover—I mean, hello! We now have a paper called *Glyph*! It used to be called something sad like *The Daily*. That's because of them. It's because of them the paper is relevant again. Plus they both have one of those 'reputation precedes them' kinda situations going on."

"Oh?"

"Yeah. Alex is apparently an ice queen. Or a bitch, depending on who you ask. Hannah's another ice queen too, but apparently like super-*super*-nice underneath—not sure how those two concepts really go hand in hand, but anyway—she's also *to die for* gorgeous. You really should be on the lookout for her."

"Are you telling me that *because* I'm gay?"

"No, I'm telling you because *she* would turn me gay." Emma whipped her head around. There was a new voice in the newsroom and it cut through the sea of chatter like a warm knife through butter. Imposing and authoritative but oddly alluring. It compelled you to listen to her.

"*There.* That's her. *Hannah.*"

She wasn't just gorgeous. She was downright stunning. Tall, blonde, green eyes—that type of stunning. Scandinavian. Hannah would turn heads without having to do very much, and in that room alone, there were at least ten people who had eyes only for her. All I wanted to do, though, was scan the room for Alex.

And there she was, leaning against the wall, arms crossed, posture relaxed, one lazy glance in Hannah's direction, utterly calm amid the bustle of activity around her. So sure of herself and seemingly certain of what she wanted and didn't want. Not remotely pressured to partake in any conversation. Whether the party came to her or not appeared to be of no consequence.

There it was again. That inexplicable draw to her. A magician's invisible thread which had attached itself to my heart without my knowledge or say-so. Emma didn't know it yet, but I was going to join her at *Glyph*.

CHAPTER 3

The familiar notes of Octavia's perfume fill the space between us. Roses and honey.

We are lounging on the dilapidated, faux-leather three-seater couch in Element. It's tucked away in a corner on the second floor, right in front of the pool table. I have one arm flung across Octavia's shoulder and she is leaning in, close enough for me to pick up her perfume. Octavia and I have bumped into each other in Element several times since being introduced. During this time, I discovered that the way Octavia describes herself and the things she likes can be terribly clichéd, sounding exactly like the sort of thing people would write on a dating website when they don't know what to say about themselves. Once, Octavia described herself as a diehard romantic who adores long walks on the beach and watching the sunset, and at first, I thought she was being ironic, but it turns out she's not. She *really* does like those things. For a medical brainiac, Octavia is a delightfully uncomplicated sweetheart and I find that I quite like being around her.

"Do you guys really do *everything* together?" I nod at her med-student mates grinding against each other on the dance floor.

"Symptom of doing the course together. The hours are long, we spend a lot of it together, and we found that we clicked. I'm happy I've got them. It's less lonely this way. Nobody understands the analogies I spout more than they can. It can be a little lame, but it's a good kind of lame."

"It's not lame."

"You're being kind."

"I'm not saying it isn't geeky when you all fondly refer to 'Thomas the Cadaver' as if he was your best mate, but it's not lame. I get it. We're all looking for somewhere to belong."

"So you think it's geeky when we talk about Thomas?"

"I think you just proved my point, but you wear 'geeky' very well. It's geeky-cute."

Octavia giggles and her face turns a slight shade of pink. It spurs me on. I enjoy making her blush.

"How's the girlfriend? Has she recovered from all the eyeballing she did the other night when you introduced her to me?" I had received sufficient glares to last me the rest of the year.

"Probably has something to do with the fact that you kept flirting with me."

Sass—I like it.

"Sure, but here's the thing about flirting...it should only have pissed the girlfriend off if *you* were flirting back."

I watch in satisfaction as Octavia's face flushes again. "Anyway, we broke up. So that's *ex*-girlfriend now." She doesn't seem too cut up about the breakup.

"What happened?"

"We're just too different. It would be less exhausting if she didn't have to keep up at every turn and I didn't have to constantly feel as if I needed energy for two."

"Ah, sorry to hear that. Definitely doesn't sound fun, or even enjoyable." Octavia's lips are close. Sweet, pretty, smart—and now single—Octavia might be exactly what the doctor ordered for the summer. "You should date me. I promise I can keep up."

Octavia's eyebrows arch upwards.

I frown. "Sorry. I thought it was obvious that I liked you and it seemed like you were interested too."

"No, no. I *do* like you. It's just...Caleb asked first."

"Caleb who?"

"Caleb. Med student, my batch. He asked me out a few weeks ago but obviously I couldn't say yes."

Through the deluge of cold water pouring over me, I ask, "Uh-huh. And are you, uh, interested in Caleb?"

"I could be."

"Are you interested in me?"

"I am."

"So why are we talking about Caleb?"

"Because...I should really give him a chance, shouldn't I?"

Is Octavia serious? Or is this some kind of reverse psychology flirt technique she's deploying to get me even more interested in her? I ask again, "Why?"

"Because he asked first?"

"And so...?"

"So, I ought to give him a shot first."

"Octavia...you're joking, aren't you?" I don't know why I bother to ask. With every answer, sweet, pretty, smart Octavia is turning into a deceptively simple riddle that I don't want or need.

"I'm not."

"So, because Caleb pressed the queue ticket dispenser first, you're going to see him first?"

"Yes."

I want to say that agreeing to your next date isn't like serving food to a line of customers. Octavia isn't obligated to date Caleb just because he happened to get in line first. Yet here she is, dead certain that this is how people approach dating. It is madness, and the sensible thing to do would be for me to get the first bus out of Octavia-town, but what is it going to cost me to wait? Back in my bedroom, I have my luggage sprawled wide open on the floor, completely unpacked even though I have a flight to catch tomorrow. It is the summer break and I am due home. Away from the sanctuary of London for two weeks, back to a town which holds parents who are unfortunately still mine and a girl who isn't. I will be so caught up, I won't even have time to think about Octavia. It will be *so easy* to agree with her. To allow her time to get this kooky plan out of her system and be ready to date me when I return. So, the next words out of my mouth?

"Okay fine, you do that, Octavia. There's still a lot of summer left and I'm not going anywhere."

CHAPTER 4

The sight of my old bedroom still gives me pause. My prison and place of refuge. It has been stripped bare, and all that remains is the bed with the study desk and wardrobe on each side of it. When I packed to leave for England, I ended up cleaning out my entire room. It was like emigration. You take what you love, throw out everything else, and leave a shell where there used to be a home.

My mother's voice travels upwards. I can hear her through the shut door. She's asking my dad if we have enough braised pork belly. Richard is in town this weekend and she wants to make sure that my brother gets to enjoy all his favorite Chinese dishes. I roll my eyes. I'm pretty certain my mother doesn't know what *my* favorite dish is, but it doesn't bother me. As long as the only thing that stings during this visit are her words, I have no quarrel with her.

Before Havenford, my family lived in a predominantly Chinese neighborhood. It was (and remains) my mother's belief that, like her, each Chinese family worked tirelessly to cultivate a perfect image that could be presented to the world, pausing for breath only when judging one another. She has therefore always had her notions of what the perfect Chinese daughter for our family would be, what *I* should have been. I should be smart (think genius) and gifted (think child prodigy). I should also be her version of beautiful (tall and slender; pale, perfect skin; long, flowy, jet-black hair; demurely dressed at all times). Just as important, I should be living the life she wanted for me—successful (but not too successful that no man will want me), married to a Chinese husband (ideally more accomplished than me, as I'll be marrying up), with a son for our firstborn.

By my mother's standards, I am a failure.

Standing at just over five feet five, I inherited my dad's broad shoulders and skin that glows warmly from being in the sun. Paired with an unchanging preference for worn-out jeans and a simple t-shirt, my appearance drove my mother to desperate measures: like installing a pull-up bar in the house and demanding that I hang from it as often as possible in a bid to stretch me out. She kept our curtains drawn at all times, till we lived like vampires, in hopes of reversing the effects of the sun on my skin. She replaced sweets with her personal homemade treat—unsweetened, lemon-juice ice cubes. *Your stupid father. Why did you have to inherit his shoulders? Boys don't want girls like that, all strong and muscular. It makes them feel inadequate. Why do you think there are so many stories about men saving damsels in distress?* This was her lament as she furiously juiced her thirtieth consecutive lemon, steadfast in her belief that muscles have no place on a woman's body; they are merely toxins to be detoxed away.

The one thing my mother felt most in control of was my academic future. It was clear from the start that I was no prodigy, so the traditional route would have to do: medicine or law, Ivy League for sure, ideally Harvard or Yale. If she could make the time to oversee my studies, then surely nothing would come between her and her dreams for me. So much time went into studying, so much pushing me to participate in as many extracurricular activities and self-improvement classes as possible, that days turned into months into years, and I was that kid who had too much to do and too little time to be, well, a kid. I didn't mind, I suppose, but I don't recall being given much of an option at all. The only thing I knew I wanted, however, was for my mother to not withhold affection when I showed no aptitude for the piano or the violin. For her not to go batshit crazy and pinch me all black and blue whenever I didn't score top marks and meet her overzealous standards. For her not to look at me with so much disdain the day she realized my prospects of making it into an Ivy League college were dwindling. For her love for me not to correspond with how well I fulfilled her vision of what she wanted her daughter to be. Yes, I would have liked all of that very much, but we don't always get what we want.

There's a commotion downstairs. The lilt in my mother's voice, brimming with joy and excitement, gives it away—Richard is home. He's the reason for her venturing into the kitchen. She usually leaves all of that to my dad, but tell her Richard is on his way and she pours all her sweat, tears, and love into homecooked dishes just for him, which was how she spent the whole of today. She's never once done that for me, not even after my move to a new continent, a faraway place I reside for fifty weeks out of every year. When my parents decided they wanted children, I think they each meant to love us equally, but an unforeseen force—their circumstances perhaps—somehow pulled each of them to a different child. My mother's love for Richard is unparalleled. All the adoration, love, and devotion she has poured into him since the day he was born makes me wonder if she gave it all away and had none left for me by the time I came along.

There's a gentle knock on the door.

"Skylar?" It's my dad. "Richard's back and dinner's almost ready. Your mom wants you to come down now."

There is another knock, more persistent this time. I barely had the chance to answer my dad the first time he called.

"Skylar. Your mom doesn't want to keep Richard waiting, his time is important." There is a pause. "And you know how insolent Richard gets when he has to wait."

I smile. *There's* the dad I know. No, we mustn't keep the boy king waiting.

/

I come out of my room hoping to find my dad on the landing, but emptiness greets me. He doesn't really stick around these days. One-on-ones seem to fill him with unease. It's hard to imagine that there was a time when they didn't. It's harder to remember that I grew up being a daddy's girl.

"I don't understand how these people got into law school, Mom." The familiar sound of Richard dissing everyone greets me as I come down the stairs. "They're just so stupid."

He had cut his teeth as an accountant for a few years before deciding that he was destined to be a lawyer, so with our mother's blessing and, more importantly, her financial assistance, he's now in his final year in law school.

"Not everyone can be as smart as you, Richard."

"But do they really have to be *that* stupid? Imagine having to be around them all the time. It's hard being the only brilliant one in the room."

I bite on my bottom lip and survey what we're having for dinner. One of my mother's traits is her dogged determination. Whether that's a good or bad thing depends on how she uses it. Today, it gifts us with an unbelievable spread. My dad pays her compliments as she enters the dining room with

Richard and the final dish. She responds with a rare, sweet smile for him.

Richard is noticeably excited as he sits down. Knowing him, he'll go for the pork and shrimp wontons first. I lift the plate and hold it out to him. One boyish grin later and a substantial portion of the wontons gone, he thanks my dad for passing the rice and gushes to my mother, who beams at him. Quietly, my heart warms a little before it pinches. This reminds me of when my family was still relatively functional—Dad and Mom talking and smiling at each other instead of going for each other's throats; Richard as a sibling instead of a stranger. If anyone asked to capture a snapshot of our family, I would tell them—this, right here, *hurry*, before it passes. Because that's all it is, a snapshot, a split second in time, a moment when we forget what it means to be angry at or disappointed with one another and ourselves.

"Auntie Eve's eldest made it onto the dean's list again. He's going to have a bright future, that one. Will make a very good lawyer," my mother announces.

Family moment over.

Richard and I trade looks. Just because we no longer speak doesn't mean I don't know what he is thinking. *This fucking thing again*, probably.

"Because he got onto the dean's list?" Richard sounds curt.

"Yes," my mother responds, clearly oblivious to the tone. "Her youngest is also going to study law. He topped his school again. Smarter than Uncle Steve's son who received a scholarship, they say."

"Who's 'they?'" Richard asks. I don't know why he bothers engaging with her. It's not like he cares for the answer, and it will only serve to irritate him.

"Auntie Eve."

"Well, obviously she'd say that, right?" I say. "She's their mom. She wouldn't exactly go around telling everyone her son is doing poorly."

"I tell everyone that you did poorly in high school, without telling them that you couldn't get into an Ivy League college, of course. And still, look, now you're in law school. In *London*."

She glows, but I can tell it's not with pride in me. It's her own pride talking—my being in law school makes *her* look good. I don't split hairs though. Measured against how she used to be, my mother is, by comparison, a nicer person today than she was a few years ago. She lashes out less and hasn't raised her hand once in the last two years. All because I got accepted into law school, never mind that it is in London. It doesn't make up for all the ways I don't satisfy her vision of what her daughter should be, but it's better than nothing. Sometimes, I hear her telling others that I'm back for the holidays, from England, where I'm studying to become a lawyer. You cannot miss the boastfulness in her voice.

"Anyway, why does any of this matter? About Auntie Eve's kids, I mean." Richard sounds annoyed. "Do we have to congratulate her kids or something? Send them a basket of fruit? Essence of Chicken, perhaps, to keep their brightly lit minds aflame? In case they get fatigued and fall off the dean's list?"

I nearly snort into my soup. My mother has always been obsessed with the benefits of drinking Essence of Chicken. In fanciful marketing speak, it's a natural food supplement which is made from the extract of chicken. If I'm asked to describe it, I will say that it's basically concentrated chicken soup, which can be pretty tasty. My mother, on the other hand, will tell you not to waste your time pondering how the supplement was brewed—all that matters is that it eliminates mental fatigue, nourishes minds, and above all else, makes us smarter. The small, stout bottles of this allegedly magical liquid were, and still are, a pantry staple and do not come cheap, so I would be hard-pressed to see my mother wanting to spend this kind of money on children who aren't her own.

"Don't be silly. Of course not. Why should we help Auntie Eve's children perform better at their studies? No, we're not sending her any." There is a pause. "Not unless our other relatives are. Then we must. Can't be seen to be stingy or worse, *poor*." To my chagrin, she turns her attention back to me. "I saw your email about your grades for your second year."

"Uh-huh."

"None of them looks like A's."

"Yeah, well, the grading system in the UK is different from ours."

"But do any of them equal the A grade?"

"No...more like disgustingly high Bs, which are still good, right?" I ask, but I know they aren't good enough for her.

"Where's the slip?"

I scrunch my eyebrows together. "Like the *actual* slip? Hard copy?"

"Yes."

"In London...?"

"Why didn't you bring it home?"

"Why would I bring it home?"

"So I can see it."

"Why?"

"To make sure you're not lying about your grades."

Had anyone but my mother said this, it would be a joke. But it's her, and she's not joking. She has probably been watching one too many soap operas. Her daughter, Skylar Cheung, scheming, lying, and, *gasp*, perhaps even sleeping her way through university—a new daytime award-winning soap coming her way this fall. I curb the eye-roll that threatens to slip past my defenses. A deep sigh rumbles through me and I pray for patience.

"Honestly, Mother, I'd find something else to lie about. Not this. I'm as invested in my grades as you are."

I am literally pulling whatever hours necessary to ensure that I get the grades I need to secure entry into one of the law firms I desire in London because if I do that, it becomes entirely plausible that I get to stay in England forever.

"But not straight A's, not even a single A."

Now that she believes me, the ever-demanding proverbial tiger mom is back. *Why aren't you on the dean's list? Why didn't you top the class? What's the point of being second best?* All her favorite questions.

"No, sorry to disappoint. I'm not *that* smart. I'll try harder."

"You're not separately holding a part-time job in London, are you?"

"What?" I flick a look at Richard whose eyebrows are as furrowed as mine.

"Are you holding a part-time job? Is that why you didn't get A's? Please tell me you didn't get a part-time job. People will just assume you come from a poor family and that's embarrassing!"

I stare at my mother. She is a daytime soap all on her own.

"No, the reason I didn't get A's is because I'm not a genius. Okay?"

My mother frowns. "You used to be so much smarter when you were young. I really don't know what happened to you. I suppose I should count my blessings that you were accepted into the university in the first place. There's still a chance that you won't turn out to be a failure in life." She shakes her head. "Auntie Eve's son made it onto the dean's list and we can't even tell them you got straight A's. So embarrassing."

"Richard didn't get onto the dean's list, either."

Richard arches an eyebrow at me, shoulders visibly tense. Again, I know what he's thinking. He's wondering why I couldn't just leave him out of my mother's inane, unspoken race against Auntie Eve and Uncle Steve to have the brightest child in the family tree. I shrug. There are two of us, and nobody said I am the sole representative of the Cheung bloodline.

"Richard will be an accountant and a lawyer. Two professions in one person. Such a smart boy."

Immediately, Richard's shoulders relax. I should get a dollar for each suppressed eye-roll whenever I'm with my family. I'd be loaded and free to live my life how I want.

"Do you need me to get you Essence of Chicken? It might make you feel better with all the studying. I know law school can be hard."

I peer over my dad's arm and consider if there's anything worth eating on the other side of the table.

"Skylar?"

"Huh? What, what?" I nearly drop the soy sauce chicken I had so delicately clasped between my chopsticks.

"I asked—do you need me to get you Essence of Chicken?"

"Oh." I do a double-take. *You were offering to do something nice, for me?* "I thought you were talking to Richard."

"Oh, he has Essence of Chicken already, and Bird's Nest too." She smiles lovingly at him, but he doesn't even look up from his food.

Of course Richard already has bottles of Essence of Chicken *and* Bird's Nest stocked up. Bird's Nest—a liquid concoction of water, rock sugar, and swiftlets' gummy saliva—in my mother's eyes, is invaluable for its health and immunity-boosting qualities. Nothing but the best for Richard, as always. Still, she was offering to do something nice for my well-being. What did she want in return? What did she want from me?

"So I'll get it for you?" she repeats.

The child in me begs to say yes—yes to her display of care and concern—but I hold back, a massive lump in my throat. My mother mistakes my silence as consent.

"I'll get it for you before you head back. Make sure you drink it; don't let it expire otherwise you're wasting my money—you've already wasted so much of it going to England—so make sure you drink it." There is a brief pause. "Maybe then you'll get straight A's and you can finally give me something to boast about."

My heart contracts. There we have it. The string that is always attached.

/

The sound of water gushing from the tap stops. I turn around and find that the plate I'm drying is the last. My dad wipes his hands dry. Everyone I know has a dishwasher, and I used to ask my dad why we didn't. Without fail, he would always respond that the best dishwasher we have is our own two hands.

"Are we done?" I ask. He hasn't said a single word since we started doing this chore together. In fact, he hasn't said much the entire night.

"Yes."

"Okay. I'm gonna head out after this." I am due to meet Emma.

"Okay." He doesn't leave. I shoot him a glance. "Have you thought about what you'll do after college?" he asks.

"Try and get a job in London?"

"As a solicitor?"

"Yeah of course. What else?"

"Your mom worries your grades won't be good enough and you won't qualify."

"Tough isn't it? Wherever will she hide her face then?"

Even though I know my dad loathes my mother's unwavering obsession with others' perception of her—*it's nobody's business but your own* he used to say—he doesn't engage. He doesn't tell me to can it, either. Tonight, his act of keeping his head under the parapet irritates me. He thinks he's keeping the peace by disengaging. To me, it looks spineless. I cannot believe that I used to see him as a strong man, a father to depend and rely on.

"Are you going to stay in London?"

I place the plate I'm holding back into the cabinet. "If I get a job, yeah."

"No, I meant in a few years. Would you still stay in London?'

"Yeah."

My dad is silent for a moment. "You should return home."

Never. "Why?"

"We're growing old. You should return home. What if something happens to us and you aren't around? It would be days before the neighbors know that something has happened."

After everything my parents had put me through, the irony of being asked to care for them once they cannot care for themselves isn't lost on me.

"Richard's still around."

"He'll be busy."

"I'll be busy too."

"You're better at dealing with stress than he is. Your mother wouldn't want to put this kind of pressure on him. Anyway, you're the daughter."

I can feel my lips start to twist and curl into an expression I know would reflect disgust at how sexist this sounds. I hide it, not wanting to hurt him. He hurts enough just by staying married to my mother. I opt for a blank look.

"I have to go, Dad. We'll talk about this next time." I exit the kitchen before there's time for him to say anything more.

/

Apart from the light streaming from the kitchen, the rest of the house is bathed in darkness. I push open the door to the sound of Richard talking and my mother's delighted laughter in response. I don't have to see them to know that her smile is wide enough to show her teeth, and her eyes are twinkling, gazing at Richard as if he is all that exists in this world. I've not seen her like this around anyone else, not even my dad who, unsurprisingly, is nowhere to be found.

"Goodnight," I call out and take the stairs two at a time. I really don't have cause to worry—my mother is far too enamored with Richard to want me to join them—but old habits die hard.

The study is occupied. Dad. Keeping himself ensconced in the privacy of the room where he will eventually fall asleep on the single bed. When I started noticing, he said that it was because he loved the cold and my mother hated it, but I knew he was lying.

I enter my bedroom and sigh. It's only been a couple of days and already, I miss my room in London. I chuck my bag down and race through my night-time routine in the bathroom. Back in my bedroom, I hold the door handle down as I quietly and firmly press the door against the frame, my slow release of the handle corresponding with how gently and softly the door shuts. I stealthily turn the lock and applaud myself for not having lost my touch. I move away from the door. I'm back at it a split second later, unlocking and relocking it, before I crawl into bed, satisfied.

Lying in bed, I find myself staring at the slit beneath the door, the dark corridor on the other side hiding the shadows of the people who may lurk outside. I lie on my back and stare at the ceiling, but sleep eludes me. I'm up again, grabbing my luggage and placing it flush against my door. Back in bed, lying on my side, I stare at the door until sleep finally comes.

Nothing like being at home during the summer break to be transported back into the body and mindset of a girl who barely survived her childhood.

CHAPTER 5

Havenford

Growing up, my dad and I created our own little morning routine. My mother was not one for waking early—odd because you would think a Type A personality would buy into the early-bird adage—and Richard always seemed to be doing his own thing. So, every morning of every day, my dad and I would have breakfast in the kitchen, we would talk—about school, work, the latest fight between him and Mom—and he would drop me off at school before work. Every morning of every day, I felt the joy of my father's love, until the day those moments ceased to exist between us, their place taken up by silence. Who knew one night could change us so irreparably?

"Cereal, please." I stuck my hand out for the box my dad was hoarding and grimaced. There was a bandage wrapped around my arm, covering up the new lines—bright red and raw—which stung with the reach. My dad raised his eyebrow as he handed over the cereal box. I pretended not to notice him noticing. Usually, I'd be bothered, but I was beyond caring right now; I had been up way too late enduring another of my mother's petty railings against me, and I'd gotten up before anyone else to wash the encrusted blood off my skin. Besides, it wasn't like my dad would say anything, anyway.

When I first started cutting, I used to bundle myself up in a sweater even if we were in the thick of summer, choosing to battle the sweltering heat as I waited on my cuts to heal and fade. He would register it, but say nothing. I soon gave up on the sweaters, partly because I didn't survive my mother and the cuts just to die of heatstroke, partly because I wanted him to see what was happening to me, and to dare him to show an ounce of love and concern for his daughter.

Instead, he finished his breakfast, roamed off and back with a freshly pressed shirt, pulling it over his white singlet. I could see a couple of aged scars peeking out at his shoulder, courtesy of my mother's nails during one of their more vicious fights. It started out like every other fight—my parents trading verbal blows with each other: my mother pulling in the greater share of the household income, his lack of support, her late nights, his preferred method of disciplining Richard with the cane, and her complete disrespect for him, her husband. I remembered Richard sitting beside me on the stairway, gasping when our mother lashed out and scratched our father. I could see it in his eyes; he feared for our mother's safety the way he feared for his own whenever he had done something to make our father angry. *If they divorce, you'll go with Dad and I'll go with Mom, okay?* he said, his face a picture of seriousness. I don't know why Richard thought what we wanted made any difference, but perhaps saying it out loud made it real enough to give him comfort. In any event, it was already understood. Between us, we had implicitly known our roles from birth—the mommy's boy and the daddy's girl.

It was therefore unsurprising, inevitable really, that my dad would be the first person I came out to. At fourteen, I had finally put a name to how I had felt since I was six, and I had told him, dead certain I could trust him. I never thought to seek his approval, only affirmation that his love would protect me. Being gay never felt wrong to me, but with the concept of heterosexuality so deeply embedded in our social and cultural influences, part of me knew that others might not see it the way I did; and in that case, I would need my father. On that day, it was autumn, and we were on the porch fixing a floorboard that had come loose, when he told me it was okay. *I love you Skylar, no matter what. You know that Daddy is always here for you*. How different things would look in six short months. I started at the top of the world with my dad's love and acceptance and ended up with all safety and security in pieces after I came out to my mother.

Now, I watched my dad as he finished his morning coffee, the dead space between us alien from what we used to have. It wasn't fair. Richard had my mother's love and protection, and I was meant to have my dad's. It was what they had taught us. It was all we had known. I swallowed my cereal and forced it past the lump forming in my throat.

My heart was meant to be broken by girls. My first girlfriend. The straight girls who don't feel the way I do. The girls who do but who aren't meant to last. The girls I shouldn't love but do anyway. My heart was *only* ever meant to be broken by girls, except it wasn't, and despite what I told myself each time my mother laid her hand on me, not everything heals with time.

/

When I joined *Glyph*, what I wanted most out of it was getting to know Alex, but a most random thing happened. I became friends with Hannah.

Despite the warmth of our initial interactions, Alex had been strictly business since then, living up to the ice queen reputation that Havenford High had bestowed on her. Hannah, on the other hand, was different.

We ran into each other one evening after school and we just got talking about everything, from the beauty of the photographs taken by Daniel—*Glyph*'s insanely talented photographer—to Havenford High's football team and cafeteria food, right down to the last movie we watched. It was Emma who called Hannah an ice queen, and while Hannah rarely exhibited that persona, I eventually knew her well enough to safely say that, like Alex, the shoe did fit. One thing that Hannah was obsessed with was maintaining our professional and personal boundaries—lest people start to believe that she reserved choice *Glyph* assignments for her friends—and *that* was when Hannah the Ice Queen appeared. It could be in the littlest things: refusing to be the one who asked for my opinion in any *Glyph* group discussion, looking wholly uninterested when I had an opinion, leaving the newsroom without saying a word to me when we were in fact meeting each other out front to head to the mall together. It could also be in the harshest actions, as I would experience at *Glyph*'s annual fall retreat.

"Skylar. *This* is what you want to submit for next week's publication?" The sound of papers hitting the table jolted everyone out of their post-lunch lethargy. "This is an account of the new policies implemented by the student government. You're *telling* me what they are, but you're not *showing* me why they're of any value to me as a student. This is an *amateur's* mistake."

I raised an eyebrow at her.

"How can you expect to be a part of *Glyph* if you can't discern the difference between the two?"

This time, there were raised eyebrows all around.

"You keep this up and I'll need to write off the prospect of you ever having a feature piece."

There was stunned silence. I never expected favors from my friendship with Hannah, but I didn't expect to not recognize her either. It wasn't in her nature to be mean. The seniors shifted uncomfortably in their chairs. My self-esteem withered.

"Okay. Surely there's no need for that," Alex said, sitting straight up.

Hannah's cold features sharpened even further. She opened her mouth, but Alex cut her off before she could say another word. "Skye, talk to a couple of students on Monday. Get their thoughts. Write that, but it's gotta be done by end of Monday, okay?"

I tossed harried glances between Hannah and Alex, then at everyone else at the table. Everyone was dumbfounded at how tense the session had become.

"Uh." I cleared my throat. "Yes, okay. I'll do that."

"Good. Fine. Now, let's talk about the recap of the football team's performance. Guys, did we really have to be that complimentary? They lost, terribly! Let's not have our reputation go down along with theirs, okay?"

Alex was usually content to let Hannah lead the *Glyph* meetings, but this time she remained squarely in control, all the way until the very end. Hannah—arms crossed, lips pursed, with an unyielding glower of irritation in her eyes throughout—couldn't be trusted to maintain any sense of calm or objectivity, not just with me or Alex, but with anyone else, and I think Alex knew that too.

Hannah eventually sought me out later that evening, presumably after the sting of the afternoon had worn off.

"I'm sorry. For being a bitch about things earlier today," she said on our way to the gym. There was only rue and regret in her eyes.

"*Were you*? Was a little hard to tell, don't you think?"

She looked sheepish. "I deserved that. I—I just didn't want anyone to think that I'm playing favorites, *especially* during the retreat. I'd hate to take away from anything you achieve in *Glyph*."

"Hannah…" I let out a heavy sigh and ran my hand through my hair. It was hard for me to be mad at her when she only had the best of intentions, however misguided. "If people are gonna talk, they'll do it, whether you ice me out or not. They've already seen us at the mall together and they're not gonna change what they think just because you didn't talk to me during the retreat. I'm cool if you want to be a little more cold or rigid during *Glyph* meetings, leave the newsroom separately, whatever, but *not* if you pull that shit again, okay? That wasn't you being objective. That was you being an asshole."

"I know, I know. I— I'm sorry, Skylar. Won't happen again, promise." She held her arms open, all sincerity. I rolled my eyes and leaned in to be wrapped in a big hug.

Yet despite the apology, I still wasn't surprised when Hannah looked uncomfortable as we entered the gym together. I could have forced Hannah to stay at my side, make good on her promise, but I knew it sat easier on her soul—or more aptly, her image—if she didn't have to. I would have preferred a little more honesty from her, but I let that go too. I had grown up with a mother who placed the utmost weight on image and perception, and who would strive for the appearance of perfection at any cost. I was not unfeeling towards Hannah's dilemma. And as emotionally bruising as her actions were, they were ultimately harmless.

The gym had been turned into a makeshift cinema and camping ground for our retreat. Having found an unoccupied corner, I spotted Emma gesticulating in the distance, hamming up a story to garner laughs. She would wonder why I hadn't joined her, but it had been a long day and I just wanted quiet. The clap of the gym doors opening drew attention—in came Alex. A rolled-up sleeping bag under her arm and a bag of chips in hand, hair still slightly damp from her shower, she started towards me. With nobody to my left or right and only the wall behind me, internally, I started to panic, but on the outside, I made sure I was the perfect picture of calm.

"Am I intruding? Seems like I'm the third wheel between you and the wall." Alex chucked her sleeping bag on the ground, gently tossed the bag of chips into my lap and sat down.

With a warm flush in my cheeks and a rush of excitement, I forced out a chuckle that could pass as sounding relaxed. "She says as she sits down."

Whatever exhaustion I felt was swiftly expelled from my system; Alex was like an adrenaline shot. My heart started to pound against my chest with a force I hadn't previously experienced, each and every beat a deep throb in my ears. My throat felt parched. I was nervous as hell. I was desperate to impress.

I gestured to the people in the gym. "This group doesn't seem to have an 'off' switch. I needed a moment to myself."

My thoughts spun out: What an awful conversation starter! Had I never chatted up a girl before? Alex, on the contrary, looked completely at ease with the remark.

"Good, then you're exactly my kind of company. Where's Emma?"

I gestured in the distance. "Somewhere over there, running through the last quarter of the energy in her tank."

Alex shot me a dubious look. "You think it's the last quarter?"

"Last third."

"Half," she said with a knowing smirk.

Laughter eased some tension. My heartbeat slowed down.

"How have you liked *Glyph* so far? Still think we're cool?"

"Yes, still exceedingly cool."

"Good. I could tell Emma was *exceedingly* excited that you decided to join."

"The girl's excited if I so much as decide to accompany her to lunch after class."

Alex laughed. I loved that I made her laugh.

"So what made you change your mind?" she asked.

"About?"

"Joining."

You. "Emma?"

Alex arched an eyebrow. I flashed a wry grin. She pursed her lips. "No offense to Emma, but she's not really a Hannah."

"Not a Hannah?"

Alex gestured in Hannah's direction. "Everyone says that Hannah and I revived the school newspaper, and I know it was teamwork, but honestly I think it revived the *second* someone like Hannah decided she wanted to try her hand at it. The number of people who tried to join that year, or sign up as contributors, was phenomenal. So again, no offense to Emma, but she's not a Hannah. Very few people are."

I chuckled. "Don't suppose you joined because of Hannah?"

"Hardly."

A hint of a frown disturbed Alex's brow before her expression smoothed over, hiding it quickly. Up until then, there were no suggestions that Alex and Hannah were anything but neutral toward each other outside *Glyph*, but signs had started to creep in.

"I may want to get into journalism in the future and figured this was as good as any place to start." Alex ripped open the bag of chips. "And you? Why were you so hesitant about joining?"

"I wasn't."

"You were." Alex shot me a knowing look. "How come?"

I didn't know if I was prepared to answer truthfully. It must have shown on my face.

"It's fine if you don't wanna talk about it. But you know, if you're hiding serial killer tendencies somewhere behind that smooth and aloof demeanor, you ought to warn me." Alex cracked a smile.

"What?" I scoffed.

"You were, after all, the person who made the remark about a serial killer's signature the first time we met."

"Second."

Alex's lips curved into a secretive sort of smile at the correction.

The answer to her question was simple enough, yet the reaction I had gotten most times for saying it out loud, it may as well have been me telling someone that I *am* a serial killer. I didn't want to give her a reason to get up and walk away, but strangely, I also felt consumed by a desire to be truthful with her.

"I had a bit of a rough time in my last school. I'm…gay."

There. It was out before I could change my mind.

My sexuality was not a secret, and while I made no attempts to hide it, I didn't shout about it from the school roof, either. I saw no need; it wasn't as if straight girls sounded the trumpet and announced their preference for boys either. Still, maybe Alex didn't know.

I stole a glance at her and breathed a sigh of relief. Her expression was relaxed.

"Came out, didn't think it mattered to anyone, but apparently it did. Classmates, tennis teammates, students who didn't even go to the same school as I did, they all had an issue with it. They got pretty cruel. Behaving as if my sexuality was a contagion they either needed to avoid or snuff out while the adults I trusted to do the right thing did absolutely nothing."

Kruger Prep had become the high school experience from hell. It started with one harmless-looking note in my locker one morning. *Sicko* it said. The next day there was another: *Stay away from my girl during training, lesbo dyke. If not, me and my friends would* love *to teach you a lesson you won't forget.* Notes turned into words sprayed across my locker—*Fucking dyke, die.* My fingers caught on broken glass and razor blades that had been emptied into my backpack, all while the grownups turned a blind eye. Time in Kruger Prep became as long as the horizon was wide, so when my dad announced that he was being relocated to Havenford, I was more than ready to leave.

Alex's forehead creased into a heavy frown.

"Anyway. I just really wanted to keep my head down here. That meant not finding a friend like Emma *and* certainly not joining any clubs or whatever. Come to school, go to class, keep to myself, try not to flunk all my classes, and go home."

"I'm sorry you had to go through that."

I shrugged. "It's done. It's in the past now. I need to move on."

Alex fell quiet beside me. "Did you?" she asked.

I raised an eyebrow.

"Move on?" she completed her sentence.

I shot Alex a wry smile, not answering her. She was a sharp one.

"Thanks, by the way," I said.

"What for?"

"This afternoon. With Hannah. You didn't have to."

Alex shrugged like it was no big deal. "She didn't mean it. You know that, right? Whatever she said, the shitty stuff. I've known her a while and she spins out sometimes. It's a thing she does when—never mind, doesn't matter. All I'm saying is that it makes her blind to the obvious, which is that you're more than enough on your own. But she cares for you. I can see that."

"I know." I gave a small, tight smile. "We're good."

Alex and I fell into a comfortable silence, passing the bag of chips between us as we watched the movie. Gradually, the chatter around us started to taper off, and by the time the movie credits started to roll, and Alex and I conceded that we too should try to get some sleep, it finally hit me that I didn't have to check and recheck my locked door. I didn't have to watch the slit of light for movement. All I had to do, *all I had to do*, was fall asleep beside Alex. I stole a final glance at the girl who thought that I was enough.

Somewhere in the crevice of my heart—my damaged heart—there was a spark.

CHAPTER 6

The dry ice makes a cloudy white veil, obscuring Emma from view. Her faint silhouette is entwined with another on the dance floor, but I can't make it out. She bursts through and stumbles forward, sweaty from dancing, giggling as she reaches for me. "Oh my god, isn't he the cutest?"

"Uh-huh, sure. Cute as a button, Ems."

"Oh my god." Emma's eyes grow large as saucers. "Skylar." She grips my hand.

"Ouch, Ems, yeah, yeah, I get it. Yes, he is *the* cutest. Please let my hand live."

"Skylar, no…" Emma says with urgency.

"Skylar."

That voice. A voice which immediately silences the club, the entire city. I would know that voice anywhere. I spin around. There she is, hair loose, deep brown eyes, a bittersweet smile. I am standing perfectly still but my heart is running a marathon.

Alex's palm is against my cheek, her caress tender. It makes my body weak. I lean into her touch. "What are you doing here, Alex?"

"To tell you I'm sorry," she murmurs. "That I've figured it out."

"Figured what out, Alexis?"

"How much I loved you," she breathes softly as her body melds into mine. "How much I still do."

She presses her forehead against mine. I close my eyes as I feel her lips meeting mine. Alex's touch burns. My lips. My skin.

She makes my heart ache with the love I have for her to a point of breaking itself…

I awake with a start.

The room is silent apart from my own breaths, heavy and rushed. I press my fingers to my lips. I can still feel Alex's lips on mine. I shut my eyes tight, willing myself back into my dreamscape. I need to be with her again, to feel her in my arms, to escape this emptiness without her.

It doesn't work. She is gone. The sun streams through the window, revealing each speck of dust that hangs in the air. This room isn't my own. It is small, the wallpaper is coming off at the corners, and there are cracks in the wall. The furniture looks old. This place technically isn't a dump, but it's far from luxurious. The bed shifts. I'm not in it alone. There's a girl in it with me, naked and fast asleep. I groan, not entirely sure whether it's regret or gratification I feel.

Last night was my first night back in London, and after the two-week purgatory in Havenford, I went to Element in desperate need of a drink, which was where I met this stranger—Jamie, I think. She's a media and communication studies student at Rockton, hates everything mainstream, capitalist and consumerist, and an objectively attractive girl who never seemed to run out of smart retorts or comebacks. She made her intentions clear as soon as she saw me. I didn't do one-night stands. Yet there I was, nursing my gloom over not seeing Alex, and now here I am, in Jamie's bed because she was there, unlike Octavia, who has yet to return. How quickly and quietly can I gather my belongings and be out the main door?

Jamie chooses this very moment to wake. She smiles. Luckily, she is still attractive even without the haze of alcohol.

There is a wicked glint in her eyes as she looms above me in bed. "If you stay for breakfast, I promise you I'll make it worth your while," she says. Her hands are already on my waist and sliding downwards.

I shouldn't stay. But Jamie's touch reminds me of how wanted and desired she made me feel last night, and how in the heady pleasures of lust, it became easier to forget that Alex existed. As the saying goes, the trick to getting over someone is to get under someone else. However, despite my past attempts, it remains a trick I've yet to master. Maybe the third time is a charm.

/

With summer officially over, Element is bustling with students. It is the first night of our final year in Rockton and although neither Alison nor I will get creativity points for where we chose to spend it, Element was reliable fun. We saw no value in fixing what wasn't broken.

Leaning against the wall, I finish my drink and place the glass on the ledge. Alison is getting her refill at the bar and Jamie—my one-night stand who has yet to leave after nearly a month—has gone off to the restroom. I spot Cam turning up with a girl I don't recognize. As Cam allows herself to be greeted by others and engulfed in hugs, her companion scans the room, alert and observant. She is maybe five feet six, seven even, slightly androgynous, with hair so dark it looks black, eyes accentuated by dark eyeliner. It takes me a moment to realize that she's looking right back at me. I break into a small smile before tearing my gaze away when a familiar face pops up in my line of vision.

"Hey, Octavia."

Octavia's face lights up the moment she sees me. "Hi." She wraps her arms around my neck and surprises me with a soft kiss on my cheek.

"Oh, uh…how was your summer?" I ask when we break apart.

"Good, then bad for a little while, then really good again."

I nod, having no idea what I am supposed to take away from that cryptic recap.

"Caleb and I…you remember Caleb, don't you?"

How can I forget? Caleb in the queue. He pressed the ticket dispenser before me, so he got to date Octavia first.

"Well, we were dating at the start of summer and it was okay at first, but then it wasn't. Another case of incompatibility, oops." Octavia doesn't seem particularly sorry about it. It reminds me of when she broke up with her ex-girlfriend; she didn't seem too cut up about that, either. "Anyway, we're done."

"You're done? With Caleb?"

"Yeah, it just wasn't my thing. So…I thought we could give this a go now?" Octavia's expression is sincere, keen, and it stumps me for a second until I recall what I had said to her before we broke for summer.

Hands snake around my waist. "Hi, baby."

Octavia's eyebrows are furrowed. I want to slap myself for suggesting to Octavia that I would wait for her, only to be off like a shot the moment opportunity came calling elsewhere. I shoot her what I can only presume to be an extremely sheepish smile.

"Octavia, uh, meet Jamie. Jamie, Octavia. Jamie is uh…" *My fuck buddy? Girlfriend? The reason you're pissed at me?*

"We're dating," Jamie says.

I groan internally and cough to clear my throat. "Jamie, do

you think you could get me a drink? Throat's feeling a little parched. I'll join you at the bar. Just give me a second, will ya?"

Jamie shrugs and obediently wanders off. Thank god. She isn't one for taking instructions.

Octavia crosses her arms. "Dating, huh? How did *that* happen?"

It's a no-brainer why and how I found my way into Jamie's bed, but why this little fling has lasted past summer, I'm not quite sure. Apart from having mind-blowing sex with each other, Jamie and I don't have much in common. Our personalities don't fit. Jamie is loud, talkative, and staunchly peddles only views which are unconventional and unorthodox. She says it's because she loves playing devil's advocate. I think she just loves arguing for the sake of arguing, and it gives me a migraine. I suppose I can simply tell Octavia the truth about how summer at home—with family and without Alex—sucked so hard that Jamie, being the first thing to come along, was hard to resist. It doesn't change the situation, but it will make me look less like the jerk who flung sweet-sounding words around like they hardly meant a thing. At the time I said them, I'd meant them.

I shrug. "It just did."

Octavia's eyebrows shoot up. She probably would have flung a drink in my face if she had one in her hand right now.

"Baby, I forgot to ask, what did you want to drink?" Jamie's voice perks up again.

"I, uh..."

"It's fine. Take your time, Skye. I'm just leaving."

I rub the back of my neck as Octavia walks off in a huff.

"Did I miss something?" Jamie asks.

I shrug again. "It's nothing. Almost dated her before I met

you. Didn't." I am getting really good at sounding like I don't care for much.

"Why not?"

"She wasn't worth the trouble."

"Shame. Maybe you should have. She's pretty hot."

I raise an eyebrow at Jamie. She grins, shrugs, and heads back to the bar, not realizing that she still doesn't know what drink I'd like.

CHAPTER 7

Despite the initial hiccup and a few chilly weeks of awkwardness that ensued, Octavia and I have managed to steer our non-existent relationship into a friendship. Most days, she behaves as if we never had a romantic run-in. Some nights, I'll catch her looking at me with a hunger in her eyes, but I don't act on it, and neither does she. Jamie has commented before on the hungry eyes, but she doesn't seem overly fussed or concerned. In fact, she and Octavia are gossiping like old ladies by the pool table right now.

I sip on my drink at the bar, idly checking out the bartender as I mull on whether to have another. I wonder if I should get her name. It seems rude to have been served by her for months now and not know it.

"We've not been introduced, not formally at least. I'm—"

"Paige!" the bartender exclaims. "I didn't think you'd make it tonight. What would you like, love?"

I glance to my side. It's the girl who came in with Cam. I already know her name *and* that she's now dating Cam, courtesy of Alison. Paige briefly tears her eyes away from me, shooting the bartender a quick grin.

"Hey, Tori, change of plans. Can I get a pint, please? The usual."

So she knows and remembers the bartender's name. Nice. Her eyes are back on me, a full smile gracing her lips. It's a lovely smile.

"Tori has stolen my thunder, but just in case she wasn't loud enough, I'm Paige."

I turn properly to face Paige. It's my first real opportunity to take her in up close. Standing there in a dark green shirt, sleeves folded up at her elbows and hip-hugging jeans, she has striking eyes. Blues. Curious, moody, and complemented by the eyeliner she has on. Paige doesn't wear her hair long, letting it come down to just under her chin. It's a little mussed up with some strands falling carelessly across her face.

I smile back. "I fear the entire club may know your name now. I'm Skylar."

Paige laughs. "Do you go to Rockton?"

"Yeah, you?"

"Same. What are you studying?"

"Law."

"Sociology."

"So, not a doctor then?" There is a slight crease on Paige's forehead. "For a moment there, I thought Cam only dated girls in the med fac," I hurry to explain, not wanting her to misunderstand and think me a snob.

"I know, her track record shows, doesn't it?" Paige accepts her drink from Tori and nods in the direction of our friends. "Not feeling the festivities tonight?"

It's true: since arriving at Element, I have spent an inordinate amount of time at the bar alone.

"I'm feeling more like home right now."

Paige laughs softly. "Don't tell Cam, but I'm feeling like that too."

"Your secret's safe with me."

Paige looks like she's about to say something, but stops. We have company—Jamie, who instantly perks up on seeing Paige.

"Oh, hello. Cam's girlfriend, aren't you? Wow, Cam's knocked this one right out of the park."

Mid-drink, I half snort into the glass. The natural flirt in Jamie is usually smoother with flattery, but it is operating way off base tonight. Thankfully, Jamie does not take the snort personally. It isn't lost on Paige, though, who shoots me an amused side-eye.

"Yes, Cam's girlfriend."

"Rockton?" Jamie asks.

"Yes." Paige doesn't bother asking the same of Jamie. She tilts her head and appears to peer around Jamie's head.

"Guys! What are you all up to?" Octavia drapes her arms around Jamie, clearly excitable. My forehead scrunches up. I still find it bewildering and slightly disconcerting that they get along so well.

"Nothing much," Paige says. "What about the two of you?"

"We were talking about the possibility of a threesome," Jamie declares. "Between us." Jamie looks at Octavia then at me.

I choke on my drink. Octavia blushes a deep crimson red. Amazingly, Paige hardly flinches. She gives me a few gentle pats on the back as I cough and nudges her pint towards me when she notices that I've nearly reached the end of mine. "Interesting, but question—why would you want to share?" She casts a glance over at me. "I know I wouldn't."

Paige's comment makes the tips of my ears burn and I gulp more of her drink than I intended. Octavia now looks as though she wishes to find a hole and bury herself in it.

Jamie's eyes narrow. "Well maybe we're just that little bit more adventurous," she says, sounding both defensive and curt.

Paige gives a casual shrug.

It annoys Jamie how easily she brushes off the jibe. She shifts her attention to me. "We're going to dance. Coming?"

"You guys go ahead first. I'll join you later."

When we're on our own again, Paige chuckles conspiratorially. "Are you going to? Join them?"

"Don't tell them, but I think not."

"Your secret's safe with me." She gestures at Tori for refills with the sweetest smile; when she turns it on me, though, it gets a mischievous edge. "So, a threesome?"

"You heard it the same time I did," I grumble.

"Not every day that the prospect of a threesome falls into your lap, and yet you don't sound keen. Not something you'd want, then?"

I haven't thought about what I wanted in a long while. Not since Alex.

"I'm not sure I'm drunk enough to talk about what I want."

I could have fobbed Paige off, kept up the pretense of trading cheeky remarks, but I find myself not doing that. She looks surprised. She tilts her head and regards me with a seriousness I can spot behind the playful shine in her eyes.

"I can race you to the bottom of a few glasses, if you like," she says.

"How smooth."

"I try."

I knock back a mouthful of the fresh pint in front of me. "I don't know if it's something I want but...it could be something I need."

Paige nods her head slowly and takes a sip of her pint.

"We should do coffee." Those words fall out of Paige so casually. She makes it sound as if we are old friends in need of a catch-up. We are not, but because she makes me feel like we are, I say yes.

/

I toss my keys onto the table and start to get ready for bed. Jamie follows and closes my bedroom door. I have an early start tomorrow, which means I need sleep; and I had to pry Jamie away from Octavia at Element. There was no further talk of threesomes, noticeably after Paige's offhanded line of questioning. While Jamie shrugged it off, Octavia had seemed more subdued.

"You weren't serious, were you?" I ask.

"About?"

"A threesome with Octavia."

Jamie starts to plant kisses along my jaw and reaches for my top. I lean against the wardrobe and close my eyes. It is obscenely late. I am bone-tired and I have a 9:00 a.m. lecture tomorrow. I hear myself sigh in my mind.

"Why wouldn't I be?"

"Didn't you think to ask me?"

Jamie pauses and pulls back a little. "I didn't think you'd mind."

"Why not?"

"I've seen the way you look at Octavia."

I feel a flush of desire when I think of Octavia.

"I've also seen the way she looks at you." Jamie pulls my hips towards her. "Why do you think we were even talking about it? She's the one who brought up how hot you looked tonight when you were talking to Paige. Urgh, that one's just a smug little tool, isn't she?"

I thought Paige had simply reacted accordingly to the smug little tool in front of her, but I doubt Jamie would appreciate my opinion, so I keep it to myself. She unhooks my bra and tosses it to a corner. Peeling my jeans off my hips, she guides me to bed.

"It would have been so hot to watch Octavia want you," she growls as she runs her tongue along my bare skin.

"Been?"

"Yeah, don't think she'll go for it. Too shy. Maybe too traditional. Shame. Would have been hot to see her go down on you." Jamie makes her way down my body.

"Doesn't bother you? Another girl going down on me?" I ask, voice raspy.

"Of course not. That's the whole point of threesomes. Watching another girl make a play for you, watching her want you, watching her fuck you and make you come when *I* am the one who has you, why would that ever bother me?"

I think of Octavia running her tongue along my bare skin and a shot of lust runs through my weary body. I arch my hips against Jamie and she digs her fingernails into my skin with a soft moan of excitement, not realizing that she's not the cause of my desire. A twinge of guilt eats away at me, but I cast it aside and wrap my legs around Jamie's back. I can feel her tongue on me, fast, skilled, speedily pushing me to the brink of my orgasm, and when I come, I imagine that it's Octavia's tongue that brings me to a shuddering stop.

CHAPTER 8

At half-past ten in the morning, it's the graveyard shift for the pub I'm seated in—The Honey Badger. I stretch my legs and take a moment to enjoy the quiet. I've never been here before. It's typically English. A lot of wood all around—tables, chairs, paneling, bar counter, what have you—floor adorned with some patches of worn-out carpeting. It's cozy. It's nice.

"Hey, Skye."

Paige stands in front of me, casually dressed in a black hoody and jeans. She texted last night about the coffee she thought we should have.

"So, did you get your threesome?" Paige asks after we return to the table with our coffees. There's a sparkle of mischief in her eyes.

I shake my head. "Nope."

"Is it in the works?"

"Unlikely."

"Hmm. What's the deal with the three of you, anyway? Not that a threesome isn't a scintillating and intriguing idea for anyone our age—"

"Isn't it always scintillating and intriguing, no matter the age?"

Paige lets out a chuckle. "That's very true. So, even though a threesome is *always* a scintillating and intriguing idea, you seem to be shopping a little close to home. A threesome with a friend is *never* a good idea."

"Are we speaking from experience here?" I ask, to which Paige simply responds with a wink. "It's Octavia and me. Bit of history there. I asked her out last summer, she turned me down for someone else, went away during the hols to give that a spin, returned telling me that it didn't work out and that she was ready to give us a try. I was already seeing Jamie by then."

"Are you…still interested in asking Octavia out?"

I am impressed at how precise Paige's line of questioning is. "Yeah, you can say that."

"A threesome hardly sounds like the way forward."

"It's not. That's entirely on Jamie."

"But you won't leave Jamie for Octavia?"

Running my finger against the rim of the mug of coffee, I mull over Paige's question. "I don't know if Octavia still feels the same way about me and I don't particularly wish to leave a girl who really wants me for a girl who couldn't make up her mind about me. Bit of a selfish bastard, really."

Paige leans back. "Nothing wrong in that. Sounds perfectly human, in fact."

"My moral compass."

"I'm a shining example." Paige's lips curl at the ends, her body language relaxed. The sunlight pouring through the window brings out the blue in her eyes.

I find myself intrigued and curious. "What's your deal, Paige?"

"Is this the part where I tell you what I put on my online dating profile?" She flashes me a grin.

"Didn't peg you for having one."

"Why not?"

"You strike me as liking things a little more…old school."

"Are you calling me old?"

I scoff. "Hardly."

"Do *you* have one?"

"I *did*. Not any longer."

"Found the girl of your dreams?"

"No, found the prospects of threesomes in real life," I say with deadpan seriousness.

Paige bursts out laughing. It's rich and delightful. "Hmm..." She smiles rather wickedly. "My *nonexistent* online dating profile would say...third-year studying sociology, contemplating a teaching career in the near future, makes a mean beef Wellington, enjoys a good laugh with her mates, and currently with a girlfriend who's probably more than she deserves."

"Does Cam know that?"

"Well, now that I've told you, I'll have to kill you."

I laugh. "So why do you think she is more than you deserve?"

Paige taps her finger against the table, thoughtful. "Cam's like...good and kind. She has an amazingly positive outlook on life and it's infectious, or at least I try to let it be. Sometimes I can be a miserable sod about it. But yeah, she's head and shoulders above anyone else I've dated before, so I'm really lucky to have her."

"What were the others like?"

"Girls who couldn't treat me right or who were emotionally unavailable."

"Oh, those."

"Which ones? The 'can't treat you right' or 'emotionally unavailable' ones?"

I think about Alex. "Both. They pull you in. They spit you out. They do it all over again. There's no rest."

"Now *you* sound like the one speaking from experience."

"I wish I wasn't." I keep a smile plastered on my face.

"And I wish I didn't know exactly what you meant about

them pulling you in and spitting you out, but I do, so that makes this potentially isolating sentiment entirely mutual." Paige tilts her head up, catches my gaze, and holds it.

Maybe it is the light framing her silhouette, the candor of the conversation, or the hint of a darker complexity, but in this very moment, there is a welcoming sense of closeness and familiarity between us.

"So which one was she? The person before Cam? Miss 'Emotionally Unavailable' or Miss 'Couldn't Treat You Right?'"

"Emotionally unavailable?" Paige seems unbothered. "She treated me really well. Older, thirty, give or take? She was fresh out of a ten-year relationship, I was fresh on the scene, and she was on the rebound. Called it off after six months, said she didn't want to get too attached."

"And were you?"

"Getting attached?"

"Yeah."

Paige chews on her bottom lip, her hands fiddling with her empty mug. "I'm very good at not getting attached," she says, her lips forming into a soft half-smile.

I nod slowly. It's a loaded statement from Paige and it invites a deeper analysis, but not today. For now, Paige appears to ponder the meaning of life at the bottom of her empty coffee mug and I'm content to just sit and watch her.

"You make a mean beef Wellington, huh?"

"I don't look it, right?"

"No offense, but you don't look like you'd enter the kitchen to begin with."

Paige grins with an impish smirk. "I'll show you one day."

The men at the bar suddenly burst into song. Paige shoots the singing party a sideways glance. It's not even close to lunchtime and these middle-aged men are already drunk, tone-deaf, and winding themselves up to the grand chorus. It is a ridiculous scene. Paige tries to stifle a giggle, which only makes me giggle. I'm not sure if it's the singing fiasco that I find funny, or bemusement I feel watching Paige as she tries to rein herself in. She presses her forehead against the tip of her fingers, looking downward at the table, the awkward body jerks giving her away even before I hear her laughter coming through. It's infectious, and it isn't long before we find ourselves laughing so hard that it hurts.

CHAPTER 9

Havenford

A few short months into attending at Havenford High, I knew the environment was different from Kruger Prep's hell. I wasn't attacked for being who I was. I had friends in Emma and Hannah, and I was even quietly nursing a crush on Alex. Havenford High had become an escape from life at home, too, and within it, I found some sense of normalcy.

"Do you want to go to the mall?" Hannah asked, slamming her locker shut.

"Sure. You need something?"

"A top, maybe two. Do you want to come over for dinner after? Mom left the good stuff tonight. You'll love it."

My mother wouldn't be pleased if I came home late. She would hurl accusations about how I treated her house like a hotel, coming and going as I pleased and not spending any time in it at all. If only it really *were* a hotel. At least I would be left alone.

"Yep, sure."

The rants would happen regardless of whether I got home at a decent time.

Hannah clapped her hands together and stopped outside the newsroom. "Great! Let me grab something real quick and we can go."

"Hannah! I didn't realize you were still around. Did you want to grab dinner tonight?"

It was Nathaniel, which meant that Hannah would be wishing she could rewind the last five seconds and change her mind about entering the newsroom. Everyone in *Glyph* knew that Nathaniel held a torch for her. She didn't feel the same about him, and given the number of times she had blown him off, the guy ought to take a hint. It was clear he hadn't.

"Oh, sorry I can't. I'm heading to the mall with Skylar."

Nathaniel wasn't alone; Alex was there too. She looked up, shot us no more than a passing glance, and went back to whatever she was reading.

"How about tomorrow, then?"

"Can't. I'm meeting some of the girls."

"Oh." Nathaniel's face fell a little, but brightened again. "Of course. You've always been real busy. My bad for not asking sooner."

"Oh yeah, a *supremely* busy schedule that Hannah *certainly* has," Alex said without looking up. A thermometer would have frosted over at her tone. Hannah ignored it.

Daniel popped his head out of the darkroom. "Hannah. Thought I heard ya. Can I borrow you for a sec?"

Hannah ducked into the darkroom. Nathaniel looked despondent as the door slammed shut on him.

Alex told him, "You *said* you were going to quit her."

"I know."

"Didn't look like you were quitting her."

"It's harder than it looks." He sounded like a lost puppy.

"She doesn't like you, Nathaniel. When you figure *that* out, it'll stop being *that* hard."

With that, she went back to her books. Didn't even greet me, as if I weren't even in the room. It stung. Alex had been friendly enough after the fall retreat. Not a "room full of sunshine" type of friendly, but there were a few hellos and quick chats about our days. Given that our last interaction had been so ordinary, it would have taken a psychic to figure out what I had done to warrant the shift in attitude from her. A psychic I was not.

"Sorry about that. You good to go?" Hannah snapped me out of my thoughts.

"Yeah..." I started to follow. I took one final parting glance at Alex. Nothing. "Okay, yeah, let's go."

/

When I went from being a straight-A student to flunking my tests with noteworthy consistency, my mother assumed a direct correlation between gayness and failure; by *choosing* the former, I was also choosing to be the latter. The fact that life at home with her had a nasty tendency to go from uneasy coexistence to murderous screaming in no time at all was irrelevant, as was the incessant bullying at Kruger Prep—although, granted, she knew nothing of what went on at Kruger Prep. With a fresh start at Havenford High, I tried harder, desperate for the academic part of my day to sail along better than the domestic part. I might not have been accepted into an Ivy League college, but graduating with decent grades was probably still a good idea. At the very least, it could stave off the future as a broken, hapless tramp which Richard had prophesied for me.

Yet I continued to muddle through classes with barely a modicum of focus. I'd often find myself sitting in an empty classroom after last period, wondering how I got through the day and how I was going to face the next one. It was how Alex found me one afternoon.

"Hey," she said with a gentle rap against the door.

Standing in the doorway with her backpack dangling from one shoulder, she might have been speaking a foreign language. Not only had she not addressed me since I last saw her in the newsroom with Nathaniel, she had also been ignoring me whenever we crossed paths. It was bewildering and hurtful. Yet the pain didn't dampen the undercurrent of joy pulsing through me now.

"Am I interrupting?" she asked.

"Nah, I was just finishing up after last period."

The hallways were deserted. Alex's eyebrows went up almost imperceptibly. "Everything okay?"

My mother had returned home the night before spoiling for a fight, and I had the stings of the cuts on my arm to remind me that nothing was okay. *Why would they want you?* she had asked when she saw me working on a *Glyph* article at the dining table.

What do you mean? I had pried open my backpack and slowly begun to pull my textbook off the dining table, gently slipping it into the backpack. I did the same for the next one and I did it all without looking away from her.

Aren't they scared of you polluting the minds of the other students with your sickness?

They don't see it that way. I'm heading to my room.

Did I say you can leave? Do you know whose house you're standing in? Mine. Paid for by my blood, my sweat, and my tears. You leave when I say you can leave. I don't know what I have done in my past life for you to turn out so wrong. You're disobedient, ungrateful, and useless. Ruining everything. Bringing nothing but shame to me...

I'd had to clench my jaw and bite on my tongue. Words, I'd reminded myself. That was all they were, coming out of her mouth. I'd stood up and took one step towards the stairs.

Did you not hear me?! You leave only when I say you can leave!

I hadn't even seen my mother's hand coming at me. I still felt it on me, though, as present as the cuts on my arm.

I smiled at Alex. "Yeah, I'm okay."

Her eyes narrowed. It caused her forehead to crease into a small frown. "Walk with me?"

I shoved my books into my bag and joined her. Her watch rattled around her wrist as she tucked loose hair behind her ear. Glasses hanging from the neck of her t-shirt—only for the really tiny words, she said, since she was otherwise blessed with near-perfect eyesight. If disheveled were a style, Alex would have made it the trend of the season. She let out a small huff of effort as she readjusted the backpack on her shoulders.

"What do you have in there? Gold bars?"

"Very funny. Textbooks. I have textbooks, and the knowledge contained in them is worth more than the value of any gold bar."

"Careful, any more of this and you might be at risk of losing your insanely cool status."

"Says the person walking beside me. Reputation by association, Skye."

I chuckled. "So why are you here so late?"

"I could ask the same thing of you."

"I asked first."

Alex tutted. "Had a terrible editorial meeting with our advisors. Needed to confirm budget numbers, but Jenny was ill, which meant nobody understood the accounts, and we kept getting the numbers wrong. Started talking about how some initiatives were way behind schedule only for it to become a question of fault. I was so over the meeting even before we got to 'any other business,' but thankfully Hannah had the sense to race through that. Do you know how she concluded the meeting? She brought it to a close by telling us that it—*the meeting*—was a pleasure. A pleasure *indeed*."

I burst into laughter. "Better?"

"Yes, better. Thanks, I needed that."

"It's been a *pleasure*."

Alex responded with a pout and awkwardly tried to swing her gold-bar-laden bag at me. "I'll show all of you pleasure," she said in a huff under her breath.

"*Ohh*...do you have a sadistic side that comes out to play when you're annoyed?"

Alex flashed me a mysterious smile. "I have hidden depths."

"I never doubted that."

Alex's smile warmed. I realized she had walked us to the newsroom. It was dark inside. She flipped the switches and flooded it with light.

"You know...I think you *really* do have a sadistic side. You just relayed a terrible meeting you've had and now we're back where it all began? I'm afraid I've unwittingly stumbled into your hidden depths."

Alex rolled her eyes, chucked her bag onto a chair, and reached over to grab my wrist very gently. I barely managed to stop myself from flinching at her touch. The sleeves of my sweater were rolled all the way to my elbows; I hadn't expected company so late in the day and I had forgotten to roll them back down when Alex started talking to me. I didn't want her to see my fresh set of wounds.

Alex led me to a door at the back of the newsroom and threw it open. I exhaled in surprise. The door had been so inconspicuous I never gave it much thought. I just assumed it led to a storage room, like how another ordinary door in the newsroom led to the unexciting but necessary darkroom. This space was different, though. It was a little bare—a modest table in the middle which could probably sit no more than four people and an old, blue couch in the corner—but was bathed in a warm light that made it cozy and inviting. Alex and I stood side by side in the doorway. It wasn't terribly wide, which meant that Alex was really close. I discreetly placed my arms behind my back.

"Cool, huh? You'd be surprised how many people don't realize this room exists. I think it's the door. It's not inviting. I've told them before, I said 'hey, here's an idea, can't we just hang up a sign that says *Fun Room*?' But nope, never took off, so it still operates like a secret portal. But thing is, even knowing it's here, most people would rather sit out in the main room—it's easier to socialize that way—but I thought you might appreciate it." Alex rested her back against the doorframe. "For days, you know, when you need some peace and quiet, but you don't want to be completely alone."

Being alone—I didn't mind. In fact, I had gotten used to it. But loneliness, the cousin of solitude, was still debilitating most days. Admitting to it, however, felt like weakness, and I didn't want Alex to see me as weak. It made me rush to put up my walls.

"I do—like this. Top marks, Alex. You know I was just finishing up my homework earlier, right? It's not like company was required for that." I kept my tone lighthearted.

"I know," Alex said simply, her hands clasped loosely in front of her. "I just felt like you shouldn't have to be alone."

Her voice was kind and devoid of any suggestion of pity. I hadn't been expecting anyone to consider what it was I needed, much less care. Caught off-guard by how touched I felt, I didn't trust my voice to hold steady.

"Alexis," I finally said, my voice hoarse, my heart tripping over itself at the sound of her name on my lips.

She seemed surprised, unused to hearing her name said this way.

Thank you—two simple words. I wanted to say them. But would Alex know the weight of what they meant when she had yet to know me? I took a breath.

"Thank you."

One moment she was quiet. The next, her eyes gentle and warm, she said, "You're welcome, Skylar."

/

Alex never quite ignored me again. Along the school hallways, she gave imperceptible nods in greeting. Out in the main newsroom area, she would be friendly enough, but never displaying the deep warmth she'd shown at the fall retreat and the afternoon when she found me in the classroom alone. Then one day after school, she joined me in the alcove, and in that space—alone with me, without an audience—she was relaxed, funny, reflective, even tender.

One afternoon turned into two, the third into the fourth, and then some more, each one pushing back at the overhanging sense of darkness that so often threatened to overwhelm me. Over time, the fleeting spark I felt for my crush transformed into something significant and far more permanent.

It was how I found myself one night, home, staring at my phone like it was the enemy. I had picked it up only to put it back down more times than I could count and occasionally, when I was a little braver, I would dial Alex's number but hang up before the call could connect. I wanted to tell her how I felt about her and see if we could take things further, but I was terrified because I was flying blind. I didn't know if Alex liked me in the same way or if she even batted for the same team. I hated uncertainty, but what I hated more was regret. That aversion trumped doing the smart thing, which was to do nothing at all.

I braced myself, picked up the phone, and dialed her number again. My heart was galloping by the time she picked up. Embarrassed, I stuttered my way through small talk, and then my mind finally gave out and went blank.

"Skye, you there?"

"Oh yeah, yeah. I, uh, I actually called because…" I mentally closed my eyes and exhaled; it's now or never. "I like you, Alex."

The words sounded so insignificant.

"As in, I *like* you."

The words still sounded insignificant.

There was silence. My heart was close to bursting.

"Skye…I'm flattered…"

My heart sank. Those were the words that preceded a no. I flattened my face into my pillow.

"But I just…I just don't do that anymore."

I stopped breathing. Alex's explanation made zero sense. What did it even mean? Do what? What did *anymore* mean? Did it mean that she *used* to do it?

"I know you might have heard that I dated some girls in the last few years…but that's in the past. I'm not like that anymore."

First, this was news to me. Second, news or not, none of it was computing, even as I dumbly repeated her words back to myself in my head.

"Okay…so what? That was a phase? You were experimenting?"

"I wouldn't call it a phase…"

"No?"

"No."

"Experimenting then?"

"Nope."

"Right, okay…" Another dead end. I contemplated hanging up. The call had gone from hopeful to embarrassing to downright weird. I needed it to be over, but Alex wasn't quite done.

"Skye, I don't want this to change things between us. I'd still like us to be friends. Can we do that?"

There was no way that kind of arrangement would end well—Alex wanting to be friends, me wanting her. I tried to visualize the expression on her face as she managed this conversation from her end of the line. All I could see was the first time she turned to look at me in the gym. My heart lurched against my ribcage.

"Yes," I said, so softly it could have been a whisper.

My head rolled its eyes at my heart.

I had no way to know if that was the right answer. It may well have been the wrong one, but at that moment, in all matters concerning Alex, I would have traded everything for anything, and I did.

CHAPTER 10

"Is that all you're going to wear?" Octavia asks.

I smooth down the tank top I've just slipped on and turn around. Alison and I are hosting pre-drinks at our apartment tonight before the usual stint at Element, and Octavia arrived early. She's made herself comfortable on my bed, propped up on her elbows, causing her barely buttoned black shirt to draw back on her shoulders to reveal an unnecessary amount of skin.

"Yeah, what's wrong with that?"

"It's cold out."

"Hmm," I say, "you can keep me warm if you like."

Octavia looks me up and down as I approach and I spot the familiar want returning in her eyes. She sits up and loosely places her hands on the back of my knees when I'm near. She runs her tongue across her lips, her mouth parting slightly. It's alluring, perhaps an invitation to kiss her. After all, she was the one discussing threesomes with Jamie. It is tempting, but Jamie's absence holds me back. I'm not sure if she would mind me and Octavia getting a head start without her, even if she's in no position to object, having been the one to offer me up on a silver platter without even asking me first.

"Where's Jamie?" Octavia asks.

I can't say I'm surprised by the question. The weight of a guilty conscience has that terrible yet effective habit of keeping people in line.

"Drinks with her tutorial mates. Why? Disappointed?"

"Didn't say that."

"Sure sounded like you are. Why? Did you want to talk to her about threesomes again?"

Octavia looks like a deer caught in headlights.

"Cause I didn't realize that's what you wanted with me."

"You're making it sound like it's a crime!" she says. She pulls her hands back to her sides.

"I'm not! I'm just expressing surprise at what you wanted. No need to get defensive."

"Well, then yes, it is." Now she sounds flippant and a little belligerent.

"Really?" I look her dead in the eye. "A threesome with me *and* Jamie. That's what you *really* want?"

No response.

"Because it sure as hell isn't what I want with you, O. I wanted to date you, *that's* what I wanted to do."

"Yeah, but I wasn't the one who found a girlfriend during the summer break." The belligerence is radiating.

"Octavia..." I tut and point at her. "Pot." I point at myself. "Kettle."

Face softening, Octavia eases off on the petulance.

I caress her cheek. "I know I made a mess with the waiting part, but this thing between us? It's still there. I know you feel it too. So why don't we give this another shot?"

She freezes like a statue.

"Okay...did I read you wrong then?" I ask, genuinely confused. "Because not too long ago, you had *your* hands on *my* legs."

"No...no. It's just that you and Jamie are, you know, still together."

"Yeah, I know. I'll end it then. Right now."

Octavia glances at me and away, confusing me further. She clears her throat. "Caleb…and I…we decided to give things another go. He argued that summer wasn't a fair reflection of how things should be. We weren't seeing each other as often so…" Her voice is almost too soft for me to hear.

I didn't see that one coming, yet it's déjà-vu all over again. I didn't think I would ever hear that name again and I still don't know who Caleb is, but regardless, I'm ready to throw him into the back of my closet and lock him up for good so that Octavia has one less reason to reject my advances. I let out a deep sigh and straighten up. Fool me once, shame on you; fool me twice, shame on me.

"Fantastic, O. Because that went soooo well the last time you decided to do the same thing. What is it? Doing the same thing over and over again and expecting different results? Oh right. Insanity." I'm working myself up. I fling open the door, and it makes a pleasing bang. "Please, don't let me keep you," I say and walk out without looking back.

There is a loud hum of voices coming from the living room. Paige is there, leaning in its threshold. Her lips curl into a soft, lazy smile in greeting. When Octavia brushes past me to join the others without a word, the smile becomes suggestive. I shake my head at how scampish she looks and step into the room where everyone is hanging out with drinks in hand. On the dining table is a solitary empty pint glass surrounded by cards which are faced downwards; it was a Ring of Fire setup.

I groan. "Not this."

"Oh yes, this." Her smile fills her whole voice.

"You sound pleased."

"I was outnumbered when we voted, so I'm making the best of a bad situation."

"How is that?"

"I only have a pinch of rum in what is otherwise a very large cup of coke and if I draw a king, I am going to dump my entire drink into that pint."

"Good plan, but what if you draw the last king?"

"Tsk, don't jinx me. You want in?"

"Yes."

"Here." Paige places her drink in my hand, her fingers grazing mine. "I'll make another."

/

Octavia half stumbles, half collides into the couch. I hold out my hand to steady her. We made landfall in Element about an hour ago, much to my surprise given everyone's best efforts to get everyone else completely and utterly wasted back at the apartment. It was like nobody had plans to go elsewhere, and yet here we are, continuing our streak of momentously bad drinking decisions. Octavia realizes that it's my hand holding her up, huffs, and stalks off unsteadily. I stare after her, frustrated.

"Girl trouble?" Alison is seated beside me, cheeks flushed, sanguine.

"I'd rather not talk about it."

"Sure." She regards Paige and Cam a stone's throw away. "It's an interesting choice, don't you think? Cam dating Paige."

"Why?"

"Have you seen the last few girls Cam's been snogging? They're just all so…" Alison scrunches up her nose and does a funny little shrug of her shoulders. "Giggly and girly. Paige is so…suave, quiet, not a girly girl. Plus she looks like a player.

Have you seen the number of girls hitting on her? Blimey, I hope Cam doesn't get her heart broken."

Alison's opinion of Paige interests me. Of all the times Paige has been in Element with Cam, her attention hardly ever strays far from Cam. Even with other girls chatting her up, the time she spends making small talk is only what one would consider polite. Paige may not radiate undying devotion, but equally, she doesn't strike me as being a player. There are plenty of those in Element, and Paige just doesn't qualify.

"Cam's a big girl, she'll be okay. So Paige isn't your type then? Even though you did just call her suave."

"Pfft. Not at all. Do you know who's my type?"

"Who?"

"That girl, Rachel." Alison points to a demure, sweet-looking brunette with shoulder-length hair. "I met her that time when we went to the LGBT lunch but didn't really think much about it until we bumped into each other on campus last week."

"What are you doing sitting here with me then?!"

Alison turns several shades redder. "She just got here. I wanted to give it a few minutes before I go over. Can't look overeager, you know? Can't look like I'm sitting here without a friend, either."

I tut with feigned disapproval. "Using me to make you look good."

Alison shoots me a sheepish grin. "So Paige doesn't seem like your type, either, eh?"

"I don't have a type."

"Sure you do. Tall, usually blonde, not too aloof, not too desperate, and definitely bordering on the feminine side. More of a girly-girl but not too girly. Sound familiar?"

"You've been taking notes."

Alison shrugs. "Just wanted to figure out what you've been looking for. Thought I did. Then you started dating Jamie."

I raise an eyebrow.

"Your height. Not blonde. In your face. Doesn't know when to call it quits. I guess the only criteria she fulfills is being feminine but not a girly-girl."

"So not my type then?"

"More like a mistake."

The snark in Alison's voice is overt. I give it a few seconds to sink in before bursting out into hearty laughter. Alison, with all the passive-aggressive politeness of a British person, certainly has her moments.

"Okay, that's my opening," Alison says in a rush. She notes Rachel to be without company now and a near-empty drink. "Wish me luck!" She vanishes.

I wander to the bar. The alcoholic buzz has waned and all I want now is a really big glass of water. The bartender places a massive cup in front of me and starts to fill it.

"Skylar."

The hairs on the back of my neck stand as Paige says my name, her voice huskier than I remember. I don't turn. "I don't think your plan worked very well."

Paige comes up beside me. She runs her hand through her hair. "No, I don't think it did." Her eyes are rueful and a little heavy-lidded from all the drinking. It's rather sexy, almost like come-hither eyes.

"Well, let's give you some credit, shall we? It worked very well in the first round, until you were no longer in charge of top-ups. 'A weak hand' is what Alison called you, I believe."

"My hands are anything but weak." Paige smirks.

I laugh, the sexual innuendo not lost on me.

"We should do coffee again," she says.

Once more, those words slip out of her mouth so casually. Before tonight, we hadn't so much as said ten sentences to each other since meeting for coffee. I would see her at Element with Cam, Cam would usually do most of the talking, and Paige and I would speak only occasionally, not so much as with each other but to the group. I had even started to think that coffee was a one-off, but here she is, asking again.

"You have my number." I give her a gentle pat on the side of her thigh as I slip off the barstool and make my way back to our friends.

CHAPTER 11

I step out into Cam's yard.

"Hi."

The sudden greeting causes me to whirl around, and Paige is leaning against the wall in a darkened corner.

"Fuck, Paige! You scared me. What are you doing out here?" I slide the patio door shut, leaving behind squeals of laughter. It's game night and everyone is inside, including Rachel, whom Alison is now dating.

"I came out for a smoke. What's your excuse?" Paige crosses her outstretched legs and takes a deep drag of her cigarette. She exhales in a slow and controlled manner.

"I couldn't endure another minute listening to Jamie and Cam debate the benefits of biking versus public transport."

"Ahh...that. Were they just about done? I'm not going back in if they're not."

"Coward."

Paige shrugs off the jibe and instead starts to recount the debate between Jamie and Cam.

"Why are you doing this to me?" I grimace. "You know I was *just* there, right?"

"Seems fair for us to suffer together. It's what friends do, right? Did you think the coffee tasted a little weird at The Honey Badger yesterday?"

My eyebrows shoot up. "Have you been standing out here pondering that? But yes, it tasted different. Different beans maybe?" I point to the multiple cigarette butts on the ground. "So, why are you really out here? Because it's certainly been a while."

Paige hesitates. "It's been a long day. Needed some peace and quiet."

"Oh..." I glance back at the living room and contemplate how to retreat.

She reaches out and hooks my belt loop with her finger before I can take my first step. "It's okay. Stay."

She looks tired and a little out of sorts, but her eyes encourage me to stay, and she follows it up with the offer of a cigarette from her pack. I light it off the tip of hers. She has on a dark blue sweater, the sleeves bunched up at her elbows and the cuffs of her white shirt barely visible. The edges of her collar are showing unevenly from beneath the sweater, with only one side tucked out. I reach over and gently untuck the other side and smooth it against the sweater.

"Everything okay?"

"Hmm." She takes another deep drag. "I got one of my papers back today. Rubbish score, off track, off topic, or perhaps the professor was off his rocker, whatever that was, just wasn't good enough. I'm not hung up on grades, but that essay does count towards a big part of my score."

"I'm sorry. That sucks. But it's just the one paper right? A portion of a module?"

Paige nods.

"Then it'll be okay. You'll get the next one."

Paige falls silent. I think of asking her what the paper was on, but doubt she brought this up for us to dissect the reasons why her paper didn't fare better.

"Want to talk about the paper itself?" I ask, to be sure.

"No."

"Want to burn the paper, then?"

"Yes."

"A funeral party for your ghastly paper."

"Nothing but the best."

"Consider it done, Paige Thomas."

The corner of her lips curls into a smile. We fall into a comfortable silence.

"Oh my word." Cam comes bursting out onto the patio at some point. "Have the two of you been here all along? You're missing all the fun inside. Come on," she coos as she leans over and kisses Paige on the lips, "don't be antisocial, baby." She wipes the smudge of residual lipstick away from Paige's mouth. She points at our smokes. "So, last one, then you're both coming back in, okay?"

Obediently, we agree and Cam leaves us, pleased.

"Asocial," Paige comments once the patio door shuts.

"Sorry?"

"It's asocial, not antisocial. Antisocial means we have no regard for society, or other people's feelings. It's also often associated with acts of hostility. Asocial, well, that just means we're not feeling social. Think introversion. It's a common mistake."

Her delivery is matter-of-fact, not snooty at all.

"For a person who's only contemplating a teaching career, you sure have this teaching thing down pat."

"Fuck, sorry. Did I sound like a know-it-all? It wasn't meant to come across like that."

"Nah, it came through just right and you've ensured that I'll never use that term incorrectly again."

The crease of worry leaves Paige's face. "So you and Octavia talking again?"

Since giving me the cold shoulder for two solid weeks after the last encounter in my bedroom, Octavia has resumed her normal programming.

"Seems like."

"What about?"

"She was gushing about how cute Alison and Rachel are. Curious about who Alison dated in the past, and when I said Alison's ex-girlfriend is a complete dick not worth discussing, she just took it in her stride and went back to gushing about Alison and Rachel and their fairytale happy ending."

"The girl is all about the positives, I see."

Octavia is currently beaming at Alison, enamored by whatever Alison is saying. It makes me wonder if they even make girls that sweet anymore.

"It's what makes Octavia, Octavia. If there's a thunderstorm, she's the fucking rainbow that shows up after, cue sunshine and all. I mean, it works, right? She's a doctor. If she loses that, then well, we're all fucked."

"True." With her back against the railing, Paige rests her elbows on top of the metal surface, the short end of her cigarette dangling from her fingers. "Alison's ex-girlfriend is a complete dick not worth discussing, huh?"

"Yup."

"Why's that?"

"Her heart belonged to someone else, but she dated Alison anyway. Even made Alison think that it was going to be 'for always.' Then randomly ended it one day with an *I don't love you anymore* and *I'm sorry*. Floors Alison."

"Fuck me. That's rough. Someone we know?"

"Yup."

"Who?"

I pause. *Might as well say it.* "Me."

A burst of laughter comes from inside. Paige gives me a friendly shove. "Fuck off. For real?" My silence tells her everything she needs to know. "Wow, you guys don't let on, do you?" she finally says.

"I think Alison tries her best to erase our past from her memory," I say, keeping my voice down. "I get it. You want to forget you ever had it, forget that you wasted your precious time on it. Makes the getting over easier, makes it less awkward between us…and it was—fucking awkward at the start, probably more so for her than me. I was just so relieved to be out of it."

"Why did you date her then?"

I allow the smoke to fill my lungs and linger. "She asked."

Paige arches an eyebrow.

"I know. I'm a real peach, aren't I?"

"Your words, not mine." Paige seems terribly relaxed about the revelation. Someone like Octavia may not have been as kind.

I grind out the last of my cigarette with the heel of my shoe. "I hated hurting her. She's a good person."

"It would have always hurt, one way or another. That's how relationships are. We don't love equally." Paige casts a look over at the house. "Besides, she looks like she's having the best time with Rachel. Couldn't have done that without you fucking off, so it's all good," she says, deadpan.

I crack a smile, then laugh. Another excited squeal of laughter erupts in the living room.

"Who was it? Who did your heart belong to?" Paige asks after a moment.

A nervous chuckle escapes me. "All the conversations we can have, and this is the one you want?"

Paige shrugs. "I think we make the mistake of asking all the wrong questions. Jamie…Octavia…sure, I have questions, but they don't seem as important."

I rest my arms against the railing and stare out into the distance. The silence feels heavy.

"There was this girl…Alex." My heart contracts. "She was everything."

I let the words sit. They seem so insignificant, swallowed up by the night, inadequate to describe the person whose mere existence fills my entire world.

"I don't really know how to describe her or what we had. All I know is that I wouldn't be here without her. I wasn't in a good place before her, then she showed up and everything changed. Everything was better after her. Everything was better *because* of her and I…I loved her. I still do."

I laugh softly, joyless. A familiar, hollow ache seeps into the fault lines of my heart. It threatens to fracture everything I have been holding together.

"I wish I could forget her, you know. Figure out how *not* to love her, want her, or need her. But ironically, all that happens is that I end up missing her more."

"It's okay to miss her," Paige says quietly.

"I don't want to."

"I know, but you know too that we can't help ourselves. Some people can be very hard to forget."

"Well, it hurts, and fucking sucks big time."

"Oh, I know. It's the worst. *They're* the worst." Paige loops an arm around my back and gives me a tight squeeze. She presses the side of her head against mine. "Want to head in and down shots until you forget about her?"

"Are you downing them with me?"

"Fuck yes. You're not the only one with something to forget.

I have Jamie's and Cam's entire debate about bikes versus public transport to erase." Her embrace tightens one more time. "Come on, I've got you."

CHAPTER 12

Jamie and I are heading to Manchester to spend Christmas with her family.

"You sure your parents are cool with this? Me visiting?" I ask Jamie on the coach. I had wanted to take the train, which would have been faster and smoother. Jamie, in typical fashion, resisted. Taking the coach isn't cheap during the festive season, but it is still cheaper than taking the train, which is how we find ourselves here, now, stuck in traffic. I mask my irritation. Neither of us is strapped for cash, but she keeps behaving like we are one minute away from going broke.

"Yeah, I was chatting with Ma the other night, we started talking about Christmas, and it sort of came out. She never seemed to mind gay people, so I just winged it and hoped that she'll be fine with her own daughter coming out to her."

"I didn't realize you were thinking about coming out."

"I didn't realize either, but when Ma asked me how my week has been, I just wanted to talk about you and what we got up to. I love you and I wanted her to know about you. I can't wait for you to meet them."

I hold Jamie's hand in mine. "Well, I'm more than happy to meet your parents." I give it a moment's pause. "I love you too, Jamie."

Jamie had said those three words just before the winter break. We were out, Octavia had brought Caleb to Element, and Jamie had observed that Octavia behaved like a dead log around him, unlike when she was with me. Jamie's eyes had sparkled, and with her arm wrapped firmly around my shoulder and her chest all puffed up, she told me she loved me. I still didn't know what it meant to be in love with anyone who wasn't Alex, but because Octavia threw Caleb in my face that evening and Jamie's confession of love was like a salve for my wounded pride, I reciprocated.

Jamie smiles and looks out the window. The coach inches forward. I bury the sigh. Jamie and I have lately found our way into too many inane, mindless arguments. Jamie channel surfing. Jamie staying over at my apartment for too many days and annoying the crap out of Alison. Jamie refusing to shop anywhere else but at the £1 shop. But today is what we call a good day. We haven't bickered once, it's nearly evening, and God willing, we will be in Manchester in an hour. This is probably the universe rewarding me for having agreed to put up with the arduous coach ride.

"I miss Manchester," Jamie says, eyes distant. "I'm thinking of moving back here after uni. Write for an indie music magazine, not the stuff of capitalists."

"And what happens when the indie acts go big?" Surely everyone wanted fame and fortune. Is Jamie going to forgo these acts when they peak? It seems like career suicide.

"I may have to follow them still. Duty calls, you know? But I can say it's because I wrote about them when they were small."

I lean in and give her a quick kiss. It's a nice change seeing her like this, full of hope and drive. Usually, her soapbox consists of gripes about the system, how consumerists and capitalists have taken over the world, and how everyone almost always becomes a sell-out in order to put food on the table. Jamie hates that her parents have insisted that she go into the world armed with a degree, and Jamie most definitely hates my degree and the future it represents. This is both fascinating and ironic, given that Jamie's dad is an investment banker. I wonder if she sees herself as payment for his sins—a cynical, resistant, tiresome atonement.

"I know you probably want to live in London, but would you consider moving to Manchester? It could be so good. You will love Manchester, I know it. Can you imagine it? I can see our lives sprawled out ahead of us. There's so much I want to show you, so much we can do..."

Jamie may be the girl who didn't leave after our one-night stand and it is anybody's guess how long we will last, but *forever*, she certainly is not. Yet I don't correct her and she talks on, excited, mistaking my silence for acquiescence. Our good days are becoming few and far between, so there is no reason to ruin a perfectly good one.

/

I take another look around the exhibit hall in exasperation. People mill about, viewing the works of art. All the time in the world with nowhere to be, but the same cannot be said for Jamie and me—we have a dinner to get to with her parents.

"Jamie, baby, we have to go," I repeat.

"Just one minute."

It has been one minute, the last few times, starting a half an hour ago. Despite the gentle reminders, her responses have been identical, as has been the lack of movement. And even though I have given us a healthy margin of time, to my eternal frustration, it appears that we are going to be late again.

"No, Jamie. Not 'one more minute.' Now. We promised your parents we would be home by 4:30. It is now 4:30 and *we are still here.*"

Jamie's parents have been dying to try out this up-and-coming restaurant we are headed to tonight and had been elated when they finally managed to secure reservations. It seemed only considerate that we heed her mom's plea to be on time.

Jamie takes a couple of steps to her left, but instead of making a move like we're meant to, she starts to read the information card for another exhibit.

"Oh for fuck's sake, Jamie. Stop pulling this shit on me. You're acting like a child with the attention span of a fucking goldfish. We need to leave. Now!"

Jamie's head whips up. Fantastic—when gentle persuasion fails, just fling a slew of insults and that is guaranteed to grab Jamie's attention. She has annoyance painted all over her face. "I heard you the first time."

"Did you? Because that was about half an hour ago, and with your lack of urgency, you could have had me fooled."

"It's not that late. Take a chill pill or something."

"How is it not that late? We were meant to be home by now."

Jamie hooks her thumbs through the loops of her backpack, planting her feet firmly on the ground. "I already told you I wanted to make full use of the free entry."

"It'll still be free tomorrow."

"But we came *today*."

"If you like this so much, we can come back tomorrow. It's not a big deal."

"But I planned for other activities tomorrow and some of those are either only free or have student discounts tomorrow!" Jamie tugs at the loops of her backpack and the shoulder straps tighten around her arms.

"Jamie. *Please*. Can we focus on the fact that we are meant to be having dinner with your parents and it is, I think, important for us to be on time instead of pursuing your incessant need to hunt down all things free and cheap?"

I regret the last comment as soon as it's out of my mouth.

Jamie's face deepens into a massive frown and her mouth opens into what I'm sure is an angry retort when her phone rings. I catch a glimpse of her flashing screen. It's her mom. Jamie starts the call by explaining how we had lost track of time. *We?* There is no bloody *we* in this, and I resent her for placing equal blame on me.

She falls silent. She apologizes and promises that we will be back in the next thirty minutes. We don't say a single word to each other on our way back.

/

Jamie stalks into her bedroom when we arrive home, ignoring her mom who hollers at us to hurry up and be ready as soon as possible. I close the door behind me and lean against it, certain that Jamie and I are about to have another fight.

Jamie whips around. "You didn't have to be such a bitch at the museum."

"There's no need for that."

"Because of you, I didn't make full use of my free entry."

"Seriously? That's what you're hung up on?" I hiss, trying to keep my voice down. "You know I would have stayed until closing if we could, but we were already late. You know how much I hate being late, and more importantly, you knew how much this dinner mattered to your parents!"

Jamie takes a few steps towards me. "My parents will live; it's just fucking dinner. They're not the problem. *You* are. Why are you so fucking uptight about this all the time?"

"I am not fucking uptight about this. It's called being considerate. You may want to try it once in a while instead of behaving like a self-entitled brat."

Jamie takes a few more steps towards me. The hostility coming off her in waves feels familiar, daunting. I avert my eyes and cast them downwards.

"Back off, Jamie."

"Oh. Does *this* bother you?" Jamie is close enough for me to feel her breath on my face.

"Yes, it does. So, back off, please."

Jamie doesn't. In fact, she comes even closer, our bodies separated by barely an inch. A triumphant snarl contorts her face into someone I don't recognize.

"Jamie...b-back off."

Push her, just push her. I will my arms to move, but they stay frozen.

"What, Skye? I'm not doing shit. I'm just talking. All I want to know is why you've always got to be so uptight and shit and spoil my fun."

I shrink back against the door. *Just push her away, Skylar!* I hear the command, but Jamie remains as close as ever. I'm on the wrong side of this closed door and nothing I say, or do, will keep me safe.

There are hurried knocks on the door. "Jamie! Are you ready? You better be. Your dad had to call the restaurant and convince them to hold the table for us. We need to go *now*!"

That interruption breaks Jamie's trance—she takes a step back. I chance the sudden reprieve and tug at the door handle, opening it to reveal her mom in the hallway.

"Jamie!" she says, eyes narrowing. "Why are you still in the same clothes? I told you to change ASAP!"

"Yes, yes Ma! Sorry! I'll change now."

I paste a smile on my face and navigate around Jamie's mom, hoping she won't notice that I'm in the same clothes.

"Are you ready, Skylar? You still have time to change if you like," Jamie's mom says more kindly to me.

My eyes dart between her and the girl in the room. The thought of putting myself at Jamie's mercy again behind the closed door is unbearable. "I-it's okay, Mrs. Walker. I'm good. Just had to freshen up that's all. I'll wait in the living room."

I force a bigger smile on my face, hoping it convinces her. Jamie's mom cocks her head slightly and when she nods and turns her attention back to Jamie, I rush down the corridor before she has anything else to say.

/

Jamie's and her parents' voices float through from the living room to her bedroom. Excusing myself as soon as we got home, I had been desperate to put distance between me and Jamie. Her parents were right to be excited about the restaurant. The food was heavenly, but no amount of good food, wine or good behavior on Jamie's part during dinner can erase the earlier incident. I bury myself deeper in the duvet, which I hoard. Sleeping apart from Jamie tonight isn't an option. There are no more spare rooms, and it isn't as if I can just crash on the couch in the living room without inviting unwanted questions from Jamie's parents, which no doubt will stoke Jamie's ire. The bolster in the middle of the queen bed will have to do, and Jamie can damn well find another duvet in her own house.

Moonlight streams into the room. I toss and contemplate whether to draw the curtains, but it's not the light that's keeping me awake. It's the memory that her behavior dredges up, like a hand unceremoniously shoved into the deepest recesses of my mind and hauling it to the surface.

I can still remember the air of disquiet when I came out to my mother. It wasn't acceptance that hung in the air, just her inability to comprehend the words I had just said to her.

What do you mean? she had demanded.

What I said, Mom, I'm gay.

What do you mean? What does gay mean?! She had started to raise her voice. She knew what it meant. She just didn't want to know it.

It means I like girls, Mom. It means I like *girls.*

Ni? Tong xing lian?! She was reaching fever pitch, resorting to asking me in Mandarin if I was gay, her eyeballs wide at the prospect that it might not have just been one giant miscommunication.

Yes.

My admission had been firm. I was not ashamed. I have never been ashamed of who I am, and I refused to allow my fear of her cow me into taking back what I said, not even as she stood over me and started to slap my head, my shoulders, my back, my face.

Sick.

Filthy.

Disgusting.

Each word is accompanied by her hand. On every inch of my bare skin. Fast, furious, packed with all the weight of her rage and revulsion. I had seen her annoyed before, angry too. Punished for having less-than-perfect grades. But this was what happened when I became the less-than-perfect daughter in her eyes. My skin started to turn an angry red and I wondered: how many hits could it endure before splitting? Ten? Twenty? Thirty? I lost count.

I searched for my dad as it happened, needing him. My eyes passed my brother standing by the front door, arms crossed, wearing a look of ugly, indescribable pleasure. I eventually found my dad, standing in a corner of the living room. Ashen. Deathly still. Seconds had turned into minutes, but his help, I realized, wasn't coming. I didn't understand—he had said he would love me no matter what.

Get out, leave! You are the devil's work. You are not welcomed here! my mother had raged on.

I was only fourteen. Too terrified to leave, too terrified to stay. I didn't know what I was going to do. I didn't know where I was going to go. I had no one. I had nothing. Still, I threw myself in the direction of the front door, wincing at the sting of the marks my mother had left on me.

Get lost, dyke, my brother sneered as he moved away from the door. *If you ever come back begging for help, I am going to take great pleasure in watching you beg first before I kick you back out onto the streets, back where you belong. Nothing but a broke, hapless tramp.*

Get out now! Before I throw you out myself! My mother looked hysterical.

I willed myself to place one hand on the door handle, twist, and pull. The air outside my parents' home would have been a biting cold that night. I knew it, but I never felt it. Instead, all I felt in that moment was her grip on my shirt, the force of being unexpectedly hauled backwards and the roughness of the carpet against my skin when my face hit the ground.

"Skye…" The mattress beside me sinks and Jamie is leaning over the bolster fort. I hadn't realized that she had entered the room.

"Baby..." She runs her fingers through my hair. I don't turn. I can feel hot tears running down my cheek, wetting the pillow. I don't want her to see me cry. I don't want her to think that I'm crying over her.

"I'm so sorry. I wasn't in control earlier. I was just so disappointed that we couldn't be at the exhibition longer. You know how excited I was about seeing it."

I don't say anything.

"I'm so sorry, baby. I promise I won't do it again. I love you. You know I'll never do anything to hurt you. Please forgive me."

I shut my eyes tight and push my face into the pillow, but not before flinging part of the duvet across the bed. I tell myself it's winter and Jamie will freeze without it. Jamie gratefully welcomes the olive branch I extend but respectfully allows the bolster fort to remain. She does, however, wrap her arm around it and me. I don't resist. Jamie's apology is more of an apology than the one I never received from my family.

CHAPTER 13

Jamie blunders by, eyes bleary and unfocused. Since downing multiple shots at home, she has displayed even less moderation in Element. She approaches the bar. Money changes hands and she has a beer *and* a shot in her hands.

"Shouldn't you maybe try and stop her?" Alison is aghast.

"Tried. Didn't work. Not her keeper."

"You two doing okay?"

"Why?"

"Sounds like more bickering than usual whenever I'm home."

That is accurate. Jamie *had* been on her best behavior during our last few days in Manchester. Quieter, less argumentative, and unexpectedly generous. That Jamie has taken leave now, and I quite miss her.

"We're fine," I say. Alison doesn't respond. "What?"

"You have been…you know…"

"What, Alison? You know you can spit it out."

"Some nights you seem to pay more attention to every other girl in Element than your actual girlfriend. Like you're bored of her."

Guilt rips through my body, not because Alison called me out, but because she had said something similar to me right before we broke up.

"I— It's not that. We have other issues."

"Okay." Alison falls quiet. "If you're not happy with her, Skye…you should tell her. You shouldn't be with her. It's not fair to either of you."

Another flash of guilt rips through me. I can only bring myself to nod.

"How are you and Rachel?" I ask.

There is a soft sigh of contentment.

"She is amazing and we completely get each other. She's a keeper, I'm telling you."

Alison finding her happiness. It brings me joy. I wait for her to turn and look at me. "I'm really, *really*, happy for you."

She smiles, eyes full of warmth. "Thanks, Skye."

I scan the room for Jamie; she's slumped face-down on the bar counter. It's only 10:00 p.m.

"Right. Comatose girlfriend. That's my cue. Duty calls." Alison shoots me a look of sympathy. "You at Rachel's tonight?" Alison nods. I scan the room and note everyone else to be caught up in their own activities, laughing, drinking, and generally still having their wits about them. "Okay, I'll see you tomorrow then. Tell the others I'm off. Night."

/

It was not an easy walk home. Except for technically being able to put one foot in front of the other, Jamie was barely responsive. Going past her place—bathed in pitch-black darkness—I lamented the fact that she didn't bring her keys with her, which meant that I couldn't just dump her at her place and leg it back to Element. By the time I had hoisted my deadweight girlfriend up three flights of stairs and onto the couch in my living room, I regretted not having left her in a heap in a corner of the club and just gotten on with my night.

It's 1:15 a.m. now and Jamie remains dead to the world. I

place my finger under her nose and check that she's still breathing. My phone vibrates in my pocket.

"Let me in," Octavia says when I pick up.

"What? Where are you?"

"Your front door. Not your main door, your front door. Someone else was coming home too so I came through with him. I was well dodgy, I tell you." Octavia giggles. "Your neighbor probably thought that too, was giving me a suspicious eye. Anyway, I've got food, so let—"

I open my front door. Octavia beams as she holds up two familiar, pale-yellow Styrofoam boxes in one hand and a massive drink in the other. She comes through the doorway without bothering to wait for an invitation and meanders down the corridor. She peers into my room and casts a curious look back at me when she realizes there is no one in it. I gesture for her to go in.

Octavia eyes the textbook and notes I have strewn on the bed. "Were you…studying?"

"When you put it like that, it makes me sound a little sad."

"It's not. I think it's hot. And you know how much I love my women and their glasses."

I choose to ignore flirtatious Octavia, the one who only comes out to play when she's had a bit to drink. She sits on the floor and opens the boxes—burgers and chips. The perfect comfort food for drunk people after a night out.

"So to what do I owe the pleasure of your visit, O?"

"We drank. We went out. You left early. Didn't feel the same without you. So, I hit that kebab place we like, got the food we like, and just hoped that you're still awake. If not, I suppose that's two burgers for me. Yay?"

I'm both touched and flattered by Octavia's decision to come over. Why is it, again, that she and I aren't dating? She fills me in on the rest of the night: people making out, guys arguing in the beer garden, the bartender who couldn't seem to get her drink orders right, Cam getting stroppy because of the numerous girls hitting on Paige and how Alison and Rachel surprised everyone by staying past midnight. It's nearly four in the morning by the time she gets up to make a move. At the door, she cracks a joke about how she'll need to share my bed if she stays any later, to which I simply lift my eyebrows in bewilderment. I can't tell if she's flirting for the fun of it or if she's serious and I'm meant to see this as an opening to make a move on her. Also, last I checked, the girl in front of me has a boyfriend. As my brain reduces itself to a series of garbled commands, Octavia leans in and kisses me on the lips without warning.

"Um," I say when she pulls away. "Not that I'm complaining, but Caleb?"

"We broke up, so..." Octavia simply kisses me again; it's hungrier than the first.

I think about Jamie in the next room, unmoving and unlikely to wake any time soon. I tilt my head up and kiss Octavia back.

CHAPTER 14

The kitchen is a mess. The chopping board with the multiple lemon slices left on it sits unattended, a sticky-looking knife by its side, and various bottles of alcohol and mixers left open and strewn about. There is only one person who can be the cause of this irritating behavior—Jamie. I locate her in my bedroom, somewhat dressed but definitely not ready, sipping on whatever drink she had made in the kitchen and scrolling through the music folder on *my* laptop.

"Skye, you've got new music. Why haven't you been sharing these with me? I've told you before, this is a big deal for me, we're supposed to religiously share our music with one another!"

I roll my eyes. "Yeah, yeah, all in your pledge to fight consumerism, isn't it? Must you *really* do this now, Jamie?" She swivels round, eyes narrowing. "I said to you an hour ago that we were leaving in an hour. But you're still here, drinking, not ready, fixated on music as fucking usual and the kitchen is a mess."

The expression on Jamie's face turns. I close the door to my room. This conversation is going south in fewer than ten seconds and it didn't seem fair to put Alison through another one of these fights.

"I said—I'll be ready." Jamie's response is terse.

"But you're not, are you? And it's 10:30."

"Why do you have to be such a bitch about this?"

"No, Jamie. I am not. It's about being on time because we promised others we would be. It's about not leaving my kitchen in a mess, again. It's about not using my laptop as if it's your own just because I didn't lock the screen. It's called common fucking courtesy, something which you seem utterly incapable of practicing."

Jamie rises from the chair and approaches me. I don't like her demeanor and start to wish I hadn't shut the door for Alison's sake.

"No. It's called *you* being a *bitch* about this."

Jamie looms in front of me. I resist the urge to shrink back against the door. "It's not. And back off, Jamie. I've told you before. I hate it when you get like this."

I hold out a hand to keep Jamie at bay, but she just flicks my hand away and keeps advancing until she has my back wedged between the door and the wardrobe right beside it. I fight irrational panic. Jamie isn't bigger than me, nor is she stronger than me, but her presence is intimidating and makes me feel sick to my stomach. I avoid her stare and hold out my hand again to keep her at a distance.

You can't just hold your hand out, Skylar. Push her away. She's got nothing in her hands. She cannot hurt you.

"S-stop it, Jamie."

God, Skylar. With a little conviction, please.

Jamie presses her body against my hand, her voice dropping an octave. "I will if you stop being a bitch about this. Admit it, you *are* being a bitch about this."

I can see my mom in front of me, my brother sneering in the periphery of my vision, my dad cowering in a corner. I can hear blood pounding in my ears, but I can't tell if that's happening now or if it's just my memories.

Just push her away, Skylar!

My arms come up and I feel them give Jamie a shove. Relief courses through my body at the sudden distance I've created between her and me. She takes a few steps back, surprised. I eye Jamie, wary, unsure of what she will do next. She still seems pissed off, but as the edge of her lip curls, her eyes give way to an expression which confuses me. Lust. Jamie is on me before I can move, pressing her lips against mine. She bats my hands away when I hold them up to fend her off.

"What the fuck!" I shove Jamie off me. "What are you doing?!"

"Come on, let's fuck and make up, Skye. Aren't you turned on by this? I think this is hot."

"No! I am not fucking turned on by this. There's no 'fuck and make up.' You want it, go fuck someone else!"

I open the door without a second's thought, entirely propelled by revulsion.

"Five fucking minutes, Jamie. Then you're leaving with us. Whether you want to leave dressed or not is entirely up to you, but five fucking minutes. That's all you're going to get."

/

When Jamie promised me in Manchester that she wouldn't lose control again, I believed her because she said she loved me. Now, her keys in my pocket weigh me down like lead.

I was careful not to let her know that I had taken her set of house keys when we left the apartment. Had she known, she would have made an excuse, delayed, convinced Alison to go ahead, and she and I would have never left. It would be like those times when we would fight, and she would refuse to leave in spite of my pleas. She would accuse me of lacking the emotional bandwidth to communicate with her, that it was my fault that we could not kiss and make up. I would let her win and she would get to stay, because it was easier that way.

Jamie's behavior normalized the instant she came out of my room and saw Alison. It was like that afternoon when she stormed out of her lecture five minutes early and repeatedly kicked the wall as she raged about the "dumb fucking professor" who didn't agree with her, but then, as soon as the rest of the lecture group dispersed through the doors, snapped back into shape like a rubber band. I'm not sure what I find more disconcerting—the fact that Jamie lost control again or that she recovered so quickly. Regardless, what I want is to pass Jamie her keys and tell her to go back to *her* home tonight. However, since arriving at Element, all I seem capable of doing is camping at a darkened corner of the beer garden.

Jamie approaches, and I inhale sharply, fighting my instinct to bolt.

"Skye..." Awkward, shamefaced and extremely apologetic. I know this Jamie.

"I don't want to hear it."

"I know, I'm sorry. I was a jerk earlier. I lost my cool. I didn't mean it."

"That's what you said the last time, but here we are, you saying sorry, *again*."

"I just got carried away. I can't help it. You know how excited I get about new music."

"Yeah, but it wasn't yours to take." Jamie's lips press into a thin hard line. "Jamie, don't. You came here to apologize. It doesn't give you the right to pick another fight." I thrust my hands into my pocket and fish out Jamie's keys. I hold them out.

"You came prepared to kick me out." Jamie's tone trembles with accusation, all remorse leaving her eyes.

I curse mentally. Why is it always a mission with Jamie? I'm an idiot for thinking that a public venue would have made any difference.

"The apartment isn't yours to come and go as you please. Same goes for the music, which isn't yours to take as you please, either." The thought that Jamie might resist even this simple request makes me anxious. "Don't make a scene, Jamie. It's unbecoming. Just take the damn keys."

Jamie's eyes narrow. She emanates something dark, like an impending apocalypse. It makes me wish I could swallow the words I just said. But then her gaze slides past me.

"Hi, Jamie."

It's Paige. I can feel her hand on my lower back.

"Hey," Jamie responds flatly. Her gaze flickers between Paige and me, then settles on Paige. Paige is silent, unmoving.

"Jamie, hey, keys." I hold up my outstretched hand to remind Jamie of what we were in the middle of.

She tears her eyes away from Paige. I can tell she is infuriated by the refusal to budge. The fact that Paige has always managed to get Jamie's hackles up just by walking into the room doesn't help the situation. "Skye…" Jamie's demeanor shifts, her tone turns pleading. "Come on, baby, I just want to talk, that's all."

One step forward, Jamie reaches for my outstretched palm with both her hands almost like a plea. I try to pull my hand away, but she refuses to let me go, her grip tightening until the keys begin to cut into my palm.

"Jamie—" I jerk my hand away with force at the sudden pain. Paige surges forward to intervene, but with my free arm I hold her back. She eases off, still tense.

"Jamie." I offer the keys to her again. "Just take the keys. *Please.*"

Again, her gaze flickers between Paige and me. Finally, she snatches the keys from my outstretched hand. "I'm going to get another drink," she says, and stalks off.

"Are you okay?" Paige asks.

"Yeah."

I'm not, but I don't see the point in making this someone else's problem. It fixes nothing. Paige granted me a reprieve, and that is more than I could have hoped for.

"I didn't realize you were going to be out tonight. Cam's not around."

"No, she's not. She's got an early start tomorrow and I had a change of plans. Can I get you a drink or something?" Her hand is still on my back. With Jamie out of sight, she turns to look at me, her eyes questioning.

"No, but thanks. I think I'm just going to head back."

"Okay, come on. Let's get your coat."

It is only when Paige and I are halfway out of the exit door that I realize that she means to leave with me. I contemplate saying something, persuading her to stay and get on with her own night, but I am tongue-tied. I can get home on my own, but the comfort of having Paige around—I don't want to be without it tonight. We are silent the whole way home.

"Can I offer you a drink?" I finally ask when we are at the door of my apartment. It's the least I can do.

"You can, and I would accept, but I think you're tired."

I am. I just want to crawl into my bed and forget tonight.

"But if you want me to stay, I will."

"I *am* tired," I say softly.

"I know." Paige takes a step closer. "How about you offer me that drink when you're next feeling up for it. Deal?"

"Deal."

Paige wraps her arms around me and hugs me tight, her arms steady, protective. I feel my muscles relax. The hallway is still and quiet, absent of the fear, panic, and stress that permeated the evening. She doesn't rush to let go. I don't rush to pull away from her either, wanting to be out here a little longer with her.

Eventually, I release the embrace. And as she leaves, I listen as she makes her way down the stairs, her footsteps growing softer the further she goes, until there is only me, the most recent memory of Jamie in my room, and how weak and helpless I felt—a familiar stranglehold I thought I had left behind.

I close myself in my room and lock the door. Tears are already running down my face as I ease myself to the floor and bury my face in my lap. I try to choke back the sobs, but they don't stop. I ram my fists repeatedly against my head, but there are only split seconds of relief each time I do so. The fleeting impermanence drives me to hit myself harder until my attention finally slides to an inconspicuous box tucked away on the bottom shelf of my nightstand. Inside, beneath the ticket stub of the first movie I watched with my first girlfriend, the funniest note I had ever received from Emma, and the friendship bracelet which Hannah had specially braided for me one evening when we were out for dinner, there is a small envelope, keeper to three new razor blades. Deep down, I recognized then it would have been a terrible idea to keep those, but I couldn't let them go. My hands reach for the box.

Skylar…

A strangled sob escapes me, triggered by the sound of Alex's voice in my head. The way she says my name when nobody is looking. My god, does she still sound beautiful.

"Alex…" I breathe, her name on my lips, surrounded by my vault of memories of her and all their fragile power.

Skylar...you need to stop.

"I can't, Alex. I can't." I exhale shakily and my body convulses into a series of uncontrollable shakes as I try to draw breath.

Skylar, look at me.

I curl my body inwards and hug myself tight. I hear her like the first time. I see her like it is yesterday.

Stop.

I choke back another sob but fight to keep my hands exactly where they are—around me and away from the box. Alex repeats herself, relentlessly without fatigue, until the dark which threatens to pull me under, stops, and the night finally stills.

CHAPTER 15

Havenford

I expected things to be awkward between Alex and me after she confusingly rebuffed my affection, but it turned out that it was only as awkward as I made it. Alex behaved no differently. Away from the alcove, I continued to feel the chilly distance she maintained between us, but inside that little room, she was like the sun, a glorious dry summer heat on my skin. Alex never saw the need to explain her selective behavior, but it didn't matter very much to me then. All that mattered to me was, in the privacy of the alcove, how hard it was to escape the sense of closeness that had come to exist between us and how happy and whole that made me feel.

Some days, we would sit in complete silence doing our homework, the atmosphere devoid of any pressure to make small talk; I would discover little things like how she loved a particular shade of pink or the way she played with the ends of her hair whenever she was stressed. Other days, we would talk, not about ourselves, but about everyone else. It wasn't in Alex's nature to be open about her opinions of others; I had to uncover them. In her tells and the words she left unsaid, I would learn what irritated or pleased her, how she liked to be teased, challenged, or placated. It was pure intuition when it came to her, and it was hard work, but it never felt like that to me.

"I should have known you were up to no good," I said, leaning over the length of the couch to ease the stack of papers out of Alex's hand. She was curled up against the corner with her legs tucked beneath her. "You were too quiet."

Alex was originally perusing a magazine but had evidently traded that for a more exciting activity—doodling with a bold pink marker along the margins of an article I had marked up.

"Oh, don't! This is such a grim article and all of this is meant to keep you afloat," she said with a proud gesture to her doodles. I raised my eyebrow. "*And* it makes me happy."

She beamed. I couldn't resist her.

"You're incorrigible." I shook my head but allowed Alex to resume work on the intricate but peaceful pattern expanding from the page's corner. She scooted in closer. Now that she had been found out, she seemed hellbent on making sure that I had a clear line of sight to each and every mark she made in pink. My skin tingled with having her near.

The door to the alcove creaked open.

"Man it's late, what are you guys still doing here?"

Emma stood in the doorway. I froze like a deer in headlights and straightened my back while simultaneously squeezing myself into the corner of the couch. I tried to introduce as much distance as I could between my body and Alex's. This was new territory for me. An interruption by Emma, and not some random *Glyph* member who would enter, assume that we were just focusing on work, then leave us alone. I had no idea how I was meant to behave.

"I'm giving Skye's article a dash of color." Alex held up the piece of paper in her hand. She didn't move away from me.

"True, she's always so serious, isn't she?" Emma sounded gossipy, but she gave me a curious glance. I felt a twinge of guilt.

"My god, isn't she?" Alex quipped back with a hint of gossip. Emma laughed.

Alex did this so effortlessly, changing up her mannerisms to suit her audience, making them think—no, *feel*—that she could be their best friend. Although I yearned to believe that I saw the real side of her, I sometimes couldn't help but wonder if like everyone else, she was merely showing me what I wanted to see.

"You're here awfully late, yourself," I said to Emma.

With a lovelorn sigh and a twirl of the tips of her hair, she said, "Got carried away chatting with Graham." She closed her eyes, still savoring her afternoon with him.

"Graham's this dude in her class. She's head over heels," I murmured to Alex.

"No kidding," she mouthed back to me with a good-natured roll of the eyes. I relaxed.

"I hear Tom asked you out to prom." Emma waggled her eyebrows at Alex. "Are you two dating?"

While prom was none of my concern, it didn't mean I liked hearing about who would have the honor of Alex's company as a date. I focused on keeping my expression neutral, polite.

"What's impressive is how fast news spreads. That was this morning," Alex said.

"Well, he is the quarterback that transforms our team from mediocre to decent, so of course this is news."

Alex laughed. "It's just prom!"

"They're calling bets on you two being crowned prom king and queen."

"Uh-huh. Sure."

The newsroom's main door opened outside, breaking Emma's attention on us.

"Hannah!" Emma called out brightly.

"Oh, hey. I didn't think anyone would still be around at this time, but I saw the lights on."

I waved, Hannah smiled, and initially looked as if she was going to enter but stopped when she saw Alex beside me. Alex, on the other hand, grew a little stiffer beside me and was a whole lot of silent as she resumed brightening up the pile of papers I left in her care. Unlike Emma, Hannah appeared to mentally note how close we were sitting.

"Anyway, I'm off now," she said without acknowledging Alex.

I raised an eyebrow, but she flashed me another smile and was gone as quickly as she had come in.

"Well, I'm going too. Mom's coming with the car, so I'm off to replay my afternoon with Graham over and over in my mind." Emma waltzed out of the alcove, seemingly oblivious to what just transpired.

The alcove's air of calm resumed.

"So you and Tom are dating now, huh?" I kept my tone light and pretended to busy myself with the pen and piece of paper. The whole point was to look like I didn't give a damn, which was a lot harder than it looked.

"Not quite. Our friends overlap. It's just prom."

"Mmhmm." I could sense a certain green-eyed monster surfacing. I shoved it back into its hole.

"You know that Hannah is not going to like this, right?" Alex gestured between us.

I was thrown. "That we're hanging out?"

"Yeah."

"Okay...why?"

"She hasn't told you?"

"Told me what?" Alex shuffled the loose papers into a neat

pile and retrieved the last piece from my hand. "Come on, Alex, you can't just say that and leave me hanging."

She placed the pile of papers on the nearby table. "Hannah and I don't really get along."

"Well, yeah, I definitely got *that*. Pretty obvious when the two of you are in the room together, you know? But surely that doesn't mean she'll have issues with us hanging out, right?"

Alex's sigh was barely audible. She turned to face me, one arm perched on the back of the couch. "We used to be best friends."

"Oh." That was news. "What happened?"

"We were too different. Hannah is Little Miss Perfect. She's got every reason to feel that way—smart, pretty, comes from a good family and with the success of *Glyph*? She can practically do no wrong and she strives very hard to preserve that image, to a point where it can all feel a little fake. And that's just not my deal."

"Is that what you thought the friendship was? Fake?" Alex's description of Hannah's behavior resonated with me, but I wouldn't go so far as to characterize Hannah as fake.

"No, of course not, but it isn't like I can take a part of her and ignore the rest. The relentless need to dress up, never a single strand of hair out of place. Obsessing about maintaining her popularity once she had it. How she behaves around guys—in the way they expect her to be so she won't ruin that perfect image in *their* heads. So fixated on becoming—and constantly *behaving* as if she was—the editor-in-chief to prove that she isn't just another pretty face. Waiting on Little Miss Perfect to tire so that the Hannah I first knew would come out? Nah, no thank you." Alex shook her head. "Anyway, she won't like this."

Alex was probably right, but it wasn't like I could do anything about it. Separating myself from her was impossible.

I shrugged. "You are riveting company."

"Oh, *am I*?"

I looked across at my article adorned with pink borders, feeling oddly cheered and comforted by it. I tilted my head towards Alex, catching her eye. "Yeah, your company can be addictive."

A smile started to form slowly on Alex's face. My heart soared. The energy between us was intoxicating.

"In that case, wanna grab dinner? I'm starving."

"Sure," I said, trying to sound cool about it when in fact my heart was doing cartwheels in my chest. Alex and I had never hung out after school before. I stood. "Let me pack up."

"I'll warn you. My car is an absolute toaster. I hate the cold."

"Uh-huh. And why are you telling me that?"

"Cause you're the one in a sweater even though it isn't quite sweater-weather today. Probably a good idea to take it off, if not it's gonna be the emergency room we're headed to because you *will* faint from a heat stroke and I will be *utterly miserable* because, as I said, I'm starving."

I flinched, blinked hard a couple of times before resuming my packing. My back was turned to Alex.

"And also, because you don't have to hide them, Skylar."

I froze mid-motion.

"Not unless you want to," Alex finished quietly.

I gave it a moment before turning around. There she was, still seated on the couch, maintaining a steadfast look of calm intensity. Alex stood up and took one step towards me, then another. I nearly forgot how to breathe.

"You were being awkward with how you held your notes earlier, like you were afraid to touch your left arm," she said gently.

I had forgotten how to speak. The lump in my throat had rendered both breathing and speaking impossible. She had my hand between hers and with a gentleness I hadn't known or experienced in a long time, she eased my sleeves up the length of my forearm. She did this slowly. I could stop her. I didn't. I didn't know how to. I didn't want to.

The scars on my forearm were erratic, unforgivingly etched into my skin and clear as day. Alex brushed her thumb against the deepest one. I was familiar with that one. It bled the longest. It was the most fulfilling. It was also the most obvious, yet this was the first time anyone made it clear to me that they were looking. I didn't know if I wanted Alex to be that person. My scars only served to highlight how broken and imperfect I was. Alex started to turn my arm toward her. I wanted to resist, knowing that she would reveal the underside of my arm, freshly littered with cuts from a few nights before. They were ugly. I didn't feel ready. I knew I should fight Alex, refuse her, but around her, all I ever wanted to do was run into a headlong collision with her. Alex traced the contours of the recent wounds, her tenderness a stark comparison to the pain that underlay those scars and the ones before. Emotions flickered in Alex's eyes before they eventually settled on a sadness that seemed to reflect the way I felt inside.

"Skylar…you need to stop," she said softly.

I saw only Alex's hand on my arm, how perfect it looked against something so harsh and unforgiving. I heard my own breaths, heavy and labored. I had no understanding of what she was saying.

Alex leaned in and dipped her head. She locked eyes with me. "Listen to me. You *need* to stop." Alex's voice was gentle but unwavering, like her gaze. With a brush of her thumb against the palm of my hand, she disarmed me with her tenderness, and bit by bit, it started to overwhelm me. A vulnerability was creeping in.

"Alexis..." I could hear the plea in the way I said her name. "I can't."

"But *you have to.*"

I tore my eyes away from her.

Her hand squeezed mine. "Skylar, look at me."

I couldn't bring myself to. There was another squeeze of my hand, tighter this time. I forced myself to look up.

"Stop," she said softly. "Okay?"

My heart felt like it could beat its way out of my chest. Alex didn't move. She said nothing more. All she did was look at me, waiting, and in her eyes, I saw a person who was more sure of me than I could have ever been in myself. She commanded a strength I couldn't possibly possess, armed with a faith that was probably, deeply misplaced. I drew a long, shaky breath. I exhaled.

"Okay."

/

The first time I stepped into a church, I did it partly out of curiosity, partly at the behest of my first girlfriend. She was Catholic, identified as a lesbian, then proceeded to tell me in church that it would be great if I'd consider a sex change because only then could we be married in the eyes of God. We broke up shortly after, and churches and I had since maintained an extremely healthy distance from one another, so when I found myself standing outside one in Havenford, I despaired a little. I had Hannah to thank for it. What began as an operation to turn down Nathaniel's advances once and for all had evolved into an awkward situation involving him, her, and Sunday service at her church. She had pleaded for me to join her so it wouldn't feel like a date.

Hannah and I eased past an elderly couple seated at the end of the pew. We were early and decided to wait for Nathaniel inside. The wooden bench creaked as we sat down. I looked around: raised slanted ceilings, tall stained-glass windows right behind the altar, with a beauty in its architectural simplicity. The pews were still fairly empty, given the time—a few families seated near the front dressed in their Sunday best, young couples nearer the back, interspersed with some individual churchgoers, and the elderly couple at the end of our pew. Were any of them like me? Gay and in church? I wasn't religious, so I was unbothered by all things concerning the scriptures and man's interpretation of the same, but regardless, it intrigued me how another gay person might have reconciled sexuality and religion. It was clear my ex-girlfriend hadn't been able to. It was also clear that she'd felt shame for being who she was, and while sympathetic to her plight, I refused to be dragged back into the closet she had barricaded herself in.

Hannah linked her arm through mine and gave it a squeeze. "I owe you big time."

"You do."

"Love you."

"Save it for your boyfriend."

"He's *not* my boyfriend and this is *church*. How can we get any safer than this?"

"There's lunch after this. Besides, he's not going to see this as church. He's going to see this as—he asked you out, you agreed to see him during the weekend and you're going out for lunch together. How did we get so far away from, 'Let him down gently please, Hannah?'"

She rolled her eyes. "Wait till you find a girl like Nathaniel, then you'll understand how painfully hard this is."

The comment caught me off guard. Me being gay—Hannah never asked, I never brought it up. We were getting along so well, I didn't want to risk ruining it. Hannah's smile met her eyes. It seemed that I should have had more faith in her and our friendship.

"So spill, you seeing anyone?" she asked.

I threw a glance around us. People were starting to trickle in, although there wasn't anyone in our immediate vicinity. "Uh…" I rubbed the back of my neck. "Should *we* be talking about this in here?"

"Here…as in…?"

"As in—here, *in church*."

"What's wrong with that?"

"You're saying your church is cool with gay people? Like I'm fine talking about it, but I'm conscious that not everyone is fine talking or even hearing about it."

Hannah mouthed a silent *ah*. She shrugged. "I think God loves everyone."

I shot her a wry smile. "You're not the Church."

Hannah appeared to ponder my comment as quickly as she threw it out. "But you *are* talking to me, not my priest, so spill. Who's the lucky girl?"

"Lucky?" I couldn't help but chuckle.

Hannah's eyes narrowed. "Yeah…? You're smart, creative, have great taste in music and you're moody-gorgeous when you scowl—"

I laughed a little too loud. "I think we need to get your eyes checked." That got me a gentle punch on my arm in response.

"Anyway, no, there's no lucky girl. I like someone, but she's not interested in me, so that's that."

"Someone in school?"

"Yeah."

"Someone I know?"

I shrugged. "You know a lot of people, Hannah," I said, hoping she would be satisfied with the response. Based on what I had heard from Alex, honesty seemed unwise.

"True. Well, her loss anyway."

"I'll be sure to tell her that when the opportunity arises."

"Tell me who she is. I'll beat some sense into her."

"Oh, I have no doubt about that. The beating."

"I'm serious."

"I know. That's what worries me." Another punch. I giggled, as did Hannah.

"Hey, what's up with you and Alex? Are you two friends or something? You were with her in the back room the other day and you seemed…tight."

"Oh." The guilt of my recent omission had caught up quick. "Um, we hang out sometimes, but only like when we bump into each other in the newsroom, that kinda thing. It's nothing." The truth died at the back of my throat. Great. Gay, and now *lying* in church. I didn't have to be Catholic to feel the full weight of judgment bearing down on me from Jesus on the crucifix.

"All right, well, keep your guard up around her, okay? She's a two-faced hypocrite and she will fuck you over when you least expect it."

My eyes widened slightly. Hannah wasn't a fan of swearing, always believing that there was a more polished way to get her point across.

"Alex and I used to be friends," Hannah continued. "Hit it off immediately the moment we met each other—freshman year—used to joke that we were like long-lost sisters. I was actually the one who convinced Alex to join *Glyph*. Anyway, things changed. It was the small things at first, like canceling on lunch, not staying back to hang out as frequently as we used to do, being closed off whenever we actually did spend any time together until finally, the only time we spent together was for *Glyph*. She never explained why, but she started to hang out with this other bunch of people in school, so I figured that's what it was. That's all I was to her—a glorified placeholder before the friends she really wanted came along. Some friend she turned out to be."

"When did this happen?"

"Junior year."

"Must be tough being co-editors-in-chief."

"Tell me about it." Hannah rolled her eyes. "Alex never displayed a single ounce of desire to be an editor-in-chief, then we fall out and suddenly she wants it? Felt like she wanted it only because *I* wanted it, as if we're ten and this is some petty rivalry or whatever. Anyway. *So. Over. It.*"

A heavy sigh weighed on my chest. Alex was wrong. Hannah wasn't simply not going to like us hanging out. Hannah was going to hate it with every fiber of her being.

/

Church with Hannah and Nathaniel went off without a hitch, as did lunch, surprisingly. I had thought I'd be home by the early afternoon, but the clock by the main door read 5:00 p.m. It turns out that beneath Nathaniel's sweet, endearing demeanor was a boy who couldn't get enough of electronic dance music, which incidentally happened to be one of Hannah's secret loves too. She doesn't usually talk about it since it's not for everyone—unlike her other love, country music—but once the secret was out, they were at it like chatterboxes. I texted Hannah, teasing her about how Nathaniel was probably already planning the next date.

"Where have you been?"

I didn't even have a chance to remove my shoes before the interrogation began. I didn't think my mother would be home until late—I overheard her telling my dad that she had two open houses to run this afternoon—yet here she was, parked at the dining table right by the main hallway.

"I told you, I was going to be out this afternoon."

"Are you deaf? I asked you where you've been."

The open houses must not have gone well.

"I was at church with Hannah. We had lunch after."

The glower from my mother made it clear that she didn't believe a single word that just came out of my mouth. It was ironic, really. Over the years, I learned how to lie to my parents without breaking a sweat. It was a survival skill for my sanity. Dating, spending nights or weekends at a girlfriend's place, you name it. But today I was being honest.

"Are you now deaf *and* stupid? Please, Skylar. Did you think I was born yesterday? Am I supposed to believe that you found religion after seventeen years?"

Having you as my mother, I'm surprised I haven't found it sooner. "Hannah wanted some company and I agreed to accompany her. That's it."

"Who is this Hannah?"

"Editor-in-chief for *Glyph*."

"And *she* wants to go to church with you?" Loosely translated, my mother was asking: *And she wants to be friends with you?*

"Yes?"

"Why?"

"We're friends?"

"Why? Did you give her money?"

"No."

"Gifts?"

"No."

"Are you doing her homework?"

"No. We're just friends, *okay*?"

"Don't know why she would want to be friends with you."

"Why not? I'm a good friend, I listen, I care."

My mother snorted. "And if they cared about you, those *girls* you called friends wouldn't have led you astray. Leading you down the devil's path. Tell me, how does a smart girl like you let that happen?"

It was the lead-in to an angry soliloquy I had heard more times than I could count. I deployed my usual strategy and remained silent, hoping she would wear herself out if I allowed her to continue, like a wind-up toy car.

"Weak. That's what you are. And too stubborn to change, only saying stupid things like how our family needs counseling when it is only *you* who needs to change. I really don't know what I've done in my past life to deserve this, to deserve a daughter *like you*."

But I was tired of her. Despite being made to endure church service, the oddball fun of being around Hannah and Nathaniel today made me feel normal. I forgot what it meant to be my parents' daughter and I was just like any other seventeen-year-old teenager—out having fun with her friends. I had wanted to hold on to that feeling a little longer, but she had ruined it.

"I wasn't weak," I said quietly.

"What did you say?"

"I said—I wasn't weak."

"Of course you are. You are just too stupid to realize that. Stupid, you hear me? Too dumb to know what's good for you. I can't believe you're my daughter."

"I'm not weak." The words were starting to pile up in my mouth, armed with a burning fervor. I kept pushing them down. No good would come of it. No good had *ever* come of it. "I'm not stupid. I didn't get led astray. It wasn't temptation. It wasn't some bad decision I made. This is how I am."

Her eyes narrowed. "It is wrong!"

"It is not!"

"It is!"

"That's what *you* think! You keep telling me to change, but why? *Why* would I turn away the one truth about me that feels right? That makes me happy? Don't you care for my happiness?"

"No!" My mother slammed her hand against the table. I flinched. "I don't! I don't care what makes you happy! Only *my* happiness matters! Mine! You hear me?!"

The impact sloshed coffee from her mug, soaking the tablecloth. She sounded so shrill. Eyes bulging, she reminded me of a spoiled brat throwing a tantrum.

"Well, that's selfish."

"You want to judge me as a mother?! How dare you tell me how to be a mother! You wouldn't know the first thing about being a mother!"

"I'd start by not judging my daughter because of who she loves."

"Love? Love?!"

In a split second, she was up like a shot, chair crashing down behind her. Her coffee spoon narrowly missed my shoulder and clanged against the wall behind me. Her eyes flashed with righteous anger. My heart slammed against my chest.

"You know nothing of love! *Do not* talk to me about love! You are incapable of love! All you do is hurt me! A hell-spawn demon sent to Earth to ruin me."

FUCK.

I stumbled backwards, avoiding her mug and the rest of its contents. A considerable amount of the coffee splashed on the floor where I had stood milliseconds ago, but the amount trickling down my arm and the drenched front of my t-shirt meant that most still found its target. The coffee was hot, but it didn't scald—did she know that? My mother stood there, chest heaving, glaring at me, unblinking. I was already halfway up the stairs before she had the chance to recover. There was a shout for me to come back followed by the frantic shoving aside of chairs. Footsteps pounding along the path I had just taken.

I slammed the bathroom door shut and locked it. I cursed when I realized what I had done. I may have taken the nearest shelter, but it wasn't impenetrable. The only keys I had were the ones to my room. The pounding started. She was screaming. Crawling into the bathtub, I drew the shower curtains and huddled in a ball, preparing myself for the worst. I shut my eyes, buried my head in my lap and forced myself to stop listening. I remained where I was even when the screams gave way to silence. I didn't dare leave, terrified that I would open the door to find her waiting outside.

Hours must have passed. The shadows in the bathroom grew longer until it was nearly dusk. Only when I heard the angry accusations, the slamming of plates on the table, could I believe that she had finally left me alone. My dad was home and my mother was busy making her displeasure known. Quietly, I snuck out of the bathroom and into my room.

I could hear my name, my mother calling me a lost cause, an embarrassment, a hopeless disappointment who deserved to have it beaten out of me. I strained to hear if my dad said anything. He was painfully silent. I could feel my tears gather. Lying on the ground, I shut my eyes and counted my breaths, hoping to count myself out of this degenerating state of mind. Yet the more I willed calm, the more it eluded me. As always. I sat up and reached into the recesses of my wardrobe. I extracted a single razor blade from the box.

Skylar…you need to stop.

Alex. Her voice. That afternoon.

I pressed the tip of the blade into my skin. It was easy for her to say. She didn't understand that this was the only way. I let out an involuntary sigh as I sliced my skin open. The pain felt familiar, like an old friend.

It hadn't always been like this. I was terrified the first time, cradling the blade for ages before tracing it gently across my skin, so gently that there wasn't even a hint of a cut. I did it again, and again, each time exerting a little more pressure than the last until I felt the sting. It was like a paper cut. That was the last time any of them qualified as a paper cut.

Skylar, look at me.

There she was again, but how could I stop? Where would all the pain go? I gave it a few minutes before I ran the blade slowly across my skin again.

Stop. Okay?

Alex's hand on mine. My heart grew tight at that memory. I laid my head back against the bed, eyes closed, the bloody blade between my fingers. I could almost feel her next to me as I willed the memory into existence. Her hand. Those eyes. Her strength. Her faith. Everything she possessed. Everything I lacked. Over and over again, I replayed that afternoon until the urge ebbed and faded and all that remained was her voice in my head.

I tried and failed to hide my momentary relapse from Alex the next day at school. When her disappointment showed, the guilt of letting her down, I learned, was something I couldn't bear.

I tried to explain. "I couldn't—"

"But you can."

"You don't understand…it's…" *It's the only thing that makes me feel better.* "Alex, I tried." I simply insisted. It was too hard to explain.

"Try harder."

"I'm not as strong as you make me out to be!" I wanted Alex to stop being stubborn and understand that she had set me an impossible task.

"Skylar." Alex leveled a look at me. It terrified me. It made me yearn deeply for her. "You are stronger than you think. You are stronger than anything and everything I make you out to be."

CHAPTER 16

Operation Missing Basement—if you can find the door that leads into it, you will stumble into a venue that is a mix of club and pub, where the drinks are way too cheap, the students drink too much, and the bouncer will ask you on your way out if anyone in the heap of people in the corner belongs to you, which makes you wonder if Operation Missing Person would have been a better name for the establishment. Alison and I agreed to join our ex-flatmates for their night out, and petulantly, we had insisted that all our friends come with us. A guy stumbles past us on our entry and ends up sprawled against a filthy-looking table. Better that than the floor, though; it probably harbors a super-bacteria no human can recover from. I wouldn't want to be here when the lights come on.

"This is a special kind of nightmare," Paige comments quietly. "Makes me want to turn around, head home, and hide in my room for eternity."

I burst into giggles. "Aww, don't be asocial, baby."

A wide smile appears on Paige's face. "And do I get a kiss with that?"

"You wish. I'll buy you a drink instead. It'll take the sting of the image out of your head."

"I'll need at least ten drinks."

"You're not a cheap date, are you?"

"Oh, I come very expensive." Paige gets to the bottom of the steps before me and holds out her hand to me, making sure I clear the last slippery-looking step without incident. "But for you, we can talk exceptions."

"So just the one drink then?"

"I'm not *that* cheap." Paige glances to the bar on her right, then to her left where our friends have headed. We remain where we are. "So...where's Jamie?"

It's been nearly two weeks since the incident. I've not been out. I've not seen Paige. We've texted, but neither of us has broached the subject.

"Staying in. She's not feeling well."

"You guys good?"

Jamie didn't stop calling or texting me after. She apologized and begged for a second (third) chance. She also promised me that was the last time. A part of me didn't believe her, but after her repeated heartfelt professions of love, I caved and said yes.

"Yeah, I suppose."

"Shame. Here you had me thinking that she's been ditched for Octavia."

"What would make you think that?"

"Octavia's draped all over you like a fancy side piece whenever she thinks nobody is looking."

"Nobody but you, it seems." Paige shoots me a wink. "I could ditch the entire universe and Octavia still wouldn't know how to be with me."

Paige turns me towards the bar and starts ushering me forward. "How true. Shame. Jamie doesn't deserve you and Octavia doesn't know how to hold onto to you." I raise an eyebrow and refrain from commenting. Paige grabs the bartender's attention, and without needing to ask, orders a vodka and soda for me.

"So what's going on with Octavia?" she asks.

“She kissed me. Probably broke some seal and doesn’t require ten drinks now before she can touch me.”

“Oh *did she*?” Paige feigns looking scandalized.

“Uh-huh.”

“So the threesome is back on?”

“I…don’t think so.”

“Oh?” Now Paige *does* look scandalized. “Does Jamie know about the kiss?” She breaks out in a soft chuckle when I fail to respond. “Oh, Skye…” Paige shakes her head and clicks her tongue, but you can see the smile in her eyes. No judgment there. “Probably best to fix it before it gets too messy.”

She collects our drinks, hands me mine, and we speak no more of the issue when we rejoin our friends.

It isn’t long before cold arms snake around my waist and hug me tight from behind. Honey and roses. A surreptitious kiss on my shoulder, my hair being swept to one side as I feel gentle breaths on my neck. Octavia casts a quick glance around, notes that our friends are all preoccupied, and with a gentle pull, she steers me into the nearest darkened corner. Using her height, Octavia shields us from view and kisses me, hard. It catches me off guard and causes me to let out a soft moan, which encourages her. Hands in my back pockets, tongue slipping past my lips, she pulls me firmly against her as her tongue thrusts deep. I feel my shirt riding up my back when she spreads her fingers against the small of my back. Octavia doesn’t let up, and in the brief reprieve of her pulling away, I catch Paige glancing our way, demeanor relaxed but contemplative. I notice for the first time tonight the dark brown leather jacket she has on. I make a mental note to tell her how much I love it on her. Octavia runs her thumb against my moist lips. I close my eyes and kiss her again.

/

The cold night hits my face as I wander in search of the smoker's corner in Operation Missing Basement, desperate for some fresh air. I leave behind the chaos and drunken horde. Everyone is behaving as if it's either their first night touching alcohol or their very last. Paige is straddling one of the benches as she smokes. Her lips turn into a soft half-smile when I approach.

"Those things will kill you." I sit down facing her.

"Will they?" Paige holds up the filtered end of her cigarette to my lips. I take a long drag before exhaling slowly. "Yeah, probably." Paige takes another drag of the cigarette before placing it to my lips again, letting me finish it.

There is a small pile of cigarette butts by her feet. Paige stubs out ours and I light up a fresh one. She nudges her pint of beer towards me and I trade the cigarette for it.

"What's up? You're doing that thing again."

"What thing?"

"Having beer and cigarettes for friends."

The edge of Paige's lip curls upwards. She gives me a little shake of her head with a chuckle and takes another drag of the cigarette. "Couple of your ex-flatmates were flirting with me. Cam got a little pissy and asked me about it. I told her it was nothing—exactly like all the other times she had asked me the same question about the girls in Element—but I must have sounded pretty unconvincing or something, because it very quickly escalated into an argument about how I'm not taking our relationship seriously."

"Are you? Taking it seriously?"

"Didn't realize you peg me for a player." Paige presses one hand to her chest and feigns hurt.

"I didn't. You don't have to be one to be accused of not taking a relationship seriously."

Paige looks wry. "Cam's been trying to have this conversation about our future for several weeks now, but I keep deflecting. I tell her that it's a good few months before we graduate, that there's still time, but frankly, I just don't feel ready to have it."

The cold lager coats my throat. I relish it, then nudge the pint back in Paige's direction with my finger. "Why not?"

Paige runs her hand through her hair and takes a big swig. "My dad bailed on us a few years ago. It was rough. My mum wept for months and my kid brother was confused most of the time. All that fighting between my parents, it was such an unhealthy relationship, but they insisted on staying together—for the kids, as they say—waiting on us to grow up and when I turned sixteen, my dad was out that door so fast I never saw him leave. I never got to remind him that only I had grown up and that Scott—my brother—was still a child."

Paige's face is caught between the shadows and the bright red light of a nearby neon sign. There is sadness in her eyes, interlaced with resignation. It is a new look on her.

"I told you—I'm very good at not getting attached. I don't get involved. Because all that happens is that you'll care too much, want too much, and nothing good ever comes out of that."

The cynicism on Paige's face is clear. I don't like seeing her this way, so convinced that all relationships are doomed to the lovelessness she had been engineered to recognize as the inevitable outcome.

"I know how you feel," I say gently. I scoot forward until our knees touch. "My parents…they—" The world around me briefly goes out of focus. I hate thinking about them and how they make me feel. I concentrate on the lit end of Paige's cigarette. "They have somehow managed to cause a lot of hurt and pain for me...and my brother. And sometimes I— I fear that that's all there is. Like life, you know, all hurt, all pain." I lift my gaze and force out a halfhearted smile. "But that's no way to live, is it? I guess that's why I'm always rushing to do the polar opposite of anything my parents do. I have to hope, trust, that it will be better somehow." I rest a hand on Paige's thigh. "That *we* will do better than them somehow."

Paige is pensive, her eyes not leaving mine. She can't see the images replaying in my mind. She can't relive my past. Still, feeling exposed and vulnerable, I begin to look away. Paige stops me with the gentlest hold of my hand. Our eyes are locked in a shared understanding, hers are warm and kind.

"Thank you." She lightly squeezes my hand. "I'm here, if you ever want to talk."

I give her hand a tender squeeze back in return.

CHAPTER 17

The news of Paige and Cam breaking up takes everyone by surprise. The first question on everyone's lips—why? The second—who gets to keep the friends? I am, without a doubt, on Team Paige, and she will no doubt enlighten me on the reasons for the split when she's ready.

"Have you spoken with Paige?" Alison asks as we wait for our drinks. We have been at the bar awhile. Thursday is the new Friday, so Element is more packed than usual. Rachel is keeping Cam company, but Paige has not shown up in Element since the breakup. She doesn't, as she has said in her text messages, wish to cause unnecessary tension.

I frown. It isn't the first time Alison has asked *me* the question.

"You keep asking me that."

"I just figured if anyone has spoken with her, it'd be you."

"Why?"

"Because the two of you are close? When did that happen, anyway? Cam and I saw you two the other night—when we were at Operation Missing Basement—but we didn't want to intrude because you looked so serious and deep in conversation. Cam didn't realize you two had grown close, either. We were trying to recall the last time we saw you talk or hang out, but we were struggling!"

I feel caught off guard by the revelation that Cam and Alison had been watching us. It probably is a good time to tell

Alison that Paige and I actually meet for coffee, which makes for a half-decent explanation. But I shrug with as much nonchalance as I can muster. "We probably just had too much to drink. You know how things are after one too many. Suddenly everyone's best friends."

"Tell me about it!" Alison laughs, then sighs. "I'm starting to think your girlfriend has a drinking problem."

We both look at Jamie, who is slamming tequila back like water; she has definitely kept the bartender busy tonight. She whoops with joy when she is done with the lemon slice and gets hearty slaps on the back.

"If she does, then we all might."

"Okay, fair point. Who are those people, anyway? I don't recognize them."

"Her course mates. *They're a hoot*, she says."

A minor commotion causes us to turn. A few girls stride into Element like a hurricane, brash and loud. Bringing up the rear is Octavia. She stops in her tracks and allows herself to be enveloped in a bearlike hug by one of the girls—a redhead—before leaning in for a kiss. The frown on my forehead deepens. The bartender finally hands us our drinks and I tell Alison I'll catch up.

When Octavia is within reach, I stop her. "Hey O, can we talk?"

Octavia trades multiple glances between me and the redhead before eventually telling her to go on ahead. Her reluctance stings.

I gesture at the redhead. "I didn't realize you were seeing someone else."

"Oh, yes, that's Scarlett. She asked me out earlier this week. Been keen on me for a while, apparently."

I am having a severe case of whiplash.

"So what was last week about?"

"What about it?"

"Oh, I don't know…you kissed me all through the night, said you'll text when your busy week was over? Now it seems like you were busy with another girl. Fair for me to ask what last week was about then, don't you think?"

Octavia won't meet my eyes. I pinch the bridge of my nose and sigh, tired and disenchanted with the constant chase.

"Octavia, I've been keen on you for a while, too—since summer in fact—*and* I have asked you out twice, but you appear to only be capable of being with me when I'm with someone else. Whenever I make myself available, you can't seem to run away fast enough. What's going on, O? Why do we keep doing this?"

She stares down at her hands and runs her right thumb across the side of her index finger. "You don't know the number of times I've wished I could just let go and say yes to being with you…" She rubs at a faded watermark on the wooden bar counter. I can sense Octavia fighting through her discomfort of addressing her feelings about our relationship. "But there is something very untouchable about you, and it makes me feel like I'll wake up one day, you'll be gone, and I'll be the one with the broken heart." She looks at Scarlett then back at me. "I want 'forever' Skye. With Caleb and Scarlett, I feel like I may have a shot at it. I feel safe. With you, it's just a matter of when you'll break my heart…so how can I say yes to that?"

I can see in her eyes that she wishes to be convinced, by me, that she's wrong. The inclination to feed her the idea of a fairytale ending lurks. It would be no different from the dream I sold Alison, and I am sure that if I wanted it hard enough, I could succeed.

"Nothing is forever, Octavia."

"Says who? You? Why can't it be?"

"It just can't."

"It *can*."

I straighten my back. "It's not fucking rainbows, sunshine, and puppies rolling in the fields, Octavia. Love isn't like that!"

The hope of a future with me flickers out in her eyes, giving way to sadness and disappointment. "Well it is for me! And *that* is why I'm with Scarlett, and why I went out with Caleb. They see it the same way I do, and all you've done is prove that I'm right about you."

Octavia's diagnosis of the problem between us—me—lands like a swift, unexpected, blow across my face. She isn't wrong, but the truth still hurts.

"I'm sorry, O." My apology finally fills the silence between us.

She shrugs. "It is what it is."

We look at each other, unsure about what to say next.

Jamie stumbles over and reaches for my glass. "Skye! Whatcha drinking? Oh, hello, Octavia! Still interested in that threesome we talked about?"

Octavia glances over at the dance floor where Scarlett is. She points at the redhead and mouths. "I'm just going to..."

I nod. Octavia gives Jamie an awkward pat on the shoulder and is gone.

"So whatcha drinking, Skye?" Undeterred by my dirty look, Jamie asks again at full volume.

"Nothing you should be having." I push the glass behind me along the bar, beyond Jamie's reach. I look around for her coursemates, irritated. If they're going to get her uselessly drunk, the least they can do is take care of her. They're nowhere in sight.

"I think you may have had enough for tonight. Let's go home, okay?"

"Don't be a bitch, Skye. I didn't ask to go home. I asked to have a drink. Lemme have the drink." Jamie half pushes, half leans against me.

"No." I try to hold her up and keep her steady, but it doesn't dissuade her from trying to reach the glass. "Jamie, stop it! I'm bringing you home."

She shakes my hand off her arm. "What are you getting so fucking worked up about? We should fuck. Then maybe you won't be so fucking uptight all the time."

"Don't talk to me like that. You've had a lot to drink, so I'm going to ignore what you said. Let's just get you home, okay?"

"No." Jamie roots herself to the floor. Her eyes are dark with petulance.

"Jamie—"

Ordinarily, I would be contemplating another way to coax her to come with me without making a scene, but I find myself exhausted beyond belief. My mind draws a blank. First Octavia, now Jamie. Both relationships coming to a head in less than a quarter of an hour. Why am I even bothering when, as Paige says, one doesn't deserve me and the other doesn't know how to hold on to me? It's not as if either of them is Alex.

"Jamie, can we just—" *Go home. Stop fighting. Break up.* Resignation and regret are eating at me. "You know, I think we're better apart."

Her head whips up. She expected to hear more coaxing and persuasions. Why wouldn't she? I expected tonight to go like any other.

"W-wait, w-what are you saying?"

I swallow hard and take a second to collect myself. "I'm

saying we're no good for each other, babe. We aren't happy together. We haven't been in months. All we do is fight, all you do is apologize, tell me you love me, then cue repeat." A mixed sense of disbelief and relief starts to creep into my bones.

"But *I love you.* Why are you saying all this? This is just another fight, isn't it? It's a harmless little fight. I'm drunk. You know how I get. I don't hear what I'm saying. I'm being stupid, and tomorrow I'll be better."

"But that's just it. I don't want to keep waiting for tomorrow and I certainly shouldn't have to wait for you to make it up to me every time you behave poorly or treat me badly."

"Are you breaking up with me?" Jamie's voice trembles. She sounds dismayed and hurt. Her eyes turn ashen. I feel a twinge of guilt for being the cause of that.

A disquiet hangs over us.

"Yes," I say as gently as possible.

Jamie stares at me. She is silent. Her blankness is disconcerting. I try to take one step back. With lightning reflexes, Jamie's hand shoots out and wraps around my wrist.

"No, Skye," she says through gritted teeth.

Her eyeballs are bulging and the vein in her temple pops. Jamie is furious at me. If we are home alone, I think she may even hit me. I recoil inside and feel like I might be sick. How could I have allowed myself to stay with her for so long?

"*You* don't get to decide when we're done or when you walk away. *Only I can.*" Jamie's hand tightens as she speaks, her voice dangerously low but just loud enough for me to hear.

I try to pull my hand away, but she doesn't let me. "Jamie, let go."

Jamie's grip keeps closing in on my wrist. She sinks her fingernails into my skin with a force that feels strong enough to puncture.

"I said—*let go.*"

I wrench my hand away with a force greater than the one Jamie used to reach for it. I stare at her, feeling oddly detached from the situation, emotionless and devoid of any guilt I felt mere seconds ago.

"You don't have any say in whether I walk away, and you would be a fool to think that you do, so don't you *ever* touch me like that again, Jamie. *Don't. Push. Me.*"

I stare at Jamie, unblinking. She shrinks away a little and swallows. The sight of her cowed injects a jolt of strength through me, pushing me forward like adrenaline. I brush past her, grab my coat, and walk out of Element without bothering to put it on. I ignore the drunken arrivals veering into my path, cross the street and keep going. I don't feel the cold. In about fifty meters, there will be a right turn and there will no longer be a direct line of sight between me and the building in which Element sits.

I make the turn. The street darkens without the glare of party lights and neon signs, dimly illuminated by the glow of the streetlamps. I stop almost immediately and bend over.

I am breathing hard. Sweat pours from my skin and anxiety sweeps through me like a tidal wave. I force myself to inhale a deep breath of air, hold it, release, and repeat. I remain exactly where I am until the sledgehammer of my heart finally stops bludgeoning my chest into a million pieces.

CHAPTER 18

Havenford

Throughout spring, all Emma could talk about was how excited she was that we were finally going to be seniors—turn eighteen, rule the school, leave campus for lunch, all that stuff. Me? I hated thinking about it, for it would have meant that Alex had graduated. Without her, Havenford High wouldn't be the same. I wouldn't get to randomly head out to the football field, like now, and find Alex sitting at the bleachers alone, reading. Seeing her was the simplest of joys.

"Hey," I said, hands jammed into my pockets, nervous. I checked our surroundings, worried that I was breaching her unspoken and unfathomable rule of behaving like strangers outside the alcove. An overcast sky meant that no one was on the field.

Alex looked up from her book. Putting it to one side, she leaned back. "Hi." Her smile was warm and welcoming. I breathed a sigh of relief inside as I took a place beside her.

"Your kind of book?" I asked, casually flipping her book over like my nerves weren't shot just from sitting next to her. The jacket copy said it was a medical thriller.

"Exactly my kind of book."

"Quiet aspirations to go into medicine? Or a life of crime perhaps?"

Alex laughed. "As exciting as those sound, nope, still journalism. To my dad's chagrin."

"Why's that?"

"He wants me to follow in his footsteps—he's an architect. I hate to break it to him, but the only thing I'd be good at is admiring the work of others. I'd probably be really good at imitating them. Hmm, plagiarism in the architectural field, that's probably a thing, isn't it?"

"Probably."

"Best not find out." Alex chuckled. "The only thing apparently worse than not following in his footsteps is me wanting to go to HVU, which is just a twenty-minute drive away. My parents are now wondering if I'm a well-adjusted individual, given that most kids can't wait to leave."

I laughed. HVU—Havenford University—was seriously close. It would be like Alex never left. "Why there?"

"It's a decent school."

"More than decent I'd say. I heard it's got a great program for journalism."

Alex seemed surprised that I knew. She gave a slight shrug. "It does okay."

In truth, Havenford University was more than okay, which was probably why she chose it. Alex never struck me as being anything but deliberate in her every action.

"So it's 'decent' and 'does okay?'"

Alex poked me in the arm. "You're teasing."

"I am."

"I thought you liked me."

"Alexis, I adore you, but one thing doesn't make the other untrue."

Alex just smiled. "My little sis seems excited at least. Even asked me if I'll be staying at home. That was a firm no for me. I'm not *that* ill-adjusted."

"Oh, I don't know about that. You're not even leaving our county—"

Alex skillfully lodged a quick but gentle jab in the side of my ribs with her elbow. I pressed my hand to my side and feigned a mortal wound. "Ouch, that hurt. And here I thought you *liked* me."

Her eyes sparkled. "Do you know what hurts? This."

Alex perched her right wrist on my knee and pointed at it. My cheeks flushed at the contact. "What happened?"

"Not quite sure. I think I probably got it during gym. Which is just sad. All I did was *pretend* to play volleyball."

I chuckled, which attracted a pout from Alex.

"Want me to take a look at it? One of the random life skills I inherited from being on the tennis team is the ability to determine when an injury is not life-threatening."

"Isn't that…no wait, shouldn't that be most, if not *all*, injuries? It's just tennis!"

I winked and boldly cradled Alex's wrist between my hands. I checked for swelling, and finding none, I proceeded to gently massage select areas of her wrist with my thumbs.

"Better?" I murmured.

Alex scooted in closer, her head just inches away from mine and her body now painfully close. There was a soft sigh of contentment. "So much better."

I willed my heart not to give out from beating too fast.

"I think you just pinched a nerve. Which means you will live to pretend to play volleyball again."

Alex chuckled. I gave her wrist a few more gentle rubs before easing my hold on it, fully expecting her to retract her hand, but she did not. I lifted my head and glanced at the girl beside me. Her eyes were on me. Soft and unguarded, I thought I saw in them a flicker of deep affection.

It's hard to say how Alex and I arrived at that moment. She threw the rulebook out the window when she rejected me, but she refused to let me retreat. She said she wanted to be friends, but I could not say with certainty that, at this moment, that was all we were. I may not have known what I meant to her, but I knew what she meant to me. She was that strangely fascinating girl who caught my eye in the gymnasium one random morning, whose blinding brightness reached through the veil of dark clouds around my heart. Fighting how I felt for her was like being in quicksand. Inevitable. Irrevocable. Final.

I was in love with her.

A movement beyond where Alex and I were seated caught my attention. Looking past her, I saw Hannah and Emma standing there, staring at us. Hannah's lips were a grim line and Emma wore the strangest look on her face—a blend of excitement and speculation.

I froze. "Hannah."

Alex snapped to attention. She spotted our audience and glanced upwards briefly, the tiniest fluttering of an eye-roll, before giving an almost-imperceptible shake of her head. She pulled her hand away slowly, corresponding with the speed at which I was releasing my grip.

"Later, Skye," she murmured, grabbed her book, and moved to stand up. "Hannah." Alex's greeting was rigid as she passed by and headed for the school building, leaving us there.

I rose. "Hannah..."

I took one step towards her. She took one step back.

"Hannah, please...let me explain."

Hannah threw up her hand. I stopped. She bolted off without another word.

I wanted to chase her down, but I didn't know what I would

do or say if I caught up with her. There was also the matter of Emma, standing there in front of me.

I rubbed the back of my neck. "Hey, Ems," I greeted her, unable to keep the sheepish tone out of my voice.

She pointed in the direction Hannah had gone. "Do you… want to go after her? Because she definitely didn't seem to take that well."

I shook my head.

"Okay…" Emma paused, her expression telling me that she was giving me time to change my mind. I didn't move.

"Right…so, I'm going to pretend that I didn't just see Hannah walk off in a huff because *Skye*!" Emma doled out a hearty smack on my arm, exclaiming with unbelievable enthusiasm. "*When were you going to tell me about you and Alex?!* You know how I usually pride myself on knowing who's dating who and all the gossip around school! How could the two of you have completely slipped my radar?! I was so certain that she was dating Tom, and I mean, *come on*, the two of them hardly ever talk to each other! But…" Emma tutted. "I should have known something was up when I found the two of you in the newsroom that afternoon…how close you were, how comfortable—"

"We're not dating!"

Emma frowned. "Okay, there's no need to hide—"

"I'm not. Alex and me. It's not a thing. We're not dating. I mean I want to, but she said no when I asked her. She said she doesn't do 'gay' anymore."

It felt so good to tell Emma the truth. It made *me* feel less like a dirty secret.

"Yeah…that's not uh…what Hannah and I saw. You guys looked *pretty* together. Hannah even said, 'What the fuck? Did you know about the two of them?' So…not sure what you're talking about, don't really care if Alex said she's off girls, but you both looked really caught up in each other. *She* looked really caught up in you."

I knew exactly what Emma meant—we just had one of those moments—but I didn't want to hear it. It would have hurt more to believe her. To have hope.

"She said no, Emma. She doesn't feel the same way as I do. That's that."

"Yeah…" Again with that drawl of disbelief. I wanted to tape Emma's mouth shut and tell her to quit it.

"Skye…honey." Emma placed her hands firmly on my shoulders and gave me a little shake. "People who don't feel the same way for each other don't get that look. People who feel the same way for each other do. And Skye? You two looked pretty damn picture perfect."

/

Very generously, Daniel decided to throw a party for *Glyph* right before the paper's final coverage of the year—prom night. From the outside, his parents' home was like every other suburban home with moderate curbside appeal. Inside, the house sprawled and ended at the back in a mezzanine which was gorgeously framed by floor-to-ceiling windows. Back at my parents' house, apart from the fresh coat of paint applied when we first moved in and the TV remote control that still looked brand new because it had been wrapped in plastic since day one, every piece of furniture was way past its sell-by date but not quite old enough to be retro-cool; just old. I appreciated my parents' need to be thrifty, but each time I returned home felt like I was stepping into a time warp. Comparatively, I was in awe of the chic interior design and style of Daniel's home. It oozed modern minimalist.

"Cool, huh?" Alex said at my shoulder. "The creativity gene runs strong in this family. It's why Daniel loves throwing parties. When you have a home like this, it's hard to throw a shitty one." I turned my head, mouth still slightly agape. She gave my arm a gentle squeeze. "I think Emma's looking for you. I'm gonna go say hi to Daniel."

Emma was on me in a heartbeat as soon as I was left alone. "And you said the two of you aren't together?" she whispered accusingly into my ear.

"We aren't."

"Then explain why you showed up at the party together?"

It was a good question. And judging by the looks Alex and I received when we arrived together, Emma wasn't the only one wondering. Unfortunately, I didn't have a good answer. Alex had surprised me by offering to pick me up and I was helpless to say no. I shrugged at Emma.

"Is Hannah here?" I asked.

"Yeah, I think she's in the kitchen. Have you spoken to her yet?"

"Nope."

"Seriously?"

"Yep."

"Have you even tried?"

"Geez, Ems. Of course I've tried."

"Okay, okay, sorry. I just don't understand why she would be this upset."

"She's not fond of Alex."

"Yeah sure, *but still.*"

"I know. Give me a sec, okay? I need to talk to her and I'd like to do that before she bolts again."

Hannah hadn't responded to any of my text messages and had also evaded me in school. It would have only been less than a week since the encounter, but it had felt a lot longer.

She shot me the iciest glare as I entered the kitchen. The place emptied out immediately. Anyone with a self-preservation instinct knew to leave when Hannah was like this. Presently, that would be everyone. She shot dagger eyes at the last person as he exited the kitchen, and when he did, she redirected them at me.

"Alex?! That's the girl you're interested in?! Tell me that's not it. *Please*. Make me understand what I saw the other day!"

"Hannah..."

"So it's true!" Hannah crossed her arms. "Why?! How could you? All this time. When I asked you, how could you not tell me? How could you not fucking tell me?"

"Hannah..." I tried to sound calm. "What does it matter who it is?'

Of course it mattered. That was why I didn't tell her.

She shot me a dirty look. "*Because*. Because it is *her*. Alex. Fucking Alex Clarke. I can't believe this. That's the girl you want? All the girls in the world and *that's* the one you want? How could you keep this from me?!"

"Why are you so fucking angry at me?!" I retorted, taken aback by the strength of Hannah's reaction.

"Because you know how I feel about her. I *hate* her. Do you understand that? How can you betray me like this?"

"It's not like that. Don't say that. I'm sorry I didn't tell you sooner. This thing with Alex...I just stumbled into it. It happened before I knew about your history with her, and I know I should have just told you, but seeing how the two of you are, it was just easier not to say anything."

The apology didn't erase the hurt on Hannah's face. I felt ridden with guilt.

"I can't do this. I don't know how I'm supposed to be friends with you when she—"

"Don't make me choose. Hannah, please." I tried to reach for her hands, but she kept her arms crossed. "I don't have a choice when it comes to Alex…I love her."

A look of dismay flashed across Hannah's face, and then she turned away from me. I knew deep down that I had just dug the inevitable grave for our friendship.

Hannah took a few steps towards the kitchen door. She stopped. "She will hurt you, Skylar. It's what she does."

I shut my eyes tight, my heart falling over itself to deny what my ears were hearing. "She won't. You're wrong, Hannah. I know she won't."

"And I can't stop you."

With that, she was gone and I was alone in the kitchen. It hurt. I didn't think loving Alex would come at the cost of a friendship, not like this.

A hand settled on my arm as I left the kitchen. I turned, hoping it was Hannah. But there was Alex. My heart raced at the sight of her, all thoughts of Hannah vanishing. It didn't matter how many times I saw Alex or that we had already spent some time together getting to the party. She would always set my heart racing.

"There you are. I was wondering where you went. Everything okay?"

"Yeah."

"You sure?"

"Yeah, I'm sure. You found Daniel?"

"Yep, eventually. He thinks that this is going to be his 'best party ever.'" She laughed as she handed me a drink. "Come, I found a perfect spot for us."

Alex led me upstairs to the daybed on the mezzanine. From it, we watched the sunset—a shattered sky of blue, pink, and orange—and as a comfortable lull fell between us, the frenetic party energy around us faded into the background like white noise. We weren't short on space, but Alex's body was pressed right up against mine, her breathing slow, deep, soothing.

"Excited about prom?" I tried to take my mind off how close her body was.

"I'm excited about my dress. Does that count?"

I held out my hand and gave it a tiny mid-air wobble. "Not sure. You could wear your dress at home and still be excited."

Alex gave me a gentle shove in mock annoyance. "Be supportive!"

I laughed. "Aren't I always?"

"Yeah, you are actually."

Alex surprised me with the seriousness of her response. I had meant to sound light-hearted. I gave her a gentle shoulder bump. "So, what is the color of your dress?"

"Silver, cuts off at the shoulders. It's a really simple one actually. Nothing fancy."

"I'm sure you'll look gorgeous in it."

"Wait till you see me in it tomorrow night, Miss Feature Piece."

I blushed. "It's nothing."

"Don't do that. It's not nothing. You earned it."

I ran my hand through my hair. "Okay. Anyway, I'm sure you'll look gorgeous in your dress. Honestly, you could come in tattered shorts and t-shirt and I'm sure you'll still find a way to look gorgeous."

Alex fell silent and I cursed at myself for not maintaining boundaries.

"Thank you," she finally murmured. We locked eyes and smiled at each other.

Alex rested her head against my shoulder and it nearly caused me to leap out of my skin. Alex's head. On my shoulder. It was unprecedented. I threw a hurried gaze around us. *Everyone* was here. I held my breath before releasing it shakily, afraid that any sudden movements would result in Alex pulling away. I wanted her to stay. I cast another furtive glance around the room, curious if anyone was paying attention. I caught Emma's eye. Discreetly, she mouthed the words "picture perfect" and mapped out the shape of a rectangle with her fingers, as if to frame us in a snapshot. I shot her a glower which had the undesired countereffect—she approached us with a camera.

"Hey you two, can I take a pic? One for the memories as they say."

I shot Alex a look, nervous.

"Go for it." She smiled for the camera without moving away. Emma scurried off triumphant.

Alex rested her hand on my arm when we were alone again. Her hand was soft, warm and the longing it ignited in me was indescribable. I groaned internally. It was difficult to avoid getting caught up in her affections. I could hear Emma's voice in my head and wondered for a moment if she was right, my innermost hopes slowly surfacing. Believing that Alex felt the way I do was a dangerous path. As I stared transfixed at her hand on my arm, I struggled to retain some semblance of ownership over my feelings for her.

Alex brushed her thumb against my scars, eyes cast downward. "What happened?"

A simple question. A surge of memories which blurred into a black hole of loneliness.

"I— I've always known I felt differently about girls. I'm lucky in that sense, having always known who I am. But everything changed when I came out." A searing pain caused my heart to recoil into isolation. I stopped.

"It's okay," she said. "We don't have to talk about it if you don't want to."

But I did. I wanted to tell Alex everything.

"I mean, I wasn't naïve," I continued. "I didn't think it was *all* going to be okay, but the way I was shunned by nearly everyone at school and how my parents reacted and rejected me..." I heard myself laugh; it sounded so sad. "That was rough. And it was lonely, yet every time I thought I hit rock bottom, I'd find a new low. The first time I did it, I think it was because I wanted someone to notice, to ask me what happened, to fix it. Nothing happened. I did a couple more. Nothing changed. But I just kept at it. Don't know why. Probably still wanted some attention, until one day I realized that I was doing it because it made *me* feel better."

I closed my eyes, an involuntary sigh escaping my lips. "It's an affliction. It hurts enough to distract me, and then it equals—melds—with what I feel inside. I bleed. The pain follows. I bleed the pain out of my body and at some point, there's peace, and it is quiet."

Alex lifted her head off my shoulder, her fingers still caressing my scars. I opened my eyes to find her looking at me with not a single shred of judgment or wariness. Where others had looked away, she did the exact opposite.

"I'm all fucked up with nowhere to go." Nobody could hear us. It sounded so confessional. My secrets, my fears—Alex could have them all.

"No, you're not." I didn't believe her, and I thought my cynicism didn't show, but her grip tightened around my arm. "Stop that."

"You're always telling me to stop, Alexis."

My voice was soft and teasing, but the truth was that I would have done anything Alex wanted me to do. Not quite able to bring myself to refuse her, whether for fear of losing her, the fear of not being good enough for her, or simply because she seemed more certain of how life should be lived than I was, all that power to command me to her will, she could take, and I would have given—freely—for no other reason than her wishing it so.

"And you should listen to me." Alex's tone mirrored mine. I chuckled, the dull ache of sadness in my heart replaced by one of affection. "I know it hasn't been easy," she said after a moment. "I'm proud of you."

Alex was the first person to ever say that to me, and I basked in the unbelievable warmth.

"You know he wants a family someday." Alex nodded at Daniel across the room. "I assumed it would have been with his boyfriend, but I assumed wrong. Said he'll marry a girl when the time comes."

"Even if he doesn't love her?"

"I don't know. I didn't ask. I suppose he'll love her in some way."

"But not the way he'll love a guy?"

"Probably not," Alex said. When I failed to respond, she pressed, "You don't agree with what he's doing?"

"No, I don't," I admitted.

"Not everyone can be brave, Skye." There was no reproach in her tone, only a hint of melancholy. "Some are just braver than others and sometimes, there isn't much of a choice to begin with."

It would be years before I realized how much I disagreed. The decision of who we should love, what we should be, is always ours, never anyone else's. The fact that it is a difficult decision, or that people would disagree with it, doesn't rid us of our autonomy. At that time though, I accepted her logic without question.

Alex started to run her finger along my skin. She traced a path starting at the topmost scars, past my wrist and finally down to the tip of my fingers. I turned my hand to reveal my palm to her when she ran out of real estate. The mood between us was shifting.

"Don't you wonder what happens if you choose to be brave and it all doesn't work out? All that fight and for nothing?" she asked.

"Then I'd rather find that out myself. Beats sitting around and wondering what if, don't you think?"

Alex tilted her head to face me. There it was again—a deep affection in her eyes, but this time apparent and unwavering, unlike the last time. She covered my palm with hers. Fanning each and every spark she had ever lit in my heart, she set me on fire with her touch. I tentatively clasped her hand. She rested her head against the crook of my neck and in the silence, with her hand still in mine, there was the gentlest fleeting caress of her thumb against my skin.

I didn't know if Alex was coming or going that night, or if her constant push and pull had finally converged with every word said and every touch made, folding into each other to send us into freefall. All I knew was that unrequited love can be cruel. It craves attention without relief. It desires affection without respite. Above all else, it makes demands on the heart without reciprocation. I thought I couldn't bear to love Alex any more than I already did. But I could. The first time, every time since, and by the time we were through that night, she had all of my heart.

/

I never cared very much for formal events—too bothersome to dress for, too tedious to endure in the company of people who don't interest you. That wasn't the case for Havenford High's prom night. There was Alex and she didn't just interest me; she infused my every waking thought.

She had dropped me off at home after Daniel's party and we parted with an impossibly long hug in her car. I was up all night after, turning over each piece of the night's events in order to decode what had happened. Unsuccessful and sleep-deprived, I remembered at the sight of seniors trickling into the gym that I still had a cover story to write for *Glyph*. I bent down to scribble shorthand descriptors of the prom venue in my notepad. When I looked up, Emma, with the most determined look on her face, was making a beeline.

"Spill," she said, not even bothering to say hi as she sat down. "What is going on between you and Alex? Everyone's talking about last night!"

"What about it?"

If looks could kill, Emma's would have eviscerated me.

"Fine. About how inseparable and physical the both of you were, *with each other*. Someone made a comment to Hannah and she almost bit their head off."

I blinked. The first mystery decoded—whatever happened with Alex at Daniel's party didn't just happen in my head.

Emma snapped her fingers. "Skye? Hellooo? This is the part where you, you know, tell me what's going on?"

I clocked a bunch of fresh faces walking through the door but didn't note anything of interest for *Glyph.*

"I wish I knew, Ems. I keep thinking about last night. I can't *stop* thinking about it. I don't know what's going on, or what Alex is thinking. All I know is that she was just..."

"All over you."

I shot Emma a look, lips pressed into a firm line.

"I've got eyes, dude. So did everyone else in the room."

"Yeah, well, if only eyes can tell me what's going on with Alex..."

"I'm ready to start drawing hearts around your names."

"Oh, shush."

"But I really ship the two of you."

I couldn't help but crack a smile. Throngs of people were coming through the door at full pelt now. The gym was filling up fast and the DJ took that as his cue to ramp up the volume. The Havenford High prom night committee certainly knew how to throw a good party; no expense was spared in decorating the gym and the entire corridor leading up to it. A figure stepped through the doorway and while I had long committed her to memory, no amount of time spent imaging how Alex would look on her prom night could match the girl who showed up. The simple silver dress, classic and lovely as it was, would have been nothing on another person. Alex was a dream made real. A split second later, Alex was joined by a taller, bulkier person—Tom. She turned to him, smiled widely and linked her arm through his. They had matching corsages to boot. Scanning the room on entry, Alex surveyed her surroundings before her eyes eventually landed on mine. I watched as her hand tightened around Tom's arm. It was slight, but unmistakable to me. Her gaze dropped and shifted quickly to her group of friends as she ushered Tom along with her.

"Alex is here!" Emma announced.

"Uh-huh…"

"Geez, sound a little more excited why don't you?"

I couldn't. My mind was running at a million miles per hour as it tried to comprehend what my eyes took in. I tried to fool myself into believing that nothing was wrong, but I knew the truth, and so did my gut—I had watched Alex shut me out, in real time. My heart sank. I honestly thought that she and I had broken through that.

"Come on, Skye." Emma tugged at my arm, too distracted by the activities around her to realize that I was in turmoil. "Let's make the rounds. Get some on-the-ground feedback from the school!"

The next thirty minutes were a blur. I was on autopilot, letting Emma ask most of the questions, dutifully jotting down the responses, politely laughing at jokes that didn't seem funny.

"Alex!"

Emma. In her wildly misguided efforts to play Cupid, she had subtly steered our path to wandering Alex. It made me sick with anxiety and hope. Alex and Emma hugged and gushed about prom and I could only stand by, unmoving, my fingers clutching my pen and notebook. Before I knew it, Emma had shoved me forward and the only screen I had between my thoughts and reality vanished.

I shoved my anxiety to one side and cracked a hesitant smile at Alex. "Hey, you," I said softly.

Alex steeled at my greeting. "Hi."

My heart winced. I waited a moment, hoping for more. The split second of silence between us was nothing like the old, comfortable ones. This one was awkward, painful, and deafening. I started to wish that the gym floor would open and swallow me.

"You look good, Alex." A compliment, I hazarded, to lighten the mood.

"Thanks." Brusque.

I searched her eyes for an answer, but she looked right through me, her lips drawn into a hard line. We had done this song and dance before, but it had never felt this brutal. Ignored me when we weren't alone, sure. Behaved coldly in response to me straying beyond her rules of our engagement, fine. But she had never looked right through me as if I didn't exist. My heart was beating hard against my chest. I looked to Emma to step in to break up the awkwardness and allow me a graceful exit, but she seemed just as confused.

"Alexis…" My voice was strained.

"I need to find Tom," she said, already looking around.

There was an ensuing tightness in my chest. I was desperate to hold on to Alex's arm, to let my tears find their way to the surface and to beg her to stay. At the same time, I was overwhelmed by the need to barricade myself behind a wall of concrete and steel, refusing for Alex to see how quickly, and easily, she could take me apart, if this was how she was going to be. Through gritted teeth, I said, "Fine. If that is where you need to be, don't let me stop you."

Emma and I watched as she glided away through the crowd on long strides towards Tom. With each of her steps, my resolve crumbled more, giving way to a violent ache which welled up from a bottomless place within me.

"What the fuck just happened?" Emma exhaled.

"Nothing." *Everything.*

"What the fuck, Skye?"

"Nothing, Emma. We didn't say shit, we didn't do shit. So, yeah, absolutely nothing happened."

"Skye, you know that's not what I—"

"*I know*, Emma. But what do you want me to say?" I hissed. "That I just got royally fucked and I didn't even see it coming? Or that I was naïve and idealistic enough to believe that last night meant anything, that it changed *anything*? Or that she just ripped my guts out and I have no fucking clue what to do or how to feel?!"

Emma took a step towards me, her hand reaching for my arm.

"Don't." I recoiled. "If you do, I don't think I can—"

"Skye…"

"I just need a moment."

I left the gym. Braced against the lockers in the corridor, I clung to whatever construct of hope I had when it came to Alex. *She will hurt you, Skylar.* Hannah's words rang in my ear. *It's what she does.* I had to believe that behind her actions lay a very good explanation, but my dread grew. I willed my legs to take me away from the gym. I had all I needed to write the article for *Glyph.* Nobody would miss me if I left. Yet the muscles of my heart flexed, sending a new direction to my legs. I walked, a glutton for punishment, back toward Alex.

From a corner, I watched as she drifted from conversation to conversation, an invisible radius doing its job to keep her away from me and firmly in Tom's embrace.

"Skylar…" There was urgency in Emma's voice when she found me. "I overheard Alex and her friends talking. They were grilling her about last night—apparently they caught wind of it from one of the *Glyph* guys—I..." Emma paused and swallowed. "I heard her say that there's nothing going on between the two of you. That she's only messing with you because it's great to be wanted..."

I shook my head very slowly. Emma sounded like she was speaking underwater.

"Skye..." Emma said softly as she wrapped her hand around my arm, worry etched in her voice as I remained silent.

I had my eyes squarely on Alex. I wanted answers but there was only confusion.

Alex was back with her friends. I caught their side glances this time, the whispers, the smirks. I turned away, jaw clenched. I felt my face burn with heat. How could I have been so blind? Someone like Alex could never love someone like me.

I turned back in their direction. Alex's cold, steely eyes were on me now, taking away whatever warmth she had shown before, and then some more. She caused the tightness in my chest to turn into pain. I could still feel her touches from the night before, each one an imprint on my heart, and each one a bigger one than the last. I chased the intangible warmth of that memory. I wanted to outrun the darkness I knew was coming.

Alex looked *at* me, then threading her fingers through Tom's hair, she kissed him.

I always knew that my heart was meant to be broken by girls, Alex. I just didn't expect it to be broken by you.

CHAPTER 19

Another letter in my mailbox today, along with some twigs and dead leaves. Courtesy of Jamie. It started with a mailbox stuffed full of branches and leaves the very first day after we broke up, accompanied by a crumpled note:

> *I hate you. We're perfect for each other. How can you not see that? I HATE YOU.*
> *P.S. I wanted to dump melted ice cream in your mailbox, but the tub was too big and I was too impatient to wait for it to melt.*

A few days later, it was stones, and another angry letter. The mailbox has gotten less full two weeks in. I figure it is either very tiring for Jamie to continually fill my mailbox with junk or she has simply run out of things to put in it. I am just grateful that she hasn't been patient enough to wait for her tub of ice cream to melt. Alison would never speak to me again.

Jamie's letters tend to waver between anger and sadness. Some days I'm treated to a more remorseful ex who simply wants another chance. Today, it is Angry Jamie. Scanning the letter, *bitch*, *fuck you*, and *go fuck yourself* are the vocabulary of the day.

There is a gentle rapping on the main entrance door. I pull my eyes away from the letter to find Paige standing outside.

I open the door. "You're early."

Despite keeping in touch through text messages, today is the first time Paige displayed any desire to physically emerge from the hole she has been in and even then, we are simply hibernating in my apartment.

"Hi." She leans in to give me a kiss on my cheek but stops short when she realizes that I am standing there with a slip of paper in one hand and dead leaves in the other. "Okay…do I want to know what this is?"

I pass Paige the letter and busy myself with the twigs and dead leaves. "Fuck me," she mutters to herself as she reads. "Why didn't you tell me about this?"

I wave the comment away. "You've had your own shit to deal with. I can manage Jamie."

"I'm sorry I haven't been around much."

"Paige." I frown at her. "You have absolutely nothing to be sorry about."

"Regardless, can I make it up to you by placing a couple of broken eggs in Jamie's letterbox?"

"It's okay. I'd rather you not."

"Because I can."

I toss the leaves out the door. "I have no doubt, but it's really okay."

"Fine, then I shall take great pleasure in doing this at least." Holding up Jamie's note, she decidedly rips it right down the middle and tosses the crumpled pieces into the bin. Together, we head upstairs to the apartment.

/

Paige polishes off another glass of vodka and soda. She stands up, retrieves my empty glass along with hers, and wanders off to the kitchen. We have successfully ploughed through more than half the bottle just shooting the breeze.

"Did you want to talk about Cam?" I have wanted to ask since she got here, but only now does the question seem possible.

"We can talk about anything whenever you want, Skye, but really, what is there to say?" She flexes her forearms and twists the ice tray. The soft clink of ice cubes hitting the bottom of our glasses is steady and measured. She turns. "Cam and I fought, she accused me of not being committed to our relationship, of being another one of those girls who played the field, and I ran out of steam explaining to her that her fears were unfounded, again. I'm in a relationship, not an inquisition, for goodness sake." Paige runs her hand through her hair, sighing. "So, I may have accused Cam of being crazy-paranoid and I think that was the last straw." She shoots me a sheepish look. "Word of advice: *never* call Cam crazy-paranoid."

"You could've just been honest with her. Told her what you told me."

Paige shrugs. "Then what? Give her a reason to have hope, because which girl doesn't want to believe that she's the one who changes it up? When it all comes out in the wash, it's Cam who gets cheated out of a relationship she deserves."

I nudge Paige's foot. "Take notes, because that's what a self-fulfilling prophecy sounds like."

She chuckles, affectionate, and pushes back against my foot. "Fuck off, Skye. And do *you* want to talk about Jamie? I know break-ups never end well, but twigs and leaves in the letterbox *does* seem pretty extreme. Could make the list of top ten break-ups of all time."

"Top ten, huh?"

"Oh, for sure."

We chuckle over that.

"There's not much to talk about, really. I mean, there's a lot I could say, but at the end of it, none of that really matters. Our relationship was beyond toxic. I allowed it to go on for too long—that's on me—but it's done and all I've got to do now is ride out the Angry Jamie wave, twigs, branches, gravel, and all."

Paige takes a sip from her glass, the familiar twinkle surfacing in her eyes. They are lovely in a different way tonight, and it's the first time, I realize, she's not wearing eyeliner and eyeshadow.

"And Octavia? What's going on with her now?"

"It's simple with Octavia. Been there. Didn't get that. Not sure how much I wanted it anyway. Tapped out. What?" I ask, amused by how amused Paige seems.

"Nothing, it's like you've been running around exorcising all your demons, with great vim and vigor."

"Ohh..." I shake my head with a grin. "You have no idea the demons I have inside."

"No?" Her eyes shine with keen interest.

"Nope."

"I'm intrigued now," Paige murmurs and approaches.

I keep my smile pleasant, neutral. "If anyone knew what they were, nobody would want me."

"Oh, Skye..." Paige brushes a few loose strands of hair away from my eyes. There is something so tender in the way she does so, it makes me shy. "I think you'll find that a lot more people want you than you realize. That's not the problem. It's that you don't seem to want any of them enough."

"Rubbish," I mutter, holding on to good humor.

"You know it's true. You're welcome to deny it, of course." Paige's expression isn't so much a smile as a rather suggestive smirk that teases at the edge of her lips. It isn't arrogant or self-righteous, only a charming playfulness that is beginning to win me over. She's born with a terribly unfair advantage.

"You know it's that kind of behavior that keeps getting you into trouble with Cam, right?"

"What?" She laughs, warm with a touch of cheek. "What did I do now?"

"You do this thing with your lips. It's not a full smile, it's like a half-smile, a secretive smile of sorts, but it drives girls wild. I've seen it. I think it's also that brown leather jacket of yours. The one you wore when we were out at Operation Missing Basement. It makes you look insanely hot. I mean, you even had my *very* straight ex-flatmates flirting with you."

Paige tilts her head. "Did you just say insanely hot?" Her voice gets a husky edge. It stirs up a reaction in the pit of my stomach.

"No..."

She waits on my answer, but it's clear from her eyes—now a little heavy-lidded from drinking—that she's processing what she just heard. I notice how her hair has become tousled from us lounging on the couch. It's messy in a sexy way and it would probably only get sexier if I could run my fingers through it and push it back. I feel a deep flush come on and my throat runs dry.

I cough and hurriedly gulp a considerable portion of my drink. "I-I'm just telling you why you keep getting into trouble with Cam."

There is a ringing silence that hangs in the kitchen, and the racing of my heart which causes the blood to rush in my ears. Suddenly unsure of how to behave, I push myself off the kitchen counter, meaning to head back to the living room.

"Do you remember how we were like the last time we were out together?" she says when I'm nearly out of the kitchen. "Sitting outside, drinking, smoking, just talking…just being…us?"

I stop and turn to look at Paige. The pensiveness in her eyes has been replaced by an intensity which causes the hairs on the back of my neck to stand and the muscles in my body to awaken and gravitate towards her. My tongue and the words on the tip of it get tangled up in each other.

"Cam had been so insistent, so utterly convinced that there was something going on between us—because for two people who don't appear to speak much to each other, we were a lot more than casual. Too close for *her* comfort. It appears I failed to put her mind at ease."

"Okay…" I will my body to move but it refuses me. "Why…" I falter, suddenly unable to focus with Paige this close, unable to comprehend this sudden emergence of feelings of conflict and attraction. "Why are you telling me this?"

"Why did you just tell me that my brown leather jacket makes me look insanely hot?" Paige's voice is soft and low, like a caress in the night. It sends shivers down my spine.

"I— I don't know."

The kitchen is obscenely warm. It is as if someone had turned the oven up and left its door wide open.

Paige leans forward until her lips meet mine. They are soft, tentative, and I feel myself melting into her kiss without resistance. Paige exhales gently when we part. I'm not sure she remembered to breathe during our kiss. I don't think I did either.

"I don't want to fuck us up, Skye…"

I gently cup her face, caressing the side of her jaw. "That makes two of us…"

Paige wraps her arms around my waist with her hands clasped together at the small of my back. She presses a kiss against my forehead. “Do you want to stop?”

I can sense her longing and restraint as I wrestle with my own conflicting feelings. This friendship—we are so good at it. Yet this attraction, surfacing, new but seemingly old, as if it has been lying in wait all this time, waiting for me to come to my senses. Or perhaps this is just me losing my senses.

I run my hands up Paige’s back, past her shoulder blades and up to her neck. Her shirt is soft against the palm of my hands. The feel of her hair—smooth and thick—between my fingers. I tilt my head up and shove all my worries and concerns into the corners of my mind. “I just want you to kiss me again.”

She does, and this time, her kisses are no longer tentative.

CHAPTER 20

I close the door behind me. It took every ounce of willpower to stop myself from unbuttoning the shirt Paige had just put on. I held firm, and with a grumble, she allowed the opportunity to pass—she had to head to morning tutorials. It was the most restraint either of us had displayed in twelve hours.

Down from our initial rush of oxytocin, we attempted to have a grownup conversation about what we should do, if we should shelve our hook up under 'random occurrences' and continue being friends (or try to do so, at least), but each time it got too difficult to decide, she would kiss me—sometimes I would kiss her—and that would be us dealing with it.

There is a soft rapping on the door and I fling it open, ready to tell Paige off for being incorrigible, ready to fling her into bed again. My face falls.

"Jamie."

"Skye..." Lips downturned with eyes sad like that of an abandoned puppy. A puppy who busied itself dumping dead foliage into my mailbox for days. Annoyance begins its slow seep into my veins.

"I see you decided to take a break from stuffing shit in my mailbox and talk to me instead."

Jamie turns a few shades of red. "You didn't want to talk to me," she mumbles.

"Not sure how I'm meant to respond to, 'Fuck you, bitch,' and, 'I hate you,' or proclamations that we're meant to be because *you* are the best I'll ever have. Did you want me to say, 'Oh yeah, fuck you too?'"

"I know, I know." Jamie tugs at the straps of her backpack. "I'm sorry. I just, fuck, I just lost control. You know how I lose control sometimes. I just couldn't bear losing you. Please let me make it up to you."

"Stop throwing shit into my mailbox and we're good. Now, if you don't mind."

I have one hand on the door. Jamie's hand whips out to keep it open. I arch an eyebrow. She hurriedly drops her hand.

"Sorry, sorry. I just want to talk. Can we talk please? We broke up and it's been so hard for me to process this. I just want to process this with you, talk it through."

Jamie's eyes are pleading. There are dark rings beneath her eyes. She looks like she hasn't slept in days and she seems genuinely apologetic. The door to the apartment opposite mine opens and my lady neighbor shuffles out with her recycling in hand, sending a cheery hello our way before making her way down the stairs. I sigh. This isn't the most convenient place to speak with Jamie.

"Okay, come in. I've got to be somewhere in a bit, so not too long, okay?"

It's a lie, but I don't want her overstaying her welcome.

"Sure, sure. I'll just say my piece and go. Thank you, Skye, for hearing me out."

That is uncharacteristically polite for Jamie, but I figure it's part of her apology tour. I position my body between her and the start of the corridor; there's no reason why the apology tour can't take place near the vicinity of the main door.

"Not even a coffee, huh? Heh." Jamie's voice grows weaker when she realizes that she isn't going to get further than a few feet from the door. I don't respond.

"Uh, right…" There is another tug of the straps of her backpack. Jamie clears her throat. "I'm sorry for what I said to you that night, for how I behaved. It wasn't right. I was drunk and you were just trying to get me home. I should have followed and not made a scene. I know how you hate that. I know you hate how I can get. I shouldn't have grabbed you like that. I shouldn't have lost my cool. I can see that now. I'm sorry. I really am. I know I need to change, and I'll work on it. I'll get better. You'll see. I'm going to change and be the girlfriend you deserve."

My eyes narrow. "Jamie…" I resist the urge to fold my arms and take a step back, lest a change in body language antagonizes her. "I appreciate what you're saying, I really do. I accept the apology but…this doesn't change anything. You know that, right?"

"Doesn't it? I said I'll get better and be the girlfriend you deserve. Isn't that what you've wanted all this time?"

"Jamie, it doesn't change anything I said that night. Being together. Us. This. This is not something I want anymore. I think it's great that you want to change, but I still believe it's best we stay apart. We're not healthy for each other. We just keep bringing out the worst in each other, and this relationship is nothing but toxic for us."

"How can you say that?!" She sounds like I have stabbed her.

"How can you not see?" I ask, keeping my tone as level as possible despite the increasingly rapid palpitations of my heart.

"I was made for you!" Jamie's fingers are now wrapped tightly around the straps of her backpack.

"Hardly." The word slips out, sarcasm and all.

Jamie falls silent. If not for the look I see in her eyes, I would have lauded myself for the feat I pulled off—Jamie, speechless, a world's first—but I have been with her long enough to know when we have turned the corner, for better or for worse. This is certainly, most definitely, for the worse.

"Is it because you're fucking Paige now? Is she that good a lay? The two of you *just couldn't wait* to jump each other's bones, could you?"

I'm taken aback. "How—"

"How did I know?" Jamie's eyes flash. "Because she sauntered out of here earlier, looking all pleased with herself. Just-been-fucked hair and all. I've been waiting for you to come out since this morning so that we could talk. Little did I know you had 'overnight fucking' scheduled."

"Jamie. Leave Paige out of this. She has nothing to do with it." I cast my eyes at the door behind her. The fool I was to have let her in. I take a few slow steps toward her, unwilling and increasingly nervous. I hate having to approach her when she is combusting. "I also think it's time for you to leave." I fight hard to steady my voice.

Jamie doesn't move. In fact, she stiffens up, eyes daring me to touch her. She knows my secret, and she knows just how to abuse me with it.

"Make me. I'd like to see you try."

The sickly feeling in my stomach churns. "Come on, Jamie, there's no need to be like this." I swallow the lump in the back of my throat and nervously place a hand on her shoulder.

To my surprise, she is compliant and allows me to maneuver her towards the front door. The relief is short-lived. She digs her heels in as we near it, staring me down, wordlessly challenging me to do something about my problem—her. She smirks, takes one small step back and bolts around me and into my bedroom. The sinking feeling drags me into the deep with it. I ponder walking out the main door and leaving Jamie in my apartment.

If she wants to stay so much, she can stay here for all I care. It is a terrible idea, of course. Who knows what Jamie will do to the apartment? I steel myself. Paige has just left. Alison spent the night at Rachel's and is therefore unlikely to return soon. So, as much as I hate this, I need to make this work, alone.

I approach my room warily and find her standing far away from the door, back glued to the wall.

"Jamie." I point in the direction of the main door. "Please leave."

"No."

"You have clearly overstayed your welcome. Leave. *Please.*"

"No."

"Jamie..."

I want to scream. All I want is her out of the apartment.

I take a deep breath and reach across for the strap of her backpack. I yank it and step aside as Jamie stumbles forward. She catches her balance and turns back, getting right up in my face.

"We're not done talking, Skye."

Fear and dread start to permeate the edge of my consciousness. I *need* her out. Now.

"We *are* done talking."

Without making eye contact, I grab her shoulders and push. She immediately becomes a deadweight leaning forcefully against me. Unlike the last time, every step towards the main door is a slog. She resists every step of the way, alternating between apologies, insults, and begging me to let her stay. The mixed sense of frustration, desperation, and hope grows inside of me with every step I clear.

I am so close.

One moment I can see the door, the next I have the wind knocked out of me. I collapse into the metal shoe rack in the corridor. When my head clears, I realize just how hard she shoved me into the wall.

"You don't get to break up with me!" She stands above me, leaning in as she speaks. Panic starts to claw at my chest. This is too close. It is too much. I throw my hand out and shove Jamie. Like a release valve, the panic ebbs.

Jamie stumbles back, surprised at first. Then her face twists into a sneer.

"What are you going to do, Skye? Try and push me out of here again? We both know I'm stronger than you, or do you need me to pin you down in bed again and show you? I can fuck you better and harder than Paige can. Did she fuck you real good last night? Did she make you scream? Give me another chance and I'll show you just how much better I am. Oh I assure you, I am *sooooo* much better than her at fucking you."

I stagger to my feet. "I said—leave Paige out of this."

"You're not answering the question, *Skye*. Did Paige fuck you real good last night? Did she make you beg? Did she make you scream? *Is she a good lay*?"

I growl in exasperation. My back is throbbing from the fall. I press my hand against it and allow myself a moment to draw solid breaths.

"Paige is more than anything you'll ever be."

"You don't get to leave me for that cunt!" Jamie lunges and shoves me onto the ground. Her knees dig into the side of my ribs, all her weight on me.

Sick! Filthy! Disgusting! You are not my daughter! You are an abomination! My mother's face flashes in front of me. My brother stalking off in the distance as she continues to hit me.

Jamie has the fabric of my shirt in her hands. The material strains and tears.

You deserve to have this beaten out of you. My mother's hand raised high before she swings it at me. I squeeze my eyes shut.

I'll kill you before I let you leave! The kitchen knife glinting in the fluorescent light. White knuckles, my mother's death grip on it as she points it at me. The stainless steel blade inches away from my heart.

My breathing is erratic. The panic is crippling, debilitating. It is a black hole and I feel like I can die from the sheer strength of it. I am shaking.

My heart seems to implode, and an indescribable fury and rage pours into my system. Like the blood in my veins, it fills every inch of me, becoming a part of me. It is cold. It feels cruel, and powerful.

I fling Jamie off me like a ragdoll.

The panic—gone.

"I am so goddamn *sick* of you and your fucking *bullshit*!" My hands find a fistful of her sweater and the waistband of her jeans and I haul her up. She still has her stupid backpack on. She tries to resist me, her hands flailing, but effortlessly I drag her, kicking and screaming, towards the front door.

"Skye! Skylar! I'm sorry! I'm so sorry! You know I have no control whenever this happens! I can't help myself! Skye, please! Stop, this hurts!"

"You should have thought about that before you behaved like a brat that needed to be taught a lesson," I say between my gritted teeth, part releasing Jamie to open the front door.

Jamie strikes my jaw with her open palm and shoves me off her before I can restore my grip on her. She comes at me again, one arm pushing me up against the wall, the other snaking underneath my shirt. "Come on, Skye," she breathes hoarsely into my ear. "Don't resist this. You love the way I fuck. It's the reason you never left me for Octavia. Why would you leave me now for Paige?"

I fling Jamie to the ground in disgust. I want to smash her smug little face and wipe that smirk off it. I crouch down. "I didn't keep you around because you were a good fuck. I kept you around because Octavia never said yes. And for the last time—" I make a fist and cock it back. "Leave. Paige. Out. Of. This." I land a punch squarely in her ribs with every pause. She curls into a ball. I stop speaking, but my fist continues to find the soft flesh of her sides again and again.

Don't think I won't do it. I will kill you before I let you ruin everything. I can still hear the threats coming from my mother's lips. Some nights I wonder how it would have felt if the slim profile of the blade had slid into my skin, past my ribcage and into my beating heart.

I wrap my fingers around a thin cylindrical item. The rod that had dislodged from the broken shoe rack. Cold relief. I bring it up past my head.

He doesn't deserve you, Skylar. He doesn't deserve your love. I see him. My dad. In a corner. Doing absolutely nothing to help me. Beads of sweat drip from my forehead. I'm on my knees, one hand on Jamie's chest to keep her down. I brace for the reverberations of the rod I know will come when it connects with the human body.

She doesn't deserve to live. If anyone should have died that night, it should have been her. I see her. My mom. Her eyes—deranged and manic. Sweat pricks at the corner of my eyes. I am painfully aware of the tightness of my arm. I can hear my breathing. It sounds labored, rough. I want someone to feel my pain. I want to unleash my rage on someone.

Jamie throws her hands up and turns her face away. I have finally wiped that smirk off her face and given her a taste of her own medicine—fear. She looks terrified beyond belief.

I feel my grip falter.

Was this what she saw too?

I give my head a rough flick and try to shake the sweat from my eyes.

Why didn't she stop?

I choke back a sob and feel my body weaken.

How could she not stop?

Jamie is unmoving beneath me, her chest heaving hard, still terrified. The rod—now warm in my hand.

Let her go.

My arm trembles.

You'll become just like her if you don't.

I hold back another strangled sob. My reasoning head for my broken heart.

Closing my eyes, I will myself to stagger up from my knees. I fling the door open and point. "Leave," I say to Jamie, filled with wretched desperation for her to listen to me just this once. "*Leave,* Jamie. Before I change my mind and do something I regret. *Get. Out.*"

Jamie scrambles towards the doorway on all fours and all but throws herself through it. I slam the door shut and its automatic lock slides into place with a resounding click.

I stagger into my bedroom, my grip grows increasingly tight around the metal rod. The emotions inside me feel uncontrolled and unwieldy. I am mad at my mother for doing what she did. Mad at my dad and Richard for doing nothing. Mad at Jamie for pushing me. Hating how weak I felt. Hating how close I came to giving in to the anger. I slam the rod down against the table. Nothing but a dull thud, and I barely feel the impact. It falls to the ground by my feet. One by one, I grab the hefty textbooks on my table and send them hurtling towards the wall. One massive swipe and the items on the table clatter to the ground. Nothing. Like clockwork, my fist finds the door of the wardrobe. I hear the softest splinter and the pain of wood on bone only lightly aches in my knuckles, but still, nothing. It does nothing for the emotions which threaten to break me from inside out.

My eyes fall on the box below my nightstand. Crumpling down beside it, I unearth the small envelope and tip out its contents—razor blades, gleaming and beckoning like an old friend. Without a single hesitation, the tip of the metal breaks my skin, biting before the familiar pain of dragging a blade through flesh starts to set in. Eyes one hundred percent focused on the bright blood which starts to trickle down the side of my arm. I inhale sharply. I have forgotten how much this could hurt.

Skylar...

"Alex, no." My heart shatters when I say her name. "You're not here. You don't get to do this anymore."

The day after Alex showed herself out of my life, I woke up, drunk off my face from the liquor in my parents' cabinet, and I despaired that I couldn't remain in that stupor forever. First came the heartache that wouldn't abate, then the anxiety when it became clear that Alex wasn't returning. I had been slowly drowning in the dark until she showed up, my midnight sun. I thrived in her light, and without it, I feared it was inevitable that I'd soon be lost again, so I kept going back. Back to my vault of memories of her, playing them back whenever life felt rough, unbearable, and out of my control, hoping it would be enough to keep the darkness at bay.

I bury the blade in my arm again and pull it toward me with slow deliberate forcefulness. I wince and repeat that action. There is the barest hint of impending relief, teasing me, urging me to do it again.

Skylar, listen to me. You need to stop.

Her words, her will, rigidly imposed on me without allowances, imbued with the power I had freely given to her, which she eventually wielded to hurt me. After everything she had done, still I let her in. Beholden. Dependent. It is a warring uncertainty which eats me up from inside out. Feeling like I'm intrinsically and irrevocably bound to a girl who broke my heart just so I can keep from drowning in the dark. She saves me with one hand and shoves me down with the other.

"I gave you everything Alex…I— I can't."

I want to be held, comforted, but the room is empty, missing the one person I truly want, and need, even though she decided years ago that my heart could, and should, be broken.

Skylar, look at me.

"Alex, *no*." I exhale sharply. "I just can't do this with you anymore."

Every battle I have waged with the instinct to hurt myself, I did it because she asked me to, but what is the point of it all if she's no longer in my life?

The cacophony quiets. I give it a moment and run the blade through flesh again. I wait. Relief eludes me. I bite on my bottom lip, brace myself and do it again. Only pain greets me, and it isn't even the metaphorical kind. No, there is just searing hot pain in all its physical urgency and none of the numbing satisfaction that used to follow. I release a guttural growl of frustration and fling the blade away. I clench my fist and release a hiss of pain. I glare at the bloodied blade on the carpet. I mean to be annoyed that it hasn't done the one job I had set for it, but instead, I'm annoyed at it for hurting me so much. I glance between the bloodied blade on my right, the fresh cuts on my arms and the two remaining clean blades on my left. I blink and glance between the blades and my arm again. The blades don't call to me like they used to. I have no desire to pick them up.

I close my eyes and take a few deep breaths. The unprecedented realization ripens. After all these years, the relationship between me and those silver blades, done. I thought we were forever. The world around me stills. I open my eyes. The room is bright with the morning sun that streams through the skylight. I stare at the five red lines etched on my skin. I stare at the blades on the floor. Still nothing.

I run my tongue across my lips, push off on my good hand and stand up. The wreckage in my room isn't pretty. I note with mortification the sizeable dent in the drywall—courtesy of my law textbook—and the splintered wardrobe door right next to it. There is also the matter of the unfixable shoe rack which I will need to explain and the bloodstains on the carpet.

As I bend down to pick up each of the razor blades and begin to wrap them in random pieces of paper, I ponder if Alison and I ever considered the necessity of a first aid kit. Maybe? I toss the carefully compressed ball into the bin in my room. I stare at it, an innocuous white ball grazed with slight traces of blood, nestled among scrap paper and trash. I blink, turn and make my way out of the room without sparing any further thought or care for it. If I am to ensure that Alison, on returning home, doesn't suffer an aneurism from the mere sight of my room, I figure I best not dawdle. The cleanup operation starts now and first on the list: unearthing one elusive first aid kit.

part / two

CHAPTER 21

Nine years later

This is how I shall pass into the afterlife: in the office, when the clock strikes midnight and the last of the oxygen supply finally runs out, confined to my castle made out of paper and a moat built out of law books. I rub my eyes with the base of my hands. I can't believe I'm in the office on a Sunday and that this has been the routine for the last five weekends. At least tomorrow is a bank holiday. Thank heavens for small mercies.

My phone vibrates violently against the desk, startling me. It is probably my office roomie, Lexi, calling to check if I'm still alive. But it's Paige.

"Hey, how's the event coming along? Bristol any fun?"

"Skye."

I sit up immediately. Unlike her usual calm self, Paige sounds sick with worry.

"What's wrong?"

"It's Scott. I need you to—" There's some shuffling on the other end of the phone and mumbling. "I need you to go to Scott's house. He called me and he wasn't making any sense. He just kept crying and freaking out, saying he did something terrible and he doesn't know why."

I am already on my feet, shoving work into my bag even before Paige has finished. "Okay, I'm going. Text me his address."

"Okay, done. I'm driving back now."

I check the text message. "Paige. *Paige.* Hold on, I can get to him in under half an hour. It's really late for you to be driving back now. Can you sit tight? Just give me half an hour, I promise I'll call you back ASAP."

There is nervous silence.

"Paige?"

I know she is deliberating.

"Paige. Trust me. I will find Scott."

"Okay, okay. Call me."

/

There is light coming from one of the windows, but apart from that, the entire house is still. I ring the doorbell. Silence. I try it again, rapping my knuckles against the door. It is a good few minutes before I hear footsteps coming down the stairs and the sound of the door being unlocked. Standing in the doorway is a dark-haired boy, tear-streaked, and obviously a bit drunk. I don't have to ask. I know this has to be Scott.

The resemblance between the siblings is striking; it must be the eyes. Scott came to London a little over a year ago, studying philosophy and economics at university, but I have never actually met him. Paige and I keep talking about how we should arrange something, and how excited she was for me to meet her little brother, but our busy schedules have made planning difficult. I wish these were better circumstances.

My eyes flicker from Scott's face to his arms. He has a scrappy-looking bandage wrapped loosely around his wrist, a bloody patch already starting to form and spread. I draw in a sharp intake of breath. I exhale slowly.

"Scott…?"

"Y-yes?" His voice is unsteady. He looks lost, ready to slam the door shut in my face.

"Scott. I'm Skylar. Your sister, Paige, she called me. She's worried about you. She wanted me to check in on you."

"Oh." Scott falters. "Oh god, I'm sorry. I just called her without thinking. She was on speed dial and I just wanted someone to talk to. I didn't want her to worry. I didn't mean to trouble you so late at night. God, I'm so stupid." Scott's words come out in a rush. So much regret and apology. My heart aches for him.

"Hey, hey..." I gingerly step towards him, my hand reaching for his. "It's okay. It's no trouble at all. Trust me, you don't know the hours I keep. Is anyone at home?"

"No, my flatmates went away for the weekend. Something about a bender."

"Okay, can I come in and sit with you for a bit then? I can take a look at your hand too."

Scott tucks his hand behind his back and looks down at his feet. He mumbles so I can barely make out the words: *Not sure what you can do about this*, is what I think he said.

"Or do you want to come over to mine? I was going to order something to eat. I don't know about you, but I'm starving. Just pulled an all-nighter."

Scott looks uncertain. It dawns on me that he can well say no, to both letting me into his house or coming with me. I am, after all, just a stranger who showed up at his door claiming to know his sister.

"Do you want to, uh, you know, text Paige? I promise I'm not trying to abduct you."

Scott digs around in his pockets for his phone and rings Paige.

"Yeah, she's here. Can you describe how she looks?" Scott listens, eyes intent. "I just wanted to check that she's who she says she is." There is a pause. "I don't know, sis. Perhaps I got lucky tonight and somehow scored *two* visitors and the first one isn't the woman you sent? I didn't want to follow the wrong woman home and leave you to fend for yourself in this cruel world."

Scott falls silent and I can only imagine that this is because of the tirade of frantic and clipped reprimands coming through from Paige. Having unflappable composure is what Paige is famous for among our friends, but I've seen what lies on the other side of it. She can be reckless, easily agitated, and impossible to reason with. All it takes is finding her trigger, which is easier said than done for the woman who actively resists getting overly involved. With Scott though, I would reckon that there has already been a swift disassembling of that said composure.

He finally hangs up the phone and shoots me a woeful, weak smile. "Your home sounds like a fantastic idea."

/

"Here, have another swig. This is going to sting." I nod in the direction of the chilled bottle of vodka. I give Scott a moment before I run the antiseptic swab across the cuts on his wrists. There are only two and, thankfully, based on my own experiences, they aren't too deep and a trip to the hospital won't be necessary. He flinches and grimaces, his grip tightening around the bottleneck. "Sorry, sorry. This is the last of it, I promise."

Scott takes another swig.

I retrieve the antiseptic cream and begin to apply it on the freshly cleaned wounds. With his skin now rid of blood, I can see that these aren't his first. There is another cut, recently healed, a thin faint line. I run my thumb lightly against it.

"First time." A drunken confirmation from Scott. "Don't

know why there was so much blood tonight. Wasn't like this last time."

"You know when they say the first cut is the deepest?"

"Yeah…?"

"They clearly weren't referring to this."

A brief silence then Scott's laughter fills the room. "Did you just make a really bad joke about cutting?"

I grin and shoot him a wink.

"Was it the same for you?" Scott's eyes cast downwards to my arm. The scars on it are faint now, but they're there. Visible to anyone who pays attention or who is actively looking.

"Yeah. First was a baby cut."

"Do you still…?"

"No." I finish wrapping Scott's wrist, taping the end to hold it in place. "I haven't in a very long time."

Putting away the med kit, I sit back down beside Scott at the dining table and allow the syrupy-cold vodka to coat the back of my throat. "Want to talk about it?"

"I dunno. I feel pretty stupid about this now. I'll sound really stupid talking about it."

"Hardly."

"You're just being nice."

"No, seriously. I mean it." I run a finger through the condensation that has formed on the vodka bottle. "Thing is, you don't just rock up to a sharp edge or object and think, *Oh fancy that, I think I'll just hurt myself today if you don't mind.* Whatever it is, you may think it trivial, childish, or insignificant, but clearly it isn't. It matters to you, and that makes it important."

Scott runs his good hand through his disheveled hair. He chews on his lip, deep in thought. I can see now—his eyes are a dark blue, a shade deeper than Paige's.

"I just feel so lost." A crease of despair cuts through Scott's words. "I feel like everyone's got their lives together and I barely know what I'm going to do with mine. Paige's career is taking off. Mum is getting serious with her boyfriend. Everyone's just moving on. Even my dad. Done such a banging job, remarried with another family and all."

I watch him fidget with his fingers and I realize I have been mindlessly running my fingers along the ridges of my scars. It is like reading braille. The scars are a language of their own.

"I think it's okay not to know what you're going to do yet. Most of us don't, not when we're young—heck, not even when we're old. Try not to worry too much about that." Scott exhales sharply and purses his lips. "I would also tell you that nobody's moving on from you. I don't know your mom, but I know Paige, and believe me, *moving on from you* aren't words that exist in her vocabulary. But I don't think it's me you need to hear it from. Have you spoken to her about this?"

"I wanted to, tonight, after…you know. I saw all that blood and thought, shit, I really messed up this time. So I did, but I don't think the words came out too well and all I did was make her panic." Scott wrings his fingers.

"Hey, hey…it's okay. It's totally okay. Paige would have wanted you to call, even if you didn't know what to say. Never stop doing that, okay?"

Scott nods, running his hand through his hair again. "I don't even know why I did it again tonight. I hated it the first time, it hurt so much, but when I dropped the glass in the sink and it broke…I-I…"

I cover Scott's hand with mine. "There's no rush to figure this out."

"No overnight fix?" Scott asks weakly with a boyish smile.

I chuckle softly. "God, no. I wish human beings were that simple. The work we do on ourselves…geez, it's hard work, but it's worth it. That much I know."

He goes quiet again. I'm sure he's tired now that the adrenal rush has worn off. I scribble my number on a piece of paper.

"Here, take this. If you want to talk, see a friendly face, or just tell someone you're about to teeter off the edge again, anything, you can always give me a call. I may not pick up immediately because of work, but I *will* call you back."

Scott grips the piece of paper between his fingers. He nods.

"Do you want to get some rest? I can get the pillows."

Scott nods again and rises to head over to the living room. He pulls his legs towards him and curls up on the couch. I tuck him in under a large throw.

"Did Paige sound mad on the phone?"

"No, she's not mad. Just worried sick. Don't worry about it." I run my hand gently through his hair. "You just rest now, okay?"

Scott nods his head one last time before his eyes flutter shut, and he surrenders to sleep.

/

The buzzing of the phone on the nightstand jolts me awake. I roll over in bed and reach for it. It's Paige. It's also five in the morning, barely two hours since I crawled into bed.

"Hey, is everything okay?"

"I couldn't sleep," she says.

"That's okay." I rub my eyes. "I'm here."

"And…I'm at your front door." There is a slight pause. "I'm sorry. I know you have Scott and he's safe, but I couldn't sleep. I just couldn't stop thinking about him, so I drove back instead.

I thought of going home first, but I really wanted to be here for him when he wakes."

I get out of bed and move quietly across the living room, past a sleeping Scott, and open the door to find one very exhausted-looking Paige.

"I'm so, so sorry. I wouldn't have come here if I didn't feel like I was going to explode with worry."

"Don't apologize. It's okay. I get it." I reassure her with a smile and a hug. Paige immediately identifies the sleeping form on the couch, gives him a once-over, and notices his freshly bandaged wrist peeking out from under the throw. "Is that…?"

"Yeah. I thought we'd talk about it tomorrow. You would have rushed out in the middle of the night if you had known."

"I would have."

"I didn't want you to drive this late in the night, alone."

"It's okay…" Paige murmurs, her hand resting on Scott's head as she kneels beside him, her head slightly bowed.

"Don't be too hard on him."

"I won't." She doesn't move. I can't see her face.

"Paige…" I come up from behind her, leaning downwards and wrapping my arms around her. "Don't be too hard on yourself." Forgetting myself, I press a kiss against the top of her head.

She holds my hands and responds by pressing a kiss into one palm. "I'll try." We break apart awkwardly as she rises. "I should let you get back to bed."

"You must be shattered too." I nudge my head in the direction of my bedroom. "Come on."

"It's okay." Paige gestures to the shorter end of the L-shaped couch. "I can take the other end. I don't want to disturb you further."

I shrug. "It's a big bed and whatever's left of the couch is inhumanly short."

Paige gives pause and considers the situation before following me. Crawling back into the warmth of the bed, I watch as she shrugs off her jacket before slipping under the covers. I contemplate scooting further to the edge of my side but think myself silly for worrying; Paige and I aren't going to sleep with each other just because we're lying in the same bed. Ages ago, we decided we were better as friends, and since then, we have only slipped up once. In my defense, she showed up at dinner looking devilishly gorgeous and we had a bit to drink. That was maybe three, four, years ago. Still, keeping a healthy distance in bed is probably wise.

As we lie in bed, I can tell from Paige's breathing that she is still awake.

"Skylar…" she murmurs as she turns on her side. I do the same and we face each other. "Thank you for getting to Scott tonight."

"You don't have to thank me. I'm always here for you."

Her voice softens with a smile. "As I'm always here for you."

She reaches across and lays her hand on my arm where my scars rest. The way she moves is deceptively calm, but I can see her eyes—alert and watchful—and the little crease on her forehead. She's not saying it, but I know she's worrying, probably stressing, about whether I'm fine and if she should ask this time. I've never gone into the details about why my scars exist, but I still remember the nights when I would feel her gaze on my arms as we lay in bed. I would look at her and know that she was there for me, even if I didn't feel like sharing. With this wordless exchange that has the power to invoke an old intimacy between us, she has a way of calling forth a vulnerability I keep at bay.

She brushes her thumb across the faint ridges. We know that they won't reopen, but sometimes I think Paige doesn't know how to be anything but tender when she touches my scars because of the memories which she believes accompany them, and when she does that, she exposes my heart and she keeps it safe.

CHAPTER 22

A rush of hot air escapes the oven. I tilt my head and expertly avoid the steam facial my oven is keen to provide free of charge. The Yorkshire puddings are ready, and they join the slab of roast beef on the countertop. The gravy simmers on the stove. I take stock of the food, satisfied. Paige left earlier this afternoon with Scott in tow, but she should be back shortly. I have my dad on the line as I finish up.

My dad and I speak once every month. I don't remember exactly when we started, but he called one day sounding rather down. He vented and griped—about life, work, and my mother—and it was the longest one-way conversation I think I have ever had with him or anyone else. Month after month he would call, and it would be more of the same. He talks, I listen. It's mostly about him, and he never asks me about anything that isn't work-related. Over the years, I have come to understand his life intimately while he still has no idea what mine looks like in London. The routine is personally unfulfilling and tedious, but time and time and again, I pick up the phone because he's my dad and I still love him.

"Come again, Dad? Why is it World War III between Richard and Mom?"

"She's annoyed at him for not spending time with her."

"But he does, right?"

Richard moved to Havenford a couple of years ago with his wife, Karen. It delighted my mother to have him near and to not have to wait months between visits.

"He's always tired when we meet him. Says it's work stress."

"Doesn't that make her happy? She's always saying, *Very good! At least they want you!* whenever I tell her that work is stressful." I roll my eyes as I recall the conversations. I've given up explaining to my mother that that is hardly the way anyone measures success. "Anyway, his energy levels aside, he's making an effort to spend time with her, isn't he?"

"But we're always meeting for lunch or dinner at restaurants."

"So? What does it matter where you guys meet? At least Richard's making the effort to see you and Mom, right?"

"It means he's not coming to our house."

"So…?"

"So your mom is saying that our neighbors talk. They gossip, they tell tales behind her back, she's the parent who has been abandoned by her children. It's embarrassing for her."

I frown. While I don't completely agree with my mother's belief that Chinese families (and *only* Chinese families) are constantly judging and competing with one another, I had assumed that she would be less concerned about it in Havenford, seeing as the majority of its residents are white. It seems my mother has not been able to shake her roots regardless of zip code or demographic.

"So let me get this straight. It isn't that Richard hasn't spent time with her. It's that he is not *perceived* or *seen* to have spent time with her because nobody—nobody being the neighbors—sees her at restaurants, but everybody—everybody being the neighbors again—sees her driveway and the lack of cars parked in it every weekend. So, it doesn't matter whether Richard makes an effort to see her. What is relevant is the number of people who see him seeing her?"

There is only silence at the other end of the line, which speaks volumes. Typical—everyone else's perception of my mother takes precedence over everything else that should matter to her. I don't envy Richard's position, but then again, being our mother's favorite comes with perks. She'll be over this in a few weeks and back to loving him with pure devotion.

"Is she taking it out on you?" I ask with a sigh. Richard and I may have grown up and left, but our parents are still stuck with each other.

"A little."

"How are you coping?"

"Just living one day to the next."

"Dad..." The doorbell rings. "One second." I turn off the speakerphone function and cradle the phone against my ear as I open the door. Paige leans in and gives me a small peck on my cheek.

"Dad, you remember what I said last time? It's okay to leave her. Perfectly fine to have that divorce. Richard and I are more than equipped to deal with this now. You should give yourself the opportunity to be happy."

Leaning against the wall, I break into a smile as I watch Paige briefly struggle with her coat and scarf. I stretch out my hand and catch the falling scarf before hanging it on the rack.

"Dad? You there?"

"I should go, Skylar. You said you had guests, and I heard the doorbell—"

"It's fine."

"No, no. We'll talk next time. I need to drive your mom to the hair salon anyway. I can never remember the way and she'll only get angrier if we're late, like the last time. Bye, Skylar."

There is an abrupt click and the line goes dead. I let out a soft growl of frustration.

"That again, huh?" Paige has been leaning against the opposite wall, watching me.

It isn't the first time my dad has brought up how unhappy he is with my mother. The conversations all have the same outcome: I try to convince him to leave her, he resists and tells me that he cannot wait for the day he dies because only then will he finally be free.

"Yeah."

"Any progress?"

"No." I toss the phone down onto the entryway table, mildly grumpy, and make a start towards the kitchen. "Did you get Scott home all right?"

Paige is close behind. "Yep. Mum's there with him now. I called her last night and she took the first train out. She told me to get some rest. You hungry? I thought we could order—" She catches sight of the gravy simmering on the stove, the roast beef resting on the countertop beside the Yorkshire puddings, baked potatoes, and the piping-hot vegetables. "I thought you had a pile of work that rivaled the height of Mount Everest."

"I did." I grab plates and start to set the table.

Paige grabs a spoon and gives the gravy a quick taste. "And you still found time to cook a heavenly roast." She takes the pan off the heat. "You are totally wife material. How do I get a woman like you?"

"You did. Get a woman like me. But last I checked, you thought we were better as friends."

There is a long look from Paige as she strains the gravy into a gravy boat. A musing affectionate smile teases her lips. "*We*, Skylar, we. Last I checked, it was a collective decision in Venice. Remember? Stayed up all night, talked, saw the sunrise, reached a mutual agreement over a most excellent espresso."

I don't argue. Her account is accurate. Venice happened during the summer after graduation. Done with university, away from our friends, a weekend filled with nothing but her, me, and us traipsing along cobbled streets and winding canals, drinking way too much coffee during the day, and exploring and discovering each other in new ways during the night. *We're really good at this, aren't we?* she had said on our last morning there as we pondered the future that lay ahead of us in London. We had been hooking up for months without labeling what we were. *What?* I asked. *Being there for each other,* she said. Paige was fraught with concern at her last-minute decision to forego teaching for a culinary career, and I was quietly panicking inside at the prospect of not having a successful career as a solicitor; making it in London then seemed like a tall order, but knowing we could lean on each other made the seemingly impossible manageable. *Yeah, we are,* I replied. And then she confessed, *I'm terrified of losing that.* And I confessed that I felt the same way. We both understood how much emotional baggage each of us would have brought to a relationship.

Paige selects a bottle of wine from my stash and returns with two glasses.

"How are you?" I ask.

"Wishing I could have a cigarette."

I shoot her a sympathetic look. Paige quit smoking a couple of years after we graduated. "How's Scott?"

"He's better. Still a little hungover. Says you plied him with way too much alcohol."

"There's a lot more to *that* story, I assure you."

Paige smirks. "Yeah, I know." She pours the wine into the glasses and takes a slow sip. I start to ladle food onto her plate. "We talked. It was a good talk, I think. Told him that even though things are changing and life is happening, it doesn't mean I'll stop being there for him. I'm his sister. I'm not going anywhere. He says he understands that. I hope he does." She lets out a deep sigh. "I didn't even know he felt this way. I'm his older sister. He should never have to think or worry that I'd abandon him. He should always know that I'll be there for him, no matter what."

"I know." I reach over and pat her hand. "It happens, though. We're all very busy at the moment. I'm not saying it like it's an excuse, just that it's only natural for some things to slip. I think it's more important to focus on the fact that you showed up. You're here for him."

She looks unconvinced.

"Paige, I said it last night and I'll say it again—don't be too hard on yourself. Scott called. You showed up. Different city, middle of the night, and you still showed up. I don't think a hurricane could have kept you away. That's what matters. You're the sister who will always show up. Even if you forget that, I won't."

Paige cradles the wine glass between her hands. "You know, my mum wanted me in the same town after my dad left us. I lied to her and said I didn't put Bournemouth on my application form because the course wasn't as good as the others I had selected. I did actually, and I had been accepted, but I didn't choose to stay because by then I was tired of being at home. I felt like the parent to both my mum *and* Scott and I wanted a fresh start, some semblance of normality. I tried to tell myself that leaving was good for her. She'll toughen up, learn that she was on her own when it came to Scott, that Scott will be fine… But really, all I was then was selfish."

"But there's nothing to make right here. This is not penance. These aren't your sins to pay for. You know that, right?"

I watch her push the food around on her plate, that familiar wry smile fixed on her face. It is her polite way of disagreeing with me. She can be so stubborn sometimes.

I click my tongue. "Can't talk sense into you."

The smile tilts toward an impish smirk. I feel a surge of affection for her.

"I saw it wasn't the first time he cut himself," she says, serious once more. "I asked if he wanted to see someone about this, but he didn't seem keen, so I didn't push. I didn't want him to feel pressured and clam up." The little crease on her forehead reappears. "Did I do it wrong? Am I supposed to push him to get help?"

I give yet another thought to my past, triggered by last night's encounter with Scott and which has stuck around for the better part of today. Apart from Alex, I didn't want to open up to anyone else. I force myself to ignore the yearning that inexorably trails her memory.

"It might not work to push him when he's not ready. Probably better if he's open to it himself. Some space to breathe might be good for him too, as long as he knows that there are people who care for him and who are here to talk whenever he's ready. We'll keep an eye on him, okay?"

Paige nods slowly.

"For what it's worth, he wanted to call you immediately last night, after it happened, and he was still willing to talk about it today. I think that's a good sign. He's not sweeping it under the rug and saying it's nothing. It's not like he's gone off to sit in the dark, which some people do, for a very long time."

Paige's tired eyes soften further.

"Now eat your dinner before it gets cold. I didn't slave over the stove and my laptop at the same time for nothing."

With a small salute of her fingers, the food starts disappearing off Paige's plate.

"Did you mean it, then? That day, when you came over...and you said you were all right, that everything was fine?"

The question catches me by surprise. Our university days. She means the time I showed up the evening after we got together, post-fight with Jamie, a slew of fresh cuts on my arm. The worry in her eyes I'll never be able to forget. I did everything in my power to assure her that everything was fine.

So I'm not the only one who has had the past on her mind today.

"I always wondered if...if I should have pressed the issue. But you seemed so sure and I...I wasn't sure I would have known what to do, either."

"I meant it. Everything was fine."

That look again. A sea of calm on the outside, her eyes and the smallest hint of a frown on her face telling an entirely different story.

"I promise it was."

Paige taps the stem of her wine glass. "Okay," she finally says. But she doesn't pick up the glass. "I would have, you know, sat in the dark with you." Her voice is quiet. "I don't mind the dark."

I reach out and squeeze her hand. "I know."

CHAPTER 23

The din in the reception area is deafening. Between the multiple conversations that are taking place all at once, the constant clang of cutlery against plates, and the clink of empty glasses being assiduously collected by the servers, I can barely hear myself think. Lexi's team—the Media and Technology practice—is hosting an event tonight, and even though I'm not obliged to attend, Lexi twisted my arm. I begrudgingly accept the fresh glass of champagne she brings over.

"Amazing, isn't this?"

"The champagne is."

"And you thought you wouldn't fit right in." With a delighted smirk, Lexi relieves a passing server of yet another glass of champagne and hands it to me as a backup. "Listen up, I only have a few seconds. I love you for coming, hon, and I know how you *abhor* this shite. But there's this chick behind you—across the room—who's been checking you out for the last ten minutes. I have no idea who she is, but more importantly, she's coming over, so I'm going to make myself scarce. Aren't you ecstatic that you're not on my team so you have less reason to worry about conflicts of interest with a potential client? Good luck!"

Just like that, Lexi is gone, leaving me exposed to whoever is approaching from behind.

"Of all the places I thought we would meet, I confess…this wasn't it."

I freeze. The one voice from Havenford I never got to hear again no matter how hard I willed it, and now, despite the seven billion people which existed in this world, despite the entire ocean which was meant to be between us, *here*, in London, at a work function that I nearly decided not to attend. I turn around slowly.

Dark blue dress, deep brown eyes, hair blown out, skin looking gorgeously sun-kissed.

"Hi, Skye. Kinda feels like serendipity, don't you think?"

Maybe so. But given that she has been on my mind again lately, it feels more like pure fucking irony. Alex smiles and immediately I am transported back to the first time we met, in the gymnasium of Havenford High. Bored out of my skull. Rolling around in my mental cage of despair until she spoke and snapped me out of it. The hustle and bustle around us fades to black and there is only her in this big room full of people, with more than a decade of silence between us, and I am seventeen again.

"Alex..." The love in my heart escapes on the syllables of her name.

There are so many things I want to do. I want to slap myself and prove that it isn't a dream. I want to grip her arm in case she vanishes into thin air. I want to wrap my hand around my heart and stop it from beating so hard and fast. My grip tightens around the stems of the champagne glasses in my hand. I take a breath and smoothly extend one of them to Alex.

"Champagne?"

"Delighted."

Alex brings the glass of bubbly to her lips, its golden hue catching the light as she takes a delicate sip. I can't take my eyes off her. So much of her is familiar. Her eyes, voice, the curve of her lips. So much of her is new. She never used to wear makeup. Also, the perfectly manicured fingernails. The high heels. Jewelry—each piece perfectly curated for her outfit, but making it look like no effort at all. She is the ice queen all grown up, and the strength of her allure—at least to me—does not appear to have faded with time.

What the fuck is she doing in London? "So…what brings you to this event?"

"A colleague with the stomach flu. I'm here for the other one so she doesn't get lonely. Arm candy, I guess."

"You're talking as if you work here. In London." I laugh, but my nerves are slipping past my defenses.

"I do."

I nearly drop my champagne glass. I peer at the name tag she has on and get flustered at how awkward I must look. What is it with name tags and how they are never located anywhere sensible or appropriate? Either on someone's chest, middle of it, near someone's hip, or nowhere at all. There it is. Her name. Her company—*Pulse*. A London publication.

Oh my god. She's here. She's really *here.* "Huh. You're a long way from home."

"Says the person who's been here longer."

Who gives a fuck about how long I've been here? Why are you *here?* "So, what brought you here then?"

"Got bored with Havenford, moved, spent a couple of years in New York before accepting a job."

"Big move."

"Yeah, I really wanted to stretch my legs, see the world. We both know Havenford isn't small, but you're not exactly going to see the world staying there. New York was freeing."

"And London?"

"Exhilarating."

"How long has it been? London."

"Hmm, three, nearly four years, give or take?"

All this time…

"And you?" Alex asks. "I had to hear from the others that you were going to London. You never told me."

"We weren't talking then, Alex," I say, a small smile gracing my lips.

She takes a smooth sip from her glass. "How long have you been here? Twelve years?"

"Give or take."

"So you crossed an ocean and decided you didn't want to come back?"

There was nothing to go back to. "Something like that."

"In it for the long haul?"

"Most likely."

"Everything you wanted?"

"Yes, it has become that, actually." Alex arches an eyebrow. "I came to London to get away. At that time, it was what I needed. A means to an end. But with time, I haven't thought about wanting to be anywhere else."

Alex is about to respond when she's interrupted by a phone ringing. She fishes her phone out of her clutch and glances at the screen. "Sorry, I have to take this." Cradling the phone against her ear, she places her hand over the mouthpiece. "Is there a quiet spot around here?"

I show Alex the way, then am ready to heed my instinct to bolt. She's the one person capable of reducing me to an incoherent mess, so I should excuse myself. But her hand comes to rest on my arm. Her touch burns the way it burned in my dreams, and I forget that I am meant to walk away. Her voice grows tender and caring. "How is she?" she says. "Oh, good. I'm glad to hear she's feeling better. What did the doctor say?" There is a pause. "Poor baby, sounds like all she needs is rest. She must be happy that she's not going to school tomorrow, though." Alex laughs. "Okay, give her kisses for me, will you?" Another short pause. "Love you too."

Lawyers are taught not to jump to conclusions. I race to this one: Alex married an Englishman and they have two kids. I gulp down whatever is left in my glass. I need something stiffer than champagne.

"Sorry about that," Alex says when she hangs up.

"It's cool. You got kids?"

"What?" Alex cocks her head. "As in, you're asking me if I have kids?"

"Erm, yeah? Sounded like you had kids?" I gesture at the phone in her hand as if it would magically speak up and confirm the fact.

Realization dawns on her face. "Oh no, no, no. That was my sister. *She* is married with kids. Kid, actually. We were chatting yesterday and her daughter—my niece—had a really high fever, so they went to see the doctor this morning. Everything's fine now."

The rock under which Alex buried my heart lifts an inch.

"I don't have kids. I'm not married. Heck, I'm not even dating right now."

An imaginary stick props up the rock.

"By circumstance or by choice?"

A split second later, Alex laughs, her entire face lighting up with seemingly genuine joy. Like magic, the heaviness of the past seems to lift and I forget that she was the one who placed the rock on my heart in the first place.

"I like what you did there. The polite way of asking if I'm happily or bitterly single."

I wink, which seems to delight her. She peers past me at the room behind us, the event still in full swing, then at her watch.

"You have to go?" I ask, my heart falling.

"No, but I'm feeling quite done with this shindig."

By that, I assume Alex means that she is done with me too and that assumption stings more than I would care to admit. I'm not ready to be done with her, yet I'm unwilling to suffer another rejection at her hands. I vacillate between letting her go and asking her to stay. If it took me more than ten years to bump into Alex by chance, am I willing to wait ten more to find her again?

"Want to get out of here then?"

Alex bites her lip, eyes flickering between me and the room behind me. I brace myself.

"You sure? Don't you have to stay? It's your firm's event."

"Nope, it's not my team's event. No three-line whip here. Sure you're done with it?"

"Yeah, I'm sure." Alex allows me to relieve her of her champagne glass, our eyes making contact as her fingers lightly graze mine. "I was done with them as soon as I saw you."

With that, it feels like someone grabbed all of the heartstrings I had ever had bound to Alex, bunched them up in their fist, and gave them a good hard yank, causing me to stumble blindly past the hurt she caused and straight into the quicksand of emotions which knows only love for her. It wouldn't be the first time Alex makes me feel like the center of her universe. It wouldn't be the first time she set me up for another trip straight into a black hole, either. In fact, all of this would be perfectly in form for Alex, and the inescapable truth is that it would be perfectly in form for me to want her all the same.

CHAPTER 24

Paige scoops a couple of parboiled brussels sprouts out of the pot and gives them a once-over. It's our regular fortnightly Monday get-together with our friends, and we're alone in Alison's and Rachel's kitchen. Paige is preparing dinner while I busy myself with tracking her movements intently, seconds away from blurting out that I had met Alex no more than just a few days ago. She lifts the pot off the stove and tips the brussels sprouts into the colander. I swallow my words and head to the fridge instead.

Paige's eyes light up when I return with a bowl filled with ice cubes. "Sure I can't convince you to consider a change in your choice of career?"

"It's okay, you're all the chef we need."

Sous-chef to be specific, at Eleven Sticks, a well-established restaurant which serves everyday Chinese cuisine, tastefully elevated without straying too far from its down-to-earth simplicity.

Paige soaks the brussels sprouts in ice water. Alison wanders into the kitchen, presumably to check on our progress. She glances over at Paige's chef's knife roll on the counter. "There is something inherently scary about you carting a set of knives around, even if you are carrying it around in a very lovely looking pouch. It's like my nan offering me a peek in her delicate-looking clutch and me finding pepper spray."

"The psych eval wasn't a prerequisite to our friendship," Paige says.

"Indeed, which now gives me cause for concern."

"I can assure you Paige is of the soundest mind," I say.

"Says the person who *bought* the chef's knife roll for her."

Alison gets laughingly distracted by the rest of our friends, who have followed the smell of food into the kitchen.

"How's Lexi?" Paige asks me.

"Is Lexi that girl you're dating now?" Octavia asks.

"Nope, Lexi's a colleague at work."

"And the other girl? What's her name again? I can't remember."

I don't have the heart to remind Octavia that since I've known her, apart from one anomaly, she's yet to remember the names of any of the women I've dated. I often wonder if it is deliberate, refusing to accept that I am seeing anyone else unless it is her.

"It's okay. I'm no longer seeing her."

"That's fast. Didn't you just get with her earlier this year? What happened? Did you grow tired of her already? Couldn't maintain your interest?" Octavia's tone is friendly, albeit heavily laced with sarcasm. Paige calls it the scorn of Octavia, my price for not wanting her enough to wait for her in university, and when I finally had her after, not wanting her enough to keep her. I catch Paige smirking to herself as she deftly splits the brussels sprouts down the middle with her knife.

"It wasn't like that, O. I just, you know, we just had very little in common. You know what that's like right?"

Octavia makes a softly scornful noise.

"Cut her some slack, O." Cam holds up a piece of chocolate to Paige's mouth, who accepts it. "Skye wasn't dating anyone for what, two years before she got with that woman. It was becoming somewhat of a desert for her, if you know what I mean. So who cares if it was fast? She needed to find her oasis, a warm spot to bury her head at midnight."

I nearly die of embarrassment, while Paige nearly chokes on the chocolate in her mouth from laughing.

"Honestly, guys, isn't it way too early for this? We've not even started on dinner!" Alison chastises.

"Not really," Rachel says. "It's never too early for this, is it?"

"Gasp! Where is my fiancée and what have you done with her?" Alison wraps her arms around Rachel, who plants a loving kiss on Alison's nose.

"Fine, fine," Octavia grumbles in response to Cam's comment. "How's casual dating working out for you, Paige?"

"Oh, you know...casual." Paige shrugs. "I think I've got a more meaningful relationship with my kitchen at Eleven Sticks than with the women I've met."

"I keep telling her that she can do better," Cam says.

"That's easy for you to say. Where on earth am I supposed to find that woman? Randomly pull her off the street?"

"Don't be daft. That makes you look quite mad. Try one of your diners instead."

Paige clicks her tongue. "*Anyway*. Did you girls manage to find your gowns over the weekend?" Her question is directed at Alison and Rachel. They announced their engagement over the summer and are planning to have an early spring wedding next year. I have been bestowed the grand title of being Alison's best woman.

"Yep," Rachel says. "We found several dresses we liked. We'll probably visit another shop before making a decision. Speaking of which, we were hoping to get some opinions on the flowers. Anyone interested?"

Octavia and Cam immediately perk up, titter excitedly about themes, and just like that, they stream out of the kitchen as quickly as they entered, leaving me and Paige on our own.

"Another shop?" Paige asks. "Weren't the three over the weekend enough?"

"You say it, but I'm the one who followed them to these shops. Imagine how I felt getting the text today that they might want to check out a couple more."

"Good prep for your own, I suppose."

I scoff. The thought of having a wedding crosses my mind about as often as me thinking about how I'm going to ring in the New Year—it happens no more than once a year, it's fleeting, filled with a brief dash of hope, expectations and aspirations before the numerous year-end deadlines in my work calendar send me plummeting back to reality.

"What?" Paige tosses a handful of toasted almonds into the pan of brussels sprouts she had been sautéing.

"I'm sorry, but weren't you present for the part of the conversation where Cam told everyone just how sad and alone I am?"

"Please. I repeat what I've been saying the whole time we've known each other. It's not that you're unwanted. It's that you don't seem to want anyone enough."

I roll my eyes, which gets me an almond flung in my direction. "Doesn't matter anyway," I say. "I've never really thought about it—having a wedding. Chinese families have massive ones. Big ballroom. Multiple tables. The entire family tree of distance relatives present. All eyes on you. Celebrating you. I was never going to get that, you know?"

Paige nods. She understands that I have had a strained relationship with my parents since coming out to them and the uneasy status quo I have achieved by permitting them to behave as if they never got told.

"I think you'll love it, though. Clearing in the middle of the woods, fire hearth on the side, benches, maybe some fairy lights, the setting sun with dusk quickly settling around you. Surrounded by friends you now call family."

Paige surprises me with the description. I surprise myself even more at finding her vision agreeable.

"Speaking of weddings, how was the bachelorette party at Eleven Sticks?"

"It was great. The bride-to-be called our menu 'exquisite.'"

"Damn right it is." I am bursting with pride. It wasn't so much Eleven Sticks' menu as it was Paige's. Malcolm—head chef at Eleven Sticks—decided he'd let her take the lead for that event.

"How was work today?" Paige asks.

"Same old, same old. My favorite senior associate was up to her usual shenanigans today. Delegated her way out of a file she hated, tried to muscle her way into my portfolio, all in a hard day's work. Lexi has again offered to dig up dirty little secrets on our 'friend' here and take her out of the running for partnership on the basis that I have no balls to do it myself."

Paige bursts out laughing. "That is *hardly* the reason why."

"Uh-huh. You try telling her that."

Paige looks at me fondly. "How was Lexi's event by the way? The one she dragged you to."

Despite having spent the better part of the evening deliberating how I was going to come through with the big reveal, my mind still goes blank at Paige's question, taken aback by the fact that she had unwittingly placed a loaded question right at my doorstep.

"I, uh..." I cough and clear my throat. "You wouldn't believe who I bumped into." I cough again. "I, uh...bumped into Alex."

The soft hum of the oven fills the kitchen for several long seconds.

"As in *the* Alex?"

"Yeah."

"Okay..." Paige scrutinizes the carrots she had left to one side. "What's she doing in London?"

"Working, apparently. She's been here for quite a few years."

"Okay. So, what happened?"

Paige is now paying the bowl of potatoes an unhealthy amount of attention.

"We went for a drink, that's all."

"How was it?"

Alex and I found ourselves in a nearby speakeasy where we stayed for a few hours catching up. As she ran through the last ten years of her life in broad strokes, I remember feeling desperate to ask her only the questions which still mattered to me after all this time—did you ever love me, and if you did, why did you hurt me? But each time I battled through my revolving slate of feelings—confusion, elation, pain, longing—and thought I found the courage to ask, I would falter. I walked away from Alex that night no more enlightened about her than I was at seventeen. I still can't quite place a finger on the kind of person she is, what she's thinking, how she truly feels about the things that matter, and most frustratingly, how she felt or feels about me. Yet despite all that, despite the fact that the thirty-year-old in me—having already had her heart broken by this woman—should know better now, my skin still sighed and hummed at her touch when she hugged me goodbye.

"Strange. Confusing. I don't know what it means yet. I'm still working it out."

There is a slight nod from Paige. "Did she seem happy to catch up?"

"I think so."

"And were you…happy to see her?" Paige's eyes are trained on me, still gentle, but I feel like they are searching for all the answers I'm not verbalizing.

I can't meet her gaze. I look at a stray toasted almond on the floor instead and think about the way my feelings for Alex selfishly shoved their way to the surface—and everyone else out—when I saw her.

"Yeah…I was."

"When are you seeing her next?"

The answers to Paige's questions don't exist. Not without a Magic 8-Ball.

"I don't know. She didn't say. Maybe never. Wouldn't be the first time." The past cuts into me, reopening old wounds. I shove it back down the hole from which it welled up.

"Hey…" Paige comes close.

"It's okay. I'm fine," I say gruffly. "I just need some time. Whether to figure it out or to get over seeing her again, I don't know."

Paige draws a deep breath and it looks like she wants to say something, but instead, she nods and pulls me close for a quick hug.

"I just need to manage my expectations, you know? It—"

"—helps with managing the disappointments," Paige finishes for me. The small smile on her face is gentle. "I understand." Then she gives me another quick squeeze. "Dinner's ready. Call the hounds, will ya?"

CHAPTER 25

There is a frantic flapping of hands as Scott tries to wave away the tenner I whipped out.

"No, no, shoo! I asked you out, it's my treat."

"Aww come on, Scott, now it'll just look like I'm getting my toy boy to pay. What kind of stingy ass cougar am I then?"

"What?!" Scott gapes at me. I wink at him. He recovers and resumes waving my tenner away with great defiance and a glower.

"Okay, okay." I retract my money.

Scott rushes to pay for our drinks. "You know the cougar comment is not believable for you, right?" he says when we find a free table.

I pretend to look offended. "Didn't think there were standards to fulfill."

Scott rolls his eyes. "No, I meant—have you met you? You with your Asian genes. You could go to class with me and convince everyone that you are *my* age."

"Then go to work and have great difficulty convincing anyone that I am *my* age. A client once asked me, 'How long have you been working here?' I said six, and she went, 'Aww, six months, good for you!' and I had to tell her I meant years. I can't wait to say thirteen, because surely then it'll be obvious that I'm talking about years."

Scott bursts out laughing. "One can hope."

"Indeed. So… How have you been?"

"I, uh…" Scott repeatedly shovels his hand through his hair. "I've been okay. I wanted to say thank you actually. For that night. I never did thank you. I wanted to, quite a few times after, but I didn't want to bother you. I mean, you probably gave me your number because it was the right thing to do. Probably thought, *Uh-oh, what have I done and what am I going to do with him when he calls?*"

I chuckle. "I can assure you I'm not a charity. I gave you my number because I wanted to."

Scott blushes a little, but he also looks relieved. "Okay. Well yes, thank you. For everything that night."

"Well, you're very welcome." I reach for his hand and inspect the scars on his wrists. "They've healed nicely." Scott nods. "And how are you feeling?"

"A little bit more positive? Paige has been over an awful lot, so I'm sure that's helped, but with her work schedule and all, it's obviously taking a toll on her. I told her yesterday she needs to stop. It's not her fault I did this, but she won't listen."

No, she probably wouldn't.

"I haven't been able to stop thinking about it, though." Scott seems embarrassed.

"In what sense?"

"I'm not sure. I—" He ploughs his hand through his hand again, more violently than before. He exhales with force. "I'm not saying I'll do it again, but I can't stop thinking about how oddly comforting it felt, and I've been too scared to say that out loud because I think Paige will lose her marbles if I did."

Quietly. Paige will quietly lose all her fucking marbles.

Scott starts peeling back the edges of his coaster. "It helped. You and Paige showing up, me not being alone after, it helped. And yet having the both of you there, in some strange way, just took that comfort away. I'm not saying I didn't want the two of you there—please don't misunderstand—I'm really glad you came, but all I'm saying is that when it started, it felt so good. Now, I'm not sure what I'm to make of it. I'm rambling. I'm sorry. Am I making sense?"

"Yeah, you are." I smile, making sure he's looking at me. I want to reassure him. "I know it's hard to put in words, but I understand. I think I do, anyway. You found something that brought you comfort, almost instant gratification, but there's a part of you that knows you shouldn't be doing it—it's probably why you called Paige in the first place—so what do you do now? How do you stop something that makes you feel good in the worst of times?"

Scott looks at me expectantly.

I tilt my head. "I feel like you're looking for me to give you the answer."

"Do you have it?" he asks with a boyish grin.

Talking about the one thing that most certainly reminds me of Alex at a time when she's magically reappeared in my life—again, the universe cannot help but remind me of the irony of my situation.

"I don't really have answers, or a one-size-fits-all solution. I can only tell you what it was like for me."

"I'd…like that, if you don't mind. It's nice…talking about it with someone else who might understand."

I take a sip of my drink, mulling on where to start.

"I was in a world of hurt before I started cutting. Between coming out, family reacting badly, being bullied at school, flunking my classes, and loneliness, I remember looking at the blade and thinking—that will hurt more, and if it does, maybe it will dull this constant pain. Instead, I felt relief. Every cut felt like I was punching a release valve into my body, made me feel like I was capable of bleeding the pain out of it, and the next thing I knew, that was the new normal for me. I didn't know how to stop, not even when I grew tired of the recovery process. Those were tough. Trying to both hide and care for the wounds. Avoiding the questions and the creeped-out looks. Worrying if this was the time I had gone too deep and nicked a nerve beyond repair. Frustrated that once the wounds healed, it would be a matter of time before I fell into the cycle again..."

I'm no longer ashamed of my history with cutting, but it is an emotionally heavy, and deeply personal, conversation which I wouldn't have with just anyone. Describing my journey to Scott is strange and affecting. Other than Alex, I've not volunteered this information to any other person. It's also surprising that it's him across the table. If anything, I've figured it would have been Paige. But she's always seemed to understand me perfectly, even without the words said out loud.

I'm taken by a strong urge to break eye contact with Scott, but I push through the discomfort and maintain it. "I felt like I couldn't live with the scars and yet without them, I wasn't living at all. Then this girl showed up in my life and fuck, did I like her. She saw me, she saw these," I throw a quick glance at my scars, "she told me I needed to stop, and I did."

Scott's eyes narrow and I wonder if he thinks that I've just given him the solution—wait for someone to give a damn. Why not? The notion of being saved is a deeply attractive proposition.

"For the longest time, I believed that this girl was why I stopped, that *she* was the solution. I created...such an inextricable bond between her and my strength to resist. Take her out of the picture, what was I? It's easy to feel like you're nothing without someone. But the day I relapsed, a few cuts in, I just didn't want it anymore. I stopped. On my own. No girl in sight. I was beyond done."

Scott's eyes are fixed on me, unblinking.

"The truth is that all the girl did was *ask* me to stop, but the *actual* act of stopping? That was all me. Her faith may have set me down the path, but at the end of the day, the strength to stop came—and still comes—from within. Nobody—not even she—can want for me what I didn't want myself.

"But I won't lie, it wasn't an easy journey. Even after that, I still had to take moments to remind myself that I didn't need her this way. This road to recovery, Scott? I can't promise you that it will be smooth or that it will be straight. But if you want to be on it, then I would say this—in the short term, try your hardest to resist, do whatever you need to do to cope in a healthy manner, lean on friends, call on family, fight the urge, whatever works for you. And in the long run? Work on getting to the heart of the matter, understand what's driving your pain, and when you do, sit in it for as long as you need to, be kind to yourself, and let yourself heal."

He remains silent, his eyes attentive and warm.

I let out a sheepish laugh. "I'm sorry. It was a bit of a prattle, wasn't it? I didn't want to say 'just stop' or 'don't worry, you'll figure it out,' because to be honest, I think that's pretty unhelpful. Apart from dishing out a quote like a walking, talking meme, what fucking value is that going to be?"

"No, no, no," Scott interjects. "Don't apologize. Please don't apologize. I'm glad you told me. To hear about this from someone else…it makes me feel…" He pauses. "It makes me feel a little less fucked up."

"Oh, Scott…" I reach out to hold his hand. "You are *not* fucked up, okay?" Seeing the despondent look on his face, I add, "And if you still feel that way, then hey, here's a little secret, *we*—all of the human race—we are all just that little bit fucked up. Some of us are just better at hiding it than others."

Scott cracks a small smile. He runs his thumb against his pint of beer. "Did you see anyone about this?"

"No. Couldn't talk to my parents. Was in a school which didn't give a shit, and I was too young to know who to turn to." I shrug. "I had to make do."

Scott is quiet. "Paige asked if I wanted to see someone."

"And what do you think of that?"

"I don't know. I fucked up, but I don't want to make a mountain out of a molehill. I also feel like something could be wrong with me, for me to do this to myself."

I cover his hand with mine. "Hey. You didn't fuck up and there is *nothing* wrong with you. We all just get a little bit lost sometimes, okay?" I squeeze his hand. "I know how scary it can get, but there is absolutely no rush or pressure. You can see someone when you're ready, but remember what I said, yeah? If you feel that urge and you want to take your mind off things, you can call me. I'll be here. Well, not literally, physically here in this pub…unless it's happy hour then all bets are off, you know?"

Scott bursts into a soft chuckle.

"And you can definitely always call Paige, urge or not, bored or not, whether in need of entertainment or not, you know, the whole spectrum, especially since she's pretty much behaving as if the entire thing was her fault."

Scott's grin gets sharper and more rakish. What is it with these Thomas siblings? Both of them are blessed with terribly devilish grins and are so easy on the eye.

"Yeah, definitely when I'm in need of entertainment," he says.

"Haha, that's a good lad." I look at Scott. He seems satisfied to leave aside the harder subjects alone for the rest of tonight. "So, tell me, since I'm the cougar in this relationship, how was school today? Do you know how much I miss being twenty, twenty-one? Has Paige even told you what we got up to at Rockton? Oh my goodness, no? Man, do I have some stories for you."

CHAPTER 26

The traffic light turns green. The sound of the black cab's tires, slick against the wet road, lulls me. I close my eyes.

As much as Alex has dominated my every waking thought for nearly a month, I have managed to resist reaching out, a feat, considering my younger days. Still, the relief I felt when I received her text was powerful; it was a proposal to join her at a networking event she couldn't get out of and then grab drinks after.

Showing up, I had wondered if Alex would merely greet me then feed me to the wolves. To my surprise, she didn't, and when she followed that up with introductions and going as far as telling her friends—the girls from work—that our friendship went way back to high school, I was beyond astonished. The Alex I knew kept me a secret, so much so that seeing us speak was equivalent to the sighting of a unicorn, yet there she had been in front of her friends, introducing me like it was the most natural thing in the world. Even so, I couldn't say I enjoyed the friends. Fifteen minutes in, I figured out why. They reminded me of Alex's friends back in high school—cliquish, gossipy, and bitchy.

"Claudia certainly took a shine to you." The observation is put to me, inviting comment as the cab slows to a stop at another traffic light.

"The entire room was shiny to Claudia. She's indiscriminate."

I catch a side glimpse of Alex, seated beside me in a little black dress, her legs accentuated by the heels she is wearing with her hair clasped back loosely. She looks gorgeous. We are on our way to her home. The plans for us to grab drinks have been swiftly abandoned for a night in, because her feet are killing her. I'm not complaining, and I would have been out of my mind to turn her down. In all the time Alex and I have known each other, this is the most personal invitation that she has ever given me.

"Oh, Claudia *definitely* discriminates. At our last event, she started talking about needing to set a 'style slash looks' code to accompany the dress code. Anyway, she doesn't usually spend that much time with one person, especially someone who isn't a client. She must have found you really cute. Even told me to bring you along for future events."

I'm not a betting woman, but if I had to, I am willing to bet that I just heard shades of possessiveness in Alex's voice.

"I'm happy to be brought along, if it means that I get your company for the evening."

I don't check to see how Alex takes my comment, but I feel pretty certain that she may have smiled. It's still in her voice when the cab pulls up to the curb and she says, "Come on, this is me."

/

Alex's apartment is surprisingly eclectic. A fair bit of light wood, white walls, with splashes of color introduced by the photographs, art, and trinkets she has on display. Her black-leather couch sits on a massive sprawling maroon shag rug in the living room with a rack of dresses neatly lined up in a corner. Alex's apartment is open concept, and the living area neatly flows onwards to the dining area, then the kitchen, before ending at a small archway to the side which presumably leads to the bedroom. Her dining table is piled high with magazines and copious papers with her familiar scrawls; the kitchen counters, however, are noticeably empty apart from a long row of tea boxes.

I pick up a novel from the coffee table and flip it over in my hands. "Still into the medical thrillers I see."

"You remembered."

"You're a difficult person to forget." I make eye contact with Alex. She doesn't look away, but retrieves an already open bottle of white wine from her fridge, discharging the charged moment.

"What did you think of the venue tonight?"

"Questionable."

"Urgh, I know right?" Alex hands me a glass of wine and gestures in the direction of the couch. "They were going for upscale and fancy, but I think it just looked gaudy. Reminds me of too many first dates." Alex makes a face.

"That bad, huh?"

"The bars or the dates? Never mind, my answer is the same." Alex sighs. "So few good men left in the world now, and even fewer good women it seems."

I briefly stop in my tracks, then continue on my way to the living room. "Why does it matter to you how many women are left in this world, good or bad?" I ask, sitting down on the couch.

"Why would it not?"

I narrow my eyes at her, confused, but with the slightest tremor of wretched realization at what I have stumbled upon. "Well, it shouldn't matter to a straight woman."

"Correct. But it matters to me."

Words escape me. I smooth down the length of my trousers and perch the wine glass on my knee. Alex makes herself comfortable beside me on the couch and takes another sip of her wine. She behaves as if she hadn't just dropped a massive truth bomb into my lap. I smooth down the length of my trousers again.

"So you're..." There is a monumentally pregnant pause. "Bisexual?"

Alex cocks her head with a glint in her eye. "Come again? I don't think I can hear you."

A flush is flaring upward from my neck.

She laughs. "My, my. Have I just found the chink in your armor? Nothing fazes you, but bisexuality...watch out."

"That's not true. There are other things that faze me."

"No, there aren't. It's one of the things I like about you."

Against my wishes, my heart sets off on another race of its own.

"What's your deal with bisexuals then? Don't like them?" Alex asks.

"I didn't say that. I just, you know, find them challenging."

"Why is that?"

"You just never really know where their hearts, or preferences I suppose, lie."

"With the person they're seeing. Isn't it as simple as that?"

"I suppose." I shrug. "Look, I get that it's not about gender. But it's still a difficult one for me to wrap my head around. If I dated a bisexual woman, I can't help but think: Will she love sleeping with a guy more? Is this for fun? Will she wake up one day and realize that she wants what's conventional? You take all that, plus the fact that bis literally, *mathematically*, have doubled their playing field, I mean, that's a lot to process."

Alex holds my gaze. She releases the clasp holding her hair back and it tumbles onto and past her shoulders. Leaning back against the side of the couch, she crosses her legs, causing the hem of her dress to ride up just a smidgen. Another flush comes on.

"Well, if *I* were dating you, I can assure you I wouldn't be thinking those thoughts."

My heart lurches forward and catapults towards Alex as if she had the gravitational force of the sun. I swallow hard and fight to remain calm and collected, acting as though the implied suggestion barely raises my pulse. It also helps that I find Alex's comment highly worthy of an eye-roll—we could have dated before, but she didn't want it.

"What?" Alex asks.

"Nothing. Just thinking that the last time we talked about this, you were saying you didn't date girls anymore. So, fancy that."

Alex levels a steady gaze on me, from which I can't look away. "Ten years is a long time, Skye. Things change."

"It would seem so," I echo, caving under the sense of missed opportunity.

"Are you seeing anyone?" Alex asks.

"Why? Are you looking to date me this time?"

My heart thunders against my chest. Alex smirks. It is suggestive, sexy. It makes me see her through new eyes. It makes my cardigan feel unbearably warm and stuffy. With our history, it is easy to get caught up in the emotional connection that keeps me tethered to her, forgetting the physicality of it all. Until now. Alex takes another slow sip from her wine glass. I want to kiss her.

I clear my throat and try to ignore that thought. "I'm not seeing anyone."

"Looking?"

"Uh, I don't know if I'm looking. The last few haven't exactly gone well. We date. It's great. Then at some point, they want more, but I don't. An ironclad heart with teeth, as one of my exes kindly summarized what it was like to date me. It is *absolutely* lovely, really."

"I would have never attributed that either to you or your heart."

I smile. Of course Alex wouldn't. I was putty in her hands.

"It's been a long time. Things happen, hearts break, you find your first love, you never find your way back."

Alex falls silent and appears to mull on my choice of words. She loosely places her hand over mine. "Give me a few minutes? I'd really like to take my makeup off before it permanently becomes part of my face."

"It'd be a lovely face," I start to say only to receive a smack on my arm. I flash her an equally playful grin. "But of course, take your time."

I cast another glance around Alex's home, standing to get a closer look at an architect's sketch framed on the wall, accompanied by her dad's signature. A montage of family photographs hanging near it; a well-traveled bunch with a deep love for ski trips. Multiple pairs of shoes—most of them high heels—by her main door. A stash of luxury-brand paper bags, folded up and shoved between the wall and dress rack.

"You're studying my apartment like I'm about to give you a pop quiz." Alex stands in the archway by the kitchen—her skin fresh-looking, soft, natural, disarmingly beautiful—studying me the way I studied her apartment.

"Just trying to figure you out, Alexis."

I surprise even myself with my honesty.

"Oh?"

I give a slight shrug. "You don't give away much. Never have. So forgive me while I try to work this one out."

A smile starts to form on her lips. It makes them look really kissable. "And has my apartment been of assistance?"

"Apart from the fact that you appear to be a little messier than I thought you'd be, I think I might need my money back."

Alex pushes herself off the wall and walks over, smiling. "Fuck you." She grabs the bottle of wine when she passes the kitchen counter.

"Ohh, language. London has changed you, my love."

"It's made me hard."

"So hard."

Chuckling, I point at a photograph on the wall. A familiar face. Her sister's. "Wow. She was just a kid last time I saw her."

"Can you believe how grown up she looks now? *And* she's got a kid. Funny how things work out. Our parents thought she would be the wild one, but she's all settled with a family and I'm behaving like the vagabond who has gone off to see the world and seek out new experiences."

"Havenford, New York, now London. A columnist at an up-and-coming London publication. Seems like seeking out new experiences has suited you fine." I extend the wine glass in my hand when Alex offers up the bottle she's holding.

"Dad's the architect who wanted me to follow in his established and very secure footsteps. I would have been good at it, he still says," she says as she tops me off before setting the bottle down on the dining table behind us.

"Was he disappointed when he finally realized you weren't going to?"

"A little, but he got over it. Father first, businessman second, he says. He didn't agree with my choice, initially. As a father, he felt that I was making things unnecessarily difficult for myself—trying to be a writer in a market already bursting at the seams with them—but he supported it ultimately, well not 'it,' but me. He made moving to New York easier than it should have been. Supported me through the more financially challenging times when I was just starting up. He even started buying all the magazines I wrote for, and when my mom reminded him that I don't get a cut of *those* profits, he confessed that he wasn't doing it for me; he just loved looking at the latest fashion trends." Alex laughs out loud, her joy apparent. "I loved it, though. I loved that he found a way to reconcile his expectations with what I wanted and found a way to see fashion the way he saw what was beautiful in his craft."

I nod at the clothes Alex has on display. "They *are* beautiful. Much like your little black dress, which I love, by the way."

Alex looks pleased. I wonder if it's my validation of her style or just, as always, the attention I pay her. She reaches out and runs her thumb against my cardigan right above the cuff of my sleeve, picking a piece of lint from it as she does so.

"Can I get your opinion? I love what you're wearing. I want to get a cardigan for my dad, for his birthday. His is molting and dying a bad death, I swear." Alex makes a start towards her laptop on the dining table.

I take another sip of wine. "Are you suggesting that I have the style of an old man?"

"God, no." She flips the screen open and pauses to look at me, fingers poised over the keys of the keyboard. "It was a race between your cardigan and loafers tonight—which I loved more and which I'd take off you first."

How suggestive.

"I think I come a little more expensive than that, Alex. At

least offer me a third glass of wine before talking about taking my clothes off."

There it is again—another suggestive smirk. My pulse races. Alex can take my cardigan off right now and have it all for herself. In fact, I would welcome it.

CHAPTER 27

There is a quiet pop and gentle hiss as I push open the entrance door of Eleven Sticks and let myself in. The restaurant has just closed its doors for the night and already the dining area is spick and span with tables set for tomorrow's lunch service, plates and cutlery glistening under the bright-white lights which only come on after the last customer has left. Otherwise, its elegant, black-and-gold color scheme is warmly lit, making it a comfortable but classy venue.

"Hi, Skylar," says a lady in her late sixties, from behind the till. Mrs. Li, matriarch of this establishment, and mother of the head chef and owner, Malcolm.

"Hi, Mrs. Li." I approach the counter. "You well?"

"As long as this restaurant continues to make money, I will be well. Otherwise, oh, I don't know, we might find ourselves out on the streets."

Mrs. Li is joking. Eleven Sticks is doing so well, the Li family has been contemplating opening a second restaurant.

"Sit, sit." She gestures at one of the tables and heads for the kitchen doors. "Have you had your dinner?"

"No—" Mrs. Li is already in the kitchen and the only response I get is the sound of the doors quietly swinging shut. I check my phone; there's a message from my dad hours ago telling me to call him back, but I haven't found the time at work.

She is already back with a plate of food in hand. "Here. Paige assumed you hadn't had dinner so she made you something before the kitchen closed."

She watches me dive in. It's easy to miss having decent Chinese food wherever I am in the world, but Eleven Sticks does a fine job of satiating me, and my pleasure satisfies Mrs. Li. She steps away briefly and returns with a pot of tea and two porcelain teacups.

Lifting the teapot, I carefully pour the piping hot liquid into the teacups. "How was business today, Mrs. Li?"

"Very good. Very brisk. We had high turnover rates for both lunch and dinner. Has been like this for nearly the entire week, so I'm happy. I did have someone come in today, look at the menu, and ask for *Singapore noodles*! Can you believe that?" Mrs. Li looks absolutely aghast. "I told the lovely gentleman that he will have better luck with the Chinese takeaway down the street, but good heavens no, *not* in Eleven Sticks!"

I burst out laughing. I used to think that Singapore noodles actually originated from Singapore until one of my cousins set the record straight. Singapore is a food paradise, and while there may be some dishes which bear *some* vague similarity to Singapore noodles, there is definitely no such thing as Singapore noodles in Singapore.

"How do you like the pork?" Mrs. Li asks with interest. "Paige has been trying out a new recipe. We're thinking of putting it on the menu, and who better to comment on it than a Chinese girl?"

"Mm, I was just thinking I haven't had this before. It's delicious. All that flavor with a hint of chili that's just right. Suits the market too. Wouldn't work if it's too spicy."

Mrs. Li nods, her approval apparent.

"Ma," a male voice calls out from across the restaurant. It's Malcolm. He beams and raises a hand in greeting. I wave back.

"Ah, right. I'm sorry but you'll have to excuse me, dear. One of the girls made a slight mess of closing tonight so we'll need to get that sorted."

"It's okay, Mrs. Li, I can self-entertain, although nothing can quite match the pleasure of your company."

Mrs. Li's laughter fills the air and her eyes twinkle with delight. She gives my arm a gentle slap. "That silver tongue of yours is going to get you into all kinds of trouble with girls one day."

"I'm afraid it already has."

She laughs again, shaking her head. In Mandarin, she mutters something about me being a delightful rascal before leaving me to enjoy Paige's cooking. I finish up dinner, check the time, and figure I can squeeze in a quick call to my dad.

"Hey, Dad."

"Hi, Skylar, just finished work?"

"Yeah."

"You home?"

"No, just waiting for a friend before we head off together."

"A friend from the office?"

"No. University. She finishes late most nights. She's a chef."

He clears his throat. "Your mom and I will be visiting you in England."

The sudden change in topic doesn't surprise me. If it isn't about the safest topic—my job—I am guaranteed a non-response. Whether my dad is terrified to uncover the truths he is keen to forget or has entirely zero interest in my actual life, I have yet to ask, but I suppose the net effect is the same. Until then, my dad continues to excel at his greatest skill—avoidance.

"Is everything okay?"

"Yes, why wouldn't everything be okay?"

"Because I've been here for more than a decade and you've yet to visit once."

"You know your mother doesn't wish to spend that kind of money."

"Sure. I'm cool with that. What's changed?"

"Your brother's going to be in Europe then London that week for work, so he won't be able to return for Chinese New Year. Your mother decided we'll have the reunion dinner and celebrate in London instead."

And there we have it. The reason. *Her* reason for being a mother. The cold war between her and Richard has officially come to a close. I haven't been reason enough for my mother to fly into London, but Richard is different.

"Did you think to ask me if I had booked *my* flights home before deciding on this?"

Without fail, I have returned home for Chinese New Year every year since starting work. I had already booked my flights for the upcoming trip.

"Uh, oh..."

"It's fine." No point shooting the messenger. "Nothing that cannot be fixed. Right, when are you in London?"

My dad lists the dates. "Can you sort out our flights?"

"Can't Richard do that for you? He's flying here too."

"We're not flying together. He's going to Europe first. Anyway, you know what your mom is like. Richard says he's busy and that's that. Also, you're the daughter."

I roll my eyes, hard. That reason gets more inane each time I hear it. I look over at Mrs. Li speaking with Malcolm. Son or daughter, it doesn't matter, Mrs. Li would rag on any of her children who wasn't pulling their weight.

"Dad, you have to stop running around saying that—this whole shit about me doing things because I'm the daughter. It makes you sound sexist."

"N-no, I'm not."

"Uh-huh."

"It's just the way things are! Girls are more filial, caring, and kind—"

"Yeah, I rest my case. You know, you could have just said: 'Skylar, do you think you can help us sort out our flights? I would ask your brother, but as you know, he's not very good at thinking about anyone else but himself and wilts at the mere thought of stress, unlike you, who can multitask and eat stress for breakfast.' Now, how about that instead? Empowerment instead of repression. Nothing about daughters versus sons, man versus woman, just you seeing who's capable enough to get shit done?"

Another bout of silence fills the line. My joking tone aside, he knows what I've said is true, but my dad is not a great forward thinker and would prefer if I stopped opening up difficult conversations.

Paige comes through the kitchen doors, her tired face lighting up when she sees me. My heart warms. It's late, work has been a bitch, and I'm not nearly feeling patient enough to conclude this call on a pleasant note, but seeing her makes me feel charitable.

"What I'm saying is—I'll sort out your flights, Daddy."

"And—"

"And yes, no business class, cheapest economy seats around, even if the flight times are horrendous, so you won't hear Mom griping about the prices all throughout the flight. I've got you. I have to go now, but love you, okay?"

"Love you too."

CHAPTER 28

There is a certain rhythm to my meetups with Alex. When she rears her head, we meet for several consecutive days before she vanishes. Give it a couple of weeks, and we'll do it all over again. It reminds me of how she was with me in high school.

Alex and I are at The Honey Badger tonight. Given how fondly and frequently I speak about it, she has been keen to see this seemingly iconic pub. I was happy to oblige, as ever, until my friends decided that a quick drink at The Honey Badger was exactly what everyone needed on a cold, dreary Sunday evening. I had thought that they would have the decency to stay away when I revealed that I was already there, *and* that I wasn't alone, but the suggestion that I was with someone worth hiding away was what singlehandedly propelled all of them out of their homes.

Alex finally stops ignoring how I drum my fingers against the table.

"You're jittery. Do your friends bite or something?"

"What? No." It doesn't matter; even if I had said yes, Alex would probably just bite back. "Gotten up to anything exciting since I last saw you?"

"Does a blind date count as exciting? One of my friends set me up with some banker dude last weekend."

That is the fifth guy Alex has mentioned in the last few months. Running through men—and only men—the way she runs through the latest fashion trends, I've been having doubts as to whether Alex is really bisexual.

"So how was it?"

"Kept wanting to talk about the stock market, but it's not like I write for the financial column. Shame, though. He wasn't bad-looking. Decent fashion sense, expensive suit—probably Italian—good taste in accessories. Gorgeous watch."

"Sounds like he ought to be in somebody's column."

"He was trying way too hard. A lot of words, a lot of pomp. When it wasn't about the stock market and how he was making a killing on all his investments, it was about his perfect suburban upbringing."

"He must have felt desperate. You can be a very difficult girl to impress."

Alex frowns. "Am not. Well, it didn't work. Consider me very unimpressed."

"Skye!"

Like mini-tornadoes, my friends tumble into the seats around us, smiles all around as they greet Alex. A hand rests briefly on the edge of my shoulder in greeting. I lean back slightly, knowing exactly who it is. "Did lunch go all right?"

"Yeah, it did," Paige murmurs, as she shoots a glance at Alex.

There are quick introductions and an even quicker exchange about what everyone wants to drink before Paige and Rachel head to the bar.

"So you guys know each other from college?" Alex asks.

Alison, Cam, and Octavia all look confused.

"University. She means university. They call it college in the States."

"Oh…kind of, I suppose," Alison says. "Apart from me and Skye—we were flatmates in our first year—we met each other in this gay club near our campus. I suppose we kind of bumped into each other and never quite separated."

Cam lets out a short laugh. "That's one way of looking at it. It's probably more accurate to say that Skye and Alison just kept turning up because Skye *really* wanted to date Octavia."

"You never told me that," Octavia says to Cam. She turns to me. "Maybe we should have conserved some of that persistence for the latter part of that summer, eh?"

"Aww come on, O, I got there eventually, didn't I?"

"Yeah in our mid-twenties when both our jobs were eating us alive. What is it that you lawyers say? Oh, right, I plead momentary insanity."

I let out a short laugh and roll my eyes at the jab.

Alex sits up straight. "Wait. The two of you dated?"

"Yep. Skye also dated her and her." Cam points at Alison, then at Paige, who is just returning from the bar. "Well, not sure if the two of them consider it dating. Do you actually?" Cam is looking at Paige, who for one split second appears uncomfortable with the question, but then smoothly shrugs it off with one of her rakish smiles.

"Don't get me wrong, we are *all* very civil about this," Cam says breezily.

It doesn't sound like it, but I'm unable to object right now, being in the hot seat.

"I'd say," Alex purrs. She seems fascinated by the information she has stumbled upon, one edge of her lip curled into a smile. She gives me a chastising look for my having left out what she considers to be really important information. I shrug. Out of the corner of my eye, I catch Cam accepting her drink from Paige with a discreet caress of her hand.

"So, Alex. What brings you to London?" Cam asks, arm now slung across the back of Paige's chair.

"Work. I write for *Pulse*, their fashion and lifestyle columns.

Been in New York a while, so thought I'd trade that in for London."

"How long have you been here?" Rachel asks.

"Several years."

"Cool. And you and Skye know each other from…?"

"School. Before college. But we lost contact when Skye came here, so it's been good to reconnect."

"Oh, I bet it was," Paige pipes in.

I shoot Paige a stare. She sounds genuine enough, but I am certain I caught a snarky undertone. The moment is already passed, as another conversation fills the void.

"All good?" I ask Alex.

"Yup." She takes a slow sip of her wine. "So did you or did you not date Paige?" Alex lowers her voice so nobody can overhear.

I flash her a wry smile. "It was…complicated."

"How so?"

"We hooked up. It went on for a bit but we ultimately decided we were better as friends."

"Because?"

I glance at Paige and back at Alex. "We just are?" Alex shoots me a long look. "Paige and I were friends first and we were very close. Getting together…well, it was probably just going to fuck everything up, so we didn't."

"How can you know that being together doesn't work?"

I shrug. "We were really young? Still in college and all. I…I don't think we wanted to take that risk. Trading a certainty for a possibility. It—" I find myself looking at Paige. She's laughing at something Rachel is saying and Cam is leaning against her. "It wasn't something we were prepared to lose."

"Hmm, okay." Alex seems thoughtful.

"What?"

"I'm surprised, that's all. You were always the brave one." Alex's line of sight travels between Paige, Alison, and Octavia. "Anyway, I'm surprised. If you asked me to guess who you dated here, I think I'd only have guessed Octavia. She definitely looks like your type. Doesn't she remind you of Hannah? Blonde, tall, pretty eyes?"

"If I didn't know better, I'd say you're suggesting that I was totally into Hannah in high school but we both know that's not true. *Anyway*, how would you know what my type is anyway?"

"Wild guess."

"And what's yours?"

Alex angles her body towards me. With one arm on the back of her chair, her body is very close to mine. Her loose-fitting t-shirt dips low. I avert my eyes from the soft swell of her chest.

"Cute. My type is really cute."

"Cute?"

"Yes."

"That tells me absolutely nothing. I mean, how does one even describe cute without immediately thinking about puppies?"

"Oh, those are *adorable*."

"Right okay, not cute then."

"Cute is like…you know, someone who is good looking, and when they smile, probably with a dimple or two, like yours—" Alex reaches out and startles me by lightly touching my jaw. "That smile completes the entire look. And personality, can't forget that. You just know that when they speak, it's going to all click together because they'll say something really funny, like witty-funny, which is totally part of the 'cute' package."

"Like that redhead at the bar." Octavia gestures at a woman waiting for drinks. "Sorry, couldn't help but overhear."

Alex looks over at the bar. "Oh yeah, definitely."

"Are you guys creeping or something? You're all staring at that woman at the bar," Cam asks across the table.

"Trust you to think we're creeping. We're not. Just us agreeing on what a 'cute' person looks like," Octavia says.

"Oh, that. Ugly but adorable. Cute is totally ugly but adorable."

"So…all those times you called me cute, you really meant that I was ugly but adorable?" Paige asks, inviting laughter from the group. Cam ruffles Paige's hair. I can feel my forehead furrow at Cam's display of affection. It is closely accompanied by an unexplainable surge of jealousy.

"Paige, honey, I think it's safe to say that you don't qualify for Cam's version of 'cute.' You're closer to Alex's version of cute than you ever will be to Cam's."

"You're being far too kind, Octavia," Paige says.

"Why, I think Octavia's just paying compliments where compliments are due, wouldn't you agree, Skye?" Alex covers my hand with hers. That touch, with one swift yank, instantly grounds me and commands my attention.

"I, uh…" Everyone is looking at me, probably expecting a sarcastic quip or two, but with the heat coming off Alex's palm and me still trying to process an emotion I have not felt in quite some time when it comes to Paige, all I can manage is a cough and an awkward shift in my seat. It causes Alex to cock her head in curiosity and Paige to turn her attention from Cam to me, her eyes seeming to dissect and categorize everything from Alex's hand on mine to how flustered I must appear to be.

"Yeah," I finally manage to say a little hoarsely. "Yeah, exactly that."

/

It's not a late night at The Honey Badger. With Alex swiftly in a cab, Paige and I make our way back together. Exiting the tube station near our apartments, it is a short walk home for us, first stop hers, then mine. We have done this walk more times than we can count.

"So that's the infamous Alex, huh?" Paige zips up her jacket, hands jammed in her pockets, her hair looking a little windswept.

"Hmm, yeah."

"She's smaller than I imagined her to be."

"What is *that* supposed to mean?"

"You have a thing for girls taller than you, but I guess she's taller than you in heels. Just about, anyway."

I chuckle. "I don't have a thing for taller girls."

Paige merely smiles in response. She knows I know that she is right. We fall into a comfortable silence as the brisk night air hits our cheeks.

"How are things going with her? Cleared the air yet? She certainly seemed quite cozy with you."

Paige and I don't discuss Alex much. In the past, it was because I could hardly bring myself to say her name on most days, for that act alone would invoke a multitude of raw feelings and tears. These days, I'm too busy building a wall around those old memories because the constant uncertainty I feel around Alex can hardly withstand my own scrutiny, much less that of an outsider. Paige, while understanding, sees Alex only as someone who didn't treat me well, and she leans hard into her tendency to judge her for it.

"It's surprisingly hard to find a moment to dredge up old shit like, *Did you love me? Did you play me? How did it feel, fucking me over?* Anyway, I don't think her affection means anything. It's just Alex being Alex."

"Like it means nothing that she's now bi?"

I may have aired my skepticism about Alex's bisexuality rather strongly in the few conversations we've had about her. Unlike me, Paige has been surprisingly generous towards Alex on the matter of her sexuality.

"Honestly, I don't think she's bi. She probably *thinks* she's bi, but all I hear are the copious number of men she's been on dates with."

"Are you choosing to see what you want to see? Convince yourself that she's not bi so you can stave off that feeling of hope? Manage the disappointment?"

"That's bollocks."

"Is it?" We slow as we reach the entrance of Paige's building complex.

"What's up with you and Cam?"

Paige runs her fingers through her hair and smooths it down. "What about me and Cam?"

"I think it's fairer to say that the two of you were the ones getting cozy. I didn't realize the two of you are getting back together."

"Who said we are?"

"I know the signs."

Paige smirks. "Why? Jealous?"

"Please." I roll my eyes. "You're welcome to date whoever you want." I applaud myself for sounding like I don't care.

A deeper smile plays at the edge of Paige's lips. She toys with the keys in her pocket and regards me, unflinching. "This casual dating thing…it gets old, Skye. It may have been fine at the start, what with my hideous schedule, but when I have a more meaningful and fulfilling relationship with my kitchen, then something's obviously not working. Between the growing responsibilities at Eleven Sticks and the still disgustingly late nights…if I'm going to give my time away on the one day and evening I have to myself, surely I ought to give it away to something, *someone*, worthwhile."

"And how does Cam fit in this?"

"Well, we still get along. And she's been reminiscing, admitting that she might have been hasty in breaking up…talking about giving us another go. She thinks we can work, long-term."

I see where Paige is headed and feel a twinge of envy. But why shouldn't it be Cam? Vivacious, nice, emotionally available Cam who will treat Paige right. It *should* be Cam.

"Are you? Give this a go with her, I mean?"

"I don't know. Cam, she—" Paige shakes her head. "I don't know. Maybe."

"Hmm." I stare at Paige's neatly crossed feet as she stands leaning against the main door. There it is again, another surge of jealousy. It doesn't make sense. When Paige first ventured back into the dating pool after Venice, I felt the odd surge of jealousy, but those spikes of emotions ultimately flattened out with time. So why have they returned with the reintroduction of Cam as Paige's girlfriend? It is human nature to want what others have. Paige and Cam have been friends as long as Paige and I have, and with their shared history, I wonder if the prospect of Paige and Cam having a serious future together is what triggers me.

"Are you going to try? With Alex?" The question makes me look up. "The way you looked at her tonight…every time she spoke…"

"Why? Jealous?"

Paige chuckles, her head dipping slightly in a way that makes her long dark lashes stand out. "Oh, you're welcome to date whoever *you* want, Skye."

The cheeky use of my own words against me evokes a deep fondness.

"You know, I always knew Alex was special, but seeing the two of you tonight… There's a way about you around her, almost as if you would cast everything aside for her, no matter the time that's passed and in spite of what she's done. It's still a little hard to comprehend. I've seen you in and out of relationships, and you *have* walked away from others for less."

I don't rush to respond. It's not easy, stringing together an explanation of why I feel so deeply bound to Alex.

"I don't think that I'm an easy person to love. With everything that has happened, I can't help but feel some days that I'm just damaged goods. And the places my head goes, they can get so dark, that I don't think anyone can ever bear to see them. Heck, Octavia caught a glimpse and she went running for the hills. 'Too difficult to love, even harder to keep,' she said." I shake my head. "But Alex…she saw me at my worst, Paige. She was the first to see *me*—scars and darkness and all—and she didn't flinch. She made me feel like she liked me, loved me even, and I was lost to her right from the start. I see her now…and it still feels like I am."

My heart is split into two, feeling both heavy and light at the same time.

Resting her head against the glass, Paige holds my gaze. "I don't know if you remember this, but there was that time when we went out for drinks after you and Octavia broke up. Halfway through the night, you wondered if there was a miracle cream that could remove all the scars on your arms. Because they were nothing but ugly reminders of how imperfect and broken you are."

"I remember." How could I not? Paige had told me that night that there was nothing broken about me because when scars and lesions heal, in their place grows a stronger body, a stronger heart, and that she'd sooner have me as-is than what I was before—pristine and allegedly whole. The way she saw my scars was beautiful.

"It was the most you had ever said about them—your scars," she continues. "You didn't dwell on it too much, and I didn't want to force the conversation, but it made me realize that you've only ever seen so much of your own darkness that I don't think you understand how much light you radiate. But it's there. In the way that you hold space for others. In the way that you've held space for Scott. And it's that very darkness that you think makes you imperfect, and broken, that makes your light even more special, Skye. They are an indivisible whole and if you think for a single second that you—scars, darkness, and all—are difficult to love, then you would be quite wrong."

I look away, my heart feeling impossibly vulnerable. "You don't know that..."

"I do." And after a pause, "Alex won't be the only one who sees you and loves you for who you are... I don't want to see you hurt again."

Paige's voice is so tender it hurts. Without thinking, I reach out and grip the tip of her fingers. I give them a gentle squeeze. I mean to pull away, yet somehow—I don't know if it is Paige's doing or mine or both of us combined—our fingers become intertwined. They fit like they did the first time she held my hand, as they did years after when we fell into bed again with each other, even though neither of us had displayed any indications of wanting to rekindle Venice.

"Paige…"

I hear the way I say her name. It sounds like a soft plea for restraint, laced with a hint of desire. I take a breath. I release it. The gentlest of kisses falls on my lips, and with that, Paige seizes control of all the breath in my lungs, and the moment she breaks away, I want her lips back on mine. Her breathing has grown long and deep, her eyes intensely focused on mine as her hold on my hand tightens. I can see the slight creases at the side of her eyes and I know she's not a fan of them—too much of a reminder that she's growing old—but I've always thought that they just made her even more alluring. Slowly, Paige leans in but bit by bit I see the doubt creeping in as her mask slips. Whether she is starting to reconsider the kiss or the possibility of my rejecting her, I don't wait around to find out; I clear the distance and meet her halfway. We kiss like our first time. A touch of hesitation, chased by a sense of abandon, and finally stripped of all sense of reason.

As we kiss, I hear the buzz of the main door opening, the erratic jangle of her keys unlocking her front door. I kick it shut and we stumble into her apartment. She already has her hands under my shirt, raking her fingernails across my skin as I have her pressed up against the wall. I grip her jacket and push it off her shoulders, with a moment of hilarity as its arms get tangled up with her clothing and we struggle to get it off her.

"I think your jacket has a mind of its own…"

Paige laughs softly, breaks the kiss for a moment, and makes short work of her jacket. She pushes off the wall, and in an instant, it's now me pressed up against it, with both my hands pinned above my head.

"Now, where were we?" she murmurs as she dips her head and begins to run kisses along my neck, exploring my skin with her tongue whenever she feels my legs giving away.

Only minutes pass, but each feels like blinding torture with the way I want her. Finally, Paige releases my hands and I thread my fingers through her hair and bring her lips back to mine. I kiss her, tenderly to start with, then each passing second more deeply and raw than the last as we make our way over to her bedroom, leaving a trail of clothes in our wake.

The back of Paige's legs hit the edge of her bed, and I wrap my arms protectively around her waist. The bed shifts as she lies down on it, pulling me on top of her. She sighs in contentment as my body sinks into hers. There is not a breadth of space between us. My hands are on her breasts, her hips, her thighs, each touch growing increasingly urgent. I slip my fingers downward between Paige's legs and she thrusts her hips forward, eyes fluttering shut, a soft moan escaping her when they enter her. She drops her hips, momentarily exposing my slick fingers to the cool atmosphere before enveloping them again with another thrust, this time accompanied by her own fingers finding their way inside me. The ease at which Paige and I find our rhythm, bodies tangled up in each other as I press into her and she arches against my touch, it is as if we have never been apart at all.

I close my eyes, biting on my lip, my body awash with the pleasure she brings me. I want to be in this moment, with her, for as long as I can. I can feel Paige getting close, and when she starts to tense up, the familiar hitch in her breath before she comes apart, I let myself go too.

CHAPTER 29

Those fortnightly Monday dinners were a routine Paige, Alison, Rachel, Octavia, Cam, and I developed to ensure that our friendship didn't suffer from the demands of work and life. We catch up, have a laugh, and have fun. All the usual suspects around me tonight. I also have Paige, ignoring me and fawning over Cam like her life depended on it. I had to find out from Alison a few days ago that Paige and Cam have gotten back together.

It's been nearly a week since Paige and I slept together. We've not seen or spoken since, but given our slip-up, the lack of contact wasn't necessarily a cause for concern. I had been prepared for things to be a little awkward, but I also expected that, like the last time, we would get past it. Although we were awkward for a short while then, behaved as if each touch would ignite into full-blown sex, we were eventually good again. No fuss, no muss. A healthy physical distance between me and Paige, even the radio silence the past week, would therefore have been perfectly understandable, but her behaving as if I'm not present at all is not.

I'm mostly annoyed, because last I checked, we were both consenting adults who slept with each other. A smidgen of guilt, however, reminds me that I'm not in a position to cling too tightly to my moral high ground—I was the one who left Paige's apartment without telling her. I texted her as soon as I was home, but admittedly, skulking out in the middle of the night was not my finest move, even if it did seem far less complicated than us talking about our slip up; it's not like we weren't already familiar with the path of resolution.

Paige excuses herself to take a call. I give it a few minutes before following her out. She is pacing the sidewalk, engrossed in her conversation until she looks up and sees me standing there, waiting for her.

"I'm going to have to call you back," she says before hanging up.

"I could have waited."

"It's fine." Paige fiddles with her phone, waking the screen and sleeping it again.

"I'm sorry," I say after it became clear that a two-worded response was all I was going to get.

"For?"

"Last week. Leaving without saying goodbye. I had an early start, you were sleeping, and I didn't want to disturb you, so I thought I'd text you instead."

"Oh, right. That. Yeah, no big deal." Paige shoves her phone into her back pocket and jams her hands into the side ones.

"I wanted to text you this week, but uh, work got away from me."

That isn't entirely true. I had time to text—and I wanted to—but maybe the complete lack of contact from Paige bothered me more than I realized.

"It's fine. I was busy anyway."

Paige's gaze flickers between me and the restaurant door. I get the sense that she is ready to head back inside, but her short responses unsettle me and I want to make things right.

"Did you…I don't know, want to grab dinner or something next week?"

Paige's lips are pursed. "Probably not. There's Cam, and it's a busy period for the restaurant. Not sure when I'll have the time."

She has never had issues juggling time between the restaurant, dating, and me. I don't see how Cam changes the situation.

"Okay...how about the week after?"

"We'll see. I don't know. That's a lot of stuff that Cam and I want to do together."

I feel my chest grow tight. I lean against the wall, my hands tucked behind my back. "Paige, if you don't want to grab dinner, just say it. You know how I hate shit like this, when people don't say what they want or don't want."

"Okay, fine." Paige crosses her arms, her jaw squared. "You know I don't have a lot of free time outside of the restaurant, I've already told you that. So bottom line is—I'd rather spend it with Cam."

Paige's answer hurts in the way I expect a knife to hurt when it's rammed into my chest. I wait to see if further explanation is forthcoming. There isn't any.

"That's it, huh? So is that also your grand fucking explanation for your behavior tonight, then? Treating me like you don't fucking know me because you're too busy spending all your free time with your girlfriend?" I forcefully inject a sense of irritation into my delivery, not wanting the hurt I feel inside to bleed into my words.

"Yes, that is my *grand fucking explanation*." There is a flash of anger in Paige's eyes. "News flash, Skye. I like my girlfriend, she makes me happy and I'd really like to make it work with her this time. So I'm sorry if it means that I'm only looking at her during dinner."

I step away from the wall and straighten my back.

"Stare at Cam all you want. That's not what I'm pissed off

about, and you know it. You are my best friend. We were this before we were ever anything else and we have broken and healed ourselves repeatedly to protect that, no matter the cost, but what you're doing here..." There is an imperceptible shake of my head, I steel myself and fight back the tears. "This isn't about Cam. This is about your decision to arbitrarily up and leave as if our friendship means nothing to you."

"No more arbitrary than your decision to up and leave in the middle of the night."

"How is that the same?"

"How is it not?"

"We both knew what we were doing and what the deal was! There was *nothing* arbitrary about me leaving."

Jaw clenched, Paige remains quiet. Stubbornly so. It is beyond infuriating.

"Fine, be like that then." Hand on door, I push it open and leave Paige outside. I pay her no mind when she returns. Instead, it is Cam who glances up, alternating gazes between me and her other half seated beside her, before she finally looks away.

/

Scott inhales his fries at a speed so unnatural I can't help but watch in fascination. I told him we were having dinner, but I'm starting to think he heard me say we're having breakfast, lunch, and dinner.

"The fries aren't going to up and run away. Don't choke."

"These are amazing." Scott unabashedly eyes my portion.

I signal the waiter for another batch. "I think you're just hungry."

Scott pulls a long face. "The trials and tribulations of being a student in London. I'm sure you don't remember it, but it's a hard life." He takes a massive bite of his burger. As he chews, he reminds me of a blissed-out hamster which found a quiet corner to work its way through its stash of nuts. He looks obscenely pleased with himself.

"Have you kissed and made up with Paige?" he asks.

I groan inwardly at his choice of words. Kissing was what got us here in the first place.

"Nope." I pick at my fries. "How do you know about it, anyway?"

"I'm her favorite brotherly confidant."

"It's not hard when you're her only brother."

Scott takes another massive bite of his burger. "I asked her if she wanted to come for dinner tonight, seeing it's a Sunday and all. She said you two aren't talking right now, then got stupidly cross with me when I asked why. What did the two of you fight about?"

I take an exceptionally long time to carve a slice of my steak and chew it.

"Right, I take it that *you* don't want to talk about it either." He chuckles. "It's all good, but sort it out and kiss and make up, okay? You're pretty much the only person she's mentioned before I came to London and she sent you out on the 'Scott search party,' so I'm thinking you're pretty important to her."

The food feels bland in my mouth now. Despite everything Paige and I have been through, I worry that we will not survive this. Sure, we've had our fair share of fights over the years. But the ferocity behind her words that night, the way she had already seemingly withdrawn and checked out of our friendship, it felt like we were breaking up somehow, which is a ridiculous notion. We have to be together in the first place, but then again, nobody ever said breakups are exclusive to couples.

"How is she?"

"She seems okay. Busy as usual. A little more stoic than usual, but that's not unusual at all. It's her default mood. She and Cam are back together, did you know?"

I give a stiff nod. "How are things with you?"

"We managed to convince Mum that she shouldn't move to London! She was here last weekend and you should have seen Paige's face. Completely drained of *all* color." Scott chortles. "But I'm good, I'm better. It's getting better. Mum and Paige are still all like: *What do you need? What can we do? Scott Thomas, do I have to physically move to London to clean your room?!* I feel like one lucky sod to have them in my life. Especially Paige. She's always taken such good care of me, even after she left for London. She may not think so, but I do."

It is clear that the Thomas siblings are fond of each other. How nice it must feel, I think, to have family who would always be in your corner.

Scott mushes his fry into the ketchup. "There's a student counseling service on campus. I'm thinking of making an appointment."

"Yeah?" I say, pleasantly surprised at Scott's willingness to see someone so soon.

He nods. "I still get…anxious—when I'm on my own. But I don't want to freak out each time Mum and Paige get busy and stop texting. I've also got all these thoughts, these feelings, which Paige can *never* know about." He halts. "Wait, you can't tell her about this either, okay?"

"I know. Let's not give your sister another reason to tear herself apart."

"Exactly. So yeah, thought I'd talk to someone about it. Thought I'd start with the counselor."

"It sounds like a good place to start. I'm super-proud of you, Scott. Whatever you're doing, it's very brave."

He turns properly bashful. "Bugger. Don't you go getting all soft on me, now." He stuffs a couple more fries into his mouth, but I catch the smile on his face. It's heartening. "Can I ask you something?"

"Anything."

He nods at the marks on my arms. "Does anyone ask about those?"

"Not really. You'd be amazed how easily others overlook these things or how quickly they assume it's either my cat or dog, but they don't ask if I have a pet, but it's fine. It's not their cross to bear."

"I feel rubbish looking at mine sometimes."

"Because it reminds you of what happened?"

"Yeah. Makes me wish that these scars would just vanish."

"I know the feeling. I get those thoughts too. Usually comes on the days when I'm feeling shitty about myself. But I'll say to you what Paige once said to me—those scars don't say anything about you. There's nothing wrong with you. When scars heal, all that remains is a stronger body, a stronger heart." My heart grows soft at the thought of Paige. "She'd say the same to you. About you."

"With a lot more scolding or nagging, I'm sure." Scott laughs, which only makes me laugh. "Can I ask you something else?"

"Of course."

Scott shoots me the cheekiest grin. "Can we get the bread and butter pudding before we go?"

I burst out laughing. "Good grief, I'm going to go broke feeding you. Remind me to tell Paige to do better in the 'feeding you' department, please. But yes of course you can have that. You can have as much as you want."

CHAPTER 30

The drive from London Heathrow into Central London isn't the longest or worst drive I've endured. Not up until my parents' arrival in London. The first five minutes were decent enough. It was the amount of time required to wave to my parents, say hi, offer to take their luggage, and ascertain that they were alive and well from the flight. It has been a swift decline since.

The glorious thing about being in London is that it has done wonders for counteracting my mother-related stress. Distance has not made my heart grow fonder of her, but it has made coexistence on the same planet bearable. It also grants me unbelievable patience and fortitude for the times I visit her at home—charge up, conserve, spend it all in one visit, repeat. London is my sanctuary, though, and having her tread on it feels like an invasion. As my parents got into my car, I secretly hoped the reserve I have built up since I last saw them would be sufficient for a weeklong visit.

Interestingly, conversations in the company of both my parents have, over time, taken on a fairly standard format, but I guess it's no surprise. My mother never stops enjoying being the center of the universe while making Richard the center of *her* universe, and my dad continually wishes he doesn't exist in the same solar system as my mother, so like a mental checklist, I can always count on them to tick it off in the following order:

Time Spent	Topics covered
Negligible	Polite inquiry about my job
5%	Direct line of questioning about my salary (which, much to the chagrin of my mother, I always respectfully decline to answer because it's crass)
5%	Indirect, but not so subtle, hints at the gifts and holidays I could fund for them because they're too cheap to do it themselves
40%	In-your-face moaning about: • Not having enough money (my parents live a *very* comfortable life) • Relatives being calculating about money • Children not giving them money • Wanting more money
40%	Richard (largely my mother's segment and time to shine): • Richard doing great and grand things (it is a low bar; Richard not quitting his job, again, counts) • Richard not paying them enough time and attention (but forgiven because he is busy doing great and grand things) • Richard's wife being the devil that stops him from visiting (very untrue, I've met his wife, she's lovely, wonder why she married him)
5%	Mother getting Hulk-level angry when I politely remind her that Richard is just a self-centered brat who has no time for anyone but himself
5%	Grumpy childish silence

In clockwork fashion, we have gone through *all* of our favorite topics during the car ride into Central London and I am currently met with my mother's grumpy childish silence. I sigh internally and wonder if it is considered abuse to dump your physically able, financially independent parents by the roadside.

"How much further is it to your place?" my dad asks.

"My place?"

"Yes, aren't we going there?"

Oh. Fuck. "No…we're not."

"What do you mean we're not staying at yours?" my mother asks, agitation and accusation sharpening her tone. As usual, she goes from zero to really pissed off in a nanosecond.

"Erm, I booked a room for you at a hotel. It's in a great spot, right in the middle of London, and not stupidly priced."

"But *why* aren't we staying at your place?"

I would have asked the question another way—what have you done for me to deserve an invitation into a home I have made my own?

"Because the hotel is more convenient. It's nice too."

"How can it be nice when it costs money?"

"It can easily be both. They are not mutually exclusive."

"Don't be smart with me, Skylar. I didn't put you through law school to argue with me. Hotels are expensive."

"This one is not *that* expensive."

"It still costs money."

"You don't have to spend a single cent. It's all paid up."

"That's still money. If you have money to spend on a hotel, why can't you give that money to me?"

"Mother…if it's money *worth* spending, then it's money well spent. You're in a very nice hotel, right in the middle of London with the tube station just a two-minute walk away."

"We won't take the tube. It costs money. We'll just walk."

"*Everywhere?*"

"We have time."

I sigh again. "Time is money" is a concept my mother is incapable of grasping.

"Then at least the hotel is central. You won't be going anywhere without getting on a tube if we were at mine." *Not that you will ever be allowed in my home.*

"Can you cancel the hotel reservation?"

Probably. "No."

I hear a grunt of disapproval, followed by silence. I check the rearview mirror. My mother is looking downwards.

"What's the name of the hotel again?" she asks without looking up.

I say the name and spell it out for her.

"Richard says it's a very nice hotel," she says, "nicer than his. I sent him the hotel name so he knows where to find us."

Of course it's nice. I wasn't going to put my parents up at a cheap, second-rate hostel. If she keeps up this behavior, however, there is a first time for everything. I make another passing glance at the rearview mirror. The woman in the backseat glances down at the message on her phone, purses her lips briefly, and then a smile graces her lips, transforming her entire face. My dad used to tell me that my mother was beautiful when she was young, that he was one of many suitors who tried for her hand. It was the most joyous moment when she chose him. I can see how it might be possible.

"Skylar." Her voice, however, is like a scalpel.

"Yes?"

"Book another room for your brother when we get to the hotel. His hotel is so far away. Better that he stays with us. He says he can cancel his hotel without additional charges. Use my card later for his room. See whether you can arrange an adjoining room."

I sigh quietly under my breath. This is going to be a very, very long week.

CHAPTER 31

It is day three of having my parents in London, and the way I have shown them the city so far reminds me of the way I used to spend my free days with Jamie back in university; the cheaper the activity, the better the experience. Richard, the prodigal son, has just arrived at the hotel, and the delight on my mother's face was indescribable, a stinging reminder that it is only his company she longs for. Before his arrival, any spare time outside of work that wasn't spent on them was scorned as filial impiety, but now, my existence cannot be further from her mind. My dad and I make a break for the café in the hotel lobby, where the atmosphere is far less stifling.

"Why don't you have a look at the menu and see if there's anything you'll like?"

I nudge the menu towards him. It is second nature for my dad to leave the ordering to my mother. He isn't without preferences, but with her constant criticism of his decisions, over time, he has stopped picking up the menu entirely.

He pushes the menu away. "It's okay."

"You should." I edge the menu back towards my dad. "She's not here and I'm no tattletale. I think you'll find some rather superb options on there." He relents and opens the menu.

"How's Mom?" I ask after we have ordered. The mood between them during the last few days has been decent, even if he has been rather somber. His spirits did, however, immediately brighten as soon as we were out of the room.

"She's been okay the last few days."

"And the days before?"

There is a soft sigh. It's an unhappy one. "You know how your mom gets."

"I do. It's why I'm asking."

"My colleague invited me on a fishing trip a few weeks ago. She got really mad when I told her about it because I didn't ask before I said yes. I told her she was welcome to join us since she was invited too, but she refused."

"Did you go anyway?"

"No…"

I keep looking at him, saying nothing, so he knows I won't be satisfied with a dodge.

"I am only inviting trouble if I did," he admits. "She was also making snide remarks about how the house wasn't going to clean itself over the weekend."

She has two hands, two legs, functioning as perfectly as her mouth. She can clean it herself. "Did you want to go?"

"Of course I did. I get along pretty well with this colleague. It would have been nice to do something interesting over the weekend for a change."

"You should, next time. Say yes. Don't change your mind. Go."

"Your mom isn't going to magically change her mind about it."

"Who cares about what she thinks?"

"You're not the one at home. You don't know how she gets."

I'm pretty sure I have a clear idea of what my mother is like when she doesn't get her way. I'm surprised my dad doesn't think that I would.

"I've told you before. Richard and I aren't kids anymore. Your reason for staying together now only serves as an excuse for your unhappiness."

"I married your mom. It's my duty to stick with her, through thick and thin, until death do us part."

Or until she becomes the death of you. "You shouldn't stay with her out of some twisted sense of duty, Dad. You're doing nobody any favors."

"What your mom has been good at her whole life is working. She's never been good at taking care of herself. It's only going to get harder for her the older she is."

"She's also not a hundred years old. She'll figure it out."

"She still struggles with electronics like her phone, her laptop..."

"Then she'll either figure it out or get by without it. It's not like she's got a bustling social life."

My dad shoots me a withering look. My last comment was unkind.

"It's fine. I'll get by. My only wish is that she goes before me so I may enjoy my last years without her. But if she doesn't... then, well, perhaps I may enjoy myself in Heaven."

"Dad..."

"Anyway, how's work?"

I purse my lips at the sudden change in subject. "It's all right. Stressful a lot of the time, but I'm still enjoying it."

"Do you ever think about coming home?"

It is my parents' wish for me to return home one day. My mother believes that it is my duty to care for her in her old age, and my dad probably believes that his life (and his burdens) will feel more manageable if I am around.

"I haven't really thought about it."

I haven't spared a single thought about returning home. In comparison, I've spent a lot of time pondering whether it's time to move from renting my own apartment in London to buying one.

"It's not as simple as it sounds, anyway. I'm an English-qualified lawyer. I can't just randomly join a law firm in the States."

"I know," my dad says. He sounds cut up. "You should still think about it."

"Why?"

"What?"

"As I said—why? I'm perfectly happy here. Job's great. Apartment's great. Friends who love me like family."

"You're far from family, and your friends are not family. You should know that."

"Can't say I do."

"What kind of answer is that? Of course they're not family."

"Because they're not blood?"

"Yes."

"They have celebrated my successes and commiserated with me over my failures, religiously, for more than ten years. They are there when I want them to be, they are there when I *don't* want them to be, and I love them for it, and they have loved me as I am from day one."

"I know you are different from us—"

"I'm not different, Dad, I'm gay!" I'm exasperated by the persistent refusal to acknowledge my unchanging sexuality.

"Fine, this lifestyle of yours..."

I contemplate grabbing the napkins on the table and giving him a good thwack on the head.

"It's wrong, and your friends' ability to love you for that doesn't make them family. It makes them enablers."

Enablers. Against my will, there is a short burst of laughter in my head.

"What happened to you?" I ask, shaking my head. "You weren't like this when I first came out to you."

"What do you mean?"

"I was fourteen, told you I was gay, you hugged me, said you'd love me no matter what, even joked that you were glad that you didn't have to worry about me getting pregnant."

My dad frowns.

"Remember? We were at home, out on the porch and you were fixing the floorboard that had come loose? It was fall and you were complaining about how the leaves would need to be swept up before Mom returned from work?"

Still he continues to frown. It is disconcerting.

"I don't remember this," he finally says.

"Come on, Dad. You're kidding, right?"

"No, I really don't know what you're talking about."

An overwhelming sense of dismay overcomes me. My heart plummets. Every forbearance I have shown my dad since I was fourteen—forgiving him for the years he stopped speaking to me, allowing him to lean on me as he struggled with his loveless marriage, letting it slide the numerous times he selfishly wrapped himself up in his ignorance instead of getting to know me—I did it because of that day on the porch, in the hopes that he would eventually come around and be the father I remembered growing up with. I have even excused him for betraying my trust and breaking my heart when he abandoned me when I most needed him, all for a memory which I have religiously held on to since I was a teenager and which he appears to have forgotten. I laugh softly in disbelief and run my fingers through my hair. I feel like I have been duped.

"Do you think we should go soon? Your mom's probably wondering where we've disappeared to."

I can't believe my ears. Here I am reeling from the discovery, and already, my dad has moved on from it as if it is of little to no significance.

"Only if you want to go. Richard's with her, anyway." I am in no hurry to return to my mother, but I am not desperate to hang around with my dad. I watch him wrestle with the decision to stay in the café. This is ludicrous. What my parents have is a marriage. What they don't have is a relationship.

I add, "Look, you can tell her it was me. Teatime. The Brits do it all the time and I'm sufficiently English for the family."

With a soft clink of metal against ceramic, my dad stirs his coffee, even though he's already sweetened and thoroughly agitated it. He's struggling with the moral quandary of throwing his only daughter under the bus to spare himself a further fiery maelstrom from his wife. Tapping his spoon three times against the top of the cup, he places it back onto the saucer and busies himself with the arrangement of the sugar sachets to his left. Smoothing out the creases of the first one, he rights its direction and straightens it neatly in its holder. I take a sip of my coffee, sit back, and watch him do the same with the next.

CHAPTER 32

Alex shrugs off her coat and allows me to take it for her as we enter the restaurant. She finished work earlier than expected and we've still got another hour to go before our dinner seating. She refuses the waiter's attempt to seat us at the bar while we wait, insisting on the booth in the corner.

"How are the parents?"

I flash a pained smile. "Trying. They've been in London barely three days and already I'm ready for them to leave. My mother is a little peeved that I'm not joining them for dinner tonight, but she got over it as soon as she saw Richard."

Alex laughs. She checks her watch. "There's still time to join them."

"What? And miss dinner with you? I think not."

Alex looks pleased. "How's work been?"

I shake my head. "I have a client—Mr. Forty Percent. He's a real prize, that one. No matter the type of work, the size of the project, he'll always ring me up after we've issued his invoice. He'll start by telling me in so many ways how we're a poor excuse for lawyers for needing to work in teams instead of having only one lawyer per file, then asks for a forty percent discount. It's the same rude and insulting call with him all the time—which I had to endure today—all because he's too cheap to pay us, but too important a client to drop."

"Sounds like a complete douche. Someone should tell him that *he* is the poor excuse for a client and that he's lucky to even have *you* on his files."

Hearing Alex, she reminds me of the times I would cling on to that fierce belief of hers—in me—so tightly, as if my entire self-worth depended on it.

"Maybe I should dial you in the next time he calls."

"Maybe you should."

It's an amusing thought, Alex putting Mr. Forty Percent back in his place with her cold, caustic words. The waiter announces his arrival by carefully placing the drinks in front of us. Alex leans forward and grabs both, handing me mine before she settles back comfortably beside me, legs crossed with one foot touching my shin.

I take a sip of my drink. "And how's your week been?"

Alex fills me in on the recent deadline she had to meet where her writing came across as flat and every picture for the article was either underexposed or irredeemably ugly. Waking the screen of my phone, I bring up the magazine and flip to Alex's article.

"The pictures aren't that bad."

Alex leans in, slipping her arm under mine and looping it through to get closer. One hand on my thigh, the other moving the article showing on the screen as the phone rests in my palm. She is so close I can smell her perfume, faint after a day's work.

"You didn't tell me you got a *Pulse* subscription." She peers at me, lips just beneath mine, the lack of space between us, slowly but surely, sending my body into a state of want. There are these moments, brief flashes, where you think if you kissed someone, they might kiss you back. The lack of apparent mutuality is terrifying, and when you have history to boot, the fear becomes paralyzing.

"Mmm, I don't think there's a rule requiring me to tell you

everything. I will agree with you, though. This article isn't your best."

There is a mock gasp. "You did not just say that!"

"You'd just call me out if I'd said it was amazing."

Alex sips her drink. "True. I called Peter out on it."

"Peter?"

"This guy who asked me out on a date."

And just like that I am back on Earth, reeling from the ice-cold bucket of water. *Girlfriend* or *girl-friend*, Alex behaves as if the two concepts are entirely interchangeable.

"Right…so who is this Peter? Another blind date?"

"No, actually. He works in the accounts department. Emails about my repeatedly unpaid expenses, one thing led to another… my expenses were paid and I'm going on a date with him."

"Killing two birds with one stone. Terribly efficient of you."

"Can't you tell? All I wanted to do was get my expenses paid."

I chuckle. Alex is joking, mostly anyway. As the saying goes—there's a grain of truth in every joke, and my take on her joke is that there is a whole chunk of it in this one.

"You're bound to him for life, then. First date bombs. There go your paid expenses. Break up. There go your paid expenses."

There is a soft groan. "Don't say that. Now I've got to quit my job before I can quit him. You've dated half your social circle and I don't see you getting into this type of trouble." Alex pretends to pout.

"For starters, they don't pay my expenses."

Alex gently bumps her shoulder against mine. "I'm serious, how are you friends with *all* your exes?"

I shrug. "Lesbians. It's a thing."

Silence, then another playful shove in the ribs. "Come on, get real. I'm sure it's not."

I laugh hard. "I don't know! I've not done a study on it. I just know that I am friends with all but one of my exes, and I know *my* exes are friends with most of *their* exes too."

"I don't believe you. I've yet to see that myself."

"You might if you *actually* dated girls."

Alex stiffens against me and just like that, all the humor drains from our conversation. I groan inwardly. Those words have been on the tip of my tongue all these months, and with them out in the air, they are nothing short of dismissive. I may as well have called Alex a fraudulent bisexual. This wouldn't have happened in the past; I used to be so much more careful around her, afraid to inadvertently do or say the wrong thing. The waiter hustles over when Alex raises her head and makes eye contact. A familiar sense of dread starts to bubble up; I am seventeen and we are in high school all over again. Meanwhile, Alex exchanges words with the waiter. I expect her to ask for the bill and cancel dinner, but instead I hear her tell him that she'll have another Manhattan and nearly jump when she gives my thigh a gentle squeeze and asks if I want the same drink. Her arm is still looped through mine, hand still on my upper thigh.

Eyebrows raised, she asks when the waiter is gone, "Are you done taking potshots at my sexuality?"

"I wasn't—"

"Oh, you were."

I cast my gaze downward at the hand that is still on my thigh, and I feel a deep flush come on. Am I still in trouble? Am I not? Do I give a fucking damn as long as Alex doesn't walk out on me and continues keeping her hand on me?

"I'm sorry," I say quietly. "I know how that came out."

"Is that what you think? That me identifying as bi is just for kicks? Wearing it like a fashionable accessory for a season or two?"

"No..." I sound weak disagreeing, because that is exactly what I was saying. "The truth is—" I run my hand through my hair. "It's just been a challenge seeing you as anything but straight, Alex. It's been, what, months? Multiple dates, always men. This is not an excuse and it certainly doesn't excuse what I said, but...it just didn't seem like you're actually into women."

Her lips draw into a firm, straight line, and her eyes are unreadable. I rest my hand on hers and gently brush my thumb against her skin. I can't explain what possesses me to do this, as we are in the middle of what I can only call a strong disagreement, but words don't suffice.

"Alexis, I'm sorry. Please don't be mad."

She still doesn't say anything and I brace myself for the long dreary wait of her shutting me out in the cold.

"I am. All right? Into women," she says without pulling away. "But what does it matter if I'm into them? If they aren't out there, available and going on dates with me, there's nothing I can do about it." She shoots me a sideways glance and with one look, I feel wretched. Alex is evidently unhappy.

I sigh, regretful. "I'm fucking useless at this, aren't I? I'm sorry. I just... It's just easier for me to deal in absolutes when it comes to this—"

"But it's not just one hundred percent straight or—"

"—when it comes to *you*."

Whatever Alex means to say, she doesn't. I brush my thumb against her skin again. The last time we were like this, side by side, bodies flushed, silences which had more to say than words, she made me feel like we were inevitable. I had given her all of my heart at the end of that night, and by the next, by her hand, it was in pieces. Yet all this time and it doesn't feel like I'm over her. All this time and once more, the possibility of being ruined by her again. My heart has waited a lifetime for her and hurt twice over because of her, but still, I want it. I want her.

Because it's Alex and I know no other way.

I briefly tighten my grip on her hand, then before I can change my mind, I dip my head down and kiss her.

Because what's another lifetime of hurt if I can have her?

A split second later, palm pressed to my cheek, Alex kisses me back and when she does, I remember how it felt loving her. It was hard, fast, and cripplingly all-encompassing.

CHAPTER 33

Given a crowded restaurant at the peak of its dinner service and without a single empty table in sight, I thought it would be a hard task locating my parents, but all I had to do was look for the only two elderly Asians looking completely out of place in La Chimère, a fancy French restaurant.

"Interesting choice for our reunion dinner. Didn't think either of you liked French food."

"It was Richard's recommendation. He said it would be a shame if we didn't eat here before we left," my mother says. I had meant to make reservations at Eleven Sticks, which seemed appropriate for a Chinese New Year reunion dinner, but decided against wading back into the complications with Paige. It wouldn't have mattered, anyway. Richard's recommendation would have trumped mine, even if I'm the one living in London.

I flip the menu in curiosity. I've heard of La Chimère and have always figured it wouldn't be cheap, but I can't help but balk a little, anyway. Were my pathologically cheap parents aware of the fact that La Chimère only has tasting menus and that the price of the *cheapest* one is at least three digits? I presume they were not, because they would not be caught dead in such an expensive place, regardless of the occasion. As my mother often says, her heart will ache at the cost, and by virtue of that, she will never be able to enjoy herself, however good the food.

"Does this happen to be Richard's treat?"

The effort to keep the sarcasm out of my voice is almost beyond me. Richard has never paid for a single one of these family meals. I used to think he might develop some sense of shame and at least feign the act of reaching for his wallet or fighting for the bill, but he never does.

"Don't be silly. Why would we make your brother pay?"

With parents like my mother, why would he know shame?

"Where is Richard, by the way?"

"He's just gone out for a smoke."

"Thought you didn't like that."

"I don't, but he's so stressed at the moment. The last thing I want to do is nag him now."

Speak of the devil—Richard returns. It's intriguing how he never seems to have evolved with time, looking like the same pouty, arrogant, and self-important boy I saw at home last year and the years before. I don't bother getting up to greet him. He doesn't bother asking for anyone's opinion when he flags down the waitress and orders for the table.

"Richard made partner. Did you know? We're both so proud of him."

A smug look crosses Richard's face. It's annoying. Richard's path to partnership wasn't exceptional, normal at best, maybe even a little slow given that he's practicing in a medium-sized outfit in Havenford. However, his mere presence has this unexplainable power to neutralize the overachieving Chinese in my mother. Can't top the class? No problem, one must accept that there are smarter people out there in the world. Can't gain entry into a prestigious law firm? No bother, not everyone can spot talent, *and* it is easier to rise to the top in a smaller firm, anyway. I find it fascinating the allowances she makes for him, even if I do loathe the inequity between her treatment of him and me.

"Oh, how wonderful!" I muster up whatever fake enthusiasm I can conjure up with such short notice. "It's about time, right?"

"I don't see you getting partnership," Richard says.

"Who says I won't? And honestly, if I had already made partner at my firm, you'd have to accept that I'm extraordinary and pretty much more awesome than you."

Richard ignores the jibe and starts to sing his own praises to my mother. He says something about his European clients who are very pleased by his promotion, then something else about how jealous the other associates in the office are; I tune him out like white noise and flag down the waitress for a double vodka and soda to pass the time. The fragility of Richard's ego demands that he be given time and space to remind you of his greatness. It is no surprise that dinner becomes all about Richard, and by the time the petits fours arrive, he's already busy complaining about his wife.

Apparently, Karen has been the most difficult partner, someone who curbs his ability to succeed. She fails to understand his need to entertain clients in unsavory bars, drinking whiskey until he stumbles home drunk at four in the morning. She is also annoyed that she continually has dinner on her own every night, falls asleep in an empty bed, and wakes to a dead log of a husband.

"I'm working so hard, my hours are so long, and Karen can't even iron my shirts for me! She says she barely has time to manage the household chores, so how is she supposed to manage mine?" Richard wears a long sulk.

The sight of a formally dressed, grown man sulking in a fancy French restaurant is good for my soul in a laughter-inducing way. What's funnier is that Richard paints Karen as an unfeeling, demanding simpleton housewife, but that can't be further from the truth. Karen's also a lawyer, and when Richard met her, he couldn't be prouder. Karen was sweet, bright, and independent, and she came from a well-to-do family. Richard thought he had landed himself a trophy wife, another achievement on the long list of accolades which would follow him—only they didn't. When Karen made partner before Richard, he smarted. When Richard resorted to moving to Havenford for a shot at making partner somewhere, he was so busy spinning tales to mask his insecurities that he failed to see that Karen sacrificed her bright future at her previous firm for him. Even then, Karen has simply landed on her feet and gained an equally successful legal career in Havenford. I'd say that she is more than entitled to tell Richard to iron his own clothes. In fact, maybe he should be ironing hers.

"Oh, Richard, I didn't know you were so unhappy in your marriage!" my mother says, gripping Richard's hand tightly. Far too blinded by her love for Richard, my mother will never see Karen the way I do. "It's not right. You deserve the world!"

Frankly, my mother's love for Richard is downright off-putting. I'm thankful for having passed on the coffee and opted for a double whiskey on the rocks instead.

The waiter is hovering by our table, patiently waiting for a lapse in conversation to introduce our last bites for the night. A text message flashes up on my phone screen, waking it. I whip it off the table. It's Alex. And it has been two days since I kissed her and she kissed me back, a moment I have been replaying non-stop in my head. Dinner with her was magical. We parted with some giggles and a lot more kisses. We even made plans for tonight. But not once did we talk about what the kisses meant. I imagine the worst and assume she's texting to cancel, but she's not. She's confirming where we're going to meet. I sag with relief, briefly, before grinning to myself like an idiot.

"I want a divorce, Mom."

There's no way in heaven or hell that my mother is going to take that well. Everything that is Chinese in her will fight this. The embarrassment of Richard's divorce will be too much to bear. It will feel like nothing but humiliation to her after the very public, well-attended, and expensive Chinese wedding dinner she blew a hole in her pocket for. I hammer out a text to Alex, confirming our meet-up point and telling her that I can't wait to see her, then shove my phone into my pocket. Ordinarily, I'd wait for her response, just to be sure. But a potential rupture between my mother and Richard? I am so not missing this. To my amusement, the waiter who served our petits fours is *still* waiting by our table. He raises his eyebrows when I wave him off. I nod my head with a small smile. Much as I would love to know what I'm eating, he would have waited the rest of the evening to say his piece. I think I spot relief in his eyes when he finally retreats.

"Oh, Richard. Surely it's not that bad…you're just angry now."

"No, I really *do* want a divorce, Mom. Do you know what makes her truly terrible? When I told her that we should just separate, sell our home, and we'll split it fifty-fifty, she said no!"

"What? Why?!"

"Because her father won't allow it! She says the house is his investment too and he refuses to sell in the current market conditions. We'll all take a loss."

When Richard and Karen moved to Havenford, they wanted this beautiful, massive, turn-key home in a highly sought-after location. They would have bled through their noses to afford it, but they really wanted it, so Karen's dad offered to stump up a wad of cash by selling some of his stocks, but he had stressed that it wasn't a gift, merely a different way for him to invest his cash. Richard and Karen agreed; they signed a contract agreeing on each of their respective shares of the house, and everyone went home happy. At that time, I wasn't surprised that Karen's dad would want the terms laid out in a contract, but I *was* surprised that Richard was fine with it. I thought he would have found it unnecessarily cold and unloving—but he's a lawyer, so it isn't like he didn't understand what he was getting himself into, either.

"He cannot be serious. He's going to hold you to that deal?"

"Yes!"

"How can he be so stingy? I never thought he'd ask for the money back!"

"I didn't think he would, either! Karen and I have been married *for years.* Doesn't that count for anything? He's so heartless."

Wading into the middle of this flurry of emotions seem unwise, but the whiskey in me cares very little for caution. "Erm, I'm *pretty* sure the whole point of having a contract is to deal with situations like this? You know, high tensions, hurt feelings, poor memories…I see this *all the time* with my clients."

"Skylar! How can you be so unfeeling? This is your brother we're talking about and his cruel wife and despicable father-in-law are holding his house ransom!"

Only with my mother can divorce negotiations be dramatized so much they're fit for television.

I exhale deeply. "Richard, if Karen's father won't sell, what's he proposing?" I ask, hoping to instill a sense of calm and decorum at our table. We are in a posh restaurant after all. My parents may not be used to dining in one, but that's no reason for us to come across as uncouth patrons.

"He's proposing that they buy me out."

"At today's market price?"

"Yes, but—"

"There. It's not ransom," I say to my mother. "It's what's fair."

"Fair? You think this is fair? They're going to leave your brother broke and homeless. All because he wants to divorce that terrible woman who won't even iron his shirts! It *is* ransom! If she really loved your brother, she wouldn't let her father do this, and your brother is right to divorce her. Richard, we'll support you no matter what. You know you can always move back home and stay with us for as long as you need."

Allowing my brother to go through with his divorce—seems like nothing is sacred to my mother anymore. And sadly, the irreconcilable divide between mother and son continues to remain elusive.

Richard breathes out, finally calm. "Okay, Mom." He reminds me of a little boy who just threw a temper tantrum to get his way. He concludes the riveting discussion on his impending divorce by signaling for the bill.

The waitress who has been tending to my drinks returns with the bill. She looks around the table trying to determine who is picking up the tab for tonight's dinner. Richard reaches into his pockets, and I kid you not, if he pulls out his wallet, I would have given him my support in the upcoming dark, difficult days of divorcing his wife. But out comes his pack of cigarettes. He excuses himself with some comment about being really stressed out. My mother looks at me expectantly, as does my dad. Still as stagnant water, neither of them moves. I sigh and gesture to the waitress, who wears an expression that can only be interpreted as sympathy as she hands me the bill.

Didn't choose the restaurant.
Didn't choose the food.
Didn't choose the company.
Didn't have a choice about the bill.
Family—where might I find one of those?

/

Alex is waiting in the hotel lobby by the time I return with my family, and at the sight of her, my spirits soar. Who cares about the shit show that was dinner when I get to spend the rest of my night with her? I introduce her to my parents. Richard is outside smoking.

"Hi, Mr. Cheung, Mrs. Cheung."

My mother squints at Alex. "You look familiar. I think I've seen a photo of the two of you in Skylar's room before. Did you go to the same high school?"

Alex seems pleasantly surprised and her gaze flickers to me. "Yes, we did. I'm working in London now."

"Okay, well, isn't that nice? Skylar has a friend in London! It's nice to meet you, Alex. Where—"

"Mom!" Richard calls out from behind us. He's standing at the main lobby door. A strong gust of wind blows around him, and he pulls his coat tight. "I'm going to meet a client. You go ahead without me. I'll see you tomorrow morning for breakfast."

"Okay, Richard. Wait—don't forget! Midnight!"

He already has his back turned. He gives her a thumbs-up sign and waves.

Alex's face contorts into a look of confusion. She swiftly recovers and wears nothing but a pleasant smile when my mother turns back to her.

"So where are you girls going? Do you need cash, Skylar?"

I stare. It's like she's forgotten about the insanely expensive dinner that I just paid for. "Erm, no?" I spy another part-confused, part-amused expression creeping onto Alex's face.

"Are you sure?" my mother asks, her face a picture of earnestness. "Not sure where you're going, but I just want to make sure you're not short on anything."

I continue to stare, now flabbergasted.

"We're just going for coffee, Mrs. Cheung. Nothing fancy, so I'm sure we're good." Alex flashes my parents one of those smiles that can charm anyone.

"Seems very late for coffee, but have fun, anyway. And Skylar—"

"Midnight?"

"Yes."

Unable to help myself, I mimic Richard's response and give her a thumbs-up sign. It satisfies her. "Night, Mom. Night, Dad," I say, keen to hustle my parents off before my mother's comments got any weirder.

"Goodnight, Mr. and Mrs. Cheung."

Alex chuckles when my parents are at the elevators and out of earshot. "Is there something you'd like to tell me? Are you broke?"

"I just paid for dinner at La Chimère."

"Did *that* make you broke?"

"I guess it did."

We giggle.

"Seriously, though. What was that about giving you money?"

"An odd mixture of love and making good first impressions. She wants you to think of her as generous, and she likens money to love."

"You got all that in one question, huh?"

I shrug. "Yeah," I say, my tone gentle. "My mom can be pretty complex."

"Seems like you read her just fine."

"No, I only know her triggers because I've triggered *a lot* of them before. I can't tell you why, but I can tell you what *not* to do."

"Huh, okay. And what's the deal about midnight? Is it a curfew or something? Do I have to return you by then or risk you turning into a pumpkin?"

"Nah, quite the contrary. The Chinese believe that on the eve of Chinese New Year, the longer the children stay awake at night, the longer their parents will live, so at minimum, my mom would like Richard and me to stay up past midnight."

Alex chuckles. "Does anyone ask the children what *they* would like?"

I enjoy the pointedness of Alex's comment. Waving at my parents who finally disappear into the elevator, I turn to face her and give her the full, knowing smile I've been holding in.

"Hi," she responds, smiling warmly.

I brush my fingers through her hair and wonder if a move to lean in and kiss her would be welcomed. Alex has not given me any reason to think that she would reject my advances, but I worry anyway, about the possibility that the night we kissed had been a one-off or worse, a mistake in her mind.

"Hi." I greet her with a kiss on the lips. My heart pounds in panic, but when she smiles into the kiss and her hand finds the back of my neck, that panic gives way to elation as I start to realize that all of this could be real, permanent.

"Mm, hello." Alex kisses me again. "What's this I hear about a photo in your bedroom?"

"The one Emma took of us at Daniel's?"

"Oh, wow. Talk about a blast from the past. Do you still have it?"

"Yeah, I do."

"You should show me sometime. It's the least you could do for your one, solitary friend in London."

We turn to leave the hotel lobby. "No shit, and I thought I was overthinking it." I laugh as I slip my arm around Alex's waist.

"Nope, you weren't. Basically, I'm it for you."

"Right…" I shoot her a cheeky sideways glance. "Could have done worse, I suppose." I pull Alex close as she playfully tries to push me away. "Where would you like to go?"

She drops a tender kiss on my cheek. "I thought we'd just walk around and see where the night takes us?"

"Sure." A chilly breeze rushes in with the opening of the main doors as I turn to kiss Alex, but with her lips on mine, I never once feel the cold.

CHAPTER 34

It is nearly last light when I reach my parents' hotel, all set to spend my last reserve of patience and fortitude during our final evening together. Come tomorrow afternoon, they will be on a plane home to Havenford and my life will resume. Alex is relatively free at the moment—being in between deadlines—and the idea of spending this weekend with her sounds glorious.

The hotel is bathed in a deep golden hue and everything around it looks warm and soft. I can't help but linger, wrapping my coat tightly around me to keep out the chill. It won't be long before the sun slips below the horizon, and a few more minutes of peace and quiet before seeing my parents can't hurt. A shout cuts through the courtyard. It sounds familiar. I turn my head and find Richard pacing the outside seating area of the hotel bar. He doesn't have his coat on, his hair is unkempt, and he has his phone pressed tight against his ear.

"I already said—I'm trying my goddamn fucking best!"

I jam my hands in my pockets and strain to hear what he's saying.

"What the fuck do you want me to do?"

Behind the anger, I can hear Richard's plea. I stop. I tell myself to walk on and leave him alone, because he's not my problem; he's certainly never made me his.

"Don't fucking tell me that. There's no salvaging this. Holding me to this fucking home isn't going to be that magical cure, and that's that!"

Yet against my better judgment, I approach Richard as he flings his phone down on the table and downs his drink.

"What do you want?" he asks when he sees me.

"No need to bite my head off. Just came to see how you're doing."

"*Awesome.* Everything is just *awesome*, can't you see?"

"I don't need this shit from you, Richard." I level a stare at him. He looks like he wants to argue but thinks better of it. I order us another round of drinks.

"Was that Karen?"

"Yeah."

I watch him rip open a fresh pack of cigarettes. He offers me one, but I decline.

"I have to ask—why are you so hung up on shit like the house?"

Richard inhales deeply, holds it in before exhaling slowly. He hasn't told me to shut up, so I continue.

"You guys got help from her dad. It's fair. The deal she made for the separation is fair."

"I know. I know." Richard rakes his hands through his hair. He looks like he wants to pull it all out.

"Then why make such a big deal of it at dinner? You know how much our mother dotes on you. You know how she feels about money. You know she was going to make a big deal of it as soon as you said it. What are you looking for? Her approval? You don't need her approval to divorce Karen. Richard, you could do it, she could hate it, and she would still love you. Hell, you could murder someone, and our mother would come as soon as you call, help you clean up the fucking dead body, and if that wasn't enough, she'd give herself up for you."

"I know." Richard looks dejected, defeated by life almost.

"What's going on, man?"

"I don't know."

"Yeah, you do. I'm not asking you what you're going to do. I'm asking you what's going on."

Richard jabs out his cigarette and lights up another.

"We've been trying to get pregnant for years. It's expensive, and it's hard to keep going like this. I told Karen we should sell the house, downsize, take the money, and keep trying, but all she says is that very little of that money is ours. With the market conditions, even if her dad is willing, we wouldn't have much after repaying our mortgage and returning what we owe her dad. He won't give the money away, and she won't ask for it for us. Some family, huh? All the love they have, they have it saved up only for each other." Richard's bitterness is apparent.

"Don't," I say softly.

"Don't what?"

"Don't be like Mom. Money isn't love, Richard."

"Money can give me a kid!"

He looks like he doesn't mean to shout and takes another long drag of his cigarette to calm his nerves. Richard and I don't look alike. He took after our mother as I did after our father. Hardly anyone would have guessed that we're siblings. Yet whenever Richard loses his cool, lets his temper slip and get the better of him, I'll see it. How alike we are. His anger feels so familiar.

"Might. *Might.* A kid can't salvage a broken relationship. You should know better than that, after what we went through."

"It was going to be different…" The hardness in Richard's eyes give way to a longing. It erases the scowl on his cheeks. "I wanted to give my kids the childhood I never had. I told myself I'll be better than our dad. No yelling, no canings, nothing I had. My children will never know fear. Only joy."

In that moment, my brother briefly sheds the damage of his upbringing.

"You were lucky," he says. "You didn't have to suffer the way I did."

The statement is preposterous. "Our mom wasn't a saint. You know that, right?"

It's clear from the confusion on Richard's face that he doesn't.

"Fourteen? Mom beat the crap out of me?" *You stood by and did absolutely nothing.*

Realization dawns on his face. I wonder if Richard remembers what he did or didn't do. "It was just that one time. I got it all the time growing up."

"That you saw, Richard. It was the one time anyone saw what was happening. What had been happening." Again, he looks confused. "She'd hit me when no one was watching."

"Oh."

I shrug. "It's a long time ago."

Richard runs his thumb across the rim of his glass. He is quiet for a long while. "I'm sorry. I didn't know."

Yet still there was the one time you knew, and you did nothing. "It's fine. You just wanted to get out. I get that."

It's funny how Richard and I used to be close. The strife between our parents, when it first enveloped us, brought us together—closer and closer until it eventually became a noose. No one understood more than me how desperately we each needed to escape.

Richard falls quiet again. "Mom wasn't happy then, you know? That time when you were fourteen. Work was hard, she and Dad were in such a bad place, and they were fighting all the time. I'm not saying this to forgive her actions…"

I don't have the heart to tell him that he is, even when he thinks he's not. Our dad, the villain in his story. Our mother, his defender, from birth onward. Of course he would find a way to excuse her actions. I'd be disappointed if he didn't even try, after everything she has done for him.

"Mom just had her own problems, that's all," he finishes.

Don't we all? "I know. It's fine. As I said, it's a long time ago." I check my watch and signal the bartender for the bill. "You coming for dinner?"

"No, I've got a work thing tonight. Just spent the day with Mom to make up for it, but she still seemed pretty annoyed. Probably cause it's the first day of Chinese New Year." He shrugs. "Nothing I can do, anyway. It's not like I can tell my clients no because my mom thinks she's more important."

I chuckle. "She'll get over it." I slip some money into the bill holder and make a move to get up. "Listen, I hope you and Karen work it out. I'm not sure either of you want this divorce. Nothing wrong if you do, but best be sure. You know how Mom would perpetually remind you of the fact that your wedding cost her an arm and a leg, so it would be nice if the woman sticks around." I roll my eyes. Richard smirks. "Anyway, we're in the twenty-first century and wives can refuse to iron their husband's shirts, there's nothing wrong with her wanting to have dinner with you, and as for the house…stop treating it like some battleground. Her unwillingness to sell or to force her dad to sell doesn't correlate with the love she has for you. It correlates with the damn market, and she's just doing her best to do right by you *and* her dad. Same goes for her not forcing him to give her the money. You guys need the money, so talk it out and figure it out, hard as it may be." I down the last remnants of my drink. "Don't get mad at me, dude, just telling you how I see it."

"I'm not—mad. I know."

He smiles to prove the point. I smile back. It will be the last time I see him before he flies home tomorrow.

"Cool, right, got to run because our parents are waiting. I'll see you when I see you."

/

My dad answers the door when I buzz the room. Eyes wary, he doesn't say hi and shuffles back down the entryway before I've even stepped in.

I hang my coat on the rack. There are only a few lights on, and the room is quiet. "Hey, Dad..." Following him, I can feel an uneasy balance hanging in the air, latching its grip onto me with each step I take. It is *too* quiet. "Where's Mom?"

He doesn't reply.

"Da—"

The words die in my mouth when I clear the length of the entryway and see my mother seated on the single-seater couch to my right. Something is wrong. She doesn't look right: stony demeanor, lips drawn into a harsh line, eyes dark with accusation behind her glasses. Her delicate fingers curl into the edge of the armrests.

I try to shake the unexplainable sense of fear creeping in. "Hi, Mom," I force myself to say.

"Did you move to London for her?" Her voice cracks like a whip across the room.

I flinch.

I shove my hands into my pockets, clench them for a few short seconds, unclench them for another few short seconds. I repeat the action.

"What do you mean?"

"Did you move to London for that girl? *Alex*." She spits Alex's name out.

"No."

"Don't lie to me."

"I'm not."

"You must think I was born yesterday. You knew her in high school. You are both here, in London, *kissing* and *touching* each other. I saw you last night, *with her*, when I went back down to the lobby!"

It feels like the wind has been knocked out of me. The accusation in her eyes is parting like a curtain to reveal what lies beneath. My breaths grow short and my body turns cold despite the stuffy heat of the room's radiators. I feel sick in the stomach.

"I-I…" I whip my head around the room searching for my dad. I find him in the other corner, the farthest he could be from me and my mother. He wears a blank look. I face my mother and turn my back towards him. He is useless to me, whereas she demands all my focus.

"How can you still be like this? I thought sending you away to England would cleanse you of your sickness, but I should have known that devil girl would have her claws in you, that she would have a hand in this!"

The tips of my mother's fingers have become dangerously white. Her inner rage is surfacing, and soon, it will drain her of all reason. The pounding in my ears and my chest rivals her shouts and competes for my attention. Out of the corner of my eye, I see the door at the end of the entryway—and the distance between me and it seems to stretch.

I take a small step away. "I didn't move to London for Alex. None of this has anything to do with her. I've always been *like this*."

The cup on the table beside my mother is in her hand one second and hurtling towards me the next. I duck, my hands coming up behind my head as it vanishes behind me. The sound of glass shattering fills the room. I feel a blow across my face, and I stumble. There is another, heavier than the first, and the side of my face throbs. Her hands are everywhere. On my head, my face, then my body and my back when I'm on the ground, crawling away on my hands and knees. I focus on the door at the end of the entryway. She has my skin pinched between her fingers. I fight the pain and keep heading for the door. She grabs my hair and yanks me back.

I'll kill you before I let you leave! My mother's younger self brandishes the knife as she screams at me. I shut my eyes tight. This can't be happening. All these years I have spent outrunning my memories, I thought I had outrun her.

There is another rough slap across the side of my head. Brutal, vicious, and uncontrolled. My mother has no intention of holding back.

She will kill you before she lets you leave, Skylar.

There's a part of me that Jamie teased out from the dark crevices of my heart. It's the part of me I thought I had buried—righteous rage. And it's trying again to get out.

Do you see him? Standing in the corner? A coward then, a coward now. Weak.

One by one, my mother's blows start to land in dull thuds. I feel no pain, only an increasingly cold, collected sense of calm.

That's it, Skylar.

The next time my mother's hand lands on me, I grab it. I squeeze her wrist and rise to my full height. I tower over her. Age has made her frailer, smaller. Funny how I could never see that until now.

"How dare you!" She wrenches her hand away from me. I let her.

I sneer. "How dare I what? Stop you? Stop you from killing me? I'm doing you a favor, *Mother*. You should be grateful."

"Grateful? For a daughter like you? You're insane! What you have is a disease! I should report you and have you disbarred."

"For being *gay*?"

"Yes, for being a homosexual."

I laugh. How ludicrous a suggestion. I would like to see her try—then everyone would let her know how stupid she sounds. "And *I'm* the one who's insane? Just listen to yourself."

She glowers at me and raises her hand, but I catch it in the air. "Do that one more time," I said, "and I'll show you what it *really* means to hit someone."

I hear myself, completely devoid of warmth. *Go on, show her what you're truly capable of.* My mother shrinks away from me, creating as much distance as she can, but I have her hand in a viselike grip. Fear flashes on her face. Maybe she'll stop if I let her go.

Just then, a crushing grip closes on my shoulder and an involuntary gasp escapes my lips. There is no one else in the room but my father. Shoving my mother aside, I wrench free of his hand.

"Nice of you to finally show up. It's amazing how frequently you continue to disappoint the only person who loves you."

There is a brief moment of doubt on his face and then it's gone, replaced by annoyance and then anger. The vein in his forehead pops out. It fuels my wrath. That expression. That look. It should be one he saves for his wife when he finally decides to leave her. Neither he nor my mother is entitled to their anger at this very moment. It belongs *to me.*

Yours. All yours.

Like the last time I saw Jamie, an open invitation for me to give in to my darker nature.

"You're just like Richard," my dad says, voice trembling. "Children who aren't in control of their tempers and with no respect for their parents."

"Respect is earned, *Dad*, and you have done such a fine job of squandering your opportunities. I think you broke Richard as a kid. All those beatings, or have you forgotten?" I look at my mother. "Has *she* forgiven you for hitting her precious son? I get why you've not left her. Why would you? When you're exactly like her."

My father raises his hand.

"Hit me like you hit Richard, and I'll hit you like I meant to hit her." Both my fists are tightly balled up and cocked. All that rage and raw power inside me, straining to get out.

My father falters, his raised open palm trembling into a clenched fist. My mother, teeth slightly bared as her heavy breaths come through in loud, sharp hisses. As an eerie silence descends in the room, a dawning realization creeps into my bones and my skin crawls. I was wrong. Richard's anger doesn't feel familiar *just* because of how alike we are. It is familiar because of *them*—our parents. So deeply unhappy they were with one another that it didn't satisfy to only take it out on each other; they had to take it out on the child the other loved most. In the way our parents felt entitled to their anger, the same would come to pass for Richard and me. But in a world where I have every reason to be angry, the truth is that all I am is one fistfight away from becoming my mother. All I have done to leave her behind, I would squander in a matter of minutes—seconds, even. I would be giving her the opportunity to steal from my future the way she has already stolen from my past.

I clench my fist until I feel my nails digging into my skin. I unclench it. My heart is beating hard. I can hear my breathing, ragged from exertion. I look at the door at the end of the entryway and back at my parents. I blink. I clench my fist. I unclench it. I take a step towards the door.

"If you leave, don't ever think of coming back!" my mother screeches.

The further away I get from her, the faster I walk, until I reach it.

"I will *never* forgive you, Skylar! *You hear me?* I will *never* take you back!"

My mother stands in a plain line of sight, her bravado returning with the distance. I smile bitterly at the woman who suddenly seems so small and insignificant.

"You still don't get it, do you, Mother? I left Havenford for London because of *you*. I was ready to leave you when I was fourteen, and I've spent more than half my life preparing for this." I place my hand on the handle and open the door without hesitation. The light from the corridor outside floods in. "I've got this."

CHAPTER 35

Apartment 9B.

I have my hands in my coat pockets, one of my fists wrapped loosely around a bunch of keys, as I stare at the alphanumeric characters on the intercom system. It is drizzling and the rain droplets are icy cold against my cheeks. The entrance to the building offers little cover.

There's a rush of heavy footsteps from behind me, a rustle and the clink of metal.

"You coming?" the man asks; he's already halfway through the door he just opened.

I nod and press my hand against the door's cool glass surface. "Thanks."

"No worries. Have a good night."

"You too."

He vanishes through the door where the stairs are. He must live on one of the lower floors. I'm in the elevator and it's a short ride to the ninth floor. I wonder if I should head back down.

With whiskey clinging to me like a bad girlfriend, I emerged from my apartment for the first time in days. It was meant to be simple. Out the door, down a moderately long street, past Paige's apartment, liquor store at the end of the street. Yet here I am—apartment 9B, where Paige lives.

I ring her doorbell. It's close to midnight and she should be back by now, but everything is still. I'm ready to leave and return home. It was a mistake to come here.

There is a short burst of wind and Paige's door is flung open from the inside.

"Skye? What are—" Her forehead creases.

She reaches out towards me and runs her thumb gently across my cheek, her forehead now deeply furrowed. She sees the gash under my eye.

"What happened?"

Snippets of the latest encounter with my parents come up in the form of sharp flashes in my mind. The looks on their faces when I entered the room. The raining blows. The unforgiving snarl on my mother's face as I walked out. How quickly my strength left me the second I was out the door. The way I wanted to crumble on the floor and bawl my eyes out but couldn't, not until I was home and safe.

My heart hurts from sadness, agony. I shrink back.

"I-I'm sorry. I have to—" I turn away, but falter when a sharp pain courses through my arm. Paige's hand is on it and her eyes narrow. She adjusts and holds my wrist instead. When I don't react, she gently pulls my arm towards her and rolls up my sleeve. I look away as the bruises on my arm are revealed, wishing that I hadn't come here.

"Who did this?" Paige's tone is clipped, raw.

"I should go."

"Skye, no. Tell me who did this to you." I can hear the urgency in her voice. Her eyes have turned wild and her body bristles with unchecked tension. "I need to know who did this to you."

"Parents." My voice trembles and cracks. "M-my parents. My mom…she saw me with Alex…"

"Where are they?" Paige has already launched herself through the door. I hold my hands out against her torso.

"Paige, don't."

"*Where are they?*"

"They're gone. They're already gone! *Paige*. Please don't go." I choke back a sob. "I need you here."

The pressure of Paige's body against my hands immediately eases, her sense of recklessness abating, but I see her. She is torn, agitated, and at a loss. She reaches out and with her hand around my back, we're in her apartment.

"Did they hurt you anywhere else?"

She sounds calm enough, but I can hear it, the underlying sense of frantic worry. I point at my shoulder. She lifts my sweater and releases my arm from its confines. The bruises on my shoulder are a mix of deep purple and yellow, angry looking. Paige runs her hand over them and I wince at even the slightest touch. My skin feels tender and weak. I awkwardly slip my hand back into the sleeve of the sweater and pull it back down, unable to look at Paige, whose gaze is squarely on me. The emotions bubbling underneath the surface make me uncomfortable. All the time spent building the wall around my heart, yet no amount of time or will in the world seems capable of protecting me from this pain. It makes me want to polish off another bottle of whiskey so that I can forget.

"Skye…" Paige places her hands lightly on my hips. She dips her head down and tries to make eye contact. "Skye, please look at me." Her anxiety rolls off her in waves. She brings her palm to my cheek. How gentle her hand feels in comparison to my mother's. "I need to know if you're okay."

The tenderness and care in Paige's voice cuts right through any semblance of strength I have left. Something in my body splinters and breaks. My vision starts to blur from tears. Paige crosses the last gap between us, fingers threading through my hair, one arm wrapped tight around me. I loop my arms around her neck, my fingers clasped.

"I've got you, Skye. I'm here."

/

The migraine hits so astoundingly hard that I regret waking up at all. I'm in Paige's bed in last night's clothes. The room is still dark, but I can see from the sliver of sunlight cutting through the blinds that the day is ripe. The pounding in my head keeps going like a bongo drum. I turn and bury my face in the pillows. Paige's side of the bed is cold, but it still smells like her.

She stayed up with me—through the tears, the truth of my history with my family, and a blunt account of the final altercation. When I worried that she would be disconcerted by the cold rage I unleashed on my parents, she soothed me. When I sank too deeply into the pain of older memories, she brought me back. And when I finally had too much to drink, she told me everything was okay, that I should close my eyes and rest.

I drag myself out of bed and crack open the door. Paige is seated at the dining table, flipping the colored pages of a large bound book; it looks like a culinary magazine.

"You're up." She sets aside what she's reading. "How are you feeling?"

I join her at the dining table. "Like I drank too much." My eyes widen at the time. It's just past 2:00 p.m. "Paige!" I jolt out of the chair and grimace at the sudden movement. "Fuck. Lunch service."

"Mmm yes, exactly what I said to Mrs. Li today."

"W-wait, what? No, I didn't mean 'fuck lunch service.' I meant: Fuck. Period. Lunch service. Period."

"You lawyers and your commas and full stops," Paige says, affectionate and unexplainably relaxed.

I can only dumbly repeat myself.

Paige covers my hand with hers. "Don't worry about it. I spoke with Mrs. Li this morning. She was the one who told me, 'Fuck lunch service,' no full stops, no commas, nothing. Okay, perhaps she said *forget* instead of *fuck*, but we were on the same page. Told me to take the entire day off if needed. It's just one day, she said, and I quote, 'Let her son do some work for once.'"

Guilt chafes at me. "I'm sorry about this. I didn't mean to inconvenience you."

"Don't say that. You're not an inconvenience. Just between you and me, I'm glad to have a Saturday off for once. I feel like the last Saturday I had off was when I was a student. Here, this should help." Paige places a glass of water in front of me along with a box of aspirin. "I'm going to make a fresh pot of coffee and order us some lunch."

I pop an aspirin and give Paige's apartment a sweeping gaze. Involuntarily, I close my eyes as I recall the last time I was here. How different things already are. Clothes on the drying rack that don't belong to Paige. Snacks that aren't to her taste littering the dining table. And with the exception of the magazine she had been perusing, books and magazines she wouldn't ordinarily read. All Cam's. I spy my phone on the coffee table and retrieve it. Alex messaged to suggest dinner places for next Saturday. She thinks I'm busy with work until then. I didn't want her to see me like this, and I wanted to give my bruises time to fade.

Paige slides a mug of piping hot coffee across the table, along with a familiar bunch of keys. "They slipped out of your hoodie, but they don't look like the keys to your flat."

I run my thumb against the jagged edge of the keys. "They're not. They're keys to my bedroom back home. Needed to make sure she couldn't get in when she was angry." Closing my hand around the metal, I allow the cool surface to soothe my heart like a balm. "I feel like I should do something."

"What do you mean?"

"Call my parents, say something, make it right."

"Why? If someone has to make it right, it's them. You did nothing wrong."

"Then why does it feel like I did? Why don't I feel better? This should be a moment of triumph, besting my abuser, something like that. But the whole fucking week—in pain over what they did when I'm drunk out of my mind and in pain over what *I* did in the cold light of day... I just fucked up everything I had left with my parents just to get here. A fucking pyrrhic victory is what I got, but nothing is ever fucking linear is it?"

"Then what would be the fun in that, eh?" Paige says, the cynic in her coming out. She leans back in her chair and cradles her mug. "When my dad left us...I remembered thinking, *Good, now we can all move on. Scott and I can start afresh with our mum*. I was in a holding pattern up until then, hoping my parents would mend, dreading—but also wishing for—the day when he'd finally decide to leave. So, imagine the relief when he finally ballsed up and left us. Fuck, Skye. I felt like I had won the fucking lottery. But for months, my mum couldn't stop crying, and I couldn't stop worrying. I thought she was more broken away from him than with him. The penny also dropped when I realized that Scott was going to grow up without his dad. It made me feel like we had somehow lost in a lottery I allegedly thought we had won. So, as you say, nothing is ever fucking linear, is it?"

"Yeah, it would seem so," I murmur.

Paige is watchful as I take a slow sip of my coffee. "Why didn't you call me? When this happened."

"I…" The explanation stays rooted at the back of my throat.

"I hate that I wasn't there for you."

"I wanted to."

"Then why didn't you call?" Her repetition is gentle.

"Because it's not where we're at right now."

"Skye—"

"Don't. Please." I am exhausted, and my stomach churns. "Don't tell me I should have because yes, it was all I wanted to do. It was all I wanted to do all week, okay? But I didn't know how, and every time I thought I did, I stopped myself because I wasn't sure if you'd come."

There is so much hurt on Paige's face. I hate what I just did.

"I—" She bites on her lip. "I'll always be here for you. You have to know that."

"Do I?" My accusation feels valid even if it doesn't seem fair. "With everything that's been happening, it's been a little hard to figure out where we're at. I couldn't just scroll through my list of contacts, pick out your name, call, and hope that we'd be okay. I couldn't do that to myself, not like this, *not for this*, and you'd be asking too much of me if you expected it."

I squeeze back the tears that have gathered in my eyes. Why am I still crying? I am so tired of crying. All I have done is cry the entire week.

"I should have been there for you."

Her regret cuts me deeper than her hurt.

"It was my decision not to call."

"But it shouldn't have come to this…" Paige runs her hand through her hair, frowning. "I'm sorry. Skye, I am so sorry. Fuck, all I have wanted to say to you of late, every time I think about you, is sorry, and I should have just said it instead of fucking around with it. I…I just haven't been very good at 'us' recently."

"I don't think either of us have been."

Paige reaches across the table and covers my hand with hers. "I will always be here for you. No matter the fights. No matter what happens. *Nothing* can ever change that."

"I know." I grip the tip of Paige's fingers and give them a gentle squeeze. Another well of emotion looms within me, and whether I am okay with it or not, fresh tears are going to follow. "God, I'm so sick of crying."

"Mm, so was my shirt from last night," Paige says lightly. She lets out a soft chuckle at my half-hearted slap of her hand. "It's good, though. Crying. Scientifically proven to release endorphins and oxytocin."

"You're like a walking encyclopedia, you know that? Sure you don't want to reconsider a switch and go back to teaching?"

"That's your polite way of calling me a geek."

I laugh.

"Still love me though, right?" she asks, her fingers now gripping the tip of mine.

"Always."

CHAPTER 36

The night is still young when Alex and I return to her apartment after dinner. I'm grateful when she hands me a glass of white wine instead of my usual coffee. Being the dedicated tea drinker that she is, Alex only has instant coffee in her home, and it is rather shit.

Alex sits down beside me with her back against the side of the couch and her legs across my lap. She leans in and presses a kiss against my cheek before resting her head against my shoulder. "Mm, it's a crime that you still smell this good after a long evening. Remember what I once said about bottling you up?"

I do because I, in turn, bottled up that memory for safekeeping. We were in the mall one day after school, wandering through the perfume and cologne aisles, when Alex declared that I was the most delicious-smelling object for miles. I'm surprised she remembers.

"Yeah, I don't think they've learned how to do that yet." I press a kiss against her head.

Alex lets out a soft sigh; she sounds content. Her hand caresses my arm.

"I can barely see them now."

I look at the faded scars on my arms where her fingers are. "Nothing time and sunlight couldn't fix."

There's another gentle brush of her fingers. "I'm proud of you, Skye."

I fall silent. Those words used to fill me up and cause my

heart to swell until I felt whole, but they don't do that tonight; they don't appear to have the same effect.

"I meant to ask earlier," she says. "Did your parents get off all right?"

I see my parents again, standing in the hotel room, a yawning gap between them and me. The sense of disappointment and sadness continues to permeate my thoughts. I cough. "Yeah, they did." Richard hasn't called me to inform me of our missing parents, so it is a fair assumption.

"Everything okay?"

"Yeah. It was just a little rough having them here, knowing they still don't accept that I'm gay."

"Did you guys talk about it?"

"Not really, but it's obvious and hard to ignore. I get stupid comments like my mother asking me why I need to rent a two-bed when I live alone. In her mind, if I'm not with a guy, then basically I'm forever alone. Doesn't matter if I've already come out to my family. Denial's my mother's superpower, but it's getting old."

"My sister asked jokingly if I've found a nice English man yet. I was tempted to say 'No, but I've found a nice American woman,' but I didn't. I don't think she'll know what to do with that info. Tell Dad? Tell Mom? Forget I ever said it?"

"You don't think she'd be okay with it?"

"I don't know."

"And your parents?"

"Don't know about that, either."

"So you don't think you'll tell them?"

"What they don't know can't hurt them."

"But it also means you're hiding who you are."

"Honestly, I've not really thought that far. It's going to be a difficult conversation one way or another, but for now, the distance helps. It's much easier this way, and it's not like the secret is hurting anyone."

"That's...convenient."

Alex pulls her knees back, stands up and goes to the kitchen. She's barely drunk more than a few sips of her wine, so it can't be time for a refill.

I'm up in a shot and right behind her, reaching for her hand. "Alex..."

She allows me to turn her around. Her lips are tight. I know I need to apologize but feel reluctant. What does Alex intend to do? Keep the truth hidden until she's ready to settle down, and even then, keep the truth at bay if she ultimately marries a guy? I push aside my misgivings.

"I'm sorry. I didn't mean it like that. It's just that I've never stopped wondering if I made a mistake coming out to my parents. All it did was hurt them, and had I just kept my mouth shut, I would have allowed them to stay in their bubble and I would have their love. Hearing you say what you did...it just made me feel like I *did* make a mistake, that I lost everything I had with them for a mistake."

Alex's eyes soften. "Being brave wasn't a mistake."

"Yeah, well, it's not like I'll know what could have been." I shrug. "What's done is done."

She gently presses her palm against my cheek. "For what it's worth, I liked you for who you were."

There is an undeniable pinch in my heart, but I give her a teasing smile. "Now why didn't you tell me these things in high school, huh?"

Alex tilts her head to one side then kisses me without comment. She places her wine glass on the kitchen counter before kissing me again, but slower this time. Gradually she parts her lips and deepens our kiss. It makes me hungry for her. I stifle a soft moan that threatens to escape. I gently press Alex against the kitchen counter and feel her hands tighten around me as I begin to run kisses down her exposed collarbone and shoulders. I can hear her breath growing short before she pulls me back in for another long kiss. I slip my hand under the hem of her top and caress her lower back. Alex arches her body against me and digs her nails gently into my back.

"Bedroom," she commands and extracts herself from my arms.

Catching up with Alex, I wrap my arms around her waist from the back and pull her back into my arms. Pushing her hair away from her neck, I press my lips against her soft skin. We fall onto her bed, its cool sheets enveloping us as we take our time, kissing languidly. Alex reaches up and removes my hair tie, running her hands through my hair as it tumbles and falls around us. I have my hands splayed on both sides of her, placing a trail of kisses from her chin to the soft rise of her chest; she smells decadent. Alex's breathing turns erratic and as my hands slowly wander downward and slip under the clothing that separates us, I can feel her grow impatient, her kisses more insistent. Without saying a word, she has my shirt off. I smirk and slide her top upwards, just enough to reveal her stomach, before running my tongue across it in an excruciatingly slow manner.

"Skylar…" Alex growls. You can hear the demand in the way she calls my name.

I pause whatever I am doing to make eye contact with her. Now entirely devoid of my kisses and touch, Alex tries to make the best of her poorer situation.

"Clothes. All of them. Off."

I press another soft kiss against her skin and lift myself up so that my mouth is right by her ear. "You're always telling me what to do, Alex."

"And you appear to have stopped heeding me entirely."

Chuckling, I make quick work of all of Alex's clothes and rest the length of my body against hers. "I only ever do as you ask," I say before putting my mouth to good use, starting right from the top. Alex's back steadily arches into my touch, increasingly forceful the further down I go. She digs her nails into my back, her moans filling the room.

"Touch me..." Alex finally gasps, her face half-buried in the pillow, fingers twisted up with the bedsheets.

"I already am." I know what Alex is asking, but I want her to say it.

"No, not like this."

I run my hand down between Alex's legs and rest it on her inner thigh. "I want you to tell me what you want."

Alex thrusts her hips downwards to seek out my hand but I move it away every time she does. She groans and finally she says, "Fuck me, Skylar." Threading her fingers firmly through my hair, she makes eye contact. "I want you to fuck me."

And because I always do as Alex asks, this time is no different. In fact, I spare no expense. My fingers, my tongue, for as long as Alex wants, however she wants, and all for her pleasure.

/

Alex's bedside lamps cast her room in a soft glow. Satiated, she lies curled against me on the bed, legs tangled up in mine with her head on my chest. The branches of the trees outside sway with the wind, their shadows dancing on the walls. She is really here. It is her body pressed against mine. Her taste on my lips. It is all real, yet surreal.

In university, each summer I was home, I would catch myself searching for Alex. Along every street, around every corner, in every place we had ever been together. The back of every girl with her height, her frame, her dark brunette hair, the face of every girl whose profile resembled hers—yet I could never find her, and after every summer, I would bury the very notion of her. It hurt too much not to. My conscious hunt for Alex lessened with time. I had come to accept that I may never see her again, that I would never find closure. Yet now here she is, in my arms, fingers caressing the length of my torso, giving me everything I wanted since the day I met her. Are we so different after these years apart that we can only make it work now, so many years after it began?

"What happened? You and me. In high school."

Alex's touch slows. My heart speeds up. The silence in the room becomes thunderously loud. I take a deep breath.

"I told you I liked you, you said no, and I accepted that, but that night at Daniel's, before prom…everything you did…how we were together…only to hear that you were just messing with me. Were you?"

"It was such a long time ago, Skye."

"I know, and I have struggled to ask you this. Because it's been so long. Because it *seems* so trivial to ask this now, but it's not. Not to me. And if we're going to do this—whatever this is for us—I can't avoid talking about it forever."

A deep exhalation of breath, but she doesn't dispute it. She sits up and pushes her pillow into an upright position. She rests against it. A few eternities pass.

"When you showed up, I had already made up my mind.

This—dating girls—was too much trouble, more trouble than it was worth. I was done with girls, so I said no to you. I should have stayed away, I really should have, but who doesn't want to feel wanted? Then there was being wanted *by you.* It was different, special. You didn't feel like a person who would pick anyone off the street to love. You were so closed off. That to be picked—chosen—by you must be something special, then. I couldn't help myself. I kept coming back to it, to you… only to realize that there were these feelings which had crept up on me."

I turn my head away slightly. Alex's admission stings.

"That night after Daniel's, there were all these questions, demands for answers by everyone else. The rumors spread like wildfire. Overnight. Less than twenty-four hours. That's all it took. Tom was asking, my friends were pushing, and there was just too much to get through…" Alex slips her hand beneath mine. "If only to explore what could have been possible for us. It wasn't a leap of faith I could make then."

"You could've just walked away. You didn't have to say a thing about it. It's one thing not to be honest with me. It was something else entirely to do what you did."

It was cruel. The hurt returns with the memory of the betrayal—Alex reaching for Tom, Alex's eyes on me, Alex kissing Tom—all of it re-injected into my veins and spreading.

"I know, and ever since I saw you that night at your firm's event, whenever we talk about our past, I've been meaning to apologize."

"Well, you certainly didn't lead with it."

It is Alex's turn to look away. "No, I didn't. And the more time we spent together, the less I knew how."

I remain silent. My eyes briefly flutter shut when I feel her hand on my cheek and the shadow of that hand reaching inward and laying claim to my heart.

"I'm sorry, Skye."

Our eyes meet. There it is. That deep affection just beneath the surface, telltale signs in her eyes, feelings she harbored for me that I would have killed to know were true all this time. She leans in and kisses me. It is tender, chaste, and heart-stealing. Everything I imagined our first kiss would have been. My heart splinters.

The mattress shifts and Alex straddles me. Her kisses grow longer as her hands roam my skin, our bodies sinking back into bed. Lingering touches which turn more purposeful with every kiss, Alex soon pins my body down with hers and spreads my legs. She holds me down like gravity. Yet I'm overwhelmed by an inexplicable sense that something is amiss. I don't know what to do but cup her face. I think of asking her if she's missed me the way I've missed her and whether she has thought about what we could have been. I think of confessing to her that I gave her everything, and that some days, I've wished for some of it back. I pull Alex in and kiss her. I allow the words to elude me.

She responds by kissing me back so deeply, I think she wants to swallow me whole. Her slender fingers start to fill me, increasingly urgent with each thrust. Softly, I groan. I feel my body give in as it bends to Alex's will, and she wastes no time in taking what I am willing to give. She has her thigh between my legs, moving it in time with every thrust. With each deepening stroke, it feels like she is crashing into me, desiring to push me into oblivion, and if that is true, it is what I want too. Every single thought and worry I have had about her. Every ounce of hurt and pain she has made me feel. I want to forget. I want Alex's hand to tell me everything she never could.

CHAPTER 37

The weather held up against all odds. Alison's and Rachel's big day arrived, and a collective sigh of relief greeted the clouds' final parting and the rays of sunshine that peeked through into the gardens, just as the brides said *I do*.

Alex loops her arms around my neck as we wait for dinner. She is in a one-shoulder, dark-purple dress: perfect, not a crack in her veneer. She kisses me lightly on my jaw.

"The girls from work have two spare tickets to a play this Wednesday evening. They asked if we'd like to join them. I said we would, unless you have something else on, but I don't think you do?"

It doesn't sound like there's much of an option, and it disregards whether I care for the company of the girls from work. I have already met them a few times, and my original assessment is the same—I don't like them. They are vapid. People say you are the company you keep, so looking at Alex, I wonder if there is a part of her that *is* like her so-called friends, a side which I've failed to see. I've asked her before how they became such firm friends, and her reasoning was simple—they were the first people she knew in London, and better to have them as friends than enemies in a political work environment. Convenience and value, it would therefore seem, are the qualifying foundations of being Alex's friend.

I mentally skim through my week's calendar. "We've got your office gala dinner..."

"That's on Friday."

I grow fatigued just thinking about the social activities lined up for next week, and instead of dwelling on it anymore, I press a kiss against Alex's forehead. "Which play is it?"

"*Girls' Night Out*."

"All the plays in London and *that's* the one they choose?"

"They thought it would be cute. Girls' night out watching *Girls' Night Out*."

"Was everything else sold out?"

"Don't be unkind."

"I'm not. But Alex, even your baking trays have more depth than *that* play."

She purses her lips, angles my head so that she has my sole attention. "Wednesday evening." She kisses me. It is long and slow. "We are going," she says as she pulls away.

"My word, did the waterworks come on for you guys?!" Cam shows up out of nowhere with Octavia, tissue in hand. "Paige was convinced I was going to cry my mascara off. So glad I proved her wrong."

"There's still the rest of the night," Paige says, cheeky and incorrigible. Dressed in dark trousers and a white cotton polo shirt, paired with a casual navy blazer to complete the look. Eyeliner accentuates her striking blue eyes, and she can still perfectly muss her hair. It's like a day hasn't passed since the first time I saw Paige in Element—she's still impossibly attractive.

Cam points to her own eyelashes. "Watch these babies hold up. What do you think, babe? How does a spring garden wedding sound to you?"

There is the fastest flick of a glance in my direction before Paige smiles at Cam, smooth and relaxed.

"I think there are several steps between now and then, don't you think, babe?"

Cam, eyes glistening with adoration, runs her hand through Paige's hair and kisses her. "How about it, Alex? How does a spring wedding sound?" She adds a wink.

"I'm more of a summer girl myself." Alex strokes the back of my neck. "What do you think?"

Octavia snorts. "Probably whichever season Skye learns to stay interested in the relationship."

Paige's tone goes cautionary. "Octavia…"

Alex laughs. "Oh, I wouldn't worry. I don't think we have a problem with that." With her hand, she guides my face towards her and gives me another lingering kiss, this time slipping me a little tongue before she pulls away. It is a blatant display of affection that makes me feel self-conscious in front of my friends. To my relief, the shrill tinkling of the bell draws everyone's attention. Dinner is commencing shortly and we have all been asked to find our table and take our seats.

/

Alone outside, under the archway leading to the hotel's gardens, I welcome the silence. After five hours of festivities, the soft rustle of leaves and the crunch of gravel under the soles of my feet are comforting.

"Out here all on your own? Don't be asocial, baby."

Her warmth wraps itself around me.

"I could say the same to you."

I lean my back against the side of the archway and take in Paige's side profile. It used to be its own mystery. I would try to catch every movement at the edge of her lips, every flicker of expression in her eyes, and every dip and tilt of her head, so certain that I could read her yet constantly filled with doubt that I had nothing figured out. We make eye contact.

Reaching out, she leans in and tenderly brushes her thumb under my right eye. She's done this a couple of times now, nurturing my healing process. "How are you holding up?"

I shrug.

"No rush. I was just checking in."

I bite my bottom lip. "I thought maybe my dad might check in on me. About time we had our regular call…but he hasn't. Don't even know why I thought he would. He's always been a constant disappointment to me. Why should it be any different this time?"

"Because you love him. We hope even when it's futile. Did you want to call him?"

"I don't know. I still don't know what I want to do with them." I nudge the gravel around with the toe of my shoe. "Scott was over the other day. Told me that it's going well with the counselor, shared some stuff they've been working through during their sessions as he foraged through my pantry." We both give a breath of laughter at the inside joke. "Sounds like he's getting on well with her."

"Sure seems like it. I'm glad. He can always switch, of course, but it's good that he has that stability right now."

"How are you holding up?" I ask.

Paige casts a long look across the darkened garden lawn and folds her arms. "I was so relieved when he told me he was seeing the counselor. After Cam and I got back together, he became even more adamant about not taking up more of my time. I didn't know what to make of it. Didn't know what the right decision was. But I knew he knew how tired I was from work and that it would be in his nature to try and care for me in his own way, but really, for this, the only person he should be taking care of is himself. I agreed that we'd reduce how often we met up, every couple of days initially, and when everything seemed fine, we spaced it out to every fortnight, but I never wanted it to get any less frequent than that. I didn't trust that I was doing the right thing then, couldn't stop worrying that I would somehow irreparably fuck him up because I wasn't reading the signs. You know, the sort where he was crying out for help and I couldn't see it to save my life."

"That's a lot to put on yourself," I say softly.

Paige runs her hand through her hair and it falls carelessly across her eyes. "I am responsible for him, even more so after our parents' divorce. Don't get me wrong, I don't care for Scott out of a sense of duty—I love him—but he's my little brother."

"That's still a lot to put on yourself," I repeat. "I'll tell you that he's equally responsible for himself, but for what it's worth, Paige, I don't believe you could ever irreparably fuck Scott up. I've seen you with him. I've seen the way you love. You're there. You're present. So is your mom. And you both care so deeply for him. In time, he's going to be okay."

Paige turns and I can see it in her eyes—she believes me this time.

"So...you and Cam are talking about weddings, huh?" I ask. "Seems serious." *And obscenely fast.*

There is a short burst of laughter and Paige shakes her head. "I think girls just love to talk about weddings *at* weddings. It's easy to get swept up in the moment, and Cam got carried away on a tidal wave."

"You're avoiding the question, love."

Paige chuckles. "Maybe I should be asking *you* if you and

Alex are talking about weddings. The two of you certainly look happy together."

I laugh, hard. "What was it you said to Cam? I think there are several steps between now and then, don't you think, babe?"

"Uh-huh." Paige scuffs the heel of her shoe against the gravel. "And how's it going? With Alex." She doesn't look at me.

"Good, I think."

"You think?"

"We spoke. About what happened."

"And?"

"She says she had feelings for me..." I purse my lips. "She didn't know what she and I were, or could be, but her friends weren't reacting well to the rumors...so she couldn't bring herself to find out."

"That's it? Alex—caving to peer pressure," Paige says. It's the same snarky undertone I caught when she met Alex at The Honey Badger.

"Don't be unkind. High school can be really stressful. She apologized."

"After *you* brought this up."

"Yeah, but—"

"So she couldn't even apologize on her own. Is she going to blame that on peer pressure too? Has she even acknowledged how *much* she hurt you?"

Since having the long-awaited talk with Alex and actually getting answers from her, I had expected the bliss of closure. With all the torment and speculation now put to rest, all I have wanted to do is accept Alex's apology and move on. Yet that inexplicable sense of something remaining amiss continues to plague me. It hovers like a lingering doubt, casting dissatisfaction over every good moment, and now here Paige is, dredging up these disquieting thoughts and dissecting all that has and has not been said.

"Don't do this."

"Do what?"

"Paint her out to be some selfish bitch who didn't give two fucks about me."

"No, she did that all on her own and you know it. You just refuse to see it. You keep putting her on some pedestal like she's God, unfairly comparing all your relationships to this great big love that is Alex such that none of them—not even ours—stood a chance. But she's not a god, Skye. There is no great love story. She was just a selfish bitch who didn't give two fucks about you."

I take offense to the bitterness of Paige's rebuke.

"I didn't singlehandedly call off our relationship, Paige. *We* agreed to stay friends. *You* agreed that neither of us was ready. *You* accepted that it was more important for us to protect what we already had."

Paige levels a hard stare at me. "You didn't give me much of a choice. You had already made up your mind."

"What a fucking convenient excuse now, don't you think?"

"You were already walking away, Skye! You walked away then and you've been doing that ever since. You just did it to me again."

"And you never asked me to stay! You. *Never.* Asked me to stay. Not then. Not after. Never."

Paige and I stand there, our breaths unsteady, the atmosphere thick and heavy with all the words that never found air until tonight. I roughly brush away tears. How are we fighting again? We had just made up. I don't want to fight, but I can't bear to stay.

"I can't do this. Not again." I turn away.

"Skye." Paige grabs hold of my hand. "Skye, don't. I'm sorry. I just…I just don't want to see you get hurt again."

I try to pull away and Paige's grip tightens. "I can't do this," I stubbornly repeat, my heart walling up.

"Skye, please—"

"No, I mean it. I can't do this anymore. I can't stand here. With you. Fighting about Alex. This. *Us.* Please, Paige, *just let me go.*" I roughly wrench my hand from her grasp, and this time, she lets go.

CHAPTER 38

To my relief, traffic is gone by the time the wedding festivities end. I just want the night to be over. Standing outside Alex's apartment, she loops her arms around my neck.

"Everything okay? You seem a little out of sorts."

I don't know if anyone at our table caught the awkward tension between Paige and me after we returned. We had returned separately and proceeded not to say a single word to each other for the rest of the evening, a stark difference from how we had been all day. I feel pangs in my heart.

"Hmm, yeah. It's just been a long day, that's all."

"Did something happen between you and Paige?"

"Huh? Oh, it's nothing. Just a minor disagreement, no big deal."

I do my best to sound convincing, but based on the look on Alex's face, I've failed.

"Okay, then." She kisses me on the lips. "Are you staying the night?"

My bones feel heavy from fatigue. Crawling into my own bed and sleeping would feel so good. It's a bank holiday tomorrow, so there's no need to even set an alarm. Alex deepens the kiss, the tips of her fingers slipping under the untucked edges of my shirt.

"Alexis, are you trying to entice me to stay? You know you can just ask me, right? If that's what you want." Outwardly I tease, but inside, the weariness is immobile.

Alex pulls away and enters her apartment, leaving me at

the door. Kicking off her heels, she chucks her clutch onto the couch, sparing me only a brief backward glance. "You can call for a cab or you can join me in the shower. Your call."

It is hard to tell whether and how I have pissed Alex off with one seemingly innocuous remark, such that she couldn't care less where I spend the night. Or does she truly want me to stay, but can't be honest with what she wants? Either way, her careless way irks me as much as it stings.

I step into her apartment, closing the door behind me. "Tell me something, Alex. Why didn't you call me after prom? Why did it take you ten, no thirteen, years and a random meeting between us to say you're sorry?"

Alex stops in her tracks in the kitchen and turns to face me. "We've talked about this. Why are we doing it again?"

"Because I haven't asked you the one question that matters. You said the other night that you've been meaning to apologize for what you did, so I want to know—why didn't you? Right after prom. You had my number. You could have called, to explain, apologize, whatever, but you didn't. Why?"

"I didn't think an apology was going to fix it."

"But you didn't even try. Did you even care?"

"Of course I did."

"Then why didn't you call?"

"Skye..."

"No, Alex. Why didn't you call?"

Alex leans against the edge of the dining table. There is a sharp exhalation of breath. "Look, there was just a lot going on then, okay? I was getting ready to leave for college, there was Tom who wanted to spend every waking minute together, and it wasn't as if you and I were going to see each other again. So what's the point?"

"Alex." Her name sounds terse on my lips. "You went to a college that was *still* within the Havenford town borders. You're hardly well placed to use distance as an excuse."

Alex's lips are drawn. I can read her with my eyes closed. No part of her wishes to engage. I pinch the bridge of my nose and let out a soft sigh, unsure about where I meant to head with my original question. Standing in front of me is the person I've wanted since I was seventeen, but the more we talk about what happened in those years, the more hollow her apology sounds. The fog in my head grows heavy.

"Do you know what meeting you did to me? It changed… *everything*. Being around you…your light. It shone so brightly in the darkness—*my* darkness—that it felt like the sun was bleeding into my eyes the whole damn time and I loved you. The kind of love where I would have broken myself in two, repeatedly, if only for you to stay for just one second more. You could have called, given me some lame excuse instead of an apology, and I probably—no, I most definitely—would have considered it fixed, never mind what you did. But you didn't. You couldn't even do that for me—and you left me to hurt in an impossible way, in a way I can only describe as cruel."

Alex and I lock eyes.

"I never asked that of you," she says, not looking away.

"What? What didn't you ask of me?"

"*Your love.* I never asked for it."

"But you took it, and you used it. You took *everything* I was giving. A little hypocritical, don't you think?"

"No less than how you are with me right now."

"What do you mean?" I ask, exasperated at the cryptic accusation, one that feels like an attempt to subvert the original conversation.

"Paige?"

I internally flinch at the reminder of her. "What about her?"

You were already walking away! I can still hear the accusation and hurt in Paige's voice. *And you never asked me to stay! You. Never. Asked me to stay.* I can hear the same in my voice too.

"You're not done with her. I don't know what's going on between the two of you or what happened tonight, but all I know is that you see each other way too often despite the disparity in your schedules, you're uncomfortable with me kissing you in front of her, and every time the two of you fight, it feels like a couple's fight, and you never want to talk about it. You're with me, but it feels like you belong to her, so *you* tell me what's going on."

The morning I woke in Paige's bed after we had slept together, before reality hit me like a ton of bricks, I briefly contemplated how natural it felt waking up next to her and whether I could hang on to that feeling a little while longer. Running my fingers through her hair, I stole my last kiss from her and I told myself to leave.

"We're friends." *Every fucking thing we have ever done was so we could be friends.*

Alex shoots me a long look. "Sure."

"Don't be short with me. I'm not creeping around with Paige as if she's some dirty little secret or mistress or whatever. Paige and I are going through a rough patch right now. That is all. It hasn't been easy for us—having you and Cam back in our lives—and we're learning to adjust how we are around each other. But I am here, *with you*, hoping to work out what you and I mean to each other despite everything that's happened between us, so stop changing the subject."

She just stands there, arms crossed, silent.

I stick my hands into my pockets with a heavy sigh, looking down at my shoes, then back up at Alex. "Getting with you… was meant to be perfect. Everything I wanted. You. I really believed there was something more between us. Regardless of whether you asked for it, I loved you, Alex—so fucking much—and I thought that this was the kind of love that would cut right through the years and the pain as if they never existed and we would pick up where we left off that night at Daniel's. I used to think you were just scared after that night, afraid to be yourself. But that's not true, is it? You were *entirely* and *completely* yourself."

I will myself to push through and see the truth that has been right in front of me all along. Even if it is painful to look at.

"You were just selfish. Doing what was easiest and best for you. Good to me when it didn't cost you. Bad to me when it did. Whatever the cost, I would pay it and you would let me. I couldn't see what you were before. How could I? I was broken, damaged, and you were my light. But I can now. I see you and nothing has changed. *You* haven't changed. But I have."

The ache in my chest intensifies.

"I've had to make do—being without you—and I have. I like who I've become without you. I love the life I've created in the absence of you. And I could—I could change it up, change who I am…to be with you, to fit in your world, in the way you want me to, but in asking myself if I'd be willing to, I realize the answer is no. Not for you. Not anymore."

It is then my heart, shedding its past entanglement, can finally grasp what it has fought so hard to comprehend. I shouldn't have left Paige's apartment that night, not when what I wanted was to be in her arms and to feel her kisses on me when the morning came; I should have found the courage to stay. I take a deep breath: and just as Alex and I started our friendship with a truth of mine that no one knew, I share another one now, as we near our inevitable end.

"I'd sooner do that for Paige than I would for you."

Alex levels a hard look at me. She turns away and pulls out the dining chair nearest to her. It is unclear whether she is hurt, mad, sad, too proud to engage, all of the above, or if she feels nothing at all. What is clear, however, is that we are done. I scan Alex's apartment, pondering whether there's anything of mine I need to take with me. There isn't, and it makes me realize that I never truly settled in to begin with. I suppose sometimes instincts know best.

At the door, I turn to take one final look at Alex. She's seated at the dining table, legs crossed, casually flipping a magazine I know she isn't reading. Where I thought I would feel grief, I feel only relief. Once, I knew with certainty how deeply I loved her; equally certain now, I know it is time to let her go. As her door clicks shut behind me, I do just that.

CHAPTER 39

Apart from staff floating around after service ends, Eleven Sticks is quiet when I enter.

"Hi, Skylar."

I turn and see a familiar face at the cash register. "Hi, Mrs. Li."

"It's been a while. The girls have been asking after you." I toss a glance at the kitchen. "Paige is not here today, dear."

"What? Is she okay? Is she sick?" Paige would never miss a day otherwise.

"She's not sick, but I wouldn't say she's okay. She looked terrible this week, exhausted, out of sorts. Still cooked great, though. Wanted to come in today but I didn't let her. Sundays can be slow and we're only open for lunch. She needed rest." Mrs. Li cocks her head at me. "I thought she would have told you."

"Erm." I tug at the sleeves of my sweater. "We've both been busy." Paige and I have not spoken for more than a month.

"Okay…"

"Anyway, I'm sorry for bothering you. I'll give Paige a call, head over to her apartment or something. You have a great rest of the day and tell the girls I said hi." I turn to leave.

"Is everything okay? Because if there's one person who looks worse than Paige, it's you."

I have to smile. "I look that bad, huh? Shame." I smooth down the front of my sweater. "This was me trying today."

"It's not your Sunday best, that's for sure," Mrs. Li says with a knowing smile around her eyes. "What's wrong? Do you want to talk about it?"

I shove my car keys into my back pocket, thinking, what do I have to lose? I approach Mrs. Li at the counter. "I'm just having a hard time with my parents. We fought. When they were here for Chinese New Year. About me being gay. This isn't the first time, but it was ugly, and messy, and we all said things I don't think we can take back and we haven't spoken since. It feels horrible. The fight, this fallout...and I keep thinking about what I should do next, but I just don't know. I don't know if I'd be making the right decision."

"And what do you think you should do about it?"

"Leave my parents be. If they never want to talk to me again, then fine by me. They'll never accept me for who I am anyway, so life would be easier that way but...I don't think I can live with myself if I did that. Leaving them seems so...cruel, to them. They're my parents. They brought me up, raised me—for better or worse—and gave me an education. I shouldn't leave them just like that, but staying feels cruel too, to me. They'll never change. They'll never accept me and love me for who I am, so why bother? I don't understand. All I want is for them to love me. Why can't they do that?"

Mrs. Li purses her lips slightly and nods. "When I met Malcolm's dad—Charlie—my parents were so angry with me. He came from a poor background, had no higher education, was a server in a restaurant who was barely making ends meet. I loved him the moment I saw him. My parents behaved as if he didn't exist, refused to talk to me, even after we got married. It was so painful for me and I cried, I screamed, I begged, I even threatened to never let them see our firstborn. It wasn't until years after we had Malcolm before they finally accepted Charlie as their son-in-law. So many nights I would call my parents heartless, and finally Charlie said they weren't being heartless—they loved me, that's all. What I saw as conditions for their love, they saw as the way to guarantee me the good life they thought I deserved, the one they had given me from birth. To them, their daughter marrying a poor man was a one-way ticket out of that good life.

"I thought he was crazy, but he kept saying he understood them. He was the poor man who loved me and who worried he couldn't give me the good life I deserved, so why would, *how could*, my parents—the rich ones—think any differently? Crazy. Anyway, I can't speak for your parents, the same way I think Charlie couldn't speak for mine, but what I've learned is that a parent's love can be complicated business; Malcolm and I are very close, and still we've had our moments. The kind of love you want from your parents is not unreasonable, but it might be something they're physically, emotionally, and mentally unable to give because their life experiences, or lack of, have not prepared them for it. Even if they love you, their love will, in *your* eyes, always feel conditional and limited no matter what."

Tears well up in my eyes. I reach for the business cards on the counter and tap them gently to the left so they're perfectly aligned in the clear holder they're sitting in. I blink the tears away, willing myself not to cry for what feels like the hundredth time whenever I think about my parents.

"I'm sorry." Mrs. Li reaches over and gives my hand a gentle pat, her eyes warm with empathy. "I'm sure you wished for me to tell you happy things like how your parents will love you no matter what, but if you're going to make a decision, you must do it with your eyes wide open."

"I know." My voice cracks slightly. "It's just hard to hear, that's all. Doesn't make the decision any easier."

"Good decisions never come easy."

I nod. I feel numb, my head jumbled up with conflicting thoughts about what I'm to do about my parents. "Thank you, Mrs. Li, for listening. I'm going to go now, find Paige, and not keep you from closing up. I'm sorry to have taken up your time."

"Oh no, thank *you*, Skylar, for listening to an old woman talk and reminisce about the days gone by. Now go. Don't let me keep you from Paige any longer."

CHAPTER 40

"Hello?" The intercom crackles to life.

"Paige, it's me. Skye."

Silence greets me and I feel stricken with fear. My heart contracts into a tight ball and my chest compresses, urging my body to fold over, curl up, protect itself. Honestly, why do we love? All it does is hurt. After a pause, the door buzzes and pops open on its hinges. Eyeing the elevator in front of me, I wonder if I made a mistake. I steel myself and step inside.

Paige is waiting at her doorway when I arrive. When I see her standing there in distressed jeans and a plain white t-shirt, an overwhelming sense of love floods my veins and courses through every vessel, tissue, and chamber in my heart, and I feel the fool for failing to see what has been right in front of me all this time. There is no back door I will see myself out of, no excuse I can allow myself, if the only reason for seeking escape is to keep myself safe from what a love with her can do to me.

"Skye," she greets me softly.

"Hey…" I can see how tired she looks. It makes me want to run my hands through her hair. "Can I come in?"

"Of course."

Paige moves to one side and I swallow the lump in my throat as I shuffle past her. I see the dining table a few meters ahead of me. I'll get there, lean against it, look at her, a few seconds to breathe, a few seconds to calm my nerves, then I'll tell her how I feel.

I spin on my heels, no more than an arm's length away from her. "I'm done walking away from you."

The door clicks shut. Paige has one hand resting against it, her body half turned. I take a small step forward and she faces me, eyes locking with mine. Paige makes me want to lean into her and run a hundred miles in a different direction at the same time.

"I'm in love with you, Paige, and I am done walking away from you."

Paige used to say we make the mistake of asking all the wrong questions, that the hardest part is cutting through the mess and finding the single thread that holds everything together. I'd like to think that once we have that figured out, we then discover what truly needs to be said. Paige's eyebrows pull together as her eyes soften. I see a hint of the smile I have grown accustomed to catching before it forms and my spirit soars. Paige's hands are on my face—holding me close—her lips on mine, searching, crushing. I wrap my arms around her neck, breathless, and surrender to her. My heart is without armor.

I tighten my arms around her when we break apart and glance around the apartment, half expecting Cam to materialize from the shadows and put a stop to everything.

"We broke up," Paige says.

I throw another glance around the apartment. I see it now. Magazines, books, snacks, clothes—anything Cam's—all gone.

"When?"

"After the wedding. It wasn't going to work. Not when the person I want is you. Was working up to it, I promise. Terribly heartrending speech and all. Massive play to convince you to leave your first love. Bit slow to the party, it seems. I really need to work on my timing."

"I can ring your doorbell again if you like."

Paige lets out a laugh. "It's okay. I'll do better next time." She caresses my cheek, turning serious. "I want you to stay, Skye. That's what I wanted to say to you. I want you to stay, for always."

Over the years we have known each other, I have seen every measure of emotion and sentiment in Paige's eyes, but the one I see right now is the truest, the one full of the spirit of everything we've experienced together. It is a love that is pure and honest, and because words will not suffice, I can only cup her face between my palms and kiss her. I am ready to give in to what it means to love, and be loved by, Paige.

She wraps her arms around me and deepens the kiss. I thread my fingers through her hair. I miss the way she holds me, the way she kisses me.

"I've missed you," I murmur.

"I've missed you too."

Running her fingers up my neck, Paige sends a shiver down my spine. She steers us backwards and has me perched on the edge of the dining table. Grasping the hem of my sweater, she swiftly pulls it over my head and tosses it to one side. I wrap my legs around her waist and bring her lips to mine, not wanting her kisses to stop. I have my hands underneath her t-shirt and I push it up past her torso; it joins my sweater on the ground. Paige leans forward and presses her hips against mine, and in an achingly slow manner, she runs the tip of her tongue along my neck. I let out a gasp of pleasure, softly pleading, and with that, Paige discards any sense of patience. The rest of our clothes come off in a hurry and with nothing but skin on skin, I feel her fingers inside me. Deep, long strokes. My legs tighten around Paige and I loop my arms around her neck as she picks up the pace. I can feel her warm breaths falling, her teeth grazing my skin as she bites down gently on my shoulder.

I am close but I am desperate to touch her. I place my hand on hers. "Not yet," I say, voice raspy.

Paige slows. "Tell me what you want, baby." Her husky voice makes me ache even more for her.

Away from the table and at the couch, I give her a gentle push and she sits. She eyes me like I'm dessert, which is exactly how I feel about her. I'm on my knees; I'm going to show her what I want. Paige braces her feet against the coffee table, gently threading her fingers through my hair while she arches her hips upwards, against my mouth, seeking out her release. I can tell she is close. She murmurs for me to keep going. It makes me weak with desire, and when her breath hitches, I drive my fingers forward, and against the base of my tongue, her body gives way to a series of trembles and shakes which I feel in my core as if they are my own.

Paige's breathing gradually slows. Arm slung across her face, partially covering her eyes, lips slightly parted, she looks beautiful. I find it impossible to look away.

She opens her eyes and she smiles dreamily at me. A light tug at my shoulder. She doesn't speak but I know exactly what she wants. I straddle her and she swiftly takes me. Pushing my hips down against her fingers, I can feel the release building inside me. I can hear our breathing, erratic and charged with urgency. I look at her, her blue eyes catching the sunlight, which floods the room. I dig my fingernails into her back, my entire body tense one moment then in complete freefall the next as she sends me over the edge. Paige holds me close as I lean into her and ride out the last of the tremors, face pressed against the crook of her neck. In this space, there is only a blissful silence and the soft kisses she plants along my shoulder. There is only us.

Loving Paige, and being loved by her, is like stepping out in the early hours of the morning just as the sun is rising, dew clinging to the blades of grass, undisturbed by a slumbering world. Or it's like after a thunderstorm, as the cool settles around you, streets quiet, clouds parting to reveal a clear sky and the most beautiful rainbow.

You take a breath, a deep one.

The air. Crisp, fresh.

Your heart. Light, bursting,

Your soul. Fulfilled, content.

"I love you," I say when I pull back, our foreheads pressed against each other.

Paige only holds me tighter. "As I love you."

"Say it again…"

She smiles and it gives me a heart rush. "I love you, Skylar."

epilogue

Havenford

The café bustles, but quietly. A low hum of conversations carries across the space. I spot the back of the head of the man I have come to see. There is no shortage of seats, given that it is a random weekday afternoon, but still he has chosen the booth all the way at the back, away from prying eyes. I note that the seat beside him is empty.

"Hi, Dad," I say sitting down in front of him, not bothering with a hug.

The way we parted the last time we saw each other isn't the cause for this reserve, even if it is the reason for the slightly strained greeting. My family doesn't do hugs, saying *I love you* doesn't come naturally to us, and our home isn't a place you would go to for that warm fuzzy feeling. I used to think that it is because we're Asian and that's just how we're built, that we aren't genetically engineered to be effusive or expressive with our feelings. I have come to learn that it isn't our heritage as much as it is just my parents and their respective upbringings.

"Skylar." As expected, he doesn't attempt to move from his seat.

"Where's Mom?" I had asked to meet both my parents today.

"She decided not to come."

My heart sinks a little, even if that was exactly the type of behavior I had prepared myself for.

"Does she know you're here?"

The shifty look on my dad's face is all the answer I need. He watches as I order my coffee. I haven't been in this café in years, not since high school. I'm amazed it survived, its menu unchanging, the coffee still dull and flat, but it is an institution in Havenford. Taking in the appearance of the man in front of me, I can tell that the passing months have not agreed with my dad. He looks older, greyer, as if age has finally caught up with him. On days when my mother is feeling generous, she might say that my dad reminds her of a movie star she had a crush on growing up, and like this movie star, my dad will be seventy before he even starts to look his age.

"How is Mom, then?" I ask. Even in absentia, she makes caring for her difficult, having decided that showing up to meet me wasn't worth her time or effort. However, I suppose it is common human decency to check that she has not given herself a stroke from all the rage boiling inside her.

"She's still angry. You've really upset her this time."

I give a half shrug. "I could say the same for her…and you."

My dad looks away, unable, or unwilling it may have been, to meet my direct gaze. He clears his throat. "How is work?"

I mentally wave away the irritation that arises. "I didn't fly all this way to talk about work. But if you must know, it's great, I'll make partner, and I'm not leaving London. So I guess you and Mom will just have to figure out how you're going to get by, given that your investment in me as your retirement plan hasn't worked out the way you want. There's still Richard, I suppose. At least he's not gay."

That certainly gets my dad's attention. He looks hurt, and it invokes that dreaded sense of guilt inside me. I catch the apology before it can escape my lips.

"What? Too harsh? It's the truth. She's been waiting on me to come home and be her version of normal, a good daughter who will care for her through her old age so that she'll never be alone. You've been waiting on me to return and ease the burden of her for you, but I'm afraid I'm not. I was never coming home...and I think you knew that already."

My dad keeps quiet, doing nothing. He just stares at his cup of coffee.

"Do you know what's worse? It's that the both of you still think that that's going to happen, despite everything that's happened. It's like la-la land for you two. Are you really going to pretend that that night in the hotel didn't happen? How's it working out for you?"

Still, nothing. Reactionless. I swear my dad is like a snail. When confronted, his tactic is to close up and silently pray for the danger to pass. I want to reach out and throttle him.

"*Dad.* Stop staring at the damn coffee. *Look at me.* How many times are you going to do this? How many times are you going to abandon me and pretend that none of it happened?"

My dad's head shoots up. He throws harried glances around us. "I've never abandoned you, Skylar!" he hisses, visibly agitated.

"How can you say that? How can you even say that you've never abandoned me? You—" I draw a staggered breath. "You allowed Mom to beat me and threaten me with a knife when she found out I was gay. You saw the cuts on my arms growing up and you never once asked. You stopped speaking to me for years, and even when we do now, you sidestep any topic that reminds you of who I am. You could have stopped Mom back at the hotel, but all you could come up with was a raised fist, for me. You did more than abandon me, do you understand? You were meant to be *my* safe harbor, the way Mom was Richard's. Instead, you left me in the hands of a madwoman who believed that I was the reason for her unhappiness, that our family was broken because of me and who punished me for being who I am, all while knowing that you would be too cowardly to come and save me."

My dad turns his head away, unable to look me in the eye. My heart is tender from the revelation.

"I didn't feel loved and I never felt like I was enough. I spent *years* dependent on *someone else* for *my* sense of self-worth and an even longer time waiting on you to love me like you once did. Growing up, I knew only anger, pain, and loneliness, but still I found a way to love you and forgive you because the day I came out to you, you said you'll love me no matter what. You may not remember it, but you said it, and *I believed you*...I— I believed you."

I can feel the tears welling up in my eyes.

"I do love you, Skylar, no matter what." My dad presses the base of his hands to his eyes. They're wet when he moves them away from his face.

I had my heart broken by my dad, but now it breaks for him too.

"I know you believe that. But I think you've simply cherry-picked parts of me to love." I can't keep the sadness out of my voice. My dad shakes his head. "You know it's true, Daddy. We wouldn't be here. Not like this if it wasn't true. All this time, you've decided which memories you'll keep and which you'll discard. You have a version of me that you will love no matter what, but that's not me. I am so much more—I always have been—and I deserve so much more than what I got. As a parent, as *my father*, I thought you'd see that and that you'll finally get it one day. I believed you would come through for me…but you didn't."

Silence blankets our table. Around us, people get on with their day. My dad— despondent, shoulders slumped—descends into his own brand of turmoil and despair. It is the same look he wore the night I came out to my mother, when he entered my room after everything that had happened and had the gall to hold me and tell me he loved me. He reeked of resignation and helplessness. I used to believe, fervently, that he would eventually find his way. But I've learned that my hope—in him—had become my prison. It is not as if parenthood magically bestowed upon him the additional gifts of strength and courage. If his approaches to fatherhood and his marriage are anything to go by, his response to today's accusations will be to wallow in a lifetime of self-imposed misery, recrimination, and inaction.

"Daddy, this is kinda the part where you say something," I say, wrestling to not let my disappointment show.

There is an inaudible gulp. "What can I say?"

My dad sounds so utterly lost. It is shocking that I once thought parents knew everything. I sigh. "I don't know. Maybe try saying you're sorry? That you'll change and be a better father to me? After everything I've just said, don't you feel like you owe me at least that?"

"I-I am sorry. It's all my fault that things are like this and I only have myself to blame but w-what can I do now? I've already failed you—as your father—and you're not my little girl anymore."

"So? I'm still your daughter, aren't I?"

"Yes—"

"And we're still both very much alive, aren't we?"

"Well, yes—"

"So just be a better father *now*."

There is another prolonged period of my dad staring at his cup of coffee. He finally looks up. "I'm not sure how."

"Well, I can't tell you how either. There are no set rules or right answers. But it's probably in the little things, you know? Like you asking me about my day—a day which isn't *just* limited to work—and listening to me talk about it. Or something like that. The only thing that is certain is that things aren't going back to the way they were before. I don't accept that anymore. You and Mom. You're my parents. But behave badly one more time and we're done. Do you get that?"

My dad dips his head and nods. I can't tell if he has a genuine appreciation for the repercussions, or if he is simply going along with everything I've said because it is how he has conditioned himself to behave around his wife. He runs his thumbs along the side of his cup for a long while and when he finally makes eye contact again, it's different. Less resigned. More purposeful. It gives me hope that maybe it could be different this time. With him at least anyway.

He stretches his hands across the table to cover mine. "I'm sorry. That I wasn't a good father to you."

I have waited a very long time for an apology from my family. The longer I waited, the longer the list of things I felt they had to be sorry for became, and the less I cared for it. After all this time, an apology, while right and proper, doesn't do much to change the past. But at least it's there. I shrug. "You did the best you knew how."

"I really do love you."

"I love you too. I may not like you very much right now—" He flinches. I pat his hand. "*But* I do love you. *And* I certainly hope I'll grow to like you again."

He swallows, hard. "I'd like that very much too."

My dad's lips are drawn into a small smile. I smile back, with some effort.

I check my watch. "I'm going to get going shortly. I didn't intend to stay long." I catch my dad's raised eyebrows. "In the interest of full disclosure, I almost didn't come at all. I don't mean to this café, I mean Havenford. Didn't have a hope in hell that either you or Mom were going to change, but I didn't want to feel like a bitch for not trying either, so..." I shrug. "Here I am, I guess. Get in, say my piece, avoid the coffee—or mug if I'm lucky—that Mom will try to fling at me, get out."

"I'm glad you came. I think your mom was expecting an apology, though."

I let out a short snort of laughter. "Why am I not surprised? The prospect of an apology and still she didn't want to show up?"

"She wanted you to come to the house."

I can't help but laugh again. "What did she want? Me to stand in the driveway and grovel for her forgiveness?" My dad purses his lips. I laugh even harder. "No, actually she wouldn't want that. Imagine the shame. No, she'll just tell everyone how filial I am to fly home randomly to visit her. Yep, that's what she'll do."

I spy a twitch in my dad's lips. It makes me smile.

"She's going to think I met you anyway," he says. "Do you want me to tell her anything if she asks?"

"I'm not going to apologize, if that's what you're asking." I exit the booth. "Look. If she asks, you can tell her that for everything's that happened, it's forgiven—all of it—and I'm willing to give it a go with her too, *if* she's ready to have an honest and respectful relationship with me. Honestly, she's probably already in denial over what happened and I really don't need to make coming out to her a periodic event for fun and games where my prize is getting a bully with anger-management issues. If she feels like changing it up, she knows how to reach me."

My dad's mouth falls open slightly. "That's it?"

"Yeah, that's kinda it."

Silence, probably in horror at the realization that he may have to independently navigate a relationship with me at the expense of incurring the full wrath of the woman he married.

"Divorce is starting to sound like a great idea, isn't it?" I quell the chuckle that threatens to follow his discomfort. "Dad…I'm going to say this one last time, and you do with it what you will. I want you to know happiness. It's not the easiest thing—learning to be happy—but I think you owe it to yourself to try. You just need to be brave about it." I place my hand on his shoulder and give it a gentle squeeze. "I'm going to be here for the rest of the week. Call me—my schedule's flexible—but I really have to go now." I look past him and find the back of a familiar dark-haired woman sitting a few tables away. I can barely contain the joy swelling in my chest. "Because I've got a date to keep."

My dad awkwardly twists his body around to catch a glimpse of what I am looking at. "You, uh, you brought a *friend*?"

"Best friend actually, but she's also the woman I'm going to marry."

"O-Oh! Er, um…" My dad can't hide his discomfort anymore. It's so easy. We're on a potentially wild and bumpy ride going forward, and it's anyone's guess if we'll ever reach the end.

"It's okay. This is one of the 'little things' we can work on next time. Are you staying?" He nods. Leaning down, I give him a peck on his cheek. "Okay then. I love you, Daddy. Call me."

I take one final glance back at my dad when I'm out of his line of vision. He's already gone back to staring at his coffee. I shake my head, a smile playing at my lips. That entire conversation we just had, and of course that's what he does immediately after—stare at his coffee—but hopefully this time it isn't to wallow, but to contemplate how to be a better father, and how to live a fuller, happier life.

A few quick strides and I am by her side. I tenderly run my fingers through the back of her hair and envelope her in a massive hug from behind.

"Hi," Paige murmurs lovingly.

We kiss. "Hi."

"All good?"

"Yes."

She stands up. "Want to get out of here, baby? Bet you hated the coffee and thought we could grab another elsewhere."

"Mm, just when I think I couldn't love you more, you go and say something like that."

Paige laughs and I can feel her hand on my waist, pulling me close. I lean in, blissfully content to listen to the list of eclectic food places she thought we could try out in Havenford. Eclectic food places, in Havenford? That would be a first, but then again, it is the first time in ages since I have set foot in this town and felt like I could breathe. As I push open the glass door, my scars shimmer in the sunlight. I smile to myself.

There it is.

All that light inside me, and it is bursting.

Acknowledgments

To my alpha reader (the love of my life), my beta readers (and dear friends), and my indispensable editors (Beth and Sarah)—thank you, a hundred times thank you.